Praise for

DEBBIE MACOMBER

Macomber "tells the parable of women's
age-old concerns with gentle humor and charm."
—*Publishers Weekly*

"Debbie Macomber is one of the few
true originals in women's fiction....
Her books are touching and marvelous
and not to be missed."—Anne Stuart

"Macomber knows what she is doing; she is no
stranger to the *New York Times* bestseller list.
She knows how to please her audience."
—*The Statesman Journal*

Harlequin Romance®
Love stories that capture the essential dream of pure romance.

HARLEQUIN *Presents*
Meet sophisticated men of the world and captivating women in glamorous, international settings. Seduction and passion guaranteed.

Vivid historical romances that capture the imagination with their richness, passion and adventure.
Harlequin® Historical

Sexy, fast-paced stories that reflect the attitudes, desires, lives and language of women today.
HARLEQUIN® *Temptation*

HARLEQUIN *Superromance®*
Longer romance novels featuring realistic, believable characters in a wide range of emotionally involving stories.

HARLEQUIN AMERICAN *Romance®*
Upbeat, lively romances about the pursuit of love in the backyards, big cities and wide-open spaces of America.

HARLEQUIN®
Duets
A fun, entertaining "lighter side of love" read that delivers romance with comedy.

HARLEQUIN®
INTRIGUE®
Electrifying romance and heart-stopping suspense that make for an exhilarating read.

HARLEQUIN®
Makes any time special ™

DEBBIE MACOMBER
RAINY DAY KISSES

DAY LECLAIRE
THE BRIDE PRICE

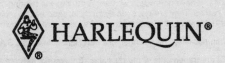

HARLEQUIN®

TORONTO • NEW YORK • LONDON
AMSTERDAM • PARIS • SYDNEY • HAMBURG
STOCKHOLM • ATHENS • TOKYO • MILAN • MADRID
PRAGUE • WARSAW • BUDAPEST • AUCKLAND

ISBN 0-373-83470-5

HARLEQUIN ROMANCE 2-in-1 COLLECTION

Copyright © 2001 by Harlequin Books S.A.

The publisher acknowledges the copyright holders
of the individual works as follows:

RAINY DAY KISSES
Copyright © 1990 by Debbie Macomber

THE BRIDE PRICE
Copyright © 2001 by Day Totton Smith

This edition published by arrangement with Harlequin Books S.A.

Visit us at www.eHarlequin.com

Printed in U.S.A.

CONTENTS

Rainy Day Kisses
Debbie Macomber

CHAPTER ONE

SUSANNAH SIMMONS BLAMED her sister, Emily, for this. As far as she was concerned this weekend was going to be the nightmare on Western Avenue. Emily, a nineties version of the "earth mother," had asked Susannah, the dedicated career woman, to baby-sit nine-month-old Michelle.

"Emily, I don't know." Susannah had balked when her sister first phoned. What did she, a twenty-eight-year-old business executive, know about babies? The answer was simple—not much.

"I'm desperate."

Her sister must have been to ask her. Everyone knew what Susannah was like around babies—not just Michelle, but infants in general. Unfortunately Susannah just wasn't the motherly type. Interest rates, negotiations, troubleshooting, staff motivation, these were her strong points. Not formula, teething and diapers.

It was nothing short of astonishing that the same two parents could have produced such completely different daughters. Susannah figured that cases such as theirs would baffle even the genetic experts. Emily baked her own oat-bran muffins, subscribed to *Organic Gardening* and hung her wash to dry on a clothesline—even in winter.

Susannah, on the other hand, wasn't the least bit

domestic and had no intention of ever cultivating the trait. She was too busy with her career to let such tedious tasks disrupt her corporate lifestyle. She was currently serving as a junior vice president in charge of marketing for H&J Lima, the nation's largest sporting goods company. The position occupied almost every minute of her time.

Susannah Simmons was a woman on the rise. Her name kept cropping up in trade journals as an up-and-coming achiever. None of that mattered to Emily, however, who needed a baby-sitter.

"You know I wouldn't ask you if it wasn't an emergency," Emily had pleaded.

Susannah could feel herself weakening. Emily was, after all, her younger sister. "Surely, there's got to be someone better qualified."

Emily hesitated, then tearfully blurted, "I don't know what I'll do if you won't take Michelle." She began to sob pitifully. "Robert's left me."

"What?" If Emily hadn't gained her full attention earlier, she did now. If her sister was an earth mother, then her brother-in-law, Robert Davidson, was Abraham Lincoln, as solid and upright as a thirty-foot oak. "I don't believe it."

"It's true," Emily wailed. "He…he claims I give Michelle all my attention and that I never have enough energy left to be a decent wife." She paused long enough to suck in a quavery breath. "I know he's right…but being a good mother demands so much time and effort."

"I thought Robert wanted six children."

"He does…or did." Emily's sobbing began anew.

"Oh, Emily, it can't be that bad," Susannah murmured in a soothing voice, thinking as fast as she could. "I'm sure you misunderstood Robert. He loves you and Michelle, and I'm sure he has no intention of leaving you."

"He does," Emily went on to explain between hiccuping sobs. "He asked me to find someone to watch Michelle for a while. He says we have to have some time to ourselves, or our marriage is dead."

That sounded drastic enough to Susannah.

"I swear to you, Susannah, I've called everyone who's ever baby-sat Michelle before, but no one is available. No one—not even for one night. When I told Robert I hadn't found a sitter, he got so angry...and you know that's not like Robert."

Susannah did know. The man was the salt of the earth. Not once in the five years she'd known him could she recall him even raising his voice.

"He said if I didn't take this weekend trip to San Francisco with him he was going alone. I tried to find someone to watch Michelle," Emily went on. "I honestly tried, but there's no one else, and now Robert's home and he's loading up the car and, Susannah, he's serious. He's going to leave without me and from the amount of luggage he's taking, I don't think he intends to come back."

The tale of woe barely skimmed the surface of Susannah's mind. The key word that stayed and planted itself in fertile ground was the word *weekend*. "I thought you said you only needed me for one night?" she gasped.

It was then that Susannah should have realized she wasn't much brighter than a brainless mouse, innocently nibbling away at the cheese in a steel trap.

Emily sniffled once more, probably for effect, Susannah thought darkly.

"We'll be flying back to Seattle early Sunday afternoon. Robert's got some business in San Francisco Saturday morning, but the rest of the weekend is free…and it's been such a long time since we've been alone."

"Two days and two nights," Susannah said slowly, mentally tabulating the hours.

"Oh, please, Susannah, my whole marriage is at stake. You've always been such a good big sister. I know I don't deserve anyone as good as you."

Silently Susannah agreed.

"Somehow I'll find a way to repay you," Emily continued.

Susannah pushed the hair from her face and closed her eyes. Her sister's idea of repaying her was usually freshly baked zucchini bread shortly after Susannah announced she was watching her weight.

"Susannah, please!"

It was then that Susannah had caved in to the pressure. "All right. Go ahead and bring Michelle over."

Somewhere in the distance, she could have sworn she heard the echo of a mousetrap slamming shut.

By the time Emily and Robert had deposited their offspring at Susannah's condominium, her head was swimming with instructions. After planting a juicy kiss on her daughter's rosy cheek, Emily handed the clinging Michelle to a reluctant Susannah.

That was when the nightmare began in earnest.

As soon as her sister left, Susannah could feel herself tense up. Even as a teenager, she hadn't done a lot of baby-sitting; it wasn't that she didn't like children, but kids just didn't seem to take to her.

Holding the squalling infant on her hip, Susannah paced while her mind buzzed with everything she was supposed to remember. She knew what to do in case of diaper rash, colic and several other minor emergencies, but Emily hadn't said one word about how to keep Michelle from crying.

"Shhh," Susannah cooed, gently jiggling her niece against her hip. She swore the child had a cry Tarzan would envy.

After the first five minutes, her calm cool composure was cracking under the pressure. She could be in real trouble here. The tenant agreement she'd signed specifically stated "no children."

"Hello, Michelle, remember me?" Susannah asked, doing everything she could think of to quiet the youngster. Dear Lord, didn't the kid need to breathe? "I'm your Auntie Susannah, the business executive."

Her niece wasn't impressed. Pausing only long enough to gulp for air, Michelle increased her volume and glared at the door as if she expected her mother to miraculously appear if she cried long and hard enough.

"Trust me, kid, if I knew a magic trick that'd make your mother reappear, I'd use it now."

Ten minutes. Emily had been gone a total of ten minutes. Susannah was seriously considering giving the state Children's Protective Services a call and claiming that a stranger had abandoned a baby on her doorstep.

"Mommy will be back soon," Susannah murmured wistfully.

Michelle screamed louder. Susannah started to worry about her stemware. The kid's voice was pitched high enough to shatter glass.

More torturous minutes passed, each one an eternity. Susannah was desperate enough to sing. Not knowing any appropriate lullabies, she started off with a couple of ditties from her childhood, but quickly exhausted those. Michelle didn't seem to appreciate them anyway. Since Susannah didn't keep up with the current top twenty, the best she could do was an old Christmas favorite. Somehow singing "Jingle Bells" in the middle of September didn't feel right.

"Michelle," Susannah pleaded, willing to stand on her head if it would keep the baby from wailing, "your mommy will be back, I assure you."

Michelle apparently didn't believe her.

"How about if I buy municipal bonds and put them in your name?" Susannah tried next. "Tax-free bonds, Michelle! This is an offer you shouldn't refuse. All you need to do is stop crying. Oh, please stop crying."

Evidently Michelle wasn't interested.

"All right," Susannah cried, growing desperate. "I'll sign over my IBM stock. That's my final offer, so you'd better grab it while I'm in a generous mood."

Michelle answered by gripping Susannah's collar with both of her chubby fists and burying her wet face in a once spotless white silk blouse.

"You're a tough nut to crack, Michelle Margaret Davidson," Susannah muttered, gently patting her niece's back as she paced. "You want blood, don't you, kid? You aren't going to be satisfied with anything less."

A half hour after Emily had left, Susannah was ready to resort to tears herself. She'd started singing again, some of the ageless Christmas songs. "You'd better watch out,/ you'd better not cry,/ Aunt Susannah's here telling you why...."

She was just starting to really get into the lyrics when someone knocked heavily on her door.

Like a thief caught in the act, Susannah hunched her shoulders and whirled around, fully expecting the caller to be the building superintendent. No doubt there had been complaints and he'd come to confront her.

Expelling a weary sigh, Susannah realized she was defenseless. The only option left to her was to throw herself on his mercy. She squared her shoulders and walked across the lush carpet, prepared to do exactly that.

Only it wasn't necessary. The building superintendent wasn't the person standing on the other side of her door. It was her new neighbor, wearing a baseball cap and a faded T-shirt, and looking more than a little disgruntled.

"The crying and the baby I can take," he said, crossing his arms and relaxing against the doorframe, "but your singing has got to go."

"Very funny," she grumbled.

"The kid's obviously distressed about something."

Susannah glared at him. "Nothing gets past you, does it?"

"Do something."

"I'm trying." Apparently Michelle didn't appreciate this stranger any more than Susannah did because she buried her face in Susannah's collar and rubbed it vigorously back and forth. That at least helped muffle her cries, but there was no telling what it would do to white silk. "I offered her my IBM stock and it didn't do any good," Susannah explained. "I was even willing to throw in my municipal bonds."

"You offered her stocks and bonds, but did you suggest dinner?"

"Dinner?" Susannah echoed. She hadn't thought of

that. Emily claimed she'd fed Michelle, but Susannah vaguely remembered something about a bottle.

"The poor thing's probably starving."

"I think she's supposed to have a bottle," Susannah said. She turned and glanced at the assorted bags Emily and Robert had deposited in her condominium along with the necessary baby furniture. From the number of items stacked on the floor, it looked as if she'd been granted permanent guardianship. "There must be one in all this paraphernalia."

"I'll look—you keep the kid quiet."

Susannah nearly laughed out loud. If she was able to keep Michelle quiet, he wouldn't be here in the first place. She imagined she could convince CIA agents to hand over top-secret documents more easily than she could silence one distressed nine-month-old infant.

Without waiting for an invitation, her neighbor moved into the living room. He picked up one of the three overnight bags and rooted through that. He hesitated when he pulled out a stack of freshly laundered diapers, and glanced at Susannah. "I didn't know anyone used cloth diapers anymore."

"My sister doesn't believe in anything disposable."

"Smart woman."

Susannah made no comment, and within a few seconds noted that he'd found a plastic bottle. He removed the protective cap and handed the bottle to Susannah, who looked at it and blinked. "Shouldn't the milk be heated?"

"It's room temperature, and frankly, at this point I don't think the kid's going to care."

He was right. The instant Susannah placed the rubber nipple in her niece's mouth, Michelle gripped the bottle with both hands and sucked at it greedily.

For the first time since her mother had left, Michelle stopped crying. The silence was pure bliss. Susannah's tension eased, and she released a sigh that went all the way through her body.

"You might want to sit down," he suggested next.

Susannah did, and with Michelle cradled awkwardly in her arms, leaned against the back of the sofa, trying not to jostle her charge.

"That's better, isn't it?" Her neighbor tipped the baseball cap farther back on his head, looking pleased with himself.

"Much better." Susannah smiled shyly up at him, studying him for the first time. As far as looks went, her new neighbor was downright handsome. She supposed most women would find his mischievous blue eyes and dark good looks appealing. He was tanned, but she'd have wagered a month's pay that his bronzed features weren't the result of any machine. He obviously spent a good deal of time out-of-doors, which led her to the conclusion that he didn't work. At least not in an office. And frankly, she doubted he was employed outside of one, either. The clothes he wore and the sporadic hours he kept had led her to speculate earlier about her neighbor. If he had money, which he apparently did or else he wouldn't be living in this condominium complex, then he'd inherited it.

"I think it's time I introduced myself," he said conversationally, sitting on the ottoman across from her. "I'm Nate Townsend."

"Susannah Simmons," she said, holding out her hand for him to shake. "I apologize for all the racket. My niece and I are just getting acquainted and—oh boy—it's going to be a long weekend, so bear with us."

"You're baby-sitting for the weekend?"

"Two days and two nights." It sounded like a whole lifetime to Susannah. "My sister and her husband are off on a second honeymoon. Normally my parents would watch Michelle and love doing it, but they're visiting friends in Florida."

"It was kind of you to offer."

Susannah thought it best to correct the impression. "Trust me, I didn't volunteer for this. In case you hadn't noticed, I'm not very motherly."

"You've got to support her back a little better," he said, watching Michelle.

Susannah tried to do as he suggested, but it felt awkward to hold on to her niece, the bottle and everything else.

"You're doing fine."

"Sure," Susannah muttered. She felt like someone with two left feet who'd been unexpectedly ushered onto center stage and told to perform the lead in *Swan Lake*.

"Relax, will you?" Nate encouraged.

"I told you already I'm not into this motherhood business," she snapped. "If you think you can do any better, you feed her."

"You're doing great. Don't worry about it."

She wasn't doing great at all, and she knew it, but this was as good as she got.

"When was the last time you had anything to eat?" he asked.

"I beg your pardon?"

"You sound hungry to me."

"Well, I'm not," Susannah said irritably.

"I think you are, but don't worry, I'll take care of that." He walked boldly into her kitchen and paused in front of her refrigerator. "You'll feel a whole lot better once you have something in your stomach."

Shifting Michelle higher, Susannah stood and followed him. "You can't just walk in here and—"

"I'll say I can't," he murmured, his head inside her fridge. "Do you realize there's nothing in here except an open box of soda and jar full of pickle juice?"

"I eat out a lot," Susannah said defensively.

"I can see that."

Michelle had finished the bottle and made a slurping sound that prompted Susannah to remove the nipple from her mouth. The baby's eyes were closed. Little wonder, Susannah thought. She was probably exhausted. Certainly Susannah was, and it was barely after seven Friday evening. And the weekend was only just beginning.

Setting the empty bottle on the kitchen counter, Susannah awkwardly lifted Michelle onto her shoulder and gently patted her back until she produced a tiny burp. Feeling a real sense of accomplishment, Susannah smiled proudly.

Nate chuckled and when Susannah glanced in his direction, she discovered him watching her, his grin warm and appraising. "You're going to be just fine."

Flustered, Susannah lowered her gaze. She always disliked it when a man looked at her that way, studying her features and forming a judgment about her by the size of her nose, or by the direction her eyebrows grew. Most men seemed to be of the opinion that they'd been granted a rare gift of insight and could determine a woman's entire character by just looking at her face. Unfortunately, Susannah's was too austere by conventional standards to be classified as beautiful. Her eyes were deep-set and dark, which had the effect of offsetting her high cheekbones. Her nose came almost straight from her forehead and together with her full mouth made her look like a classic Greek sculpture. Not pretty, she thought. Interesting perhaps.

It was during Susannah's beleaguered self-evaluation that Michelle stirred and started jabbering cheerfully, reaching one hand toward a strand of Susannah's dark hair.

Without her realizing it, her chignon had come undone. Michelle had somehow managed to loosen the pins and now the long dark tresses fell haphazardly over Susannah's shoulder. If there was one thing Susannah was meticulous about, and actually there were several, it was her appearance. She must look a rare sight, in a two-hundred-dollar business suit with a stained white blouse and her hair tumbling over her shoulder.

"Actually I've been waiting for an opportunity to introduce myself," Nate said, leaning against the counter, looking right at home. "But after the first couple of times we saw each other, our paths didn't seem to cross again."

"I've been working a lot of overtime lately." If the truth were known, Susannah almost always put in extra hours. Often she brought work home with her. She was dedicated, committed and hardworking. Her neighbor, however, didn't look as if he possessed any of those qualities. She strongly suspected that everything in life had come much too easily for Nate Townsend. She'd never seen him without his baseball cap or his T-shirt. Somehow she doubted he even owned a suit. Even if he did, it probably wouldn't look right on him. Nate Townsend was definitely a football-jersey type of guy.

He seemed likable enough, friendly and outgoing, but from what she'd seen, he lacked ambition. Apparently there had never been anything he'd wanted badly enough to really strive for.

"I'm glad we had the chance to introduce ourselves," Susannah added, walking back into the living room and toward her front door. "I appreciate the help, but as you said, Michelle and I are going to be just fine."

"Frankly, it didn't sound that way when I arrived."

"I was just getting my feet wet," she returned, defending herself, "and why are you arguing with me? You're the one who said I was doing all right."

"I lied."

"Why would you do that?"

Nate shrugged nonchalantly. "It was apparent a little self-confidence would do you a world of good, so I offered it."

Susannah glared at him, resenting his attitude. So much for the nice-guy-who-lives-next-door image she'd had of him up to this point. "I don't need any favors from you."

"You may not," he agreed, "but unfortunately Michelle does. The poor kid was starving and you didn't so much as suspect."

"I would have figured it out."

Nate gave her a look that seemed to cast doubt on her intelligence, and Susannah frowned right back. She opened the door with far more force than necessary and flipped her hair over her shoulder with flair a Paris model would have envied. "Thanks for stopping in," she said stiffly, "but as you can see everything's under control."

"If you say so." He gave her an off-center grin and without another word was gone.

Susannah banged the door shut with her hip, feeling a good deal of satisfaction as she did so. She realized this was petty, but her neighbor had irked her in more ways than one.

Soon afterward Susannah heard the soft strains of an Italian opera drifting from Nate's condominium. At least she thought it was Italian, which was unfortunate because it made her think of spaghetti and of how hungry she actually was.

"Okay, Michelle," she said, smiling down on her niece. "It's time to feed your auntie." Without too much trouble, Susannah assembled the high chair and set her niece in that while she scanned the contents of her freezer.

The best she could come up with was a frozen Mexican entrée. She gazed at the picture on the front of the package, shook her head and tossed it back inside the freezer.

Michelle seemed to approve and slapped her hands against the tray on her high chair.

Crossing her arms and leaning against the freezer door, Susannah paused. "Did you hear what he said?" she asked, still irate. "In a way he was right, but he didn't have to be so superior about it."

Michelle slapped her hands in approval once more. The vigorous strains of the music were muted by the thick walls, and wanting to hear a little more, Susannah cracked open the sliding glass door to her balcony, which was separated from Nate's by a concrete partition. It offered privacy, but didn't hold back the melodious voices raised in triumphant song.

Susannah opened the glass door completely and

stepped outside. The evening was cool, but pleasantly so. The sun had just started to set and had cast a wash of golden shadows over the picturesque waterfront.

"Michelle," she muttered when she returned, "he's cooking something that smells like lasagna or spaghetti." Her stomach growled and she returned to the freezer, taking out the same Mexican entrée she'd rejected earlier. On second study, it didn't seem any more appetizing than the first time.

A faint scent of garlic wafted into her kitchen. Susannah turned her classic Greek nose in that direction, then followed the aroma to the open door like a puppet drawn there by a string. She sniffed loudly a couple of times and eagerly turned back to her niece. "It's definitely something Italian, and it smells divine."

Michelle pounded the tray again.

"It's garlic bread," Susannah announced and whirled around to face her niece, who appeared singularly unimpressed. But then, thought Susannah, she wouldn't be. She'd eaten.

Under normal conditions, Susannah would have reached for her jacket and headed to Mama Mataloni's, a fabulous Italian restaurant within easy walking distance. Unfortunately Mama Mataloni's didn't deliver.

Against her better judgment, Susannah stuck the frozen entrée into her microwave and set the timer. When her doorbell chimed, she stiffened and looked to Michelle as if the nine-month-old would sit up and tell Susannah who'd chosen to stop by this time.

It was Nate again, holding a plate of spaghetti and a small glass of red wine. "Did you fix yourself something to eat?" he asked.

For the life of her Susannah couldn't tear her gaze

away from the oversize plate, heaped high with steaming pasta smothered in a thick red sauce. Nothing had ever looked more appetizing. He'd grated fresh Parmesan cheese over the top, which had melted onto the rich sauce. A generous slice of French bread was balanced on the side.

"I, ah, was just cooking up a...TV dinner." She pointed behind her toward the kitchen as if that would explain what she was trying to say. Her tongue seemed to be stuck to the roof of her mouth.

"I shouldn't have acted so superior earlier," he said, pushing the plate toward her. "I'm bringing you a peace offering."

"This...is for me?" She raised her eyes from the plate for the first time, wondering if he knew how hungry she felt and was toying with her.

He handed her the meal. "The sauce has been simmering most of the afternoon. I like to pretend I'm something of a gourmet chef. Every once in a while I get creative in the kitchen."

"How...nice." Her mind conjured up a picture of him standing in his kitchen stirring sauce while the rest of the world struggled to make a living. Her attitude wasn't the least bit gracious and she mentally apologized. Without further ado, she marched into her kitchen, reached for a fork and plopped herself down at the table. She might as well eat this feast while it was hot!

One sample told her everything she needed to know. "This is great." She took another bite, pointed her fork in his direction and rolled her eyes. "Marvelous. Wonderful."

Nate pulled a bread stick out of his shirt pocket and gave it to Michelle. "Here's looking at you, kid."

As Michelle chewed contentedly on the bread stick, Nate pulled out a chair and sat across from Susannah, who was too busy enjoying her dinner to notice anything out of the ordinary until Nate's gaze narrowed.

"Is something wrong?" Susannah asked. She wiped the edges of her mouth with a napkin and sampled the wine.

"I smell something."

From the look of him, whatever it was apparently wasn't pleasant. "It might be the TV dinner," she suggested hopefully, already knowing better.

"I'm afraid not."

Susannah straightened and carefully set the fork beside her plate as uneasiness settled over her.

"It seems," Nate said, sounding as if something was wrong with his nasal cavity, "that someone needs to change Michelle's diaper."

CHAPTER TWO

HOLDING A FRESHLY DIAPERED Michelle on her hip, Susannah rushed out of the bathroom into the narrow hallway and gasped for breath.

"Are you all right?" Nate asked, his brow creased with a concerned frown.

She nodded and sagged against the wall, feeling light-headed. Once she'd dragged several clean breaths through her lungs, she straightened and even managed a weak smile.

"It wasn't so bad now, was it?"

Susannah paused and glared at him. "I should have been wearing an oxygen mask."

Nate's responding chuckle did little to improve Susannah's mood.

"In light of what I just experienced," she said righteously, "I can't understand why the population continues to grow." To be on the safe side, she opened the hall linen closet and took out a large can of disinfectant spray. Sticking her arm inside the bathroom, she gave a generous squirt.

"While you were busy I assembled the crib," Nate told her, still revealing far too much amusement to suit Susannah. "Where would you like me to put it?"

"The living room will be fine." The gesture had been a thoughtful one, but Susannah wasn't accustomed to depending on others, so when she thanked him, the words were forced.

Susannah followed him into the living room and found the bed readied. She laid Michelle down on her stomach and covered her with a handmade blanket. The baby settled down immediately, without fussing.

Nate headed toward the door. "You're sure everything's going to be all right?" he said softly.

"Positive." Susannah wasn't, but Michelle was her niece and their problems weren't his. Nate had done more than enough already. "Thanks for dinner."

"Any time." He paused at the door and turned back. "I left my phone number on the kitchen counter. Call if you need me."

"Thanks."

He favored her with a grin on his way out the door, and Susannah stood a few moments after he'd vacated the apartment, thinking about him. Her feelings were decidedly mixed.

Susannah began sorting through the various bags her sister had left, depositing the jars of baby food in the cupboard and putting the bottles of formula in the fridge. As Nate had pointed out, there was plenty of room—all she had to do was scoot the empty pickle jar aside.

She supposed she should toss the jar in the garbage, but one of the guys from the office had mentioned something about pickling hard-boiled eggs. It sounded so simple—all she had to do was peel a few eggs and keep them refrigerated in the jar for a week or so. Susannah had been meaning to try the uncomplicated recipe ever since. But she feared that when the mood struck her, she wouldn't have any pickle juice around, so she kept it on hand just in case.

When she'd finished in the kitchen, Susannah soaked in a hot tub, leaving the door ajar in case Michelle woke and needed her. She felt worlds better afterward.

Walking on the tips of her toes back into the living room, she brought out her briefcase and removed a fat file. She paused and glanced down at her sleeping niece and gently patted her back. The little girl looked so angelic, so content.

Suddenly a powerful yearning stirred within Susannah, one she wasn't sure she could put a name to. She felt real affection for Michelle, but the feeling was more than that. This time alone with her niece had evoked a longing buried deep in Susannah's heart, a longing she had never taken the time to fully examine. And with it came an aching restless sensation that she promptly submerged.

When Susannah had chosen a career in business, she'd realized she was giving up the part of herself that hungered for husband and children. There was nothing that said she couldn't marry, couldn't raise a child, but she knew herself too well. From the time she was in high school it had been painfully apparent she was completely inadequate in the domestic arena. Especially when she compared herself to Emily, who seemed to have been born with a dust rag in one hand and a cookbook in the other.

Susannah had never regretted the decision she'd made to dedicate herself to her career, but then she was more fortunate than others. She had Emily, who was determined to supply her with numerous nieces and nephews. For Susannah, Michelle and the little ones who were sure to follow would have to be enough.

Comfortable with herself and her choices, Susannah quietly stepped away from the crib. For the next hour, she sat on her mattress reading the details of the proposed marketing program the department had sent her. Their full presentation would follow on Monday morning and she wanted to be informed and prepared.

When she finished reading the report, she tiptoed back to her desk, situated in the far corner of the living room, and replaced the file in her briefcase.

Once more she paused to check on her niece. Feeling just a little cocky, she returned to the bedroom convinced this baby-sitting business wasn't going to be so bad after all.

Susannah changed her mind at one-thirty when a piercing wail startled her out of a sound sleep. Not knowing how long Michelle had been at it, Susannah nearly fell out of bed in her rush to reach her niece.

"Michelle," she cried, blindly stumbling across the floor, her arms stretched out in front of her. "I'm coming.... There's no need to panic."

Michelle disagreed vehemently.

Turning on a light only made matters worse. Squinting to protect her eyes from the glare, Susannah groped her way to the crib, then let out a cry herself when she stubbed her toe on the leg of the coffee table.

Michelle was standing, holding on to the bars and looking as if she didn't have a friend in the world.

"What's the matter, sweetheart?" Susannah asked softly, lifting the little one into her arms.

A wet bottom told part of the story, but also the poor tyke had probably woken and, finding herself in a strange place, felt scared. Susannah couldn't blame her.

"All right, we'll try this diapering business a second time."

Susannah spread a thick towel on the bathroom counter, then gently placed Michelle on it. She was halfway through the changing process when the phone pealed. Straightening, Susannah glanced around her, wondering what she should do. She couldn't leave Michelle, and picking her up and carting her into the kitchen would be difficult. Whoever was calling at this time of night should know better! If it was important they could leave a message on her answering machine.

But after three rings, the phone stopped, followed almost immediately by a firm knock against her front door.

Hauling Michelle, freshly powdered and diapered, with her, Susannah squinted and checked the peephole to discover a disgruntled Nate on the other side.

"Nate," she said in surprise as she opened the door. She couldn't even guess what he wanted. And she wasn't too keen about letting him inside her apartment at this hour.

He stood just inside the condo, barefoot and dressed in a red plaid housecoat. His hair was mussed as if he'd recently woken, which made Susannah wonder about her own disheveled appearance. She feared she looked like someone who'd walked out of a swamp.

"Is Michelle all right?" he barked, despite the evidence before him. Not waiting for a reply, he continued in an accusing tone, "You didn't answer the phone."

"I couldn't. I was changing her diaper."

Nate hesitated and then studied her closely. "In that case, are you all right?"

She nodded and managed to raise her right hand. It

was difficult when her arms were occupied with a baby. "I lived to tell about it."

"Good. What happened? Why was Michelle crying?"

"I'm not sure. Maybe when she woke up and didn't recognize her surroundings, she suffered an anxiety attack."

"And, from the look of us, caused a couple more."

Susannah didn't want to look at herself. Her mussed and knotted hair spilled over her shoulder like an oil slick. She too was barefoot. She'd been so anxious to get to Michelle that she hadn't taken the time to reach for her slippers or her robe.

Michelle, it seemed, was pleased with all the unexpected attention, and when she leaned toward Nate, arms outstretched, Susannah marveled at how fickle an infant could be. After all, she was the one who had fed and diapered her. Not Nate.

"It's my male charm," he explained, looking delighted.

"More likely, it's your red housecoat."

Whatever it was, Michelle went into his arms as if he was a long-lost friend. Susannah excused herself to retrieve her robe from the foot of her bed. By the time she returned, Nate was sitting on the sofa with his feet stretched out in front of him, supported by Susannah's mahogany coffee table.

"Make yourself at home," she muttered. Her mood wasn't always the best when she'd been startled out of a sound sleep.

He glanced up at her and grinned. "There's no need to be testy."

"Yes, there is," she countered and destroyed what remained of her argument by yawning loudly. Covering her mouth with the back of her hand, she slumped down on the chair across from him and flipped her hair away from her face.

His gaze followed the action. "You should wear your hair down more often."

She glared at him once more, fuming. "I always wear my hair up."

"I noticed. And frankly, it's much more flattering down."

"Oh, for heaven's sake," she cried, "are you going to tell me how to dress next?"

"I might."

He said it with such a charming smile that any sting there might have been in his statement was diluted.

"There's no need to stick with business suits every day, is there? Try a dress sometime—a frilly thing with lace and buttons."

She opened her mouth to argue with him, then decided it wouldn't do any good. The arrogance he displayed seemed to be characteristic of handsome men in general, she'd noted. Because a man happened to possess lean good looks and could smile beguilingly, he figured he had the right to say anything he pleased to a woman. As if it was up to him to comment on how she styled her hair, how she chose to dress or anything else. These were things he wouldn't dream of suggesting if he were talking to another man.

"You aren't going to argue?"

"No," she said, and for emphasis shook her head.

That stopped him short. He paused and blinked, then gave her another of his captivating smiles. "I find that refreshing."

"I'm gratified to hear there's something about me you approve of." There were probably several other things about her that didn't please him. Given any encouragement, he would probably be glad to list them for her.

Sweet little traitor that she was, Michelle had curled up in Nate's arms, utterly content just to sit there and study his handsome face, which no doubt had fascinated numerous other females before her. The least Michelle could do was show some signs of going back to sleep so Susannah could return her to the crib and usher Nate out the door.

"I shouldn't have said what I did about your hair and clothes."

"Hey," she returned flippantly, "you don't need to worry about hurting my feelings. I've got a lot of emotional fortitude."

"Strong," he repeated. "You make yourself sound like an all-weather tire."

"I've had to be a good deal tougher than that."

His face relaxed into a look of sympathy. "Why?"

"I work with men just like you every day."

"Men just like me?"

"It's true. For the past seven years, I've found myself up against the old double standard, but I've learned to keep my cool."

He frowned as if he didn't understand what she was talking about. Susannah felt it was her obligation to tell him. Apparently Nate had never been involved in office politics. "Let me give you a few examples. If a male co-worker has a cluttered desk, then everyone assumes he's a hard worker. If my desk is a mess, it's a sign of disorganization."

Nate straightened and looked as if he wanted to argue with her, but Susannah was just warming to her subject and she continued before he had a chance to speak. "If a man in an office marries, it's good for the company because he'll settle down and become a more productive employee. If a woman marries, it's almost the kiss of death because management figures she'll get pregnant and leave. She's the last one to be offered a promotion no matter how qualified she is. If a man leaves because he's been offered a better job, everyone's pleased for him because he's taking advantage of an excellent career opportunity. But if the same position is offered to a woman and she takes it, then upper management shrugs and claims women aren't dependable anyway."

When she'd finished there was a short pause. "You certainly have strong feelings on the subject," he said at last.

"If you were a woman, you would, too."

His nod of agreement was a long time coming. "You're right, I probably would."

Michelle seemed to find the toes of her sleeper fascinating and was examining them with sheer delight. Personally, Susannah didn't know how anyone could look so wide-awake at this ungodly hour.

"If you turn down the lights, she might get the hint," Nate said, doing a poor job of smothering a yawn.

"You look beat," said Susannah. "There's no need for you to stay. I'll take her." She held out her arms to Michelle, who whimpered and clung all the more tightly to Nate. Susannah's feelings of inadequacy were reinforced.

"Don't worry about me. I'm comfortable," Nate told her.

"But..." She could feel the warmth invading her cheeks. She lowered her gaze, regretting her outburst of a few minutes ago. She'd been standing on her soapbox again. "Listen, I'm sorry about what I said. What goes on at the office has nothing to do with our being neighbors."

"Then we're even."

"Even?"

"I shouldn't have commented on your hair and clothes." He hesitated long enough to envelop her in his smile. "Friends?"

Despite the intolerable hour, Susannah found herself smiling back. "Friends."

Michelle seemed to concur because she cooed loudly, kicking her feet.

Susannah stood and turned the lamp down to its lowest setting, then reached for Michelle's blanket, covering the baby with that. Feeling slightly chilled herself, she retrieved the brightly colored afghan at the foot of the sofa, which Emily had crocheted for her last Christmas.

The muted light created an intimate atmosphere, and suddenly self-conscious, Susannah suggested, "Maybe if I sing to her. That should help her go to sleep."

"If anyone sings, it'll be me," he said much too quickly.

Susannah's pride was a little dented, but remembering her limited repertoire of songs, she gestured toward him and said, "All right, Frank Sinatra, have a go."

To Susannah's surprise, Nate's singing voice was soothing and melodious. More amazingly, he knew exactly the right kind of tunes to sing. Not baby songs, but easy-listening ones, the kind she'd heard for years on the radio. She felt her own eyes drifting closed and battled to stay awake. His voice dropped to a mere whisper that felt like a warm caress. Much too warm. And cozy, as if the three of them belonged together, which was ridiculous since she'd only just met Nate. He was her neighbor and nothing more. There hadn't been time for them to get to know each other, and Michelle was her *niece*, not her daughter.

But the domestic fantasy continued no matter how hard she tried to dispel it. She couldn't stop thinking about what it would be like to share her life with a husband and children—and also manage to keep her eyes open for more than a second or two. Perhaps if she rested them for just a moment...

The next thing Susannah knew her neck ached. She reached up to secure her pillow, then realized she didn't have one. Instead of being in her bed, she was curled up in the chair, her head resting uncomfortably against the arm. Slowly, reluctantly, she opened her eyes and discovered Nate sitting across from her, his head tilted back, sleeping soundly. Michelle was resting peacefully in his arms.

It took Susannah a moment to orient herself. When she realized the sun was breaking across the sky and spilling into her large windows, she closed her eyes again. It was morning. Morning! Nate had spent the night in her condominium.

Flustered, Susannah twisted her body into an upright position and rubbed the sleep from her face, wondering what she should do. Waking Nate was probably not the best idea. He was bound to be as unnerved as she to discover he'd fallen asleep in her living room. To complicate matters, the afghan she'd covered herself with had somehow become twisted around her legs and hips. Muttering under her breath, Susannah yanked it about in an effort to stand.

Her activity disturbed Nate's restful slumber. He stirred, glanced in her direction and then froze for what seemed the longest moment of Susannah's life. Then he blinked several times and glared at her as if he felt certain she'd vanish into thin air provided he looked at her long enough.

Standing now, Susannah did her best to appear dignified, which was nearly impossible with the comforter still twisted around her hips and legs like a coiled rope.

"Where am I?" Nate asked dazedly.

"Ah...my place."

His eyes drifted shut. "I was afraid of that." The mournful look that came over Nate's face would have been comical under other circumstances. Only neither of them was laughing.

"I, ah, must have fallen asleep," she said, breaking the embarrassed silence. She took pains to fold the afghan, and then held it against her stomach like a shield.

"Me too, apparently," Nate muttered.

Michelle woke and struggled into a sitting position. She looked around her and evidently didn't like what she saw, either. Her lower lip started to tremble.

"Michelle, it's okay," Susannah said quickly, hoping to ward off the jungle yell she feared was coming. "You're staying with Auntie Susannah this weekend, remember?"

"I think she might be wet," Nate offered when Michelle started to whimper softly. He let out a muffled curse and hastily lifted the nine-month-old from his lap. "I'm positive she's wet. Here, take her."

Susannah reached for her niece and a dry diaper in

one smooth movement, but it did little good. Michelle was intent on letting them both know, in no uncertain terms, that she didn't like her schedule altered. Nor did she appreciate waking up in a stranger's arms. She conveyed her displeasure in loud boisterous cries.

"I think she might be hungry, too," Nate suggested, trying to brush the dampness from his housecoat.

"Brilliant observation," Susannah said sarcastically on her way to the bathroom, Michelle in her arms.

"My, my, you certainly get testy in the mornings," he said.

"I need coffee."

"Fine. I'll make us both a cup while I'm heating a bottle for Michelle."

"She's supposed to eat her cereal first," Susannah shouted. At least that was what Emily had insisted when she outlined her daughter's schedule.

"I don't think she cares. She's hungry."

"All right, all right," Susannah yelled from the bathroom. "Heat her bottle first if you want."

Yelling was a mistake, she soon discovered. Michelle apparently wasn't any keener on mornings than Susannah was. Punching the air with her stubby legs, her niece made diapering nearly an impossible task. Susannah grew more frustrated by the minute. Finally her hair, falling forward over her shoulders, caught Michelle's attention. She grasped it, pausing long enough to suck in a huge breath.

"Do you want me to get that?" she heard Nate shout.

"Get what?"

Apparently it wasn't important because he didn't answer her. But a moment or so later he was standing at the bathroom door.

"It's for you," he said.

"What's for me?"

"The phone."

The word bounced off the walls of her mind like a ricocheting bullet. "Did...did they say who it was?" she asked, her voice high-pitched and wobbly. No doubt it was someone from the office and she would be the subject of gossip for months.

"Someone named Emily."

"Emily," she repeated. That was even worse. Her sister was sure to be full of awkward questions.

"Hi," Susannah said as casually as possible into the receiver.

"Who answered the phone?" her sister demanded without preamble.

"My neighbor, Nate Townsend. He, ah, lives next door." The finesse with which she delivered that brilliant explanation amazed even her. Worse, Susannah had been ready to blurt out that Nate had spent the night, but she'd stopped herself just in time.

"I haven't met him, have I?"

"My neighbor? No, you haven't."

"He sounds cute."

"Listen, if you're phoning about Michelle," Susannah hurried to add, anxious to end the conversation, "there's no need for concern. Everything's under control." That was a slight exaggeration, but what Emily didn't know couldn't worry her.

"Is that Michelle I hear crying in the background?" Emily asked, sounding concerned.

"Yes. She just woke up and she's a little hungry." Nate was holding the baby and pacing the kitchen, impatiently waiting for Susannah to get off the phone.

"My poor baby," Emily said. "Tell me when you

met your neighbor. I don't remember you ever mentioning anyone named Nate."

"He's been helping me out," Susannah said quickly. Wanting to change the subject, she asked, "How are you and Robert?"

Her sister sighed audibly. "Robert was so right. We needed this time alone. I feel a thousand times better and so does he. Every married couple should get away for a few days like this, but then everyone doesn't have a sister as generous as you to fill in on such short notice."

"Good, good," Susannah said, hardly aware of what she was supposed to think was so fantastic. "Uh-oh," she said, growing desperate. "Michelle's bottle is warm. I hate to cut you off, sis, but I've got to go take care of Michelle. I'm sure you understand."

"Of course."

"I'll see you tomorrow afternoon then. What time's your flight landing?"

"One-fifteen. We'll drive straight to your place and pick up Michelle."

"Okay, I'll expect you sometime around two then." Another day with Michelle. She could manage for an additional twenty-four hours, couldn't she? What could possibly go wrong in that small amount of time?

Losing patience, Nate took the bottle and Michelle and returned to the living room. Susannah watched through the doorway as he turned on her television set and plopped himself down as if he'd been doing it for years. His concentration moved from the TV long enough to place the rubber nipple in Michelle's eager mouth.

Her niece began greedily sucking, too hungry to care who was feeding her. Good heavens, Susannah thought, Michelle had spent the night in his arms. A little thing like letting this man feed her paled in comparison.

Emily continued chatting, telling her sister how romantic her first night in San Francisco had been. But Susannah barely heard. Her gaze settled on Nate, who looked rumpled, crumpled and utterly content, sitting in her living room, holding an infant in his arms.

The sight affected Susannah as few ever had, and she was powerless to explain its impact on her senses. She'd dated a good number of men—debonair, rich, sophisticated ones. But the feeling she had now, this attraction, had taken her completely by surprise. Over the years, despite her dates, Susannah had always been careful to guard her heart. It hadn't been difficult, since she'd never met anyone who truly appealed to her. Yet this disheveled, disgruntled male, who sat in her living room holding and feeding her infant niece with enviable expertise, attracted her more profoundly than anyone she'd ever met. It didn't make the least bit of sense. Nothing could ever develop between them—they were as different as gelatin and concrete. The last thing she wanted was to become involved in a serious relationship. With some effort, she forced her eyes away from the homey scene.

When at last she was able to hang up the phone, Susannah moved into the living room, feeling almost weary. She brushed the tangled curls from her face, wondering if she should take Michelle from Nate so he could return to his own apartment. No doubt her niece would resist and humiliate her once more.

"Your sister isn't flying with Puget Air, is she?" he asked, frowning. His gaze remained on the television screen.

"Yes, why?"

Nate's mouth thinned. "You...we're in trouble here. Big trouble. According to the news, maintenance workers for Puget Air are going on strike. By six tonight, every plane they own will be grounded."

CHAPTER THREE

"IF THIS IS A JOKE," Susannah told him angrily, "it's in poor taste."

"Would I kid about something like this?" Nate demanded.

Susannah slumped down on the edge of the cushion and gave a ragged sigh. This couldn't be happening to her, it just couldn't. "I'd better call Emily." She assumed her sister was blissfully unaware of the strike.

Susannah returned a few minutes later.

"Well," Nate demanded, "what did she say?"

"Oh, she knew all along," Susannah replied disparagingly, "but she didn't want to say anything because she was afraid I'd worry."

"How exactly does she intend to get back to Seattle?"

"Apparently they booked passage on another airline on the off chance something like this might happen."

"That was smart."

"My brother-in-law is like that. I'm not to give the matter another thought," she said, quoting Emily. "My sister will be back Sunday afternoon as promised." If the fates so decreed, and Susannah said a fervent prayer they would.

But the fates had other plans.

*   *   *

Sunday morning, there were bags under Susannah's eyes. She was exhausted mentally and physically, and convinced anew that motherhood was definitely not for her. Two nights into the ordeal, Susannah had noted that the emotional stirring for a husband and children came to her only when Michelle was sleeping or eating. And with good reason.

Nate arrived around nine bearing gifts. He brought freshly baked cinnamon rolls still warm from the oven. He stood in her doorway, tall and lean, with a smile bright enough to dazzle the most dedicated career woman. Once more, Susannah was amazed at her overwhelming reaction to him. Her heart leaped to her throat, and she immediately wished she'd taken time to dress in something better than her faded housecoat.

"You look terrible."

"Thanks," she said, bouncing Michelle on her hip.

"I take it you had a bad night."

"Michelle was fussing. New tooth coming in. She didn't seem the least bit interested in sleeping." She wiped a hand over her face, certain she'd never looked worse.

"I wish you'd called me," Nate said, taking her by the elbow and leading her into the kitchen. He actually looked guilty because he'd had a peaceful night's rest. Ridiculous, Susannah thought.

"Call you? Whatever for?" she asked. "So you could have paced with her, too?" As it was, Nate had spent a good portion of Saturday in and out of her apartment helping her. Spending a second night with them was above and beyond the call of duty. "Did I tell you," Susannah said, yawning, "Michelle's got a new tooth coming in—I felt it myself." Deposited in the high chair, Michelle was content for the moment.

Nate nodded and glanced at his watch. "What time does your sister's flight arrive?"

"One-fifteen." No sooner had the words left her lips when the phone rang. Susannah's and Nate's eyes locked, and as it rang a second time she wondered how a telephone could sound so much like a death knell. Even before she answered it, Susannah knew it was what she'd most dreaded hearing.

"Well?" Nate asked when she'd finished.

Covering her face with both hands, Susannah sagged against the wall.

"Say something," Nate demanded.

Slowly she lowered her hands. "Help."

"Help?"

"Yes," she cried, struggling to keep her voice from cracking. "All Puget Air flights are grounded just the way the news reported they would be, and the other airline Robert and Emily made reservations with is overbooked. The earliest flight they can take is tomorrow morning."

"I see."

"Obviously you don't!" she cried. "Tomorrow is Monday and I've got to be at work!"

"Call in sick."

"I can't do that," she snapped, angry with him for even suggesting such a thing. "Marketing is giving their presentation and I've got to be there."

"Why?"

She glared at him. It was futile to expect someone like Nate to understand something as important as a sales presentation. Nate didn't seem to have a job; he didn't worry about a career. For that matter he couldn't possibly grasp that a woman holding a management position had to strive twice as hard to prove herself.

"I'm not trying to be cute, Susannah," he said with infuriating calm. "I honestly want to know why that meeting is so important."

"Because it is. I don't expect you to appreciate something like this, so just accept the fact that I *have* to be there."

Nate cocked his head and idly rubbed the side of his jaw. "First, answer me something. Five years from now, will this meeting make a difference in your life?"

"I don't know." She pressed two fingers to the bridge of her nose. She'd had less than three hours' sleep, and Nate was asking impossible questions. Michelle, bless her devilish little heart, had fallen asleep in her high chair. Why shouldn't she? Susannah reasoned. She'd spent the entire night fussing, and was exhausted now. By the time Susannah had discovered the new tooth, she felt as if she'd grown it herself.

"If I were you, I wouldn't sweat it," Nate said with that same nonchalant attitude. "If you aren't there to hear their presentation, marketing will give it Tuesday morning."

"In other words," she muttered, "you're saying I don't have a thing to worry about."

"Exactly."

Nate Townsend knew next to nothing about surviving in the corporate world, and he'd obviously been protected from life's harsher realities. It was all too obvious to Susannah that he was a man with a baseball-cap mentality. He couldn't be expected to fully comprehend her dilemma.

"So," he said now, "what are you going to do?"

Susannah wasn't entirely sure. Briefly, she closed her eyes in an effort to concentrate. *Impose discipline,* she said to herself. *Stay calm,* that was important above all else. *Think slowly and analyze your objectives.* For every problem there was a solution.

"Susannah?"

She glanced at him; she'd almost forgotten he was with her. "I'll cancel my early-morning appointments and go in for the presentation," she stated matter-of-factly, having arrived at a manageable decision.

"What about Michelle? Are you going to hire a sitter?"

A baby-sitter hired by the baby-sitter. A novel thought, perhaps even viable, but Susannah didn't know anyone who sat with babies.

Then she made her decision. She would take Michelle to work with her.

And that was exactly what she did.

As she knew it would, Susannah's arrival at H&J Lima caused quite a stir. At precisely ten the following morning, she stepped off the elevator. Her black eel-skin briefcase was clenched in one hand and Michelle was pressed against her hip with the other. Head held high, Susannah marched across the hardwood floor, past the long rows of doorless cubicles and shelves of foot-thick file binders. Several employees moved away from their desks to view her progress. A low rumble of hushed whispers followed her.

"Good morning, Ms. Brooks," Susannah said crisply as she walked into her office, the diaper bag draped over her shoulder like an ammunition pouch.

"Ms. Simmons."

Susannah noted that her secretary, to her credit,

didn't so much as bat an eye. The woman was well trained; to all outward appearances, Susannah regularly arrived at the office with a nine-month-old infant attached to her hip.

Depositing the diaper bag on the floor, Susannah took her place behind a six-foot-wide walnut desk. Content for the moment, Michelle sat on her lap, gleefully viewing her aunt's domain.

"Would you like some coffee?" Ms. Brooks asked.

"Yes, please."

Her secretary paused. "Will your, ah…"

"This is my niece, Michelle, Ms. Brooks."

The woman nodded. "Will Michelle require anything to drink?"

"No, thanks anyway. Is there anything urgent in the mail?"

"Nothing that can't wait. I canceled your eight and nine o'clock appointments," her secretary went on to explain. "When I spoke to Mr. Adams, he asked if you could join him for drinks tomorrow night at six."

"That'll be fine." The old lecher would love to do all their business outside the office. This time, she'd agree to his terms, since she'd been the one to cancel the appointment, but she wouldn't be so willing a second time. She'd never much cared for Andrew Adams, who was overweight, balding and a general nuisance.

"Will you be needing me for anything else?" her secretary asked when she delivered the coffee.

"Nothing. Thank you."

As she should have predicted, the meeting with marketing was an unmitigated disaster. The presentation took twenty-two minutes, and in that short time Michelle managed to dismantle Susannah's Cross pen, unfasten her blouse and pull her hair free from her carefully styled French twist. Several times the baby had clapped her hands and made loud noises. At the low point of the meeting, Susannah had been forced to leave her seat and crawl under her desk to retrieve her niece, who was cheerfully crawling over everyone's feet.

By the time she arrived back at her condo, Susannah felt as if she were returning from a war zone. It was the type of day that made her crave something chocolate and excessively sweet. But there weren't enough chocolate chip cookies in the world to see her through another morning like that one.

To Susannah's surprise, Nate met her in the foyer outside the elevator. She took one look at him and resisted the urge to burst into tears.

"I take it things didn't go well."

"How'd you guess?" she questioned sarcastically.

"It might be the fact you're wearing your hair down when I specifically remember you left wearing it up. Or it could be that your blouse is buttoned wrong and there's a gaping hole in the middle." His smile was devilish. "I wondered if you were the type to wear a lacy bra. Now I know."

Susannah groaned and slapped a hand over her front. He could have spared her that comment.

"Here, kiddo," he said, taking Michelle out of Susannah's arms. "It looks like we need to give your poor aunt a break."

Turning her back, Susannah refastened her blouse and then brought out her key. Her once orderly, immaculate apartment looked as if a cyclone had gone through it. Blankets and baby toys were scattered from one end of the living room to the other. She'd slept on the couch in order to be close to Michelle, and her pillow and blankets were still there along with her blue suit jacket, which she'd been forced to change when Michelle had tossed a spoonful of plums on the sleeve.

"What happened here?" Nate asked, looking in astonishment at the scene before him.

"Three days and three nights with Michelle and you need to ask?"

"Sit down," he said gently. "I'll get you a cup of coffee." Susannah did as he suggested, too grateful to argue with him.

Nate stopped just inside the kitchen. "What's this purple stuff all over the walls?"

"Plums," Susannah informed him. "I discovered the hard way that Michelle hates plums."

The scene in the kitchen was a good example of how her morning had gone. It had taken Susannah the better part of three hours to get herself and Michelle ready for the excursion to the office. And that was just the beginning.

"What I need is a double martini," she told Nate when he carried in two cups of coffee.

"It's not even noon."

"I know," she said. "Can you imagine what I'd require if it was two o'clock?"

Chuckling, Nate handed her the steaming cup. Michelle was sitting on the carpet, content to play with the very toys she'd vehemently rejected that morning.

To Susannah's surprise, Nate sat down next to her and looped his arm over her shoulder. She tensed, but if he noticed, he chose to ignore it. He stretched his legs out on top of the coffee table and relaxed.

Susannah felt her tension mount. The memory of the meeting with marketing was enough to elevate her blood pressure, but when she analyzed this strained tautness, she realized it came from being so close to Nate. It wasn't that Susannah objected to his touch; in fact quite the opposite was true. They'd spent three days in close quarters, and contrary to everything she'd theorized about her neighbor, she had come to appreciate his happy-go-lucky approach to life. But it was diametrically opposed to her own view, and the fact that she could be so attracted to him was something of a shock.

"Do you want to talk about marketing's presentation?"

She released her breath slowly. "No, I think this morning is best forgotten by everyone involved. You were right, I should have postponed the meeting."

Nate sipped his coffee and said, "It's one of those live-and-learn situations."

Pulling herself to a standing position at the coffee table, Michelle cheerfully edged her way around until she was stopped by Nate's outstretched legs. Then she surprised them both by reaching out one arm and granting him a smile that would have melted concrete.

"Oh, look," Susannah cried proudly, "you can see her new tooth!"

"Where?" Lifting the baby onto his lap, Nate peered inside her mouth. Susannah was trying to show him where to look when the doorbell chimed in three impatient bursts.

When Susannah answered the door, Emily flew in as if she had suddenly sprouted wings. "My baby," she cried. "Mommy missed you so-o-o much."

Not half as much as I missed you, Emily, she mused, watching the happy reunion.

Robert followed on his wife's heels, looking

pleased. The weekend away had apparently done them both a world of good. Never mind that it had nearly destroyed Susannah's peace of mind and her business career.

"You must be Nate," Emily said, claiming the seat beside Susannah's neighbor. "My sister couldn't say enough about you."

"Coffee anyone?" Susannah piped up eagerly, rubbing her palms together. The last thing she needed was her sister applying her matchmaking techniques to her and Nate. Emily strongly believed it was unnatural for Susannah to live the way she did. A career was one thing, but choosing to forgo the personal satisfaction of a husband and family was beyond her sister's comprehension. Being fulfilled in that role herself, Emily assumed that Susannah was missing an essential part of life.

"Nothing for me," Robert answered.

"In fact, I bet you're eager to pack up everything and head home," Susannah stated hopefully. Her eye happened to catch Nate's, and it was obvious he was struggling not to laugh at her less-than-subtle attempt to usher her sister and family on their way.

"Susannah's right," Robert said, glancing around the room. It was clear he'd never seen his orderly, efficient sister-in-law's home in such a state of disarray.

"But I've hardly had a chance to talk to Nate," Emily protested. "And I was looking forward to getting to know him better."

"I'll be around," Nate said lightly.

His gaze settled on Susannah, and the look he gave her caused her insides to quiver. For the first time she realized how much she wanted this man to kiss her.

Susannah wasn't the type of person who looked at a handsome male and wondered how his mouth would feel on hers. She was convinced this current phenomenon had a good deal to do with sheer exhaustion, but whatever the cause she found her eyes riveted to his.

Emily suddenly noticed what was happening. "Yes, I think you may be right, Robert," she said, and her voice contained more than a hint of amusement. "I'll pack Michelle's things."

Susannah's cheeks were pink with embarrassment by the time she tore her gaze away from Nate's. "By the way, did you know Michelle has an aversion to plums?"

"I can't say that I did," Emily said, busily throwing her daughter's things together.

Nate helped disassemble the crib and the high chair, and it seemed no more than a few minutes had passed when Susannah's condo was once more her own. She stood in the middle of the living room savoring the silence. It was pure bliss.

"They're off," she said when she realized Nate had stayed behind.

"Like a herd of turtles."

Susannah had heard that saying from the time she was a kid. She didn't find it particularly funny anymore, but she shared a smile with him.

"I have my life back now," she sighed. It would probably take her the better part of a month to recover, though.

"Your life is your own," Nate agreed, watching her closely.

Susannah would have liked to attribute the tears that flooded her eyes to his close scrutiny, but she knew better. With her hands cradling her middle, she walked

over to the window, which looked out over Elliott
Bay. A green-and-white ferry glided peacefully over
the darker green waters. Rain tapped gently against the
window, and the sky, a deep oyster-gray, promised
drizzle for most of the afternoon.

Hoping Nate wouldn't notice, she wiped the tears
from her face and drew in a deep calming breath.

"Susannah?"

"I…I was just looking at the Sound. It's so lovely
this time of year." She could hear him approach her
from behind, and when he placed his hands on her
shoulders it was all she could do to keep from leaning
against him and absorbing his strength.

"You're crying."

She nodded, sniffling because it was impossible to
hold it inside any longer.

"It's not like you to cry, is it? What's wrong?"

"I don't know…" she said and hiccuped on a sob.
"I can't believe I'm doing this. I love that little
tyke…we were just beginning to understand each
other…and…dear heaven, I'm glad Emily came back
when…she did." Before Susannah realized how much
she was missing without a husband and family.

Nate ran his hands down her arms in the gentlest of
caresses.

He didn't say anything for a long time, and Susannah was convinced she was making an absolute idiot
of herself. Nate was right. It wasn't like her to dissolve
into tears. This unexpected burst of emotion must have
been a result of the trauma she'd experienced that
morning in her office, or the fact she hadn't had a
decent night's sleep in what felt like a month and, yes,
she'd admit it, of her having met Nate.

Without saying another word, Nate turned her

around and lifted her chin with his finger, raising her eyes to his. His look was so tender, so caring, that Susannah sniffled again. Her shoulders shook and she wiped at her nose.

He brushed away the hair that clung to the side of her damp face. His fingertips slowly slid over each of her features as though he were a blind man trying to memorize her face. Susannah was mesmerized, unable to pull away. Slowly, as if denying himself the pleasure for as long as he could, he lowered his mouth.

When his lips settled on hers, Susannah released a long, barely audible sigh. She'd wondered earlier what it would be like when Nate kissed her. Now she knew. His kiss was soft and warm. Velvet smooth, and infinitely gentle, yet somehow electric.

As if one sample wasn't enough, he kissed her again. This time it was Nate who sighed. Then he dropped his hands and stepped back.

Startled by the abrupt action, Susannah swayed slightly. Nate's arms righted her. Apparently he'd come to his senses about the same time as she had. For a brief moment they'd decided to ignore their differences. The only thing they had in common was the fact they lived in the same building, she reminded herself. Their values and expectations were worlds apart.

"Are you all right?" he asked, frowning.

She blinked a couple of times, trying to find a way to disguise that she wasn't. Everything had happened much too fast; her heart was galloping like a runaway horse. She'd never been so attracted to a man in her life. "Of course I'm all right," she said with strained bravado. "Are you?"

He didn't answer for a long moment. Instead he

stuffed his hands in his pants pockets and moved away from her, looking annoyed.

"Nate?" she whispered.

He paused long enough to scowl in her direction. Rubbing his hand across his brow, he twisted the ever-present baseball cap backward as if he were catcher. "I think we should try that again."

Susannah wasn't sure what he meant until he reached for her. His first few kisses had been gentle, but this one was meant to take charge of her senses. His mouth moved over hers until she felt the starch go out of her knees. In an effort to maintain her balance, she gripped his shoulders, and although she fought it, she quickly surrendered to the swirling excitement. Nate's kiss was debilitating. She couldn't breathe, couldn't think, couldn't move.

Nate groaned, then his grip tightened and shifted to the back of her head. He slanted his mouth over hers, and moved his lips as if he were playing an intricate musical instrument. At length he released a jagged breath and buried his face in the soft curve of her neck. "What about now?"

"You're a good kisser."

"That's not what I meant, Susannah. You feel it too, don't you? You must! There's enough electricity between us to light up a city block."

"No," she lied, and swallowed tightly. "It was nice as far as kisses go—"

"Nice!"

"Very nice," she amended, hoping to appease him, "but that's about it."

Nate didn't say anything for a long minute, a painfully long minute. Then, scowling at her, he turned and walked out of her apartment.

Trembling, Susannah watched him go. His kiss had touched a chord within her, notes that had been long-silent deep within her, and now she feared the music would forever mark her soul. But she couldn't let him know that. They had nothing in common. They were mismatched.

Now that she was seated in the plush cocktail lounge with her associate, Andrew Adams, Susannah regretted having agreed to meet him after hours. It was apparent from the moment she stepped into the dimly lit room that he had more on his mind than discussing business. Despite the fact that Adams was balding and overweight, he would have been appealing enough if he hadn't looked upon himself as some kind of modern-day Adonis. Although Susannah struggled to maintain a business-like calm, it was becoming increasingly difficult, and she wondered how much longer her good intentions would hold.

"There are some figures I meant to show you," Adams said holding the stem of his martini glass with both hands and studying Susannah with undisguised admiration. "Unfortunately I left them at my apartment. Why don't we conclude our talk there?"

Susannah made a point of looking at her watch and frowning, hoping her associate would take the hint. Something told her differently. "I'm afraid I won't have the time," she said. It was almost seven and she'd already spent an hour with him.

"My place is only a few blocks from here," he coaxed.

His look was much too suggestive, and Susannah was growing wearier by the minute. As far as she could see, this entire evening had been a waste of valuable time.

The only thing that interested her was returning to her own place and talking to Nate. He'd been on her mind all day and she was eager to see him again. The truth was that she was downright nervous after their last meeting, and wondered how they'd react to each other now. Nate had left her so abruptly, and she hadn't talked to him since.

"John Hammer and I are good friends," Adams claimed, pulling his chair closer to her own. "I don't know if you're aware of that."

He didn't even bother to veil his threat. Susannah worked directly under John Hammer, who would have the final say on the appointment of vice president. Susannah and two others were in the running for the position. And Susannah wanted it. Badly. She could achieve her five-year goal if she got it, and in the process make H&J Lima history—by being the first female vice president.

"If you're such good friends with Mr. Hammer," she said, doing an admirable job of keeping her cool, "then I suggest you give those figures to him directly, since he'll need to review them anyway."

"No, that wouldn't work," he countered sharply. "If you come with me it'll only take a few minutes. We'd be in and out of my place in, say, half an hour at the most."

Susannah's immediate reaction to situations such as this was a healthy dose of outrage, but she managed to control her temper. "If your apartment is so convenient, then I'll wait here while you go back for those sheets." As she spoke, a couple walked past the tiny table where she was seated with Andrew Adams. Susannah didn't pay much attention to the man, who wore a gray flannel suit, but the blonde with him was striking. Susannah's eyes followed the woman and envied the graceful way she moved.

"It would be easier if you came with me, don't you think?"

"No," she answered bluntly, and lowered her gaze to her glass of white wine. It was then that she felt an odd sensation prickle down her spine. Someone was staring at her; she could feel it as surely as if she were being physically touched. Looking around, Susannah was astonished to discover Nate sitting two tables away. The striking blonde was seated next to him and obviously enjoying his company. She laughed softly and the sound was like a melody, light and breezy.

Susannah's breath caught in her chest, trapped there until the pain reminded her it was time to breathe again. When she did, she reached for her wineglass and succeeded in spilling some of the contents.

Nate's gaze centered on her and then moved to her companion. His mouth thinned and his eyes, which had been so warm and tender a day earlier, now looked as if they could cut through solid rock.

Susannah wasn't exactly thrilled herself. Nate was dating a beauty queen while she was stuck with Donald Duck.

CHAPTER FOUR

SUSANNAH VENTED HER ANGER by pacing the living room carpet. Men! Who needed them?

Not her. Definitely not her! Nate Townsend could take his rainy-day kisses and stuff them in his baseball cap for all she cared. Only he hadn't been wearing that for Miss Universe. Oh no, with the other woman, he was dressed like someone out of *Gentleman's Quarterly*. Susannah, on the other hand, rated worn football jerseys or faded T-shirts.

Susannah hadn't been home more than five minutes when her doorbell chimed. She whirled around and glared at the door as if it were to blame for the intrusion. Checking the peephole, she discovered her caller was Nate. She pulled back, wondering what she should do. He was the last person she wanted to see. He'd made a fool of her... Well, that wasn't entirely true. He'd only made her *feel* like a fool.

"Susannah," he said, knocking impatiently a second time. "I know you're in there."

"Go away."

Her shout was followed by a short pause. "Fine. Have it your way."

Changing her mind, she twisted the lock and yanked open the door. She glared at him with all the fury she could muster—which at the moment was considerable.

Nate glared right back. "Who was that guy?" he asked with an infuriating calm.

She was tempted to inform Nate that it wasn't any of his business. But she decided that would be churlish.

"Andrew Adams," she answered and quickly followed with a demand of her own. "Who was that woman?"

"Sylvia Potter."

For the longest moment, neither spoke.

"That was all I wanted to know," Nate finally said.

"Me, too," she returned stiffly.

Nate retreated two steps, and like precision clockwork Susannah shut the door. "Sylvia Potter," she echoed in a low-pitched voice filled with disdain. "Well, Sylvia Potter, you're welcome to him."

It took another fifteen minutes for the outrage to work its way through her system, but once she'd watched a portion of the evening news and read her mail, she was reasonably calm.

When Susannah really thought about it, what did she have to be so furious about? Nate Townsend didn't mean anything to her. How could he? Until a week ago, she hadn't even known his name.

Okay, so he'd kissed her a couple of times, and sure, there had been electricity, but that was all. Electricity did not constitute a lifetime commitment. If Nate Townsend chose to date every voluptuous blonde between Seattle and New York it shouldn't matter to her.

But it did. And that fact infuriated Susannah more than anything. She didn't want to care about Nate. Her career goals were set. She had drive, determination and a positive mental attitude. But she didn't have Nate.

Jutting out her lower lip, she expelled her breath forcefully, ruffling the dark wisps of hair against her forehead. Maybe it was her hair color—perhaps Nate preferred blondes. He obviously did, otherwise he wouldn't be trying to impress Miss Universe.

Refusing to entertain any more thoughts of her neighbor, Susannah decided to fix herself dinner. An inspection of the freezer revealed a pitifully old chicken patty. Removing it from the cardboard box, Susannah took one look at it and promptly tossed it into the garbage.

Out of the corner of her eye she caught a movement on her balcony. She turned and noted a sleek Siamese cat walking casually along the railing as if he were strolling across a city park.

Although she remained outwardly calm, Susannah's heart lunged to her throat. Her condo was eight floors up. One wrong move and that cat would be history. Carefully walking to her sliding glass door, Susannah eased it open and softly called, "Here, kitty, kitty, kitty."

The cat accepted her invitation and jumped down from the railing. With his tail pointing toward the sky, he walked directly into her apartment and headed straight for the garbage pail, where he stopped.

"I bet you're hungry, aren't you?" she asked softly. She retrieved the chicken patty and stuck it in her microwave. While she stood waiting for it to cook, the cat, with his striking blue eyes and dark brown markings, wove his way in and around her legs, purring madly.

She'd just finished cutting the patty into bite-size pieces and putting it on a plate when her doorbell rang.

Licking her fingers clean, she moved into the living room.

"Do you have my cat?" Nate demanded when she opened the door. He'd changed from his suit into jeans and a bright blue T-shirt.

"I don't know," she fibbed. "Describe it."

"Susannah, this isn't time for silly games. Chocolate Chip is a valuable animal."

"Chocolate Chip," she repeated with a soft snicker, crossing her arms and leaning against the doorjamb. "Obviously you didn't read the fine print in the tenant's agreement, because it specifically states in section 12, paragraph 13, that no pets are allowed." Actually she didn't have a clue what section or what paragraph that clause was in, but she wanted him to think she did.

"If you don't tattle on me then I won't tattle on you."

"I don't have any pets."

"No, you had a baby."

"But for only three days," she countered. Talk about nit-picking people! He was flagrantly disregarding the rules and had the nerve to throw a minor infraction in her face.

"The cat belongs to my sister. He'll be with me for less than a week. Now, is Chocolate Chip here, or do I go into cardiac arrest?"

"He's here."

Nate visibly relaxed. "Thank God. My sister dotes on that silly feline. She flew up from San Francisco and left him with me before she left for Hawaii." As if he'd heard his name mentioned, Chocolate Chip casually strolled across the carpet and paused at Nate's feet.

Nate bent down to retrieve his sister's cat, scolding him with a harsh look.

"I suggest you keep your balcony door closed," she told him, striving for a flippant air.

"Thanks, I will." Chocolate Chip was tucked under his arm as Nate's gaze casually caught Susannah's. "You may be interested to know that Sylvia Potter's my sister." He turned and walked out her door.

"'Sylvia Potter's my sister,'" Susannah mimicked. It wasn't until she'd closed and locked her door that she realized the import of what he'd said. "His sister," she repeated. "Did he really say that?"

Susannah was at his door before she paused to judge the wisdom of her actions. When Nate answered her furious knock, she stared up at him, her eyes round and confused. "What was that you just said?"

"I said Sylvia Potter's my sister."

"I was afraid of that." Her thoughts were stumbling over one another like marbles tossed out of a bag. She'd imagined...she'd assumed....

"Who's Andrew Adams?"

"My brother?" she offered, wondering if he'd believe her.

Nate shook his head. "Try again."

"An associate from H&J Lima," she said, then hurried to explain. "When I canceled my appointment with him Monday morning, he suggested we get together for a drink to discuss business this evening. It sounded innocent enough at the time, but I should have realized it was a mistake. Adams is a known sleazeball."

An appealing smile touched the edges of Nate's mouth. "I wish I'd had a camera with me when you first saw me in that cocktail lounge. I thought your eyes were going to fall out of your face."

"It was your sister—she intimidated me," Susannah admitted. "She's lovely."

"So are you."

The man had obviously been standing too long in the sun, Susannah reasoned. Compared to Sylvia, who was tall, blond and had curves in all the right places, Susannah felt about as pretty as a professional wrestler.

"I'm flattered that you seem to think so." Susannah wasn't comfortable with praise. She was much too levelheaded to let flattery affect her. When men paid her compliments, she smiled and thanked them, but she treated their words like water running off an oily surface.

Except with Nate. Everything was different with him. She seemed to be accumulating a large stack of exceptions because of Nate. As far as Susannah could see, he had no ambitions, and if she'd met him any-place else other than her building, she probably wouldn't have given him a second thought. Instead she couldn't stop thinking about him. She knew better than to allow her heart to be distracted this way, and yet she couldn't seem to stop herself.

"Do you want to come in?" Nate asked and stepped aside. The bleeping sound drew Susannah's attention across the room to a five-foot-high television screen. She'd apparently interrupted Nate in the middle of an action-packed video game. A video game!

"No," she answered quickly. "I wouldn't want to interrupt you. Besides I was…just about to make my-self some dinner."

"You cook?"

His astonishment—no, shock—was unflattering, to say the least.

"Of course I do."

"I'm glad to hear it, because I seem to recall that you owe me a meal."

"I—"

"And since we seem to have gotten off on the wrong foot lately, a nice quiet dinner in front of the fireplace sounds like exactly what we need."

Susannah's thoughts were zooming at the speed of light through her befuddled mind. Nate was inviting himself to dinner—one she was supposed to whip up herself! Dear Lord, how could she have so glibly announced that she cooked? Everything she'd ever attempted in the kitchen had been a disaster. Toast was her specialty. Her mind whirled with all the different ways she could serve it. Buttered? With honey? Jam? The list was endless.

"You fix dinner and I'll bring over the wine," Nate said in a low seductive voice. "It's time we sat down together and talked. Deal?"

"I, ah, I've got some papers I need to read over tonight."

"No problem. I'll make it a point to leave early enough for you to finish whatever's necessary."

His eyes held hers for a long moment, and despite everything Susannah knew about Nate, she still wanted time alone with him. She had some papers to review and he had to get back to his video game. A relationship like theirs was not meant to be. However, before she even realized what she was doing, Susannah nodded.

"Good. I'll give you an hour. Is that enough time?"

Once more, like a remote-control robot, she nodded.

Nate smiled and leaned forward to lightly brush his lips over hers. "I'll see you in an hour then."

He put his hand at her lower back and guided her out the door. For a long moment she did nothing more than stand in the hallway, wondering how she was going to get herself out of this one. When she reviewed her options, she realized there was only one choice.

The Western Avenue Deli.

Precisely an hour later, Susannah was ready. A tossed green salad rested in the middle of the table in a crystal bowl, which had been a gift when she graduated from college. Her Aunt Gerty had given it to her. Susannah loved her aunt dearly, but the poor soul had her and Emily confused. Emily would have treasured the fancy bowl. As it happened, this was the first occasion Susannah had even used it and now that she looked at it, she realized that the dish might have been meant for punch. Maybe Nate wouldn't notice. The Stroganoff, on the other hand, was simmering in a pan and perfect.

Her doorbell chimed. Susannah drew in a deep breath, then frantically waved her hands over the simmering food to disperse the scent around the condo before she opened her door.

"Hi," Nate said, leaning against the doorjamb. He held a bottle of wine in one hand.

His eyes were so blue, she thought, it was as if she was looking into a crystal-clear lake. When she spoke her voice trembled slightly. "Hi. Dinner's just about ready."

He sniffed the air appreciatively. "Will red wine do?"

"It's perfect," she told him, stepping aside so he could come in.

"Shall I open it now?"

"Please." She led him into the kitchen.

He stopped and cocked an eyebrow. "It looks like you've been busy."

For good measure, Susannah had stacked a few pots and pans in the sink and set out an array of spices on the counter. In addition, she'd laid out a few books. None of them had anything to do with cooking—she didn't own any cookbooks—but they looked impressive.

"I hope you like Stroganoff," she said cheerfully.

"It's one of my favorites."

Susannah swallowed tightly and nodded. She'd never been much good at deception, but then she'd rarely put her pride on the line the way she was this evening.

While she dished up the Stroganoff, Nate expertly opened the wine and poured them each a glass. When he'd finished, they sat across the table from each other.

After one taste of the buttered noodles and the rich sauce, Nate said, "This is delicious."

Susannah kept her gaze lowered. "Thanks. My mother has a recipe that's been handed down for years." It was a half-truth that was stretched about as far as it could go without snapping back and hitting her in the face. Yes, her mother did have a favorite family recipe, but it was for Christmas candies.

"The salad is excellent, too. What's in the dressing?"

This was the moment Susannah had dreaded. "Ah…" Her mind faltered before she could remember exactly what usually went into salad dressings. "Oil!"

she cried, as if black gold had just been discovered in her living room.

"Vinegar?"

"Yes." She nodded eagerly. "Lots of that."

Planting his elbows on the table, he smiled at her. "Spices?"

"Oh, yes, those, too."

His mouth was quivering when he took a sip of wine.

Subterfuge had never been Susannah's strong point. If Nate hadn't started asking her these difficult questions, she might have been able to pull off the ruse. But he obviously knew, and there wasn't any reason to continue it.

"Nate," she said, after fortifying herself with a sip of wine, "I...I didn't exactly cook this meal myself."

"The Western Avenue Deli?"

She nodded, feeling wretched.

"An excellent choice."

"H-how'd you know?" Something inside her demanded further abuse. Anyone else would have dropped the matter right then.

"You mean other than the fact that you've got enough pots and pans in your sink to have fed a small army? By the way, what could you possibly have used the broiler pan for?"

"I...was hoping you'd think I'd warmed the noodles on it."

"I see." He was doing an admirable job of not laughing outright, and Susannah supposed she should be grateful for that much.

After taking a bite of the dinner roll, he asked, "Where'd you get all the spices?"

"They were a Christmas gift from Emily one year.

She continues to hold out hope that a miracle will happen and I'll suddenly discover I've missed my calling in life and decide to chain myself to the stove.''

Nate grinned as if he found the picture an amusing one. "For future reference, I can't see how you'd need poultry seasoning or curry powder for Stroganoff.''

"Oh.'' She should have quit when she was ahead. "So…you knew right from the first?''

Nate nodded. "I'm afraid so, but I'm flattered by all the trouble you went to.''

"I suppose it won't do any more harm to admit that I'm a total loss in the kitchen. I'd rather analyze a profit-and-loss statement any day than attempt to bake a batch of cookies.''

Nate reached for a second dinner roll. "If you ever do, my favorite are chocolate chip.''

"I'll remember that.'' An outlet for Rainy Day Cookies had recently opened up on the waterfront and they were the best money could buy.

Nate helped her clear the table once they'd finished. While she rinsed the plates and put them in the dishwasher, Nate built a fire. He was seated on the floor in front of the fireplace waiting for her when she entered the room.

"More wine?'' he asked, holding up the bottle.

"Please.'' Inching her straight skirt slightly higher, Susannah carefully lowered herself to the carpet next to him. Nate grinned and reached for the light, turning it to the lowest setting. Shadows from the fire flickered across the opposite wall. The atmosphere was warm and cozy.

"All right,'' he said softly, close to her ear. "Ask away.''

Susannah blinked, not sure what he meant.

"You've been dying of curiosity about me from the moment we met. I'm simply giving you the opportunity to ask me anything you want."

Susannah gulped her wine. If he could read her so easily, then she had no place in the business world. Yes, she was full of questions about him, and had been trying to find a way to bring some of them subtly into the conversation.

"First, however," he said, "let me do this."

Before she knew what was happening, Nate had pressed her down onto the carpet and was kissing her. Kissing her deeply, drugging her senses with a mastery that was just short of arrogant. He'd caught her unprepared, and before she could raise any defenses, she was captured in a dizzying wave of sensation.

When he lifted his head, Susannah stared up at him, breathless and amazed at her own ready response. Before she could react, Nate reached behind her. He unpinned her hair, then ran his fingers through it.

"I've been wanting to do that all night," he murmured.

Still she couldn't speak. He'd kissed and held her but these actions didn't seem to affect his powers of speech, while she felt completely flustered and perplexed.

"Yes, well," she managed to mutter, righting herself. "I...forget what we were talking about."

Nate moved behind her and pulled her against his chest, wrapping his arms around her and nibbling on the side of her neck as if she were a delectable dessert. He paused long enough to answer her question. "I believe you were about to ask me something."

"Yes...you're right, I was...Nate, do you work?"

"No."

Delicious shivers were racing up and down her spine. His teeth found her earlobe and he sucked gently on that, causing her insides to quake in seismic proportions.

"Why not?" she asked, her voice trembling.

"I quit."

"But why?"

"I was working too hard. I wasn't enjoying myself anymore."

"Oh."

His mouth had progressed down the gentle slope of her neck to her shoulder, and she closed her eyes to the warring emotions churning inside her. Part of her longed to surrender to the thrill of his touch, yet she hungered to know all she could about this unconventional man.

Nate altered his position so he was in front of her once more. He kissed her gently and then his mouth began exploring her face with soft kisses that fell like gentle raindrops over her eyes, nose, cheeks and lips.

"Anything else you want to know?" he asked, pausing.

Unable to do more than shake her head, Susannah sighed and reluctantly unwound her arms from around his neck.

"Do you want more wine?" he asked.

"No...thank you." It demanded all the fortitude she possessed not to ask him to keep kissing her.

"Okay," he said, making himself comfortable. He leaned forward and wrapped his arms around his knees. "My turn."

"Your turn?"

"Yes," he said with a lazy grin that did wicked

things to her equilibrium. "I have a few questions for you."

Susannah found it difficult to center her attention on anything other than the fact that Nate was sitting not more than a few inches away from her and could lean over and kiss her again at any moment.

"You don't object?"

"No," she said, gesturing with her hand.

"Okay, tell me more about yourself."

Susannah paused. For the life of her, she couldn't think of a single thing that would impress him. She'd worked hard, climbing the corporate ladder, inching her way toward her long-range goals.

"I'm up for promotion," she began. "I started working for H&J Lima five years ago. I chose this company, although the pay was less than what I'd been offered by two others."

"Why?"

"There's opportunity with them. I looked at the chain of command and saw room for steady advancement. Being a woman is both an asset and a detriment, if you know what I mean. I had to work hard to prove myself, but I was also aware of being the token woman on the staff."

"You mean you were hired *because* you were female?"

"Exactly. But I swallowed my pride and set about proving that I could handle anything asked of me, and I have."

Nate looked proud of her.

"Five years ago, I decided I wanted to be the vice president in charge of marketing," she said, her voice gaining strength and conviction in pace with her enthusiasm. "It was a significant goal, because I'd be the first woman to hold a position that high within the company.''

''And?''

''And I'll find out in the next few weeks if I'm going to get it. I'll derive a good deal of satisfaction from recognizing that I earned it. I won't be their token female in upper management any longer.''

''What's the competition like?''

Susannah slowly expelled her breath. ''Stiff. Damn stiff. There are two men in the running, and both have been with the company as long as me, and in one case longer. Both are older, bright and dedicated.''

''You're bright and dedicated, too.''

''That may not be enough,'' she murmured. Now that her dream was within reach, she yearned for it even more. She could feel Nate's eyes studying her.

''This promotion means a lot to you, doesn't it?''

''Yes. It's everything. From the moment I was hired, I've striven toward this very thing. But it's happening much faster than I dared hope.''

Nate was silent for a moment when she'd finished. He put another log on the fire, and although she hadn't asked for it, he replenished her wine.

''Have you ever stopped to think what would happen if you achieved your dreams and then discovered you weren't happy?''

''How could I not be happy?'' she asked. She honestly didn't understand. For years she'd striven toward obtaining this vice presidency. Of course she was going to be happy. She'd be thrilled, elated, jubilant.

Nate's gaze narrowed. ''Aren't you worried about there being a void in your life?''

Oh, no, he was beginning to sound like Emily. ''No,'' she said flatly. ''How could there be? Now before you start, I know what you're going to say, so please don't. Save your breath. Emily has argued with me about this very subject from the time I graduated from college."

Nate looked genuinely puzzled. "Argued with you about what?"

"Getting married and having a family. The roles of wife and mother just aren't for me. They never have been and they never will be."

"I see."

Susannah was equally convinced he didn't. "If I were a man, would everyone be pushing me to marry?"

Nate chuckled and his eyes rested on her for a tantalizing moment. "Trust me, Susannah, no one is going to mistake you for a man."

She grinned and lowered her gaze. "It's the nose, isn't it?"

"The nose?"

"Yes." She twisted sideways and held her head at a lofty angle in order for him to view her classic profile. "I think it's my best feature." The wine had obviously gone to her head. But that was all right because she felt warm and cozy and Nate was sitting beside her. Rarely had she been more content.

"Actually I wasn't thinking about your nose at all. I was remembering that first night with Michelle."

"You mean when we both fell asleep in the living room?"

Nate nodded and reached for her shoulder, his eyes trapping hers. "It was the only time in my life I can remember having one woman in my arms and wanting another."

CHAPTER FIVE

"I've DECIDED not to see him again," Susannah announced.

"I beg your pardon?" Ms. Brooks stopped in her tracks and looked at her boss.

Unnerved, Susannah made busywork at her desk. "I'm sorry, I didn't realize I'd spoken aloud."

Her secretary delivered the coffee to her desk and hesitated. "How late did you end up staying last night?"

"Not long," Susannah lied. It had, in fact, been almost ten when she left the building.

"And the night before?" Ms. Brooks pressed.

"Not so late," Susannah fibbed again.

Eleanor Brooks quietly left the room, but not before she gave Susannah a stern look, which said she didn't believe her for one moment.

As soon as the door closed, Susannah pressed the tips of her fingers to her forehead and exhaled a slow steady breath. Dear heaven, Nate Townsend had her so twisted up inside she was talking to the walls.

Nate hadn't left her condo until almost eleven the night he'd come for dinner, and by that time he'd kissed her nearly senseless. Three days had passed and Susannah could still taste and feel his mouth on hers. The scent of his aftershave lingered in her living room to the point that she looked for him every time she walked into the room.

The man didn't even hold down a job. Oh, he'd had one, but he'd quit and it was obvious, to her at least, that he wasn't in any hurry to get another. He'd held her and kissed her and patiently listened to her dreams. But he hadn't shared any of his own. He had no ambitions, and no urge to better himself.

And Susannah was falling head over heels for him.

Through the years, she had assumed she was immune to falling in love. She was too sensible for that, too practical, too career oriented. Not once did she suspect she would fall so hard for someone like Nate. Nate, with his no-need-to-rush attitude and tomorrow-will-take-care-of-itself lifestyle.

Realizing what was happening to her, Susannah had done the only thing she could—gone into hiding. For three days she'd managed to avoid Nate. He'd left a couple of messages on her answering machine, which she'd ignored. If he confronted her, she had a perfect excuse. She was working. And it was true: she spent much of her time holed up in the office. She left home early in the morning and arrived home late at night. The extra hours she was putting in served two distinct purposes: they showed her employer that she was dedicated, and kept her from having to deal with Nate.

Her intercom buzzed, effectively pulling Susannah from her thoughts. She reached over and pressed down the button. "Yes?"

"Mr. Townsend is on the phone."

Susannah squeezed her eyes closed and her throat muscles tightened. "Take a message," she said, her voice little more than a husky whisper.

"He insists on speaking to you."

"Tell him I'm in a meeting and...unavailable."

That wasn't like Susannah to lie, and her secretary knew it.

Ms. Brooks hesitated and then asked, "Is this the man you plan never to see again?"

The abruptness of her secretary's question caught Susannah off guard. "Yes..."

"I thought as much. I'll tell him you're not available."

"Thank you." Susannah's hand was trembling by the time she released the intercom button. She hadn't dreamed Nate would call her at the office.

By eleven, a feeling of normalcy had returned. Susannah was gathering together her notes for an executive meeting with the finance committee when her secretary entered her office. "Franklin phoned and canceled his afternoon appointment."

Susannah paused. "Did he want to reschedule?"

"Friday at ten."

She nodded. "That'll be fine." It was on the tip of her tongue to ask her secretary how Nate had responded earlier when told she was unavailable, but she resisted the temptation.

"Mr. Townsend left a message."

Her secretary knew her too well, it seemed, and could read her thoughts. "Leave it on my desk."

"You might want to read it," the older woman urged, looking flustered.

"I will. Later."

Halfway through the meeting, Susannah wished she'd followed her assistant's advice. Impatience filled her. She wanted this finance meeting over so she could hurry back to her desk and read the message from Nate. Figures flew over her head—important ones with bearing on the outcome of the marketing strategy she and her department had planned. Yet, again and again, Susannah found her thoughts drifting to Nate.

That wasn't like her. When the meeting finally ended, she was furious with herself. She walked briskly back to her office, her low heels making staccato taps against the polished hardwood floor.

"Ms. Brooks," she said, as she hurried into the outer office. "Could you—"

Susannah stopped dead in her tracks. The last person she'd expected to see was Nate. He was sitting on the corner of her secretary's desk, wearing a Mariners T-shirt, faded jeans and a baseball cap. He tossed a hardball in the air and deftly caught it in his mitt.

Eleanor Brooks looked both unsettled and inordinately pleased. No doubt Nate had used some of his considerable male charm on the gray-haired grandmother.

"It's about time," Nate said, grinning devilishly. He leaped off the corner of the desk. "I was afraid we were going to be late for the game."

"Game?" Susannah repeated. "What game?"

Nate held out his right hand to show her his baseball mitt and ball—just in case she hadn't noticed them earlier. "The Mariners are playing, and I've got two of the best seats in the place reserved for you and me."

Susannah's heart sank to the pit of her stomach. It was just like Nate to assume she could take off in the middle of the day on some lark. He obviously had no understanding of what being a responsible employee meant. It was bad enough that he'd dominated her thoughts through an important meeting, but suggesting they escape for an afternoon was too much.

"You don't honestly expect me to leave, do you?"

"Yes."

"I can't. I won't."

"Why not?"

"I'm working," she said, deciding that was enough explanation.

"You've been at the office late every night this week. You need a break. Come on, Susannah, let your hair down long enough to have a good time. It isn't going to hurt. I promise."

He was so casual about the whole thing, as if obligation and duty were of little significance. It proved more than anything that he didn't grasp the concept of hard work being its own reward.

"It will hurt," she argued.

"Okay," he said forcefully. "What's so important this afternoon?" To answer his own question, he walked around her secretary's desk. Then he leaned forward and flipped open the pages of her appointment schedule.

"Mr. Franklin canceled his three o'clock appointment," Ms. Brooks reminded her primly. "And you skipped lunch because of the finance meeting."

Susannah glared at the older woman, wondering what exactly Nate had said or done that had turned her loyal secretary into a traitor on such short acquaintance.

"I have other more important things to do," Susannah told them both stiffly.

"Not according to your appointment schedule," Nate returned confidently. "As far as I can see you haven't got an excuse in the world not to attend that baseball game with me."

Susannah wasn't going to stand there and argue

with him. Instead she marched into her office with a precision step General George Patton would have admired and dutifully sat down at her desk.

To her chagrin both Nate and Ms. Brooks followed her inside. It was all Susannah could do not to bury her face in her hands and demand they both leave.

"Susannah," Nate coaxed gently, "you need a break. Tomorrow you'll come back rejuvenated and refreshed. If you spend as many hours at the office as you have lately, you'll begin to lose some of your perspective. An afternoon away will do you a world of good."

Her secretary looked as if she were about to comment, but Susannah stopped her with a scalding look. Before she could say anything to Nate, someone else entered her office.

"Susannah, I was just looking over these figures and I—" John Hammer stopped midsentence when he noticed the two other people in her office.

If there had been an open window handy, Susannah would have gladly hurled herself through it. The company director smiled benignly, however, looking slightly embarrassed at having interrupted her. Now, it seemed, he was awaiting an introduction.

"John, this is Nate Townsend…my neighbor."

Ever the gentleman, John stepped forward and extended his hand. If he thought it a bit odd to find a man in Susannah's office dressed in jeans and a jersey, he didn't show it.

"Nate Townsend," he repeated, pumping his hand. "It's a pleasure, a real pleasure."

"Thank you," Nate returned. "I'm here to pick up Susannah. We're going to a Mariners game this afternoon."

John removed the glasses from the end of his nose, and looked thoughtful. "An excellent idea."

"No, I really don't think I'll go. I mean..." She stopped when it became obvious that no one was paying any attention to her protests.

"Nate's absolutely right," John said, setting the file on her desk. "You've been putting in a lot of extra hours lately. Take the afternoon off. Enjoy yourself."

"But—"

"Susannah, are you actually going to argue with your boss?" Nate prompted.

Her jaw sagged. "I...guess not."

"Good. Good." John looked as pleased as if he'd made the suggestion himself. He was smiling at Nate and nodding as if the two were longtime friends.

Her expression more than a little smug, Eleanor Brooks returned to her own office.

Nate glanced at his watch. "We'd better leave now or we'll miss the opening pitch."

With heavy reluctance, Susannah reached for her purse. She'd done everything within her power to avoid Nate, yet through no fault of her own, she was going to spend the afternoon in his company. They didn't get a chance to speak until they reached the elevator, but as soon as the door glided shut, Susannah tried once more. "I can't go to a baseball game dressed like this."

"You look fine to me."

"But I've got a business suit on."

"Hey, don't sweat the small stuff." His hand reached for hers and when the elevator door opened on the bottom floor, he led her out of the building. Once outside, he quickened his pace as he headed down Fourth Avenue toward the Kingdome.

"I want you to know I don't appreciate this one bit," she said, forced to half run to keep pace with his long-legged stride.

"If you're going to complain, wait until we're inside and settled. As I recall, you get testy on an empty stomach." His smile was enough to cause a nuclear meltdown, but she was determined not to let it influence her. Nate had a lot of nerve to come bursting into her office, and as soon as she could catch her breath, she'd tell him so.

"Don't worry, I'm going to feed you," he promised, when they were forced to wait at a red light.

His assurance did little to smooth her ruffled feathers. Lord only knew what John Hammer thought—although she had to admit that her employer's reaction had baffled her. John was as hardworking and dedicated as Susannah herself. It wasn't like him to fall in with Nate's offbeat idea of attending a ball game in the middle of the afternoon. In fact, it almost seemed as if John knew Nate, or had heard of him. Hardly ever had she seen her employer show such enthusiasm when introduced to anyone.

The man at the Kingdome gate took their tickets and Nate directed her to a pair of seats right behind home plate. Never having attended a professional baseball game before, Susannah didn't realize how good these seats actually were.

She'd no sooner sat down in her place when Nate leaped to his feet and raised his right hand. Susannah slouched as low as she could in the unyielding seat. The next thing she knew, a bag of peanuts whizzed past her ear.

"Hey!" she cried, and jerked around.

"Don't panic," Nate said, and chuckled. "I'm just

playing catch with the vendor.'' No sooner had the words parted from his mouth when he expertly caught a second bag.

''Here.'' Nate handed her both bags. ''The hot dog guy will be by in a minute.''

Susannah had no intention of sitting still while food was being tossed about. ''I'm getting out of here. If you want to play ball, go on the field.''

Once more Nate laughed, the sound husky and rich. ''If you're going to balk at every little thing, I know a good way to settle you down.''

''Do you think I'm a complete idiot? First you drag me away from my office, then you insist on throwing food around like some schoolboy. I can't even begin to guess what's going to happen next, and another thing—''

She didn't get any further, although her outrage was mounting with every breath she drew. Before she could guess his intention, Nate planted his hands on her shoulders, hauled her against him and gave her one of his dynamite-packed kisses.

Completely unnerved, she numbly lowered herself back into her seat and closed her eyes, her pulse roaring in her ears.

The next thing she knew, Nate was pressing a fat hot dog into her lifeless hands. ''I had them put everything on it,'' he explained.

A glance at the overstuffed bun informed her that ''everything'' included pickles, mustard, ketchup, onions and sauerkraut and one or two more items she wasn't sure she could identify.

''Now eat it before I'm forced to kiss you again.''

His warning was all the incentive she needed. Several minutes had passed since he'd last kissed her and she was still so bemused she could hardly think. On cue, she lifted the hot dog to her mouth, prepared for the worst. But to her surprise, it didn't taste half bad. In fact, it was downright palatable. When she'd polished it off, she reached for the peanuts, which were still warm from the roaster. Warm and salty, and excellent.

Another vendor strolled past and Nate bought them each a cold drink.

The first inning was over by the time Susannah finished eating. Nate reached for her hand. "Feel better?" His eyes were friendly enough to warm water.

One look certainly had full effect on Susannah. Every time her eyes met his she felt as if she were caught in a whirlpool and about to be sucked under. She'd tried to resist the pull, but it had been impossible.

"Susannah?" he prompted.

It was all she could do to nod. After a moment she said, "I still feel a little foolish though...."

"Why?"

"Come on, Nate. I'm the only person here in a business suit, for heaven's sake."

"I can fix that."

"Oh?" Susannah sincerely had her doubts. What did he plan to do? Undress her?

He gave her another one of his famous knowing smiles and casually excused himself. Puzzled, Susannah watched as he made his way toward the concession stand. Then minutes later he was back with a Mariner jersey in one hand, a baseball cap in the other.

Removing her suit jacket, Susannah slipped the jersey over her head. When she was finished, Nate set the baseball cap on her head, adjusting it so the bill dipped low over her forehead.

"There," he said, satisfied. "You look like one of the home team now."

"Thanks." She smoothed the T-shirt over her straight skirt and wondered at the sight she made. Funny how it didn't seem to matter. She was having a good time with Nate, and it felt wonderful to laugh and enjoy life.

"You're welcome."

They both settled back in their seats to give their full attention to the game. The Seattle Mariners were down by one run at the bottom of the fifth inning.

Susannah didn't know all that much about baseball, but the crowd was a good size and seemed to be lending its support to the home team. She loved the organ music and the atmosphere, which crackled with excitement, as if everyone was waiting for something splendid to happen.

"You've been avoiding me," Nate said halfway through the sixth inning. "I want to know why."

She couldn't very well tell him the truth, but lying seemed equally unattractive. Pretending to focus her attention on the field, Susannah shrugged, hoping he'd accept that as explanation enough.

"Susannah?"

She should have known he would force the issue. "Because I don't like what happens when you kiss me," she blurted out.

"What happens?" he echoed. "The first time we kissed, you nearly dealt my ego a fatal blow. As I recall, you claimed it was a pleasant experience. I believe you described it as 'nice,' and said that was about it."

Susannah kicked at the litter on the cement floor with the toes of her pumps, her gaze downcast. "Yes, I do remember saying something along those lines."

"You lied?"

He didn't need to drill her to prove his point. "All right," she admitted, "I lied. But you knew that all along. You must have, otherwise…"

"Otherwise what?"

"You wouldn't be kissing me every time you want to coerce me into doing something I don't want to do."

Crow's-feet fanned out at the edges of his eyes as he grinned, making him look both naughty and angelic at once.

"You knew all along, so don't give me that injured-ego routine!"

"It feels good for you to admit it. There's electricity between us, Susannah, and it's about time you recognized that. I did, from the very first."

"Sure. But there's a big difference between standing next to an electrical outlet and fooling around with a high-voltage wire. I prefer to play it safe."

"Not me." He ran a knuckle down the side of her face. Circling her chin, his finger rested on her lips, which parted as if by demand. "No," he said in a hushed voice, studying her. "I always did prefer to live dangerously."

"I've noticed." Nerve endings tingled at his touch, and Susannah held her breath until he removed his hand. Only then did she breathe normally once again.

The cheering crowd alerted her to the fact that something important had taken place in the game. Glad to have her attention diverted from Nate, she watched as a Mariner rounded the bases for a home run. Pleased, she clapped politely, although her enthusiasm was far more restrained than that of the other spectators around her.

That changed, however, at the bottom of the ninth inning. The bases were loaded and Susannah sat on the edge of her seat as the designated hitter approached home plate.

The spectators around her were chanting, "Grand slam, grand slam!" and Susannah's voice soon joined in. The pitcher tossed a fast ball, and unable to watch, she squeezed her eyes shut. But the sound of the wood hitting the ball was immediately recognizable. Susannah opened her eyes and leaped to her feet as the ball flew into left field and over the wall. The crowd went wild, and after doing an impulsive jig, Susannah threw her arms around Nate's neck and hugged him.

Nate appeared equally excited, and when Susannah had her feet back on the ground once more, he raised his fingers to his mouth and let loose a piercing whistle.

She was laughing and cheering and even went so far as to cup her hands along the sides of her mouth and boisterously yell her approval. It was then that she noticed Nate watching her. His eyes were wide with feigned shock, as if he couldn't believe the refined and cultured Susannah Simmons would dare to lower herself to such enthusiastic approval.

His censure instantly cooled her reactions, and she returned to her seat and demurely folded her hands and crossed her ankles, embarrassed now by her uninhibited response to something as mindless as a baseball game. When she dared to glance in Nate's direction, she discovered him watching her intently.

"Nate," she whispered, disconcerted by his undivided attention. The game was over and everyone around them had started to leave their seats. Susannah could feel the color in her cheeks. "Why are you looking at me like that?"

"You amaze me."

More likely, she'd disgraced herself in his eyes by her wild display. She was mortified.

"You're going to be all right, Susannah Simmons," he announced cryptically. "We both are."

"Susannah, I'm surprised to find you home on a Saturday," Emily said as she stepped inside her sister's apartment. "Michelle and I are going to the Pike Place Market this morning and decided to drop by and see you first. You don't mind, do you?"

"No. Of course not. Come in." Susannah brushed the hair from her face and wiped the sleep from her eyes. "What time is it anyway?"

"Eight-thirty."

"That late, huh?"

Emily chuckled. "I forgot. You like to sleep in on the weekends, don't you?"

"Don't worry about it," she said on the tail end of a yawn. "I'll put on a pot of coffee and be myself in no time."

Emily and Michelle followed her into the kitchen. Once the coffee was brewing, Susannah took the chair across from her sister. Michelle gleefully waved her arms, and despite the early hour, Susannah found herself smiling at her niece's enthusiasm toward life. She held out her arms to the baby and was pleasantly surprised when Michelle happily came into them.

"I think she remembers you," Emily said, sounding amazed.

"Of course she does," Susannah said as she nuzzled her niece's neck. "We had some great times, didn't we, kiddo? Especially when it came to feeding you the plums."

Emily chuckled. "I don't know that I'll ever be able to thank you enough for keeping Michelle that weekend. That time away was just what Robert and I needed."

"Don't mention it." Susannah dismissed the appreciation with a weak gesture of her hand. She was the one who'd profited from that zany weekend. It might have been several weeks before she'd met Nate if it hadn't been for Michelle.

Emily sighed. "I've been trying for the past week to get hold of you, but you're never home."

"Why didn't you leave a message on the machine?"

Emily shook her head and her long braid swung with the action. "You know I hate those things. I get all tongue-tied and I can't seem to talk. You might phone me sometime, you know."

Over the past couple of weeks, Susannah had considered it, but she'd been avoiding her sister because she knew that the minute she called, Emily was going to ply her with questions about Nate.

"Have you been working late every night?" Emily asked.

Susannah lowered her gaze. "Not exactly."

"Then you must have been out with Nate Townsend." Emily didn't give her time to respond, but immediately started jabbering away like a blue jay. "I don't mind telling you, Susannah, both Robert and I were impressed with your new neighbor. He was wonderful with Michelle, and from the way he was looking at you, I think he's interested. Now, please, don't tell me to keep my nose out of this. You're twenty-eight, for heaven's sake, and that biological clock is ticking away every single day. If you're ever going to settle down and get serious about a man, the time is now. And personally, I don't think you'll find anyone better than Nate. Why he's…''

She paused to breathe, giving Susannah the chance she'd been waiting for. "Coffee?"

Emily blinked, then nodded. "You didn't listen to a word I said, did you?"

"I listened."

"But you didn't *hear* a single word."

"Sure I did," Susannah countered. "I'd be a fool not to put a ring through Nate Townsend's nose. You want me to marry him before I lose my very last chance at motherhood."

"Exactly," Emily said, looking pleased that she'd conveyed her message so effectively.

Michelle squirmed and Susannah set her on the floor to crawl around and explore.

"Well?" Emily pressed. "What do you think?"

"About marrying Nate? It would never work," she said calmly, as though they were discussing something as mundane as stock options, "for more reasons than you realize. But to satisfy your curiosity I'll list a few. First and foremost I've got a career and he doesn't, and furthermore—"

"Nate's unemployed?" her sister gasped. "But how can he not work? I mean this is an expensive complex. Didn't you tell me the condominium next to yours was nearly twice as large? How can he afford to live there if he doesn't have a job?"

"I have no idea."

Susannah forgot about Nate for the moment as her eyes followed Michelle. It was something of a surprise to realize how much she'd missed her. She stood and brought down two cups from the cupboard.

"That's not decaffeinated, is it?" Emily asked.

"No."

"Then don't bother pouring me a cup. I gave up caffeine years ago."

"Right." Susannah should have remembered. Michelle crawled across the kitchen floor to her and, using Susannah's nightgown for leverage, pulled herself into a standing position. She smiled merrily at her achievement.

"Listen," Susannah said impulsively, leaning over to pick up her niece. "Why don't you leave Michelle with me? We'll take this morning to become reacquainted and you do your shopping without having to worry about her."

A short shocked silence followed. "Susannah?" Emily said, after a moment. "Did I hear you correctly? I thought I just heard you volunteer to baby-sit Michelle."

CHAPTER SIX

THE MORNING WAS BRIGHT and sunny, and unable to resist, Susannah opened the sliding glass door and let the salty breeze off Elliott Bay blow into her apartment. Sitting on the kitchen floor with a saucepan and a wooden spoon, Michelle lightheartedly proceeded to demonstrate her musical talents by pounding out a loud enthusiastic beat.

When the phone rang, Susannah knew it was Nate.

"Good morning," she said, brushing the hair away from her face. She hadn't pinned it up when she'd dressed, knowing Nate preferred it down, and she didn't try to fool herself with excuses for leaving it that way.

"Morning," he breathed into the phone. "Do you have a drummer visiting?"

"No, a special friend. I think she'd like to say hello. Hold on a minute." Susannah put down the telephone receiver and lifted Michelle from the floor. Holding the baby on her hip, she pressed the telephone receiver to the side of Michelle's face. As if on cue, the child let loose an excited flow of gibberish.

"I think she said good-morning," Susannah explained.

"Michelle?"

"How many other babies would pay me a visit?"

"How many Simmons girls are there?"

"Only Emily and me," she answered with a soft laugh, "but trust me, the two of us were enough for any one set of parents to handle."

Nate's responding chuckle was warm and seductive. "Are you in the mood for more company?"

"Sure. If you bring the Danish, I'll provide the coffee."

"You've got yourself a deal."

It wasn't until several minutes had passed that Susannah realized how little resistance she was putting up lately when it came to Nate. Since the baseball game, she'd given up trying to avoid him; she simply hadn't the heart for it, although deep down, she knew anything beyond friendship was impossible. Yet despite her misgivings, after that one afternoon with him she'd come away feeling exhilarated and excited. Being with Nate was like recapturing a part of her youth that had somehow escaped her. Seeing him was fun, true, but it wasn't meant to last, and Susannah reminded herself of that fact every time they were together. Nate Townsend was like an unexpected burst of sunshine on an overcast day, but soon the rain would come, the way it always did. Susannah wasn't going to be fooled into believing there could ever be anything permanent between them.

When Nate arrived, the reunion was complete. He lifted Michelle high into the air and Susannah smiled at the little girl's squeals of delight.

"Where's Emily?" he wanted to know.

"Shopping. She won't be more than an hour or so."

With Michelle in one arm, Nate moved into the kitchen where Susannah was dishing up the pastries and pouring coffee. "She's grown, hasn't she?" she said.

"Is that another new tooth?" he asked, peering inside the baby's mouth.

"It might be," Susannah replied, taking a look herself.

Nate wrapped his free arm around her shoulder and smiled at her. His eyes, so clear and blue, were enough to rob her of her wits.

"Your hair's down," he murmured, his look caressing her upturned face.

She nodded, not knowing how else to respond, although a dozen plausible excuses raced through her mind. But none of them would have been true.

"For me?"

Once more, she answered him with a slight nod.

"Thank you," he whispered, his face so close to her own that his words were like a gentle kiss.

Hardly realizing what she was doing, Susannah leaned into him, pressing herself against his solid length. When he kissed her, it was all she could do not to melt into his arms.

Michelle thought it was great fun to have two adults so close. She wove her fingers into Susannah's hair and yanked until Susannah was forced to pull away from Nate.

Smiling, Nate disengaged the baby's hand from her aunt's hair and kissed Susannah once more. "Hmm," he said when he lifted his head. "You taste better than any sweet roll ever could."

Unnerved, and suddenly feeling more than a little shy, Susannah busied herself setting the pastries on the table.

"Do you have plans for today?" he asked, taking a chair, Michelle gurgling happily on his lap.

Michelle was content for the moment, but from experience Susannah knew she'd want to be back on the floor soon. "I...I was thinking of going into the office for an hour or so."

"I don't think so," Nate returned flatly.

"You don't?" she asked, somewhat surprised.

"I'm taking you out." He paused and surveyed her navy-blue slacks and the winter-white sweater she wore. "I don't suppose you have any jeans."

Susannah nodded. She knew she did, somewhere, but it was years since she'd worn them. As long ago as college, and maybe even her last year of high school. "I don't know if they'll fit, though."

"Go try them on."

"Why? What are you planning? Knowing you, I could end up on top of Mount Rainier looking over a crevasse, and not know how I got there."

"We're going to fly a kite today," he announced casually, as if it was something they'd done several times.

Susannah thought she'd misunderstood him. Nate loved pulling this kind of surprise. First a baseball game in the middle of a workday, and now kites?

"You heard me right, so don't stand there with your eyes as wide as Grand Coulee Dam."

"But...kites...that's for kids. Frankly, Nate," she said, her voice gaining some conviction, "I don't happen to have one stuffed away in any closet. Besides, isn't that something parents do with their children?"

"No, it's for everyone. Don't look so indignant. Adults have been known to have fun, too. Don't worry about a thing. I built a huge one and it's ready for testing."

"A kite?" she repeated, holding in the desire to

laugh outright. She'd been in grade school the last time she'd attempted anything so...so juvenile.

By the time Susannah had rummaged in her closet and found an old pair of jeans, Emily had returned for Michelle. Nate let her sister inside, but the bedroom door was cracked open, and Susannah could hear the conversation. She held her breath, first because her hips were a tiny bit wider than the last time she'd donned her denims, and also because Susannah could never be sure what her sister was going to say. Or do.

It would be just like Emily to start telling Nate how suitable Susannah would be as a wife. That thought was sobering enough to make Susannah stop short.

"Nate," she heard her sister say, "it's so good of you to help with Michelle." Her voice was a full octave higher than usual in her excitement.

"No problem. Susannah will be out in a minute—she's putting on a pair of jeans. We're going to Gas Works Park to fly a kite."

There was a short pause. "Susannah wearing jeans and flying a kite? You mean she's actually going with you?"

"Of course I am. Don't look so shocked," Susannah said, walking into the room. "How did the shopping go?"

Emily couldn't seem to close her mouth. She stared at her sister to the point of embarrassment, then swung her gaze to Nate and back to Susannah again.

Susannah realized she must look different, wearing jeans and with her hair down, but it certainly didn't warrant this openmouthed gawking.

"Emily?" Susannah waved her hand in front of her sister's face in an effort to bring her back to earth.

"Oh...the shopping went just fine. I was able to get

the fresh herbs I wanted. Basil and thyme and…some others.'' As though in a daze, Emily lifted the home-sewn bag draped over her arm as evidence of her successful trip to the market.

"Good," Susannah said enthusiastically, wanting to smooth over her sister's outrageous reaction. "Michelle wasn't a bit of trouble. If you need me to watch her again, just say so."

Her sister's eyes grew wider. She swallowed and nodded. "Thanks. I'll remember that."

The sky was as blue as Nate's eyes, Susannah thought, sitting with her knees tucked under her chin on the lush green grass of Gas Works Park. The wind whipped Nate's box kite back and forth as he scrambled from one hill to the next, letting the brisk breeze carry the multicolored crate in several directions. As it was late September, Susannah didn't expect many more glorious Indian summer days like this one.

She closed her eyes and soaked up the sun. Her spirits raced with the kites that abounded in the popular park. She felt like tossing back her head and laughing triumphantly, for no other reason than that it felt good to be alive.

"I'm beat," Nate said, dropping on the grass beside her. He lay on his back, his arms and legs spread-eagle.

"Where's the kite?"

"I gave it to one of the kids who didn't have one."

Susannah smiled. That sounded exactly like something Nate would do. He'd spent hours designing and constructing the box kite, and yet he impulsively gave it away without a second thought.

"Actually I begged the kid to take it, before I keeled

over from exhaustion," he amended. "Don't let anyone tell you otherwise. Flying a kite is hard work."

Work was a subject Susannah stringently avoided discussing with Nate. From the first he'd been completely open with her. Open and honest. She was confident that if she quizzed him about his profession or lack of one, he'd answer her truthfully.

Basically, Susannah supposed, what she didn't know about him couldn't upset her. Nate apparently had a good deal of money. He certainly didn't seem troubled by financial difficulties. But it was his attitude that worried her. He seemed to see life as just one grand adventure. He leaped from one interest to another without apparent rhyme or reason. Nothing seemed more important or vital than the moment.

"You're frowning," he said. He slipped a hand around her neck and pulled her down until her face was within inches of his own. "Aren't you having a good time?"

She nodded, unable to deny the obvious.

"Then what's the problem?"

"Nothing."

He hesitated and the edges of his mouth lifted sensuously. "It's a good thing you decided against becoming an attorney," he said with a roguish grin. "You'd never be able to fool a jury."

Susannah was amazed that Nate knew she'd once seriously considered going into law.

"Don't look so shocked. Emily told me you'd thought about entering law school."

Susannah blinked a couple of times, then smiled. She brushed the hair from his brow, determined not to ruin this magnificent afternoon with her concerns.

"Kiss me, Susannah," he whispered. The humor

had drained from his features and his gaze searched hers.

Her breath caught. Her eyes lifted and she quickly glanced around. The park was crowded and children were everywhere.

"No," he said, bracing his hands against the sides of her face. "No fair peeking. I want you to kiss me no matter how many spectators there are."

"But—"

"If you don't kiss me, then I'll simply have to kiss you. And, honey, if I do, watch out because—"

Not allowing him to finish, she lowered her mouth enough to gently skim her lips over his. Even that small sample was enough to send the blood racing through her veins. Whatever magic quality this man had should be bottled and sold over the counter. Susannah knew she'd be the first one in line to buy it.

"Are you always this stingy?" he asked when she lifted her head.

"In public, yes."

His eyes were smiling once more and Susannah swore she could have drowned in his look. He exhaled, then leaped to his feet with an energy she had to envy.

"I'm starved," he announced, reaching out for her. Susannah slipped her hand in his and he pulled her to her feet. "But I hope you realize," he whispered close to her ear, wrapping his arm around her waist, "my appetite isn't for food. I'm crazy about you, Susannah Simmons. Eventually we're going to have to do something about that."

"I hope I'm not too early," Susannah said as she entered her sister's home on Capitol Hill. When Emily had called to invite her to Sunday dinner, she hadn't bothered to disguise her intention. Emily was dying to grill Susannah about her budding relationship with Nate Townsend. A week ago, Susannah would have found an excuse to get out of it. But after spending an entire Saturday with Nate, she was so confused that she was willing to talk matters out with her sister, who seemed so much more competent in dealing with male/female relationships.

"Your timing's perfect," Emily said, coming out of the kitchen to greet her. She wore a full-length skirt with a bib apron, and her long hair was woven into a single braid that fell halfway down the middle of her back.

"Here." Susannah handed her sister a bottle of chardonnay, hoping it was appropriate for the meal.

"How thoughtful," Emily murmured, leading her back into the kitchen. The house was an older one, built in the early forties, with a large family kitchen. The red linoleum countertop was crowded with freshly canned tomatoes. Boxes of jars were stacked against one corner of the floor along with a wicker basket filled with fresh sun-dried diapers. A rope of garlic dangled from above the sink and a row of potted plants lined the windowsill.

"Whatever you're serving smells wonderful."

"It's lentil soup."

Emily opened the oven and pulled out the rack, wadding up the skirt of her apron to protect her fingers. "I made a fresh apple pie this morning. Naturally I used organically grown apples so you don't need to worry."

"Oh, good." That hadn't been a major concern of Susannah's.

"Where's Michelle?" Both father and daughter were conspicuously absent.

Emily turned around looking mildly guilty, and Susannah realized that her sister had gone to some lengths to provide time alone with her. No doubt she was anxious to wring as much information about Nate from her as possible. Not that Susannah had a lot to tell.

"So how was your day in the park?"

Susannah took a seat on the stool and made herself comfortable for the upcoming inquisition. "Great. We had a wonderful time."

"You like Nate, don't you?"

Like was the understatement of the year. Contrary to every ounce of sense she possessed, Susannah was falling in love with her neighbor. It wasn't what she wanted, but she hadn't been able to stop herself.

"Yes, I like him," she answered after a significant pause.

Emily looked delighted by her admission. "I thought as much," she said, nodding profoundly. She pushed a stool next to Susannah and sat down. Emily's hands were rarely idle, and true to form, she reached for her crocheting.

"I'm waiting," Susannah said, growing impatient.

"For what?"

"For the lecture."

Emily cracked a knowing smile. "I was just gathering my thoughts. You were always the one who would evaluate things so well. I had such trouble and you aced every paper."

"School reports have very little to do with real life," Susannah reminded her. How much simpler it would be if she could just look up everything she needed to know about dealing with Nate in an encyclopedia.

"I knew that, but I wasn't sure you did."

Perhaps Susannah hadn't until she met Nate. "Emily," she said, her stomach muscles tightening, "I need to ask you something…important. How did you know you loved Robert? What was it that told you the two of you were meant to share your lives?" Susannah realized she was practically laying her cards faceup on the table, but she was past the point for word games. She wanted hard facts.

Her sister smiled softly and tugged at her ball of yarn before she responded. "I don't think you're going to like my answer," she murmured, frowning slightly. "It was the first time Robert kissed me."

Susannah nearly toppled from her perch on the chair, remembering her experience with Nate. "What happened?"

"We'd gone for a nature walk in the rain forest over on the Olympic Peninsula and had stopped to rest. Robert helped me remove my backpack, then he looked into my eyes and leaned over and kissed me." She sighed softly at the memory. "I don't think he intended to do it because he looked so shocked afterward."

"Then what happened?"

"Robert took off his own backpack and asked if I'd minded that he'd kissed me. Naturally I told him I rather liked it, and he sat down next to me and did it again—only this time it wasn't a peck on the lips but a full-blown kiss." Emily's shoulders sagged a little in a sigh. "The moment his lips touched mine I couldn't think, I couldn't breathe, I couldn't even move. When he finished I was trembling so much I thought something might be physically wrong with me.''

"So would you say you felt…electricity?"

"Exactly."

"And you never had with any of the other men you'd dated?"

"Never."

Susannah wiped a hand down her face. "You're right," she whispered. "I don't like your answer."

Emily paused in her crocheting long enough to glance at her. "Nate kissed you and you felt something?"

Susannah nodded. "I was nearly electrocuted."

"Oh, Susannah, you poor thing!" She gently patted her sister's hand. "You don't know what to do, do you?"

"No," she admitted, feeling wretched.

"You never expected to fall in love, did you?"

Slowly Susannah shook her head. And it couldn't be happening at a worse time. The promotion was going to be announced within the next week or so, and the entire direction of her life could be altered if she became involved with Nate. Only she didn't know if that was what either of them wanted. Susannah felt mystified by all that was going on in her life, which until a few short weeks ago had been so straightforward and uncluttered.

"Are you thinking of marriage?" Emily asked outright.

"Marriage," Susannah echoed weakly. It seemed the natural conclusion when two people were falling in love. She was willing to admit her feelings, but she wasn't completely confident Nate felt the same things she did. Nor was she positive that he was ready to leap into something as permanent as a lifelong commitment. She knew *she* wasn't, and the very thought of all this was enough to throw her into a tizzy.

"I don't…know about marriage," Susannah admitted. "We haven't discussed anything like that." The fact was they hadn't even talked about dating regularly.

"Trust me, if you leave it to Nate the subject of marriage will never come up. Men never want to talk about getting married. The topic is left entirely up to us women."

"Oh, come on—"

"No, it's true. From the time Eve slipped Adam the apple, we've been left with the burden of taming man, and it's never more difficult than when it comes to convincing one he should take a wife."

"But surely Robert wanted to get married?"

"Don't be silly. Robert's like every other man alive. I had to convince him this was what he wanted. Subtlety is the key, Susannah. In other words I chased Robert until he caught me." She stopped working her crochet hook long enough to laugh softly at her own wit.

From the time she first met her brother-in-law, Susannah had assumed he'd taken one look at her sister and dropped to his knees to propose. It had always seemed obvious to Susannah that they were meant for each other, far more obvious than it was that Nate was right for her.

"I don't know, Emily," she said on the tail end of a jagged sigh. "Everything is so confused in my mind. How could I possibly be so attracted to this man? It doesn't make any sense! Do you know what we did yesterday afternoon when we'd finished at the park?"

She didn't wait for a response. "Nate brought over his Nintendo game and Super Mario Brothers cartridge, and we played video games. Me! I can't believe it even now. It was a pure waste of time."

"Did you have fun?"

That was a question Susannah wanted to avoid. She'd laughed until her stomach muscles hurt. They'd challenged each other to see who could achieve the better score, and then had done everything possible to sabotage each other.

Nate discovered a sensitive area behind her ear and took to kissing her there just when she was about to outscore him. Fair was fair, however, and Susannah soon discovered Nate had his own area of vulnerability. Without a qualm, she had used it against him, effectively disrupting his game. Soon they both forgot Nintendo and became far more interested in learning about each other.

"We had fun" was all Susannah was willing to admit.

"What about the kite flying?"

Her sister didn't know when to quit. "Then, too," she acknowledged reluctantly. "And at the baseball game Thursday, as well."

"He took you to a Mariners game...on Thursday? But they played in the middle of the afternoon. Did you actually leave the office?"

Susannah nodded, without explaining the details of how Nate had practically kidnapped her. "Back to you and Robert," she said, wanting to change the subject.

"You want to know how I convinced him he wanted to get married? Actually, it wasn't so difficult."

For Emily it wouldn't have been, but for Susannah

it would be another story entirely. The biggest problem was that she wasn't sure she wanted Nate to be convinced. However, she should probably know these things for future reference, and Emily was so much wiser in such matters. She'd listen to what her sister had to say and make up her mind later.

"Remember that old adage—the way to a man's heart is through his stomach? It's true. Men equate food with comfort and love—that's a well-known fact."

"I'm in trouble," Susannah announced flatly. Good grief, she thought, Nate could cook far better than she could any day of the week. If she couldn't attract him with her home-style cooking, then all she had in the way of looks was her classic profile. As painful as it was to accept, men simply weren't attracted to her.

"Now don't overreact. Just because you can't whip up a five-course meal doesn't mean your life is over before it even starts."

"My married life is. I can't put together soup and a sandwich and you know it."

"Susannah, I wish you'd stop demeaning yourself. You're bright and pretty, and Nate would be the luckiest man alive if he were to marry you."

Now that they were actually discussing marriage, Susannah was having mixed feelings. "I…don't know if Nate's the marrying kind," she muttered. "For that matter, I don't know if I am, either."

Emily ignored that. "I'll start you out on something simple and we'll work our way forward."

"Something simple. I don't understand."

"Cookies," Emily explained. "There isn't a man alive who doesn't appreciate homemade cookies. There's something magical about them—really," she

added when Susannah cast her a doubtful glance.
"Cookies create an aura of domestic bliss—I know it
sounds crazy, but it's true. A man can't resist a woman
who bakes him cookies. They remind him of home
and mother and a warm fire crackling in the fireplace." Emily paused and sighed. "Now, it's also true
that men have been fighting this feeling since the beginning of time."

"What feeling?"

Emily glared at her. "Domestic contentment. It's
exactly what they need and want, but they fight it."

Susannah mulled over her sister's words. "Now that
you mention it, Nate did say something about chocolate chip being his favorite."

"See what I mean?"

Susannah couldn't believe she was pursuing this
subject with her sister. Okay, so she and Nate shared
some fun times. Lots of people had good times together. She was also willing to admit there was a certain amount of chemistry between them. But that
wasn't any reason to run to the nearest altar.

For the past several minutes, she'd been trying to
sensibly discuss this situation between Nate and her
with her sister, and before she even knew how it happened, Emily had her talking about marriage and baking chocolate chip cookies. At this rate Emily would
have her married and pregnant by the end of the week.

"So how did dinner go with your sister?" Nate asked
her later that same night. He'd been down on the Seattle waterfront earlier in the day and had brought her
back a polished glass paperweight made of ash from
the Mount St. Helens volcano.

"Dinner was fine," she said quickly, perhaps too quickly. "Emily and I had a good talk."

Nate wrapped his arms around her, trapping her against the kitchen counter. "I missed you."

Swallowing tensely, she exhaled and murmured, "I missed you, too."

He threaded his fingers through the length of her hair, pulling it away from her face and holding it there. "You wore it down again today," he whispered against her neck.

"Yes...Emily says she liked it that way better, too." Talking shouldn't be this difficult, but it was every time Nate touched her. Susannah's knees had the consistency of pudding and her resolve was just as weak. After analyzing her talk with Emily, Susannah had decided to let matters cool between her and Nate for a while. Things were happening much too quickly. She wasn't ready, and she doubted that Nate was, either.

When he kissed her lightly at the scented hollow of her throat, it was all she could do to remain in an upright position. As she braced her hands against his chest, she began to push him gently away and escape. But when his lips traveled up the side of her neck, blazing a trail of moist kisses, she was lost. His mouth grazed along the line of her jaw, slowly edging its way toward her lips, prolonging the inevitable until Susannah thought she would dissolve at his feet.

When he finally kissed her mouth, they both sighed, caught in a swelling tide of longing. His mouth moved hungrily over hers. Then he tugged at her lower lip with his teeth, creating a whole new wave of sensations.

By the time Nate returned to his apartment, Susannah was shaking from the inside out. She'd walked all the way to the kitchen before she realized her intent. She stared at the phone for a long moment. Calling Emily demanded every ounce of courage she possessed. With a deep calming breath, she punched out her sister's number.

"Emily," she said when her sister answered on the second ring, "do you have a recipe for chocolate chip cookies?"

CHAPTER SEVEN

THE RECIPE for chocolate chip cookies was safely tucked away in a kitchen drawer. The impulse to bake them had passed almost immediately and cool reason had returned.

Monday morning, back at the office, Susannah realized how close she'd come to the edge of insanity. The vice presidency was almost within her grasp, and she'd worked too long and too hard to let a promotion of this importance slip through her fingers simply because she felt a little weak in the knees when Nate Townsend kissed her. To even contemplate anything beyond friendship was like…like amputating her right hand because she had a sliver in her index finger. She'd been overreacting, which was understandable, since she'd never before experienced such a strong attraction to a man.

"There's a call for you on line one," Ms. Brooks told her. Her secretary paused, then added dryly, "It sounds like that nice young man who stopped by last week."

Nate. Squaring her shoulders—and her resolve—Susannah picked up the phone. "This is Susannah Simmons."

"Good morning, beautiful."

"Hello, Nate," she said stiffly. "What can I do for you?"

He chuckled. "That's a leading question if there ever was one. Trust me, honey, you don't want to know."

"Nate," she breathed, briefly closing her eyes. "Please. I'm busy. What do you want?"

"Other than your body?"

Hot color leaped into her cheeks and she gave a distressed gasp. "I think we'd better put an end to this conversation—"

"All right, all right, I'm sorry. I just woke up and was lying here thinking how nice it would be if we could escape for the day. Could I tempt you with a drive to the ocean? We could dig for clams, build a sand castle, and then make a fire and sing our favorite camp songs."

"As a matter of interest, I've been up for several hours. And since you've obviously forgotten, I do have a job—an important one. At least it's important to me. Now exactly what is the purpose of this call, other than to embarrass me?"

"Lunch."

"I can't today. I've got an appointment."

"Okay." He sighed, clearly frustrated. "How about dinner, just you and me?"

"I'm working late and was planning on sending out for something. Thanks, anyway."

"Susannah," he said in a burst of impatience, "are we going to go through this again? You should know by now that avoiding me won't change anything."

Perhaps not, she reasoned, but it would certainly help. "Listen, Nate, I really am busy. Perhaps we should continue this conversation another time."

"Like next year—I know you. You'd be willing to bury your head in the sand for the next fifteen years if I didn't come and prod you along. I swear, I've never known a more stubborn woman.''

''Goodbye, Nate.''

''Susannah,'' he persisted, ''what about dinner? Come on, change your mind. We have a lot to talk about.''

''No. I wasn't lying—I do have to work late. The fact is, I can't go outside and play today—or tonight.''

''Ouch,'' Nate cried. ''That hurt.''

''Perhaps it hit too close to home.''

A short silence followed. ''Maybe it did,'' he murmured thoughtfully. ''But before we hang up, I do want to know when I can see you again.''

Susannah leaned forward and stretched her arm across the desk to her calendar, flipping the pages until she found a blank space. ''How about lunch on Thursday?''

''All right,'' he said, ''I'll see you Thursday at noon.''

For a long moment after they'd hung up, Susannah kept her hand on the receiver. As crazy as it seemed, spending the afternoon with Nate at the beach sounded far too appealing. The way he made her think and feel was almost frightening. The man was putting her entire career in jeopardy. Something had to be done, only Susannah wasn't sure what.

An hour later, Ms. Brooks tapped gently on her door and walked inside, carrying a huge bouquet of red roses. ''These just arrived.''

''For me?'' Surely there was some mistake. No one had ever sent her flowers before. There'd never been any reason. There wasn't now.

''The card has your name on it,'' her secretary informed her. She found the small white envelope and handed it to Susannah.

Not until her assistant had left the room did Susannah read the card. The roses were from Nate, who wrote that he was sorry for having disturbed her earlier. She was right, he told her, now wasn't the time to go outside and play. He'd signed it with his love. Closing her eyes, Susannah held the card to her breast and battled down a swelling surge of emotion. The least he could do was stop being so damn wonderful. Then everything would be so much easier.

As it turned out, Susannah finished relatively early that evening and returned home a little after seven. Her apartment was dark and empty—but it was that way every night and she didn't understand why it should matter to her now. Yet it did.

It wasn't until she stood outside Nate's front door and knocked that she realized how impulsive her behavior had become since she'd met him. She was doing everything within her power to avoid him, and at the same time she couldn't stay away.

"Susannah," he said when he opened the door. "This is a pleasant surprise."

She laced her fingers together. "I...I just wanted you to know how much I appreciated the roses. They're lovely and the gesture was so thoughtful."

"Come in," he said, stepping inside. "I'll put on some coffee."

"No, thanks. I've got to get back, but I just wanted to thank you for the flowers...and to apologize if I sounded waspish on the phone. Monday mornings aren't exactly my best time."

Grinning, he leaned against the doorjamb and crossed his arms over his broad chest. "Actually, I was the one who owed you an apology. I should never have phoned you this morning. I was being selfish and thoughtless. You do have an important job and these are anxious days for you. Didn't you tell me that you'd hear about that promotion within the next week or two?"

Susannah nodded.

"You might find this hard to believe, but I don't want to say or do anything that would take that away from you. You're a dedicated, hardworking employee and you deserve to be the first female vice president of H&J Lima."

His confidence in her was reassuring, but confusing. From everything she'd witnessed about Nate, the last thing he appreciated was hard work and its rewards.

"If I do get that promotion," she said, watching him closely, "things will change between you and me. I...I won't have a lot of free time for a while."

"Does this mean you won't be able to go outside and play as often?" he asked, his mouth curving into a sensuous smile. He was taunting her with the words she'd used earlier that morning.

"Exactly."

"I can accept that. Just..." He hesitated.

"What?" Nate was frowning and that wasn't like him. He wore a saucy grin as often as he donned a baseball cap. "Tell me," she demanded.

"I want you to do everything possible to achieve your dreams, Susannah, but there are plenty of pitfalls along the way you need to watch for."

Now it was her turn to frown. She wasn't sure she understood what he was talking about.

"All I'm saying," he elaborated, "is that you shouldn't lose sight of who you are because this vice presidency means so much to you. And even more important, count the cost.'' With that he stepped forward, gazed hungrily into her eyes and then kissed her lightly on the lips. Reluctantly he stepped back.

For a second Susannah teetered, then she moved forward into his arms as if that was the most natural place in the world for her to be. Even now, she wasn't entirely sure she understood what he was talking about, but she couldn't mistake the tenderness she heard in his voice. Once her head had cleared and she wasn't wrapped up in this incredible longing he created every time he touched her, she'd mull over his words.

Susannah woke around midnight, and rolling over, adjusted her pillow. The illuminated dial on her clock radio told her she'd only been sleeping for a couple of hours. She yawned, wondering what had woken her out of a sound peaceful slumber. Closing her eyes, she tucked the blankets more securely over her shoulder, determined to sleep. She tried visualizing herself accepting the promotion to the vice presidency. Naturally, there'd be a nice write-up about her in the evening paper and possibly a short piece in the business journal.

Susannah's eyes drifted open as she recalled Nate's words reminding her not to forget who she was. Who was she? A list of possible replies skipped easily through her mind. She was Susannah Simmons, future vice president in charge of marketing for the largest sporting-goods store in the country. She was a daughter, a sister, an aunt… And then it hit her, hard between the eyes. *She was a woman.* That was what Nate had been trying to tell her. It was the same message

Emily had struggled to get across to her on Sunday. From the time Susannah had set her goals, she'd dedicated her life to her career and pushed every feminine part of herself aside. Now was the time for her to deal with that aspect of her life.

It was the following evening after work. Susannah was leaning against the kitchen counter, struggling to remove the heavy food mixer from its reinforced cardboard box. The way she figured it, Emily's recipe for chocolate chip cookies made three dozen. After her trip to the grocery store, followed by a jaunt to the hardware store for the mixer, cookie sheets and measuring utensils, the cookies were costing her $4.72— each.

The price be damned. She was setting out to prove something important—although she wasn't sure exactly what! She'd have preferred to dismiss all her sister's talk about cookies being equated with warmth and love as a philosophy left over from an earlier generation. Susannah didn't actually believe Emily's theory, but still, she wanted to give it a try. Perhaps she wanted to prove something to herself. Susannah wasn't sure anymore. All she knew was that she had this incredible urge to bake chocolate chip cookies.

Emily had eagerly given her this recipe, and once Susannah thought about it, just how difficult could baking cookies be?

Not hard, she determined twenty minutes later when everything was laid out on her extended counter. Pushing up the sleeves of her shirt, she turned on the radio to keep her company. Next she tied the arms of an old shirt around her waist, using that as an apron. Emily always seemed to wear one when she worked in the kitchen and if her sister did, then it must be important.

The automatic mixer was blending the butter and white sugar nicely and, feeling extraordinarily proud of herself, Susannah cracked the eggs on the edge of the bowl with flair a French chef would have envied.

"Damn," she cried when half the shell fell into the swirling blades. She glared at it a moment, watching helplessly as the beater broke the fragile shell into a thousand pieces. Shrugging, she decided a little extra protein—or was it calcium?—wasn't going to hurt anyone. Finally she turned off the mixer and stirred in the flour, then the chocolate chips.

The oven was preheated exactly as the recipe required when Susannah slipped the shiny new cookie sheet inside. She closed the oven door with a swing of her hip and set the timer for twelve minutes.

Sampling a bite of the dough from the end of her finger, she had to admit it was downright tasty. At least as good as Emily's and perhaps even a little better. But Susannah considered it best not to let anyone know her secret ingredient was eggshell.

Feeling exceptionally proud at how easy everything had been, she poured herself a cup of coffee and sat down at the table with the evening paper.

It was a few minutes later that she smelled smoke. Suspiciously sniffing the air, she set the paper aside. It couldn't possibly be her cookies—they'd been in the oven less than five minutes. To be on the safe side, however, she reached for a pot holder and opened the oven door.

Immediately she was assaulted by billowing waves of smoke, followed by flames that licked out at her.

Gasping in horror, she dropped the pot holder and gave a piercing scream. "Fire! Fire!"

The smoke alarm started ringing, and she swore she'd never heard anything louder in her life. Like a madwoman, Susannah raced for the door, throwing it open in an effort to allow the smoke to escape. Then she ran back to the table and hurled the liquid from her coffee cup straight into the belly of the oven. Coughing hoarsely, she slammed the door shut.

"Susannah!" Breathless, Nate burst into her condominium.

"I started a fire," she shouted above the deafening din of the smoke alarm. Her voice still sounded raspy.

"Where?" Nate circled her table several times, looking frantically for the source of her panic.

"In the oven." Standing aside, she covered her face with her hands, not wanting to look.

A few moments later, Nate took her in his arms. Two blackened sheets of charred cookies were angled into the sink. "Are you all right?"

Somehow she managed a nod.

"You didn't burn yourself?"

She didn't have so much as a blister and told him so.

Gently he brushed the hair away from her face, and expelled his breath in a long drawn-out exercise, apparently to ease his tension. "Okay, how did the fire get started?"

"I don't know," she said dismally. "I...I did everything the way the recipe said, but when I put them in the oven they...they started on fire." By this time her voice was wobbling, like the spin cycle in a washing machine that wasn't balanced.

"The cookies weren't responsible for the fire," he

corrected. "The cookie sheets were the culprits. They must have been new—it seems, ah, you forgot to remove the paper covering from the backs."

"Oh," she whispered and the word escaped on a hiccuping sob. Her shoulders were shaking with the effort to repress her shudders.

"Susannah, there isn't any reason to cry. It was a reasonable mistake. Here, sit down." Gently he lowered her onto the kitchen chair and knelt in front of her, taking her hands in his and rubbing them. "It isn't the biggest disaster in the world."

"I know that," she wailed, unable to stop herself. "You don't understand. It was sort of a test...."

"A test?"

"Yes. Emily claims men love cookies...and I was baking them for you." She didn't go on to add that Emily also claimed that men loved the women who baked those cookies. "I can't cook...I started a fire...and I dropped part of the eggshell in the batter and...and left it.... I wasn't going to tell anyone."

Her confession must have shocked Nate because he stood up and left the room. Burying her face in her hands, Susannah struggled to regain her composure and was doing an admirable job of it when Nate returned, holding a box of tissue.

Effortlessly lifting her into his arms, he pulled out the chair and sat down, holding her securely on his lap. "Okay, Betty Crocker, explain yourself."

She wiped her face dry with the tissue, feeling rather silly at the way she was reacting. So she'd burned a couple of cookie sheets and ruined a batch of chocolate chip cookies. Big deal, she told herself with as much bravado as she could muster. "Explain what?"

"The comment about men loving cookies. Were you trying to prove something to me?"

"Actually it was Emily I wanted to set straight," she whispered.

"You said you were baking them for my benefit."

"I was. You mentioned something yesterday about me not forgetting who I was, finding myself and I…think this sudden urge to bake was my response to that. Believe me, after today, I know I'm never going to be worth a tinker's damn in the kitchen."

"I don't remember suggesting you 'find yourself' in the kitchen," Nate said, looking confused.

"Actually that part was Emily's idea," she admitted. "She's the one who gave me the recipe. My sister seems to believe a woman can coerce a man into selling his heart and soul if she can bake chocolate chip cookies."

"And you want my heart and soul?"

"Of course not! Don't be ridiculous."

He hesitated for a moment and seemed to be considering her words. "Would it come as a surprise if I said I wanted yours?"

Susannah barely heard him; she wasn't in the mood to talk about heart and soul now. She'd just proved how worthless she was in the kitchen. Her lack in that area hadn't particularly troubled her until now. She'd made a genuine effort and fallen flat on her face. Not only that, to have Nate witness her defeat had badly dented her pride. "When I was born something must have been missing from my genes," she murmured thoughtfully. "Obviously. I can't cook, and I don't sew, and I haven't got the foggiest idea of how to tell one end of a knitting needle from the other. I can't do any of the things that…normal people associate with the female gender.''

''Susannah.'' He said her name on a disgruntled sigh. ''Did you hear what I just said?''

In response, she shook her head. She understood everything perfectly. Some women had it and others didn't. Unfortunately, she was in the latter group.

''I was telling you something important. But I can see you're going to force me to say it without words.'' Cupping her face, Nate directed her mouth to his. But he didn't only kiss her this time. The hot moist tip of his tongue traced the sensitive line of her lips until she shivered with a whole new realm of unexplored sensations. All her disheartened thoughts dissolved instantly. She forgot to think, to breathe, to do anything but tremble in his arms. The fire in her oven was nothing compared to the one Nate started in her body. Without conscious thought, she wrapped her arms around his neck and slanted her mouth over his, surrendering to the hot currents of sensation he'd created. She opened herself to him, granting him anything he wanted. His tongue found hers, and Susannah whimpered at the shock of pleasure she received. The sound was absorbed by Nate. Her response, she realized, was innocent and abandoned, unskilled and unknowing, yet eager.

''There,'' he whispered, supporting his forehead against hers, while he sucked in deep breaths. His husky voice was unsteady.

He said it as if that was enough to prove everything. Susannah slowly opened her eyes. She drew in a steadying breath herself, one that caused her to tremble all the way to her toes. If she was going to say anything, it would be to repeatedly whisper his name and ask him why he was doing this and then plead with him never to stop.

He threaded his fingers through her hair and kissed her again with a mastery that caused her to cling to him as if he were a life raft in a stormy sea. Unable to keep still, Susannah ran her palms against the sides of his neck and onto his shoulders and down the length of his arms. He must have liked her touch because he groaned and deepened the kiss even more.

"Unfortunately I don't think you're ready to hear it yet," he said softly.

"Hear what?" she asked, when she could find her voice.

"What I was telling you."

She puckered her brow. "What was that?"

"Forget the cookies. You're more than enough woman for any man."

She blinked, not understanding him. Lord, she barely understood herself.

"I never meant for you to test who you are. All I suggested was that you take care not to lose sight of your own personality. Goals are all well and good, even necessary, but you should calculate the cost."

"Oh." Her mind was still too hazy to properly assimilate his meaning.

"Are you going to be all right?" he asked, as he grazed her cheek with his fingertips. He kissed Susannah's eyelids, closing them.

It was all she could do to nod.

"John Hammer would like to see you right away," Ms. Brooks told Susannah when she walked into her office Thursday morning.

Susannah's heart zoomed to her throat and stayed

there for an uncomfortable moment. This was it. The day for which she'd been waiting five long years.

"Did he say what he wanted?" she asked, struggling to appear at least outwardly calm.

"No," Ms. Brooks returned. "He just asked me to tell you he wanted to talk to you at your convenience."

Susannah slumped into the thick cushion of her high-backed office chair. She propped her elbows on the desk and buried her face in her hands, trying to put some order to her muddled thoughts. "At my convenience," she repeated in a ragged whisper. "I didn't get the promotion. I just know it."

"Susannah," her secretary said sternly, calling her by her first name—something she'd never done in the past. "I think you might be jumping to conclusions."

Susannah glared at her, annoyed by the woman's obtuseness. "If he planned to appoint me as vice president, he would have called me into his office late in the afternoon. That's the way it's always done. Then he'd go through this long spiel about me being a loyal employee and what an asset I am to the company and all that rot. Wanting to talk to me *now* means... Well, you know what it means."

"I can't say that I do," Ms. Brooks said primly. "My suggestion is that you pull yourself together and get over to Mr. Hammer's office before he changes his mind."

Susannah got to her feet and stiffened her spine. Her stomach felt like a pot of melted honey, and no matter how hard she tried she couldn't seem to stop shaking.

"I'll be waiting here when you get back," Ms. Brooks told her on her way out the door. She smiled then, an encouraging gesture that softened her austere features. "Break a leg, kid."

"I think I will, whatever happens." If she didn't get this promotion, she was afraid she'd fall apart. Forcing a calm manner, she decided not to worry until she knew for sure.

John Hammer stood up when she was announced. Susannah walked into his office, and the first thing she noticed was that the two men who were her competition hadn't been called. The company president smiled benignly and motioned toward a chair. Susannah sat on the edge of the cushion, doing her best to disguise how nervous she was.

A smile eased over her employer's features. "Good morning, Susannah…"

True to her word, Susannah's secretary was waiting for her when she strolled back to her office.

"Well?"

Eleanor Brooks followed her to her desk and watched as Susannah carefully sat down.

"What happened?" she demanded a second time. "Don't just sit there. Talk."

Susannah's gaze slowly moved from the phone to her secretary. Then she started to chuckle. The laughter came from deep within her chest and she had to cover her mouth with her palms. When she could talk, she wiped the tears from the corners of her eyes.

"The first thing he did was ask me if I wanted to trade offices while mine was being repainted."

"What?"

Susannah thought Ms. Brooks's look probably reflected her own when Mr. Hammer had asked that question. "That was my first reaction, too," Susannah exclaimed. "I didn't understand what he meant. Then he said he was going to have my office done, because he thought it was only right that the vice president in charge of marketing have a brand-new office.

"You got the promotion?" Eleanor Brooks clapped her hands in sheer delight, then pressed them over her lips.

"I got it," Susannah breathed, squeezing her eyes shut. "I actually got it."

"Congratulations."

"Thank you, thank you." Already she was reaching for the phone. She had to tell Nate. Only a few days before he had said she should go after her dreams, and less than two days later everything was neatly falling into place.

There was no answer at his apartment and, dejected, she replaced the receiver. The need to talk to him consumed her, and she tried again every half hour until she thought she'd go crazy.

At noon, she was absorbed in her work when her secretary announced that her luncheon date had arrived.

"Send him in," Susannah said automatically, irritated that her concentration had been broken.

Casually Nate strolled into her office and plopped himself down in the chair opposite her desk.

"Nate," she cried, leaping to her feet. "I've been trying to get hold of you all morning. What are you doing here?"

"We're going out to lunch, remember?"

CHAPTER EIGHT

"NATE." SUSANNAH RAN around her desk until she stood directly in front of him. "John Hammer called me into his office this morning," she explained breathlessly. "I got the promotion. You're looking at the vice president in charge of marketing for H&J Lima."

For a moment Nate said nothing. Then he asked slowly, thoughtfully, as if he wasn't sure he'd heard her correctly, "You got the promotion?"

"Yes," she repeated. "I got it."

"You actually got it." Nate's eyes were wide with awe.

In her enthusiasm, Susannah nodded several times, with a violence that seemed to dislocate her neck. She was smiling so hard, her face ached.

Throwing back his head, Nate let out a shout that must have shaken the ceiling tile. Then he locked his arms around her waist, lifted her from the floor and swung her around, all the while howling with delight.

Susannah threw back her head and laughed with him. She'd never experienced a moment of joy more profoundly. The promotion hadn't seemed real to her until she had shared it with Nate. The first person she'd thought to tell had been him. He had become the very center of her world, and it was time to admit she was in love with him.

Nate had stopped whirling her around, but he continued to grip her middle so that her face was elevated above his own.

Breathless with happiness, Susannah smiled down on him and on impulse she buried her fingers in his hair. She couldn't resist him, not now, when she was filled with such exhilaration. Her mouth was trembling when she kissed him. She made a soft throaty sound of discovery and pleasure, then lifted her head and smiled at him, noticing how deep and blue his eyes were. Her gaze lowered to the sensual lines of his mouth, and she remembered how she'd felt when he'd held and reassured her after the cookie disaster. She lowered her lips once more, lightly rocking her head back and forth, creating a friction that was so hot, she felt as though she'd catch fire.

In an unhurried movement, Nate lowered her to the ground and wrapped his arms around her. "Susannah," he moaned, kissing the corner of her mouth with exquisite care, "the things you do to me."

With a shudder, she opened her mouth to him. She wanted him to kiss her the way he had in the past. Deep, slow, moist kisses that made her forget to breathe. She yearned for the taste and scent of him to fill her so she couldn't tell where she ended and he began. This was the happiest moment of her life, and only a small portion could be attributed to the promotion. Everything else was Nate and the mounting love she felt for him each time they were together.

Someone coughed nervously in the background, and Nate broke off the kiss and stared impatiently past her to the open door.

"Ms. Simmons," her secretary said, smiling broadly.

"Yes?" Breaking away from Nate, Susannah

smoothed the hair at the sides of her head and struggled to replace her business facade.

"I'll be leaving now. Ms. Andrews will be answering your calls."

"Thank you, Ms. Brooks," Nate muttered, but there was little appreciation in his tone.

Susannah chastised him with a look. "We'll...I'll be leaving directly for my luncheon appointment."

"I'll tell Ms. Andrews."

"This afternoon, I'd like you to call a meeting of the staff," Susannah said, "and I'll announce the promotion."

Eleanor Brooks nodded, but her smiling eyes landed heavily on Nate. "I believe everyone has already guessed from the...commotion that came from here a few minutes ago."

"I see." Susannah couldn't help smiling.

"There isn't an employee here who isn't happy about your news."

"I can think of two," Susannah said under her breath, remembering the men she'd been competing against. Nate squeezed her hand, and it was all she could do to keep from laughing outright.

Her assistant closed the door on her way out, and the minute she did, Nate reached for Susannah to bring her back into the shelter of his arms. "Where were we?"

"About to leave for lunch, as I recall."

Nate frowned. "That's not the way I remember it."

Susannah laughed and squeezed him tightly, loving him all the more. "I think we both forgot ourselves." She broke away and reached for her purse, hooking the long strap over her shoulder. "Are you ready?"

"Any time you are." But the hot eager look in his

eyes told her he was talking about something other than lunch.

Susannah could feel the color working its way up her neck and suffusing her face. "Nate," she whispered, lowering her gaze, "behave yourself. Please."

"I'm doing the best I can under the circumstances," he whispered back, his eyes filled with mischievous delight. "In case you haven't figured it out yet, I'm crazy about you, woman."

"I...I'm pretty keen on you myself."

"Good." He tucked his arm around her waist and led her out of the office and down the long hallway to the elevator. Susannah was certain she could feel the stares of her staff members, but for the first time, she didn't care what image she projected. Everything was right in her world, and she'd never been happier.

Nate chose the restaurant, Il Bistro, which was one of the best in town. The atmosphere was festive, and playing the role of the gentleman to the hilt, Nate wouldn't so much as allow her to look at the menu, insisting that he'd order for her.

"Nate," she whispered once the waiter had left the table, "I want to pay for this. It's a business lunch."

His thick brows arched upward. "And how are you going to rationalize that when your boss questions you about it, my dear?" He wiggled his eyebrows suggestively.

"There's a reason I agreed to go to lunch with you—other than celebrating my promotion, which was something I didn't even know about until this morning." As she'd explained to Nate earlier, her life was going to change with this promotion. New responsibility would result in a further commitment of time and energy to the company, and could drastically alter her relationship with Nate. If anything, she wanted them to grow closer, not apart. This advancement had the potential to make or break them, and Susannah was looking for a way to draw them closer together. She thought she'd found it.

"A reason?" Nate questioned.

They were interrupted by the waiter as he produced a bottle of expensive French wine for their inspection. He removed the cork and poured a sample into the glass for Nate to taste. When Nate nodded in approval, the waiter filled their glasses and discreetly retreated.

"Now, you were saying?" Nate continued, studying her. His mouth quirked up at the edges.

Gathering her resolve, Susannah reached across the table and gripped Nate's hand. "You've always been open and honest with me. I want you to know how much I appreciate that. When I asked you if you had a job, you admitted you'd had one until recently and that you'd quit." She waited for him to elaborate on his circumstances, but he didn't, so she went on. "It's obvious you don't need the money, but there's something else, just as important, that's obvious, too."

Nate removed his fingers from hers and twirled the stem of the wineglass between his open palms. "What's that?"

"You lack purpose."

His gaze lifted to meet hers and his brow creased in query.

"You have no direction," she announced flatly. "Over the past several weeks, I've watched you flit from one area of interest to another. First it was baseball, then it was video games, then kite flying, and tomorrow, no doubt, it'll be something else."

"Traveling," he concluded for her. "I was thinking

of doing some serious sight-seeing. I have a hankering to stroll the byways of Hong Kong.''

"Hong Kong,'' she repeated, gesturing with her hands. "That's exactly what I mean.'' Her heart slowed to a sluggish beat at the thought of his being gone for any length of time. She'd become accustomed to having Nate close, to sharing bits and pieces of her day with him. Not only had she fallen in love with him, he'd quickly become her best friend.

"Do you think traveling is wrong?'' he asked.

"Not wrong,'' she returned swiftly. "But what are you going to do once you've run out of ways to entertain yourself and places to travel? What are you going to do when you've spent all your money?''

"I'll face that when the time comes.''

"I see.'' She lowered her gaze, wondering if she was only making matters worse. There was little she could say to counter his don't-worry attitude.

"Susannah, you make it sound like the end of the world. Trust me, wealth isn't all that great. If I run out of money, fine. If I don't, that's all right, too.''

"I see,'' she murmured miserably.

"You claimed you understood a few minutes ago,'' he countered with a smile. "How can you *see* again so soon?''

"It's because I care about you, I guess.'' She paused and drew in a deep breath. "We may live in the same building, but our worlds are totally different. My future is charted, right down to the day I retire at age sixty-five. I know what I want and how to get there.''

"I thought I did once, too, but then I learned how unimportant it all was.''

"It doesn't have to be like that,'' she told him, her voice filled with determination. "Listen, there's something important I'm going to propose, but I don't want you to answer me now. I want you to give yourself time to think about it. Promise me you'll do at least that.''

''Are you suggesting we get married?'' he teased.

''No.'' Flustered, she smoothed out the linen napkin in her lap, her fingers lingering there to disguise her nervousness. ''I'm offering you a job.''

''You're doing what?'' He half rose out of his seat.

Embarrassed, Susannah glanced nervously around her and noted that several people had stopped eating and were glancing in their direction. ''Don't look so aghast. A job would make a lot of difference in your attitude toward life.''

''And just exactly what position are you offering me?'' Now that the surprise had worn off, he appeared amused.

''I don't know, at least not yet. We'd have to figure out something with personnel. But I'm sure that there would be a position open that would fit your qualifications.''

The humor drained from his eyes, and for a long moment Nate said nothing. ''You think a job would give me purpose?''

''I believe so.'' To her way of thinking, it would help him look beyond today and toward the future. Employment would lend Nate a reason to get out of bed in the mornings, instead of sleeping in until nine or ten every day.

''Susannah—''

''Before you say anything,'' she interrupted, holding up her hand, ''I want you to think it over seriously. Don't say anything until you've had a chance to consider my offer.''

His eyes were more serious than she could ever remember seeing them—other than just before he wanted to kiss her. His look was almost brooding.

Their meal arrived, and the lamb was as delicious as Nate had promised. He was unusually quiet during the remainder of the meal, but that didn't surprise her. He was reflecting on her job offer and that was exactly what she wanted. She hoped he'd come to the right decision. Loving him the way she did, she longed to make his world as right as her own.

Despite Nate's protests, Susannah paid for their lunch. He walked her back to her office, standing with her on the sidewalk while they exchanged a few words of farewell. Susannah kissed him on the cheek and asked once more that he consider her job offer.

"I will," he promised, lightly running his finger down the side of her face.

He left her then, and Susannah watched as he walked away, letting her gaze linger on him for several minutes.

"Any messages?" she asked Dorothy Andrews, who was sitting in her secretary's place.

"One," Dorothy said, without looking up. "Emily—she didn't leave her full name. She said she'd catch you later."

"Thanks." Susannah took the pink slip into her office and, sitting down at her desk, punched out her sister's telephone number.

"Emily, this is Susannah. You phoned?"

"I know I probably shouldn't have called you at the office, but you never seem to be home and I had something important to ask you," her sister said, talking so fast she ran her words together.

"What's that?" Already Susannah was reaching for

a file, intending to read while her sister spoke. It some-times took Emily several minutes to get around to the purpose of any call.

Her sister hesitated. "I've got several large zucchini left from my garden, and I was wondering if you wanted one."

"About as much as I want a migraine headache." After her disaster with the chocolate chip cookies, Su-sannah planned never to so much as read a recipe again.

"The zucchini are excellent this time of year," Em-ily prompted, as if that would be enough to induce Susannah into agreeing to take a truckload.

Her sister hadn't phoned her to ask about zucchini, Susannah would have staked her promotion on it. The Italian vegetable was a lead-in for something else, and no doubt it would be left to Susannah to play a guess-ing game. Mentally, she scanned a list of possible fa-vors and decided to leap in with both feet.

"Zucchini are out, but I wouldn't mind taking care of Michelle again, if you need me."

"Oh, Susannah, would you? I mean, it'd work out so great if you could keep her two weeks from this Saturday."

"All night?" As much as she loved her niece, an-other overnight stretch was more than Susannah wanted to contemplate. As it was, Nate would proba-bly be more than happy to lend a hand. No doubt she'd need it.

"Oh, no, not for the night, just for dinner. Robert's boss is taking us out to eat, and it wouldn't be appro-priate if we took Michelle along. Robert got a big promotion, did I tell you?"

"No."

"I'm so proud of him. I think he's probably the best accountant in Seattle."

Susannah toyed with the idea of letting her sister in on her own big news, but she didn't want to take anything away from her brother-in-law. She could let them both know in two weeks when they dropped off Michelle.

"I'll be happy to keep Michelle for you," Susannah said, and discovered, as she marked the date on her calendar, how much she actually meant that. She might be a disaster waiting to happen in the kitchen, but she didn't do half badly with her niece. The time might yet come when she'd seriously consider having a child or two of her own—not now, of course, but sometime in the future. "All right, I've got you down for the seventeenth."

"Susannah, I can't tell you how much this means to me," Emily said.

By the time Susannah arrived home that evening she was tipsy. The staff meeting that afternoon had gone wonderfully well. After five, she'd been taken out for a drink by her two top aides, to celebrate. Several others from her section had unexpectedly dropped by the cocktail lounge and insisted on buying her drinks, too. By seven, Susannah was flushed and excited, and from experience, she knew it was time to call it quits and phone for a taxi.

Dinner probably would have cut the effects of the alcohol, but she was more interested in getting home. After a nice hot bath, she'd fix herself some toast and be done with it.

She hadn't been home more than a half hour when

her phone rang. Dressed in her robe and sipping tea in the kitchen, she reached for the receiver.

"Susannah, it's Nate. Can I come over?"

Glancing down at her robe and fuzzy slippers, she decided it wouldn't take her long to change.

"Give me five minutes."

"All right."

Dressed in slacks and a sweater, she opened the door when he knocked. "Hi," she greeted cheerfully, aware her mouth had probably formed a crooked grin despite her efforts to smile naturally.

Nate barely looked at her. His hands were thrust deep in his pockets, and his expression was disgruntled as he marched into her apartment. He didn't take a seat but paced the carpet in front of her fireplace like a soldier on guard duty. Obviously something was going on.

She sat on the edge of the sofa, carefully watching him, feeling more than a little reckless and exhilarated from the promotion and the celebration that had followed. She was amused, too, at Nate's peculiar agitation.

"I suppose you want to talk to me about the job offer," she asked, surprised by how controlled her voice sounded.

He paused, splayed his fingers through his thick hair and nodded. "That's exactly what I want to talk about."

"Don't," she said, smiling up at him.

His brow puckered in a frown. "Why not?"

"Because I wanted you to give long and careful consideration to the proposal."

"I need to explain something to you first."

Susannah wasn't listening. There were far more important things she had to tell him. "You're personable, bright and attractive," she began enthusiastically. "You could be anything in the world that you wanted, Nate. Anything."

"Susannah…"

She waved a finger at him and shook her head. "There's something else you should know."

"What?" he demanded.

"I'm in love with you." Her glorious confession was followed by a loud yawn. Unnerved, she covered her mouth with the tips of her fingers. "Oops, sorry."

Nate's eyes narrowed suspiciously. "Have you been drinking?"

She pressed her thumb and index finger together and held them up for his inspection. "Just a little, but I'm more happy than anything else."

"Susannah!" He dragged her name out into the longest, most splendid sigh. "I can't believe you."

"Why not? Do you want me to shout it to all of Seattle, because I will. Watch!" She waltzed into the kitchen and jerked open the sliding glass door.

Actually, some of the effects of the alcohol had worn off, but she'd experienced this irrepressible urge to tell Nate how much she'd come to care for him. They'd skirted around the subject long enough. He didn't seem to want to admit it, but she was, especially now, fortified with her good fortune. This day had been one of the most fantastic of her life. After years of hard work, everything was falling neatly into place, and she'd found the most wonderful man in the world to love—even if he *was* misguided.

The wind whipped against her on the balcony, and the multicolored lights from the waterfront below resembled those on a Christmas tree. Standing at the railing, she cupped her hands over her mouth and shouted,

"I love Nate Townsend!" Satisfied, she whirled to face him and opened her arms as wide as they would go. "See? I just announced it to the world."

He joined her outside, and wrapped his arms around her and closed his eyes. Susannah had expected him to at least show some emotion.

"You don't look very happy about it," she challenged.

"You're not yourself."

"Then who am I?" Fists digging into her hips, she glared up at him, her eyes defiant. "I feel like me. I bet you think I'm drunk, but I'm not."

He didn't reply. Instead he threw an arm over her shoulder and urged her into the kitchen. Then, quickly and efficiently, he started to make coffee.

"I gave up caffeine," she announced.

"When was this? You had regular coffee today at lunch," he said.

"Just now." She giggled. "Come on, Nate," she cried, bending forward and snapping her fingers. "Loosen up a little."

"I'm more concerned about sobering you up."

"You could kiss me."

"I could," he admitted, "but I'm not going to."

"Why not?" She pouted, disappointed by his refusal.

"Because if I do, I may not be able to stop."

Sighing, she closed her eyes and heaved her shoulders. "That's the most romantic thing you've ever said to me."

Nate rubbed a hand over his face and leaned against the kitchen counter. "Have you had anything to eat since lunch?"

"One stuffed mushroom, a water chestnut wrapped

in a slice of bacon and a piece of celery filled with something cheesy.''

"But no dinner?''

"I was going to make myself some toast, but I wasn't hungry.''

"After a stuffed mushroom, a celery stick and a water chestnut? I can see why not.''

"Are you trying to be cute with me? Oh, just a minute, there was something I was supposed to ask you.'' She pulled herself up short and covered one eye, while she tugged at her memory for the date her sister had mentioned. "Are you doing anything on the seventeenth?''

"The seventeenth? Why?''

"Michelle's coming over to visit her Auntie Susannah and I know she'll want to see you, too.''

Nate looked even more disturbed, but he hadn't seemed particularly pleased about anything from the moment he'd arrived.

"I've got something else on that night.''

"Oh, well, I'll make do. I have before.'' She stopped abruptly. "No, I guess I haven't, but Michelle and I'll be just fine, I think…''

The coffee had finished dripping through into the glass pot. Nate poured a cup and, scowling, handed it to her.

"Oh, Nate, what's wrong with you? You haven't been yourself since you arrived. We should be kissing by now and all you seem to do is ignore me.''

"Drink your coffee.''

He stood over her until she'd taken the first sip. She grimaced at the heat. "You know what I drank tonight? I've never had them before and they tasted so good. Shanghai Slungs.''

"They're called Singapore Slings.''

"Oh." Maybe she was more confused than she thought.

"Come on, drink up, Tokyo Rose."

Obediently Susannah did as he requested. The whole time she was sipping away at her coffee, she was watching Nate, who moved restlessly about her kitchen, as if unable to stand still. He was disturbed by something, and she wished she knew what.

"Done," she announced when she'd finished, pleased with herself and this minor accomplishment. "Nate," she said, growing concerned, "do you love me?"

He paused and turned around to face her, his eyes serious. "So much I can't believe it myself."

"Oh, good," she said with an expressive sigh. "I was beginning to wonder."

"Where are your aspirin?" He was searching through her cupboards, opening and closing the ones closest to the sink.

"My aspirin? Did telling me how you feel give you a headache?"

"No." He turned and answered her with a gentle smile. "I want to have it ready for you in the morning because you're going to need it."

Her love for him increased tenfold. "You are so good to me!"

"Take two tablets first thing when you wake up and that should help a little." He crouched in front of her and took both her hands in his. "I'm leaving tomorrow and I won't be back for a couple days. I'll call you, all right?"

"You're going away to think about the job I offered you, aren't you? That's a good idea—when you come back you can tell me your decision." She was forced to stop in order to yawn, a huge jaw-breaking yawn that depleted her strength. ''I think I should go to bed, don't you?''

The next thing Susannah knew, her alarm was buzzing angrily. With the sound came a piercing pain that shot straight through her temple. She groped for the clock, turned it off and sighed with relief. Sitting up in bed proved to be equally overwhelming and she groaned.

When she'd managed to maneuver herself into the kitchen, she saw the aspirin bottle and remembered that Nate had insisted on setting it out the night before.

''Bless that man,'' she said aloud and winced at the sound of her own voice.

By the time she arrived at the office, she was operating on only three cylinders. Eleanor Brooks didn't seem to be any better off than Susannah was. They took one look at each other and smiled knowingly.

''Your coffee's ready,'' her secretary informed her.

''Did you have a cup yourself?''

''Yes.''

''Anything in the mail?''

''Nothing that can't wait. Mr. Hammer was in earlier. He told me to give you this magazine and said you'd be as impressed as he was.'' Susannah glanced over a six-year-old issue of *Business Monthly*, a trade magazine that was highly respected in the industry.

''It's several years old,'' Susannah noted, wondering why her employer would want her to read it now.

''Mr. Hammer said there was a special feature in there about your friend.''

''My friend?'' Susannah didn't understand.

''Your friend,'' Eleanor Brooks repeated. ''The one with the sexy eyes—Nathaniel Townsend.''

CHAPTER NINE

SUSANNAH WAITED until her secretary had left the office before opening the magazine. The article on Nathaniel Townsend was the lead feature. The picture showed a much younger Nate standing in front of a shopping-mall outlet for Rainy Day Cookies, the most successful cookie chain in the country. In his hand he was holding a huge chocolate chip cookie.

Rainy Day Cookies were Susannah's absolute favorite. There were several varieties, but the chocolate chip ones were fantastic.

Two paragraphs into the article, Susannah thought she was going to be physically ill. She stopped reading and closed her eyes to the waves of nausea that lapped against her. Pressing a hand to her stomach, she resolutely focused her attention on the article, storing away the details of Nate's phenomenal success in her numb mind.

He had started his cookie company in his mother's kitchen while still in college. His specialty was chocolate chip cookies, and they were so popular that he soon found himself caught up in a fairy-tale rollercoaster ride that had led him straight to the top of the corporate world. By age twenty-eight, Nate Townsend was a multimillionaire.

Now that she thought about it, an article she'd read six or seven months ago in the same publication had stated that the company was recently sold for an undisclosed sum, which several estimated to be a figure so staggering Susannah had gasped out loud.

Bracing her elbows on the desk, Susannah took several calming breaths. She'd made a complete idiot of herself over Nate, and worse, he had let her. She suspected this humiliation would stay with her for the rest of her life.

To think she'd baked the cookie king of the world chocolate chip cookies, and in the process nearly set the kitchen on fire. But that degradation couldn't compare to yesterday's little pep talk when she'd spoken to him about drive, ambition and purpose, before— dear heaven, it was too much—she'd offered him a job. How he must have laughed at that.

Eleanor Brooks brought in the mail and laid it on the corner of Susannah's desk. Susannah glanced up at her secretary and knew then and there that she wasn't going to be able to cope with the business of the day.

"I'm going home."

Ms. Brooks stopped abruptly. "I beg your pardon?"

"If anyone needs me, tell them I'm home sick."

"But..."

Susannah knew she'd shocked her assistant. In all the years she'd been employed by H&J Lima, Susannah had never used a single day of her sick leave. There'd been a couple of times when she probably should have stayed home, but she'd insisted on working anyway.

"I'll see you Monday morning," she announced on her way out the door.

"I hope you're feeling better then."

"I'm sure I will be." She needed some time alone

to lick her wounds and gather the scattered pieces of her pride. To think that only a few hours earlier she'd drunkenly declared her undying love to Nate Townsend!

That was the worst of it.

When Susannah walked into her apartment she felt as if she was stumbling into a bomb shelter. For the moment she was safe from the world outside. Eventually she'd have to go back and face it, but for now she was secure.

She picked up the afghan her sister had crocheted for her, wrapped it around her shoulders and sat staring sightlessly into space.

What an idiot she'd been! What a fool! Closing her eyes, she leaned her head against the back of the sofa and drew in several deep breaths, releasing the anger and hurt before it fermented into bitterness. She refused to allow her mind to dwell on the might-have-beens and the if-onlys, opting instead for a more positive approach. *Next time*, she would know enough not to involve her heart. *Next time*, she'd take care not to make such a fool of herself.

It amazed her when she awoke an hour later, to realize she'd fallen asleep. Tucking the blanket more securely around her, she analyzed her situation.

Things weren't so bad. She'd achieved her primary goal and was vice president in charge of marketing. The first female to hold such a distinguished position in the company's long history, she reminded herself. Her life was good. If on occasion she felt the yearning for a family of her own, there was always Emily, who was more than willing to share. Heaving a sigh, Susannah told herself that she lacked for nothing. She was respected, hardworking and healthy. Life was good.

Her head ached and her stomach didn't feel much better, but at noon, Susannah heated some chicken noodle soup and forced that down. She was putting the bowl in the dishwasher when the telephone rang. Ms. Brooks was the only one who knew she was home, and her assistant would call her only if it was important. Susannah answered the phone just as she would in her office.

"Susannah Simmons."

"Susannah, it's Nate."

She managed to swallow a gasp. "Hello, Nate," she said as evenly as possible. "What can I do for you."

"I called the office and your secretary said you'd gone home sick."

"Yes. I guess I had more to drink last night than I realized. I had one doozer of a hangover when I woke up this morning." But she didn't add how her malady had worsened once she read the article about him.

"Did you find the aspirin on the kitchen counter?"

"Yes. Now that I think about it, you were by last night, weren't you?" She was thinking fast, wanting to cover her tracks. "I suppose I made a fool of myself," she said, forcing a lightness into her tone. "I didn't say anything to embarrass you…or me, did I?"

He chuckled softly. "You don't remember?"

She did, but she'd rather have been tortured than admit it. "Some of it, but most of the evening remains fuzzy."

"Once I'm back in Seattle I'll help you recall every single word." His voice was low, seductive and filled with promise.

That was one guarantee, however, that Susannah had no intention of accepting.

"I...probably made a complete idiot of myself," she mumbled. "If I were you, I'd forget anything I said. Obviously, I can't be held responsible for it."

"Susannah, Susannah, Susannah," Nate said gently. "Let's take this one step at a time."

"I...think we should talk about this later, I really do...because it's all too obvious I wasn't myself." Moisture pooled at the corners of her eyes and poured down her face. Furious at this display of emotion, she wiped the tears aside with the back of her hand.

"You're feeling better now?"

"Yes...no. I was just about to lie down."

"Then I'll let you," Nate said. "I'll be back Sunday. My flight should arrive early afternoon. I'd like us to have dinner together."

"Sure," she said, without thinking, willing to agree to just about anything in order to put an end to this conversation. She was still too raw, still bleeding. By Sunday, she'd be able to handle the situation far more effectively without all this emotion. By Sunday, she could disguise her pain.

"I'll see you around five then."

"Sunday," she echoed, feeling like a robot programmed to do exactly as its master requested. She had no intention of having dinner with Nate, none whatsoever. He'd find out why soon enough.

The only way Susannah made it through Saturday was by working. She stopped off at her office and sorted through the mail Ms. Brooks had left on her desk. News of her promotion was to be announced in the Sunday business section of the *Seattle Times*, but word had apparently already leaked out, probably

through her boss; a speaking invitation was in the
mail, for a luncheon at a conference of local salespeo-
ple who had achieved a high level of success. The
request was an honor and Susannah scribbled off a
note of acceptance to the organizer. She considered it
high praise to have been asked. The date of the conference was the seventeenth, which was only two
weeks away, so she spent a good portion of the morning typing up notes for her speech.

Sunday morning, Susannah woke feeling sluggish
and out of sorts. She realized almost instantly the
source of her discomfort. This afternoon, she would
confront Nate. For the past two days, she'd gone over
in her mind exactly what she planned to say, how she
would act.

Nate arrived at four-thirty. She answered his knock,
dressed in navy blue slacks and a cream shell-knit
sweater. Her hair was neatly rolled into a chignon.

"Susannah." His gaze was hungry as he stepped
across the threshold and reached for her.

It was too late to hide her reaction by the time she
realized he intended to kiss her. He swept her into his
arms and eagerly pressed his mouth over hers. Despite
all that he'd failed to tell her, Susannah felt an immediate warm response she couldn't disguise.

Nate threaded his fingers through her hair, removing
the pins that held it in place, while he leisurely moved
his mouth over hers.

"Two days have never seemed so long," he
breathed, then nibbled on her lower lip as if she were
a delectable feast and he was a starved man.

Regaining her composure, she broke away, her
shoulders heaving. "Would you like some coffee?"

"No. The only thing I want is you."

She started to walk away from him, but Nate reached out and caught her, hauling her back into the warm shelter of his arms. He linked his hands at the small of her back and gazed down at her, his eyes caressing and gentle. Gradually, his expression altered.

"Is everything all right?" he asked.

"Yes...and no," she admitted dryly. "I happened upon an article in an old issue of *Business Monthly*. Does that tell you anything?"

He hesitated, and for a long moment Susannah wondered if he was going to say anything or not.

"So you know?"

"That you're the world's cookie king, or once were—yes, I know."

His eyes narrowed slightly. "Are you angry?"

She sighed. A good deal depended on her delivery, and although she'd practiced her words several times, it was far more difficult than she'd realized. She was determined, however, to remain calm and casual.

"I'm more embarrassed than amused," she said. "I wish you'd said something before I made such a fool of myself."

"Susannah, I know you have every right to be upset." He released her and rubbed the back of his neck as he began to walk back and forth between the living room and kitchen. "It isn't like it was a deep dark secret. I sold the business almost six months ago, and I was taking a sabbatical—hell, I needed one. I'd driven myself as far as I could. My doctor thinks I was on the verge of a complete physical collapse. When I met you, I was just coming out of it, learning how to enjoy life all over again. The last thing I wanted to do was sit down and talk about the past thirteen years. I'd put Rainy Day Cookies behind me, and I was looking to build a new life.''

Susannah crossed her arms. "Did you ever intend to tell me?''

"Yes!'' he said vehemently. "Thursday night. You were so sweet to have offered me a job and I knew I had to say something then, but you were…''

"Tipsy,'' she finished for him.

"All right, tipsy, for lack of a better word. You've got to understand why I didn't. The timing was all wrong.''

"You must have got a good laugh from the cookie disaster,'' she said, and was surprised at how steady her voice remained. Her poise didn't even slip, and she was proud of herself.

The edges of his mouth quivered slightly, and it was apparent that he was struggling not to laugh.

"Go ahead,'' she said, waving her hand dramatically. "I suppose those charred cookies and the smoldering cookie sheets were a comical sight. I don't blame you. I'd probably be in hysterics if the situation was reversed.''

"It isn't that. The fact that you made those cookies was one of the sweetest things anyone has ever done for me. I want you to know I was deeply touched.''

"I didn't do it for you,'' she said, struggling to keep the anger out of her voice. "It was a trial by fire—'' Realizing what she'd said, Susannah closed her eyes and stopped abruptly.

"Susannah—''

"You must have got a real kick out of that little pep talk I gave you the other day, too. Imagine *me* talking to you about drive, motivation and goals.''

"That touched me, too,'' he insisted.

"Right on the funny bone, I'll bet." She faked a laugh herself just to prove what a good sport she was. She could take a joke, but she wasn't exactly keen on being the brunt of one.

Nate paused, then gestured at her. "I realize it looks bad when you consider it from your point of view."

"Looks bad," she echoed, with a short hysterical laugh. "That's one way of putting it!"

Nate strode from one end of the room to the other. If he didn't stop soon, he was going to wear a hole in the carpet.

"Are you willing to put this small misunderstanding behind us, Susannah, or are you going to hold it against me? Are you willing to ruin what we have over a mistake?"

"I don't know yet." Actually she did, but she didn't want him to accuse her of making snap decisions. It would be so easy for Nate to talk his way out of this. But Susannah had been humiliated. How could she possibly trust him now? He'd thought nothing of hiding a large portion of his life from her.

"How long will it be before you come to a conclusion about us?"

"I don't know that, either."

"I suppose dinner is out?"

She nodded, her face muscles so tight, they ached.

"Okay, think matters through. I trust you to be completely fair and unbiased. All I want you to do is ask yourself something. If the situation were reversed, how would you have handled it?"

"All right." She was willing to grant him that much, although she already knew what she would have done—and it wasn't keep up a charade the way he had.

"There's something else I want you to think about," he said when she held open the door for him.

"What?" Susannah was frantic to get him out of her home quickly. The longer he stayed, the more difficult it was to remain angry with him.

"This." He kissed her then and it was the type of kiss that drove to the very depths of her soul. His mouth on hers was hot, the kiss deep and moist and so filled with longing that her knees almost buckled. Tiny sounds interrupted the moment, and Susannah realized she was the one making them.

When Nate released her, she backed away and nearly stumbled. Breathing hard, she braced her back against the doorframe and heaved in giant gulps of oxygen.

Satisfied, Nate smiled infuriatingly. "Admit it, Susannah," he whispered and ran his index finger over the shell sweater at her collarbone. "We were meant for each other."

"I...I'm not willing to admit anything."

His expression looked forlorn. It was no doubt calculated to evoke sympathy, but it wouldn't work. Susannah wouldn't be fooled a second time.

"You'll phone me?" he pressed.

"Yes." When the moon was in the seventh house, which should be sometime in the *next* millennium.

For two days, Susannah's life returned to a more normal routine. She went in to the office early and stayed late, doing everything she could to avoid Nate, although she was certain he would wait patiently for some signal from her. After all, he, too, had his pride—she was counting on that.

When she arrived home on Wednesday, there was a folded note taped to her door. Susannah stared at it for several thundering heartbeats before she reached for it.

She waited until she had put her dinner in the microwave before she read it. Her heart was pounding painfully hard as she folded open the sheet and saw three words: "Call me. Please."

Susannah gave a short hysterical laugh. Ha! Nate Townsend could tumble into a vat of melted chocolate chips before she'd call him again. More than likely he'd say or do something that would remind her of what a fool she'd been! Damn, she thought, but it was hard to stay angry with him.

When the phone rang she was still ambivalent. Jumping back, she glared at it before answering.

"Hello," she said cautiously, quaveringly.

"Susannah? Is that you?"

"Oh, hi, Emily."

"Good grief, you gave me a scare. I thought you were sick. You sounded so feeble."

"No. No, I'm fine."

"I hadn't talked to you in a while and I was wondering how you were doing."

"Fine," she repeated.

"Susannah!" Her sister made her name like a warning. "I know you well enough to realize something is wrong. I also know it probably has something to do with Nate. You haven't mentioned him the last few times we've talked, but before you seemed to be overflowing with things you wanted to say about him."

"I'm not seeing much of Nate these days."

"Why not?"

"Well, being a multimillionaire keeps him busy."

Emily paused long enough to gulp in a breath, then gasped, "I think there must be something wrong with the phone. I thought you just said—"

"Ever been to Rainy Day Cookies?"

"Of course. Hasn't everyone?"

"Have you made the connection yet?"

"You mean Nate…"

"…is Mr. Chocolate Chip himself."

"But that's marvelous. That's wonderful. Why, he's famous…I mean his cookies are world-renowned. To think that the man who developed Rainy Day Cookies actually helped Robert carry out Michelle's crib. I can't wait until he hears this."

"Personally, I wasn't all that impressed." It was difficult to remain indifferent when her sister was bubbling over with such enthusiasm. Emily usually only got excited over something organic.

"When did you find out?" Emily asked, her voice almost accusing, as if Susannah had been holding out on her.

"Last Friday. John Hammer gave me a magazine that had an article about Nate in it. The issue was a few years old, but the article told me everything Nate should have."

A short soft sound of exclamation followed. "So you just found out yourself?"

"Right."

"And you're angry with him?"

"Good heavens, no. Why should I be?" Susannah was afraid Emily wouldn't appreciate the sarcasm.

"He probably planned on telling you," Emily argued, defending Nate. "I don't know your neighbor all that well, but he seemed straightforward enough to me. I'm sure he intended to explain the situation when the time was right.''

"Perhaps," Susannah agreed, but as far as she was concerned, that consolation was too little, too late. "Listen, I've got something cooking in the microwave, so I've got to scoot." The excuse was weak, but Susannah didn't want to discuss Nate right now. "Oh, before I forget," she added quickly. "I've got a speaking engagement on the seventeenth, but I'll be finished before five-thirty so you can count on me watching Michelle."

"Great. Listen, sis, if you want to talk, I'm always here. I mean that. What are sisters for if not to talk?"

"Thanks, I'll remember that."

Once she replaced the telephone receiver, Susannah was left to deal, once more, with Nate's short note. By all rights, she should crumple it into a ball and toss it in the garbage. She did, feeling a small, damn small, sense of satisfaction.

Out of sight, out of mind—or so the old adage went—only this time it wasn't working. Every time she turned around the sight of the telephone seemed to pull at her.

Her dinner was cooked, but as she gazed down at the unappetizing entrée, she considered throwing it out and going to the Western Avenue Deli for a pastrami on rye instead. That would serve two purposes; first, it would take her away from the phone, which seemed to want to lure her to its side; and second, she'd at least have a decent meal.

Having made her decision, she was already in the living room when the doorbell chimed. Susannah groaned, knowing even before she answered it that her visitor had to be Nate.

"You didn't call," he snapped the minute she opened the door.

He stormed inside without waiting for an invitation, looking irritated, but in control. "Just how long are you planning to keep me waiting? It's obvious you're intent on making me pay for the error of my ways, which to a certain point I can understand. But we've gone well past that point. So what are you waiting for? An apology? All right—I'm sorry."

"Ah—"

"You have every reason to be upset, but what do you want? Blood? Enough is enough. I'm crazy about you, woman, and you feel the same way about me, so don't try to fool me with this indifference routine, because I can see right through it. Let's put this foolishness behind us and get back on track."

"Why?" she demanded.

"Why what?"

"Why did you wait? Why couldn't you have said something sooner?"

He gave her a look that suggested they were rehashing old news, then started his pacing routine. "Because I wanted to put Rainy Day Cookies out of my mind. I'd made the business my entire world." He stopped and whirled to face her. "I recognized a kindred spirit in you. Your entire life is wrapped up in some sporting goods company—"

"Not just *some* sporting goods company," she returned, indignant. "H&J Lima is the largest in the country."

"Forgive me, Susannah, but that doesn't really impress me. What about your life? Your whole world revolves around how far you can climb up the corporate ladder. Let me tell you that once you're at the top, the view isn't all that great. You forget what it means to appreciate the simple things in life. I did.''

"Are you telling me to stop and smell the flowers? Well, I've got news for you, Nate Townsend. I like my life just the way it is. I consider it insulting that you think you can casually walk into my world and my career and insist I'm headed down the road to destruction, because I'll tell you right now—'' she paused long enough to gulp in a breath ''—I don't appreciate it.''

Nate's expression tightened. "I'm not talking about flowers, Susannah. I want you to look out this window at Puget Sound and see something beyond a lovely view with ferryboats and snowcapped mountains. Life is more than that spider gracefully spinning its web in the corner of the balcony. Those are everyday miracles right at our doorstep, but life, abundant life, is more than that. It's meaningful relationships. Friends. Fun. We'd both lost sight of that. It happened to me first, and I can see you headed in the same shattering direction.''

"That's all fine and dandy for you, but I—''

"You need the same things I do. We need each other.''

"Correction,'' she said heatedly. "I happen to like my life just the way it is, thank you. And why shouldn't I? My five-year goals have been achieved, and there are more in the making. I can go straight to the top with this company, and that's exactly what I want. As for needing relationships, you're wrong about that, too. I got along just fine before I met you, and the same will prove true when you're out of my life.''

The room went so still that for a second Susannah was convinced Nate had stopped breathing.

"When I'm out of your life," he echoed. "I see. So you've made your decision."

"Yes," she said, holding her head high. "It was fun while it lasted, but if I had to choose between you and the vice presidency, the decision wouldn't be the least bit difficult. I'm sure you'll encounter some other young woman who needs saving from herself and her goals. As far as I can see, our relationship was more of a rescue mission, from your perspective. Now that you know how the cookie crumbles—the pun's intended—then perhaps you'll kindly leave me to my sad sorry lot.''

"Susannah, would you listen to me?"

"No." She held up her hand for effect. "I'll try to be happy," she said, a heavy note of mockery in her voice.

For a long moment, Nate said nothing. "You're making a mistake, but that's something you're going to have to learn on your own."

"I suppose you're planning on being around to pick up the pieces when I fall apart?"

His blue eyes narrowed and bored into hers. "I might be, but then again, I might not."

"Well, you needn't worry, because either way, you've got a long wait."

CHAPTER TEN

"MS. SIMMONS, Mr. Hammer, it's an honor to meet you."

"Thank you," Susannah said, smiling politely at the young man who had been sent to greet her and her employer. The Seattle Convention Center was filled almost to capacity. The moment Susannah realized her audience was going to be so large, her stomach was attacked by a bad case of nerves. Not the most pleasant conditions under which to be eating lunch.

"If you'll come this way, I'll show you to the head table."

Susannah and John Hammer followed the young executive toward the front of the crowded room. There were several others already seated on the stage. Susannah recognized the mayor and a couple of city councillors, along with the King County executive and two prominent local businessmen.

Susannah was assigned the chair to the right of the podium. John was assigned the place beside her. After briefly shaking hands with the conference coordinator, she greeted the others and took her seat. Almost immediately, the caterers started serving lunch, which consisted of an elegantly prepared salad, wild rice and broiled fresh salmon drenched with raspberry vinegar.

She didn't think she could manage even a bite while sitting in front of so many people. Glancing out over the sea of unfamiliar faces, she forced herself to remain calm and collected. She was, after all, one of the featured speakers for the afternoon, and she had come well prepared.

There was a slight commotion to the right of her, but the podium blocked her view.

"Hi, gorgeous. No one told me you were going to be here."

Nate. Susannah nearly swallowed her forkful of salmon whole. It stuck in her throat and she would have choked had she not reached for her water glass and hurriedly taken a swallow.

Twisting around in her chair, she came eye to eye with him. "Hello, Nate," she said as nonchalantly as she could. Her smile was firmly rooted in place; explosives couldn't have budged it.

"I thought Nate Townsend might be here," John whispered, looking pleased with himself.

"I see you've taken to following me around now," Nate taunted.

Susannah ignored that comment and both men, studiously returning to her salmon, hoping to suggest that her meal was far more appealing than their conversation.

"Have you missed me?"

It was ten tortuous days since she'd last seen Nate. Avoiding him hadn't been easy. He'd made sure of that. The first night she'd come home to an Italian opera played just loud enough to be heard through her kitchen wall. The sound of the music was combined with the tangy scent of his homemade spaghetti sauce. The aroma of simmering tomatoes and herbs mingled with the pungent scent of hot garlic and butter.

Evidently Nate assumed the way to *her* heart was

through her stomach. She'd nearly succumbed then, but her conviction was strong and she'd hurried to a favorite Italian restaurant to alleviate her sudden craving for pasta.

By the weekend, Susannah would have sworn Nate had whipped up every recipe in an entire cookbook, each one more enticing than the last. Susannah had never eaten as many restaurant meals as she had in the past week.

When Nate realized she couldn't be bought so easily with fine food, wine and song—or in this case opera—he tried another tactic, this one less subtle.

A single red rose was waiting for her outside her door when she arrived home from the office. There wasn't any note with it, just a perfect fresh flower. She picked it up and against her better judgment took it inside with her, holding it and inhaling the delicate scent. The only person who could have left it was Nate. In a flurry of righteousness, she'd taken the rose and placed it back where she found it. Five minutes later, she jerked open her door and to her dismay discovered the flower was still there, looking forlorn and dejected.

Deciding to deliver her own less than subtle message, Susannah left the rose outside Nate's door. She hoped he understood once and for all that she refused to be bought!

Nate, however, wasn't easily dissuaded. The rose was followed the next evening by a small box of luscious chocolates. This time Susannah didn't even bring them inside, but marched them directly to Nate's door.

"No," she said now, forcing her thoughts back to the present and the conference. She chanced a look around the crowded, noisy room. "I haven't missed you in the least."

"You haven't?" He looked dashed. "But I thought you were trying to make everything up to me. Why else would you leave those gifts outside my door?"

For just a second her heart thumped wildly. Then she gave him a fiery glare and diligently returned to her meal, making sure she downed every bite. If she didn't, Nate would be sure to think she was lovesick for want of him.

Her employer tilted his head toward her, looking pleased with himself. "I thought it would be a nice surprise for you to be speaking with Nate. Fact is, I arranged it myself."

"How thoughtful," Susannah murmured.

"You have missed me, haven't you?" Nate asked again, balancing on two legs of his chair in an effort to see her.

Okay, she was willing to admit she had been a bit lonely, but that was to be expected. For several weeks, Nate had filled every spare moment of her time with such silliness as baseball games and kite flying. But she'd lived a perfectly fine life before she met him, and now she'd returned to that same serene lifestyle without a qualm. Her world was wonderful. Complete. She didn't need him to make her a whole person. Nate was going to a great deal of trouble to force her to admit she was miserable without him. She wasn't about to do that.

"I miss you," he said, batting his baby blues at her. "The least you could do is concede you're as lonely and miserable as me."

"But I'm not," she answered sweetly, silently acknowledging the white lie. "I have a fantastic job and a promising career. What else could I want?"

"Children?"

She shook her head. "Michelle and I have lots of fun together, and when we grow bored with each other, she goes home to her mother. As far as I can see that's the perfect way to enjoy a child."

The first speaker approached the podium, and Susannah's attention was diverted to him. He was five minutes into his greetings when Susannah felt something hit her arm. She darted a glance at Nate, who was holding up a white linen napkin. *"What about a husband?"* was inked across the polished cloth.

Groaning, Susannah prayed no one else saw his note, especially her boss. She rolled her eyes and emphatically shook her head. It was then that she noted how everyone was applauding and looking in her direction as though anticipating something. She blinked, not understanding, until she realized that she'd just been introduced and they were waiting for her to stand up and give her talk.

Scraping back her chair, she stood abruptly and approached the podium, not daring to glance at Nate. The man was infuriating! A lesser woman would have dumped the contents of her water glass over his smug head. Instead of venting her irritation, she drew in a deep calming breath and looked out over her audience. She soon realized that was a mistake. There were so many faces, and they all had their eyes trained on her.

Her talk had been carefully planned and memorized. But to be on the safe side, she'd brought the typed sheets with her. She had three key points she intended to share, and had illustrated each one with several colorful anecdotes. Suddenly her mind was a blank. It took every bit of courage she possessed not to bolt and run from the stage.

"Go get 'em, Susannah," Nate whispered, smiling up at her.

His eyes were so full of encouragement and faith that the paralysis started to leave her. Although she'd memorized her speech, she reached for the written version. The instant she read the first sentence she knew she was going to be fine.

For the next twenty minutes she spoke of the importance of indelibly marking a goal on one's mind and how to mentally minimize difficulties and maximize strengths. She closed by explaining the significance of building a mental ladder to one's dreams. She talked about using determination, discipline, dedication and demeanor as the rungs of this cerebral ladder to success.

Despite Nate's earlier efforts to undermine her dignity and poise, she was pleased by the way her speech was received. Many of her listeners nodded at key points in her talk, and Susannah knew she was reaching them. When she finished, she felt good, satisfied with her speech and with herself.

As she turned to go back to her seat, her gaze caught Nate's. He was smiling as he applauded, and the gleam in his eyes was unmistakably one of respect and admiration. The warm, caressing look he offered her nearly tripped her heart into overdrive. Yet he'd maddened her with his senseless questions, distracted her, teased and taunted her with his craziness and then written a note on a napkin. But when she finished her speech, the first person she'd looked to, whether consciously or unconsciously, was Nate.

The man was driving her straight to the loony bin.

Once Susannah was seated, she noted that her hands were trembling. But she couldn't be sure if it was a release from the tension that had gripped her when she first started to speak, or the result of Nate's tender look.

Nate was introduced next, and he approached the podium. It would serve him right, Susannah thought, if she started inking messages on her napkin and holding them up for him to read while he gave his talk. Almost immediately she was shocked by the childishness of the idea. Five minutes with Nate seemed to reduce her mentality to that of a ten-year-old.

With a good deal of ceremony, or so it seemed to Susannah, Nate retrieved his notes from inside his suit jacket. It was all she could do to keep from laughing out loud when she noticed that everything he planned to say had been jotted on the back of a single index card. So this was how seriously he'd taken this afternoon's address. It looked as if he'd scribbled a couple of notes while she was delivering her speech. He hadn't given his lecture a second thought until five minutes before he was supposed to stand before the podium.

Nate proved her wrong, as seemed to be his habit, she thought testily. The minute he opened his mouth, he had the audience in the palm of his hand. Rarely had she heard a more dynamic speaker. His strong voice carried to the farthest corner of the huge hall, and although he used the microphone, Susannah doubted he really needed it.

Nate told of his own beginnings, of how his father had died the year he was to enter college, so that the funds he'd expected to further his education were no longer available. It was the lowest point of his life and out of it had come his biggest success. Then he explained that his mother's chocolate chip cookies had always been everyone's favorite. Because of his father's untimely death, she had taken a job in a local factory, and Nate, eager to find a way to attend university in the fall, had taken to baking the cookies and selling them to tourists for fifty cents each.

Halfway through the summer he'd made more than enough money to see him through his first year of schooling. Soon a handful of local delis had contacted him, wanting to include his cookies as part of their menus. These requests were followed by others from restaurants and hotels. He had been approached by a small cookie company that wanted his recipe for chocolate chip, as well as peanut butter cookies.

Nate went to school that first year and took every business course available to him. By the end of the following summer, he had set up a kitchen and opened his own business, which thrived despite his mistakes. The rest was history. By the time he graduated from college, Nate was already a millionaire. To his credit, he'd resisted the temptation to abandon his education. It had served him well since, and he was pleased he'd stuck with it, even though everyone around him seemed to be saying that he knew more, from personal experience, than most of the authors of the textbooks did. A fact he was quick to dispute.

Susannah was enthralled. She'd assumed Nate would be telling this audience what he'd been beating her over the head with from the moment they'd met— that the drive to succeed was all fine and good, but worthless if in the process one forgot who and what one was. However, if that thought was on Nate's mind, he didn't voice it. Susannah suspected he'd reserved that philosophy for her and her alone.

When he returned to his seat, the applause was thunderous. The first thing he did was look to Susannah, who smiled softly, as touched as the rest of his audience by his personal experiences. Not once had he patted himself on the back, or taken credit for the phenomenal success of Rainy Day Cookies. Susannah would almost have preferred it if his talk had been a boring rambling account of his prosperous career. She didn't want to feel so much admiration for him. It would be easier to work Nate out of her life and her mind if she didn't.

The luncheon ended a few minutes later. Gathering up her things, Susannah hoped to make a speedy escape. She should have known that Nate wouldn't allow that. Several people had hurried up to the podium to talk to him, but he excused himself and moved to her side.

"Susannah, I'd like to talk to you."

She made a show of glancing at her watch, then at her boss. "I have another appointment," she said stiffly. She secured the strap of her purse over her shoulder and offered him what she hoped resembled a regretful smile.

"Your speech was wonderful."

"Thank you, so was yours," she said, then mentioned the one thing that had troubled her. "You never told me about your father's death."

"I've never told you that I love you, but I do."

His words, so casual, so calm and serene, were like a blow to her solar plexus. Susannah felt the tears form in her eyes and tried to blink them back. "I...I wish you hadn't said that."

"The way I feel about you isn't going to change."

"I...really have to go," she said, glancing anxiously toward John Hammer. All she wanted to do was escape with her heart intact.

"Mr. Townsend," a woman bellowed from the audience. "You're going to be at the auction tonight, aren't you?"

Nate's gaze slid reluctantly from Susannah to the well-dressed woman on the floor. "I'll be there," he called back.

"I'll be looking for you," she said and laughed girlishly.

Susannah couldn't help thinking that the other woman's laugh resembled the sound an unwell rooster would make. She was tempted to ask Nate exactly what kind of auction he planned to attend where he expected to run into someone who yelled questions across a crowded room. But she resisted the urge, which was just as well.

"Goodbye, Nate," she said, turning away.

"Goodbye, my love." It wasn't until she was walking out of the Convention Center that Susannah realized how final his farewell had sounded.

It was what she wanted, wasn't it? As far as she was concerned, Nate had proved he wasn't trustworthy; he had an infuriating habit of keeping secrets. So now that he wasn't planning on seeing her again, there was absolutely no reason for her to complain. At least that was what Susannah told herself as she headed home, taking a short side trip down by the Seattle waterfront.

Within a couple of hours, Emily and Robert would be dropping off Michelle before they went to dinner with Robert's employer. Once the baby was with her,

Susannah reminded herself, there wouldn't be time to worry about Nate or anyone else.

By the time Emily arrived with her family, Susannah was in a rare mood. She felt light-headed and witty, as though she'd downed something alcoholic, but the strongest thing she'd had all evening was coffee.

"Hi," she greeted cheerfully, opening the door. Michelle looked at her with large round eyes and grabbed for her mother's coat collar.

"Sweetheart, this is your Auntie Susannah, remember?"

"Emily, the only thing she remembers is that every time you bring her here, you leave," Robert said, carrying in the diaper bag and a sack full of blankets and toys.

"Hello, Robert," Susannah murmured, kissing him on the cheek. The action surprised her as much as it did her brother-in-law. "I understand congratulations are in order."

"For you, too."

"Yes, well, it was nothing."

"Not according to the article in the paper."

"Oh," Emily said, whirling around. "Speaking of the newspaper, I read Nate's name this evening."

"Yes...we were both speakers at a conference this afternoon."

Emily looked impressed, but Susannah couldn't be sure if it was for her or for Nate.

"That wasn't what I read about him," Emily continued, focusing her attention on removing the jacket from Michelle's stubby arms. The child wasn't the least bit cooperative. "Nate's involved in the auction."

"Da-da!" Michelle cried once her arms were free.

Robert looked on proudly. "She finally learned my name. Michelle's first and only word," he added, beaming. "Da-da loves his baby, yes he does."

It was so unusual to hear Robert speaking baby talk that for an instant, Susannah didn't catch what her sister was saying. "What was that?"

"I'm trying to tell you about the auction," Emily said again, as if that should explain everything. At Susannah's puzzled look, she added, "His name was in an article about the auction to benefit the Children's Home Society."

The lightbulb that clicked on inside Susannah's head was powerful enough to search the night sky. "Not the *bachelor* auction?" Her question was little more than a husky murmur. No wonder the woman who'd shouted to Nate at the luncheon had been so brazen! She was going to bid on him.

Slowly, hardly conscious of what she was doing, Susannah lowered herself onto the sofa next to her sister.

"He didn't tell you?"

"No, but then why should he? We're nothing more than neighbors."

"Susannah!"

Her sister had the infuriating habit of making an entire statement just by the way she said Susannah's name.

"Honey," Robert said, studying his watch, "we'd better leave now if we intend to be at the restaurant on time. I don't want to keep my boss waiting."

Emily's glance toward Susannah promised a long talk later. At least Susannah had several hours during which to come up with a way of warding off her sister's questions.

"Have a good time, you two," Susannah said lightheartedly, guiding them toward the door, "and don't you worry about a thing."

"Bye, Michelle," Emily said and waved from the doorway.

"Tell Mommy goodbye." Since the baby didn't seem too cooperative, Susannah held up the chubby hand and waved it for her.

As soon as Emily and Robert had left, Michelle started whimpering softly. Susannah took one look at her niece and her spirits plummeted. Whom was she trying to fool? Herself? She'd been miserable and lonely from the moment she left Nate. Michelle sniffled, and Susannah felt like crying right along with her.

So the notorious Nate Townsend had done it again—he hadn't even bothered to mention the bachelor auction. Obviously he'd agreed to this event weeks in advance and it had never even occurred to him to tell her. Oh, sure, he swore undying love to her, but he was willing to let some strange woman buy him. Men, she was quickly learning, were not to be trusted.

The more Susannah thought back over the details of this evening, the more infuriated she became. When she'd asked Nate about helping her out with Michelle, he'd casually mentioned that he had "something else on" this evening. He sure did. Auctioning off his body to the highest bidder, and all in the name of charity!

"I told him I didn't want to see him again," Susannah announced to her niece, her fervor causing her to raise her voice. "That man was trouble from the moment we met. You were with me at the time, re-member? Don't we wish we'd known then what we know now?''

Michelle's shoulders bobbed up and down with the effort to either cry or keep from crying. Susannah didn't know which.

"He had this habit of hiding things from me. Important information, but I'm telling you right now that I've completely washed that man out of my hair. Any woman who wants him tonight can have him, because I'm not interested.''

Michelle buried her face against Susannah's neck.

"I know exactly how you feel, kid," she said, continuing to stalk the carpet in front of the large picture window. The night was filled with the sights and sounds of the city. "It's like you've lost your best friend, right?"

"Da-da.''

"He's with your mommy. I thought Nate was my friend once," she said to the baby sadly. "But I learned the hard way what he really was—nothing earth-shattering, don't misunderstand me. But he let me make a complete idiot of myself.''

Michelle stared up at Susannah, apparently enthralled with her speech. In an effort to keep the baby appeased, she continued chattering. "I hope he feels like a fool on the auction block tonight," she said, imagining him standing in front of an auditorium full of screaming women. She slowly released a sigh when she realized that with his good looks, Nate would probably bring in top money. In past year's auctions, several of the men had gone for as much as a thousand dollars. All for an evening in the company of one of Seattle's eligible bachelors.

"So much for undying love and devotion," she muttered. Michelle continued to stare at her, and Susannah felt it was her duty as the baby's aunt to give this little one some free advice. "Men aren't all they're cracked up to be. You'd be wise to learn that now."

Michelle gurgled cheerfully, obviously in full agreement.

"I for one don't need a man. I'm completely and utterly happy living on my own. I've got a job, a really good job, and a few close friends—mostly people I work with—and of course your mother." Michelle raised her hand to Susannah's face and rubbed her cheek where a tear had streaked a moist trail.

"I know what you're thinking," Susannah added before she realized that it was unnecessary to explain anything to anyone so young. "If I'm so happy, then why am I crying? Darned if I know. The problem is I can't help loving him and that's what makes this all so difficult. Then he had to go and write me that note on a napkin." She paused and pressed her fingers to her mouth to calm herself. "He asked me if I was willing to live my life without a husband…on a napkin he asked me that. Can you imagine what the caterers are going to think when they read that? And we were sitting at the head table, no less."

"Da-da."

"He asked about that, too," Susannah explained, sniffling as she spoke. She was silent a moment and when she began again her voice trembled slightly. "I never thought I'd want children, but then I didn't realize how much I could love a little one like you." Holding the baby against her breast, Susannah closed her eyes to the tight pain that clawed at her. "I could just shoot that man."

Enthralled with Susannah's hair, Michelle reached up and tugged it free from the confining pins.

"I wore it up this afternoon just to be contrary and prove to myself that I'm my own woman, and then he was there and the whole time I was speaking I wished I'd left it down—just because Nate prefers it that way. Oh, honestly, Michelle, I think I may be ready to go off the deep end here. Any advice you'd care to lend me?"

"Da-da."

"That's what I thought you'd say." Forcing in a deep breath, Susannah tried to control the tears that sprang to her eyes. She hadn't expected to cry. The tears had taken her by surprise, and she had yet to understand their significance.

"I thought once I was promoted to vice president everything would be so wonderful and, well, it has been good, but I feel so empty inside. Oh, Michelle, I don't know if I can explain it. The nights are so long and there are only so many hours I can work anymore without thinking of getting home and the possibility of seeing Nate. I...I seem to have lost my drive. Here I was talking to all these people today about determination and drive and discipline and none of it seemed real. Then...then on the way home I was walking along the waterfront and I saw an old college friend. She's married and has a baby a little older than you and she looked so happy." She paused long enough to rub the back of her hand under her nose. "I told her all about my big promotion and Sally seemed genuinely happy for me, but I felt this giant hole inside me."

"Da-da."

"Michelle, can't you learn another word? Please. How about Auntie? It's not so difficult. Say it after me. Auntie."

"Da-da."

"Nate is probably going to meet some gorgeous blonde and fall madly in love with her. She'll bid hundreds of dollars for him and he'll be so impressed that he won't even mind when she keeps him captive until—" Susannah stopped abruptly, her mind whirling. Her head snapped up and her back straightened. "You won't believe what I was just thinking," she said to Michelle, who was studying her curiously. "It's completely crazy, but then again, perhaps not."

Michelle waved her arms and actually seemed interested in hearing about this insane idea that had popped into Susannah's head. It was impossible. Absurd. But then she'd made a fool of herself over Nate so many times that once more certainly wasn't going to hurt.

It took several minutes to get Michelle back into her coat. Susannah would have sworn the contraption had more arms and legs than a centipede.

After glancing at the balance in her checkbook, she grabbed her savings-account records and, carrying Michelle, headed to the parking garage. She'd been saving up to pay cash for a new car, but bidding for Nate was more important.

The parking lot outside the theater where the bachelor auction was being held was filled to capacity, and Susannah had a terrible time finding a place to leave her car. Once she was inside the main entrance, the doorman was hesitant to let her into the auditorium, since Michelle was with her and neither one of them had a ticket.

"Lady, I'm sorry, I can't let you in there without a ticket and a bidding number—besides I don't think married women are allowed."

"I'll buy one and this is my niece. Now either you let me in there or…or you'll…I'll…I don't know what I'll do. Come on," she pleaded. "This is a matter of life and death." Okay, so that was a slight exaggeration.

While the doorman conferred with his supervisor, Susannah looked through the swinging doors that led into the theater. She watched as several women raised their hands, and leaped enthusiastically to their feet to show their numbers. A television crew was there taping the proceedings, as well.

Susannah was impatiently bouncing Michelle on her hip when the doorman returned.

"Ma'am, I'm sorry, but my supervisor says the tickets are sold out."

Susannah was about to argue with him when she heard the master of ceremonies call out Nate's name. A fervent murmur rose from the crowd.

Desperate times demanded desperate measures, and instead of demurely going back outside, Susannah rushed to the swinging doors, tossed them open and hurried down the narrow aisle.

As soon as the doorman saw what she'd done, he ran after her and shouted, "Stop that woman!"

Abruptly, the master of ceremonies ceased speaking, and a hush fell over the room as every head in the place turned toward Susannah, who was clutching Michelle protectively to her chest. She'd made it halfway down the center aisle before the doorman caught up with her. Susannah cast a wretched pleading glance at Nate, who had shielded his eyes from the glare of the lights and was staring at her.

Michelle cooed, having enjoyed the game of cat and mouse. With her pudgy hand, she pointed toward Nate.

"Da-da! Da-da!" she cried, and her voice seemed as loud as a sonic boom.

CHAPTER ELEVEN

AN IMMEDIATE UPROAR rose from the theater full of women. Nothing Susannah did could distract Michelle from pointing toward Nate and calling him Da-da. For his part, Nate appeared to be taking all the commotion in his stride. He walked over to the master of ceremonies, whom Susannah recognized as Cliff Dolittle, a local television personality, and whispered something in his ear.

"What seems to be the problem here?" Cliff asked.

"This lady doesn't have a ticket or a bidding number," the doorman shouted back. He held Susannah by her upper arm and didn't look any too pleased with this unexpected turn of events.

"I may not have a number, but I've got $6010.12 I'd like to bid for this man," she shouted.

Her announcement was again followed by a hubbub of whispering voices, which rolled over the theater like a wave crashing on the shore. The six thousand was the balance in Susannah's savings account, plus all the cash she was carrying with her.

A noise from the back of the room distracted her, and it was then that she realized the television crew had the cameras rolling. Every single detail of this debacle was being documented.

"I have a bid of $6010.12," Cliff Dolittle announced, sounding a little shocked himself. "Going once, going twice—'' he paused and his gaze scanned the female audience ''—sold to the lady who gate-crashed this auction. The one with the baby in her arms.''

The doorman released Susannah and reluctantly directed her to where she was supposed to pay. It seemed everyone was watching her and whispering. Several of the women were bold enough to shout bits of advice to her.

A man with a camera balanced on his shoulder hurried toward her. Loving the attention, Michelle pointed her finger toward the lens and cried ''Da-da'' once more for all the people who would soon be viewing this disaster at home.

''Susannah, what are you doing here?'' Nate whispered, joining her when she reached the teller's booth.

''You know what really irritates me about this?'' she said, her face bright with embarrassment. ''I could probably have had you for three thousand, only I panicked and offered every penny I have. Me, the financial marketing wizard. I'll never be able to hold my head up again.''

''You're not making the least bit of sense.''

''And you are? One moment you confess undying love to me and the next you're on the auction block, parading around for a bunch of…women.''

''That comes to $6025.12,'' the white-haired woman in the teller's booth told her.

''I only bid $6010.12,'' Susannah protested.

''The extra money is the price of the ticket. You weren't supposed to bid without one.''

''I see.''

Unzipping her purse and withdrawing her checkbook while balancing Michelle on her hip proved to be difficult.

"Here, I'll take her." Nate reached for Michelle, who surprised them both by protesting loudly.

"What have you been telling her about me?" Nate teased.

"The truth." With a good deal of ceremony, Susannah wrote out the check and ripped it from her book. Reluctantly she slid it across the short counter toward the woman collecting the fees.

"I'll write you a receipt."

"Thank you," Susannah said absently. "By the way, what exactly am I getting for my hard-earned money?"

"One evening with this young man."

"One evening," Susannah repeated grimly. "If we go out to dinner does he pay or do I?"

"I do," Nate answered for her.

"It's a good thing, because I don't have any money left."

"Have you eaten?"

"No, and I'm starved."

"Me, too," he told her smiling sheepishly, but the look in his eyes said he wasn't talking about snacking on crêpes suzette. "I can't believe you did this."

"I can't, either," she said, shaking her head in wonder. "I'm still reeling with the shock." Later, she'd probably start trembling and not be able to stop. Never in her life had she done anything so bold. Love apparently did this to a woman. Before she met Nate she'd been a sound, logical, dedicated businesswoman. Six weeks later, she was smelling orange blossoms and thinking about weddings and babies and giving up a promising career all because she was head over heels in love!

"Come on, let's get out of here," Nate said, tucking his hand around her waist and leading her toward the theater doors.

Susannah nodded. The doorman looked pleased that she was leaving his domain.

"Susannah," Nate said, once they were in the parking lot. He turned and placed his hands on her shoulders, then closed his eyes as if gathering together his thoughts. "You were the last person I expected to see tonight."

"Obviously," she returned stiffly. "When we're married, I'm going to have to insist that you keep me informed of your schedule."

Nate's head snapped up. "When we're married?"

"You didn't honestly believe I just spent six thousand dollars for a single dinner in some fancy restaurant, did you?"

"But—"

"And there'll be children, as well. Two are probably about all I can handle, but we'll play that by ear when the time comes."

For the first time since she'd met him, Nate Townsend seemed speechless. His mouth made several movements in an attempt to talk, but no sound came out.

"I suppose you're wondering how I plan to manage my career," she said, before he could ask the question. "I'm not exactly sure what I'm going to do yet. Since I'm looking at the good side of thirty, I suppose we could delay having children for a few more years."

"I'm thirty-three. I want a family soon."

Nate's voice didn't sound at all like it normally did,

and Susannah peered at him carefully, wondering if the shock had been too much for him. It had been for her! And she was probably going to end up on the eleven-o'clock news. "All right, we'll plan on starting our family right away," she agreed. "But before we do any more talking about babies, I need to ask you something important. Are you willing to change messy diapers?"

A smile played at the edges of his mouth before he nodded.

"Good." Susannah looked at Michelle, who had laid her head against her aunt's shoulder and closed her eyes. Apparently the events of the evening had tired her out.

"What about dinner?" Nate asked as he tenderly brushed the silky smooth hair from the baby's brow. "Michelle doesn't look like she's going to last much longer."

"Don't worry about it. I'll pick up something on the way home." She paused, then gestured weakly with her hand. "Forget that. I...I don't have any money left."

Nate grinned widely. "I'll pick up something and meet you back at your place in half an hour."

Susannah smiled her appreciation. "Thanks."

"No," Nate whispered, his eyes locked with hers. "Thank you."

He kissed her then, slipping his hand behind her neck and tilting her face up to meet his. His touch was so potent Susannah thought her heart would beat itself right out of her chest.

"Nate." Her eyes remained closed when his name parted her lips.

"Hmm?"

"I really do love you."

"Yes, I know. I love you, too. I knew it the night you bought the Stroganoff from the Western Avenue Deli and tried to make me think you'd whipped it up yourself."

She opened her eyes and raised them, wide and dark, to him. "But I didn't even realize it then. Why, we barely knew each other."

He kissed the tip of her nose. "I was aware almost from the first time we met that my life was never going to be the same if you weren't there to share it with me."

His romantic words stirred her heart and she wiped a tear from the corner of her eye. "I...I'd better take Michelle home," she said, and sniffled.

Nate's thumb wiped the moisture from her cheek before he kissed her again. "I won't be long," he promised.

He wasn't. Susannah had no sooner got Michelle home and into her sleepers when there was a light knock at the door.

Hurriedly, she tiptoed across the carpet and opened it. She pressed her finger to her lips as she let Nate inside.

"I got Chinese."

Her eyes widened as she nodded. "Great."

She paused on her way into the kitchen and showed him Michelle, who was sleeping soundly on the end of the sofa. Susannah had taken the opposite cushion and braced it against the side so there wasn't any chance she could fall off.

"You're going to be a good mother," he whispered, kissing her forehead.

It was silly to get all misty-eyed over Nate's saying

something like that, but she did. She succeeded in disguising her emotion by walking into the kitchen and getting two plates from the cupboard. Opening the silverware drawer, she brought out forks, as well.

Nate set the large white sack on the tabletop and lifted out five wire-handled boxes. "Garlic chicken, panfried noodles, ginger beef and two large egg rolls. Do you think that'll be enough?"

"Were you planning on feeding the Seventh Infantry?" she teased.

"You said you were hungry." He opened all the boxes but one.

Susannah filled her plate and sat next to Nate, propping her feet on the cushion of the chair opposite her. The food was delicious, and after the first few mouthfuls she decided if Nate could eat with chopsticks she should try it, too. Her efforts had a humbling effect on her.

Watching her artless movements, Nate laughed, then leaned over and kissed the corner of her mouth.

"What's in there?" she asked pointing a chopstick at the fifth wire-handled box.

He shrugged. "I forget."

Curious, Susannah reached for the container and opened it. Her breath lodged in her throat as she raised her eyes to Nate's. "It's a black velvet box."

"Oh, yes, now that you mention it I remember the chef saying something about black velvet being the special of the month." He paused long enough to answer her question and then went on expertly delivering food to his mouth with the chopsticks.

Susannah continued to stare inside the white carton at the velvet box as if it would leap out and open itself. It was the size of a ring box.

Nate waved a chopstick in her direction. "You might as well take it out and see what's inside."

Wordlessly she did as he suggested. Once the box was free, she set the carton aside and lifted the lid. She gasped when she saw the size of the diamond. For one wild moment she couldn't breathe.

"I picked it up when I was in San Francisco," Nate told her, with as much emotion as if he were discussing the weather.

The solitary diamond held her gaze as effectively as a magnet. "It's the most beautiful ring I've ever seen."

"Me, too. I took one look at it and told the jeweler to wrap it up."

He acted so casual about it, seeming far more interested in eating his ginger beef and panfried noodles than discussing anything as mundane as an engagement ring.

"I suppose I might as well mention that while I was in San Francisco, I made an offer for the Cougars. They're a professional baseball team, in case you don't know."

"The baseball team? You're going to own a professional baseball team?" Any news he was going to hit her with, it seemed, was going to be big.

He nodded. "I haven't heard back yet, but if that doesn't work out then I might be able to interest the owner of the New York Wolves in selling."

He made it all sound as if he were discussing buying a car instead of something that cost millions of dollars.

"But whatever happens, we'll make Seattle our home."

Susannah nodded, although she wasn't exactly sure why.

"Here." He set his plate aside and took the ring box from her limp hand. "I suppose the thing to do would be to place this on your finger."

Once again, Susannah nodded. Her meal was sitting like a ton of lead in the pit of her stomach. From habit, she held out her right hand. He grinned and reached for her left one.

"I had to guess the size," he said, deftly removing the diamond from its lush bed. "I had the jeweler make it a size five, because your fingers are dainty." The ring slipped on easily, the fit perfect.

Susannah couldn't stop staring at it. Never in all her life had she dreamed she would ever have anything so beautiful. "I...don't dare go near the water with this," she whispered, looking down at her hand. Lowering her gaze helped cover her sudden welling up of tears. The catch in her voice was telltale enough.

"Not go near the water...why?"

"If I accidentally fell in," she said, forcing a light laugh, "I'd sink from the weight of the diamond."

"Is it too big?"

Quickly she shook her head. "It's perfect."

Catching her unawares, Nate pressed his mouth to her trembling lips, kissing what breath she had completely away. "I planned to ask you to marry me the night I came back from the trip. We were going out for dinner, remember?"

Susannah nodded. That had been shortly after she'd read the article in *Business Monthly* about Nate. The day her whole world had felt as if it were rocking beneath her feet.

"I know we talked briefly about your career, but I have something else I need to tell you."

Susannah nodded, because commenting at this point was becoming increasingly impossible.

"What would it take to lure you away from H&J Lima?"

The diamond on her ring finger seemed more than enough incentive, but she wasn't going to let him know that quite yet. "Why?"

"Because I'm starting a kite company. Actually, it's going to be a nationwide franchise. I've got plans for opening ten stores in strategic cities around the country to see how it flies." He stopped long enough to laugh at his pun. "But from the testing we've been doing, this is going to hit it off big. However—" he paused to draw in a deep breath "—I'm lacking one important part of my team. I need a marketing expert, and was wondering if you'd like to apply for the job."

"I suppose," she said, deciding to play his game. "But I'd want top salary, generous bonuses, a four-day week, a health and retirement plan and adequate maternity leave."

"The job's yours."

"I don't know, Nate, there could be problems," she said, cocking her head to one side, letting him think she was already having second thoughts. "People are going to talk."

"Why?"

"Because I fully intend to sleep with the boss. And some old fuddy-duddy is bound to think that's how I got the job."

"Let them." He laughed, reaching for her, wrapping his arms around her trim waist and hauling her into his lap. "Have I told you I'm crazy about you, woman?"

Smiling into his eyes, she nodded. "One thing I

want cleared up before we go any further, Nate Townsend. No more secrets. Understand?''

''Scout's honor.'' He spit on the end of his fingertips and used the same fingers to cross his heart. ''I used to do that when I was a kid. It meant I was serious.''

''Well,'' Susannah murmured, thinking fast, ''since you seem to be in a pledging mood, there are a few items I'd like to have you swear to.''

''Such as?''

''Such as…'' she whispered, and lowered her mouth to a scant inch above his. Whatever thoughts had been in her mind scattered like autumn leaves caught in a brisk whirlwind. Her tongue outlined his lips, teasing and taunting him as he'd taught her to do.

''Susannah, dear Lord…''

Whatever he meant to say was interrupted by the doorbell. Susannah lifted her head. It took a moment to clear her muddled thoughts before she realized it must be her sister and brother-in-law returning from their celebration dinner with Robert's boss.

She tried to move from Nate's lap, but he groaned in protest and tightened his arms around her. ''Whoever it is will go away,'' he whispered close to her ear.

''Nate—''

''Go back to doing what you were just doing and forget whoever's at the door.''

''It's Emily and Robert.''

Nate moaned and released her.

Susannah had no sooner unlocked the door than Emily flew into the room as though she were being pursued by a banshee. She marched into the center of the living room, stopped abruptly and looked around.

Robert followed her, looking nearly as frenzied as his wife. Sane, sensible Robert!

"What's wrong?" Susannah asked, her heart leaping with concern.

"You're asking *us* that?" Robert flared.

"Now, Robert," Emily said, gently placing her hand on her husband's forearm. "There's no need to be so angry. Stay calm."

"Me? Angry?" he cried facing his wife. "In the middle of our after-dinner drink you let out a shriek that scared me out of ten years of my life and now you're telling me not to be angry?"

"Emily," Susannah tried again, "what's wrong?"

"Is Nate here?" Robert interrupted. One corner of her brother-in-law's mouth curved down in a snarl. He raised his clenched fist. "I'd like ten minutes alone with that man. Give me ten minutes."

"Robert!" Emily and Susannah cried simultaneously.

"Did someone say my name?" Nate asked, as he strolled out from the kitchen.

Emily threw herself in front of her husband, patting his heaving chest with her hands. "Now, honey, settle down. There's no need to get so upset."

Susannah was completely confused. She had never heard her brother-in-law raise his voice before. Whatever had happened had clearly unsettled him to the point of violence.

"He's not going to get away with this," Robert shouted, straining against his wife's restricting hands.

"Away with what?" Nate said with a calm that seemed to inflame Robert even more.

"Taking my daughter away from me."

"What?" Susannah cried. It amazed her that Michelle could be sleeping through all this commotion. But fortunately the baby seemed completely oblivious to what was happening.

"I think you'd better start from the beginning," Susannah instructed, leading everyone into the kitchen. "There's obviously been some kind of misunderstanding. Now sit down and I'll put on some decaffeinated coffee and we can sort this out in a reasonable manner."

Her brother-in-law pulled out a chair and put his elbows on the table, supporting his head in his hands.

"Why don't you start?" Susannah said, looking at her sister.

"Well," Emily began, taking in a deep breath, "as I told you, we were having dinner with Robert's boss and—"

"They know all that," Robert interrupted. "Tell them about the part when we were having a drink in the cocktail lounge."

"Yes," Emily said, heaving a great sigh. "That does seem to be where the problem started, doesn't it?"

Susannah shared a look with Nate, wondering if he was as lost as she was in this muddle. Neither Emily nor Robert was making any sense.

"Go on," Susannah encouraged, growing impatient.

"As I explained, we were all sitting in the cocktail lounge having a drink. There was a television set playing in the corner of the room. I hadn't been paying much attention to it, but I looked up and I saw you and Michelle on the screen."

"That was when she gave a scream that was loud enough to curdle a Bloody Mary," Robert explained.

"I got everyone to be quiet while the announcer came on. He said that you had taken *my daughter* to this…this bachelor auction. Then they showed Michelle pointing her finger at Nate and calling him Dada."

"That was when Robert let out a fierce yell," Emily explained.

"Oh, Lord." Susannah slumped into a chair, wanting to find a hole to crawl into and hibernate for the next ten years. Maybe by then Seattle would have forgotten how she'd disgraced herself.

"Did they say anything else?" Nate wanted to know, doing a poor job of disguising his amusement.

"Only that the details would follow at eleven."

"I demand an explanation!" Robert said, looking to Nate.

"It's all very simple," Susannah rushed to explain. "See…Nate's wearing a suit that's very similar to yours. Same shade of brown. From the distance, Michelle obviously mistook him for you."

"She did?" Robert muttered.

"Of course," Susannah went on. "Besides, Da-da is the only word she can say…" Her voice trailed off.

"Michelle knows who her daddy is," Nate said matter-of-factly. "You don't need to worry that—"

"Susannah," Emily broke in, "when did you get that diamond? It looks like an engagement ring."

"It is," Nate said and reached to the middle of the table for the last egg roll. He paused and looked at Susannah. "You don't mind, do you?"

"No. Go ahead."

"What channel was it?" Nate asked between bites. Emily told him.

"It must be a slow news day," Susannah mumbled.

"Gee, Susannah," said Emily, "I always thought if you were going to make television news it would be over some big business deal. I never dreamed it would be because of a man. Are you going to tell me what happened?"

"Someday," she said, expelling her breath. She'd never dreamed it would be over a man, either, but this one was special. More than special.

"Well, since we're going to be brothers-in-law I guess I can forget about this unfortunate incident," Robert said generously, having regained his composure.

"Good, I'd like to be friends," Nate said, holding out his hand for Robert to shake.

"You're going to be married?" Emily asked her sister.

Susannah exchanged a happy smile with Nate and nodded.

"When?"

"Soon," Nate answered for her. His eyes told her the sooner the better.

She felt the heat crawl into her face, but she was as eager as Nate to get to the altar.

"Not only has Susannah agreed to be my wife, she's also decided to take on the position of marketing director for Windy Day Kites."

"You're leaving H&J Lima?" Robert asked, as if he couldn't believe his ears.

"Had to," she explained. She moved to Nate's side, wrapped her arms around his waist and smiled up at him. "The owner made me an offer I couldn't refuse."

Nate's smile felt like a warm summer day. Susannah closed her eyes, basking in the glow of this man who'd taught her about love and laughter and rainy day kisses.

The Bride Price
Day Leclaire

To friends who are there
when the crunch times are at their crunchiest.
To Felicia Mason and Carolyn Greene
with my love, thanks and deepest appreciation.

Dear Reader,

I live with an ever-changing tableau of characters—
wonderful men and women who are just like
those in the world around us. As they strive to
find happiness, they mirror our own struggle to find
our true soul mates. As their hearts are touched, our
hearts are touched. As they face life's ordeals, we
face them. I love creating strong, tender men and
spirited, determined women who fight to reach the
ultimate happy ending we all long to attain in our
own lives.

When I create my stories I try to tap in to the
universal emotions we all share. I hope you'll enjoy
the story of Piper and Gideon, two individuals who
loved each other, lost that love and now struggle to
find it again. To me that rediscovery of a love that
transcends all hardship resonates with a depth of
passion that is the core of true romance. It keeps me
returning to Harlequin Romance novels as an avid
reader because it's a journey I love to take again
and again. And I hope it's a journey you'll continue
to take with me.

Love,

Day Leclaire

PROLOGUE

Old Mill Run, Colorado

THEY ringed him like jackals surrounding a predator they were too apprehensive to take on by themselves.

Gideon ignored them, his attention focused on the more immediate danger—the man determined to beat him into the ground. Close by, the charred ruins of a hundred-year-old flour mill smoldered, the fire that had swept through it gutting a full year of painstaking renovation. Wisps of smoke invaded the circle, briefly obscuring his view, and he blinked against the sting, shaking back his sweat-dampened hair.

"I didn't burn your mill," he gritted out.

"Bull." Spencer's voice came in short, swift pants. "You were seen!"

"You're a liar!"

"Who else would have reason to do it?"

"How about you? I'll bet the insurance money will come in handy now that your old man is gone." Gideon's taunt was met by such a powerful fist to the chin that it sent him reeling.

"There is no insurance money, you bastard!" Spencer shouted. "All I had was tied up in that mill."

"I didn't burn it." Gideon stayed down, trying one final time to end the fight peacefully. It was a futile gesture, but one he felt obligated to attempt. "If you don't believe me, ask your sister."

"Leave Piper out of this. Your relationship with her is over."

Something primitive sparked to life, an elemental drive to protect and hold what belonged to him. "She's mine," he warned in a guttural voice. "She'll always be mine. No one is going to take her from me. Not even you."

"No?" Challenge was met with challenge. "You've ruined me and I swear I'm going to make you pay. You're garbage, Hart. You always have been. Always will be."

It was the final straw. Gideon had spent too many years fighting to protect his name and reputation. He'd be damned if he'd let Spencer destroy it now. Not over something he didn't do. Picking himself off the ground, he wiped the blood from the corner of his mouth. And then he attacked.

The next several minutes were vicious, neither man giving ground. The crowd surrounding them called encouragement to Spencer, quick to side with the town's golden boy. Gideon made the mistake of moving too close to the edge of the circle and was rewarded with a staggering slam to the back. Boots shot out of nowhere, pitching him off balance. But he'd been in his fair share of barnyard brawls, all with the odds against him, and he'd managed to come out on top. If he wanted to win this one, he'd have to find a way to even the current odds.

Finally he managed to knock Spencer through the circle, scattering the crowd. It was the opening he needed to finish the fight. He balled his hand, prepared to put his opponent down when a brutal kick swept his feet out from under him. Gideon went down hard, momentarily stunned. He suspected he'd cracked at least one of his ribs. It hurt to breathe, hurt to move. Not that he had any choice. In another second Spencer would be on him. Rolling, he forced himself to his feet.

They were close to the river now, near a ten-foot drop-off. It was either him or Spence, and he was damned if it was going to be him. Gathering every last ounce of energy, he drew back his arm.

Someone grabbed him from behind and he roared in frustration, shaking them off with an ease that had to come from an excess of adrenaline. Or perhaps it came from pure testosterone. All he knew was that something within him was raging out of control. Free once again, he launched himself at Spencer, ending the battle with a single, powerful right hook. Spence went down without a sound, hitting the ground with painful force.

And then the surrounding jackals went mad and Gideon disappeared beneath the ravenous pack.

CHAPTER ONE

Denver, Colorado
Five years later...

THE board meeting wasn't going the way he'd planned.

Gideon Hart folded his arms across his chest and regarded the chaos breaking loose around him. The owners and representatives of the three companies he'd recently purchased had already come to blows. Two nursed black eyes, another a swollen jaw and a fourth a chipped tooth. One was so drunk, she could be poured down the elevator shaft and into her limo. And the caterer he'd hired to provide them with lunch had decided to join the drunken mêlée by gulping from a bottle of his best Lafite Rothschild, after which she'd managed to set the dessert table on fire while attempting to ignite the crêpes Suzette.

But the pièce de résistance had to be the arrival of Piper Montgomery.

He hadn't expected her to crash the party. Hell, he hadn't expected to see her ever again. But she erupted from the elevator with all the determination of an avenging angel, dressed in a yellow so brilliant, it looked like a flaming sun had exploded to life in their midst. How long had it been since they were last together? Four years? Five? His mouth twisted. Five years, two months and twelve days. But who was counting?

She paused inside the doorway and lifted the Leica camera strung around her neck, snapping off a quick series of shots. Nothing had changed, it would seem. Photography was still a vital part of her life, her take on the world around her expressed through a Carl Zeiss lens. Lowering the camera, her gaze swept the room, no doubt searching for him. Damn, but she looked good. Her hair was shorter than before, just clipping her shoulder blades, though still ruler-edge straight and still streaked with shades of blond ranging from sun-bleached white to a light sandy brown. She also had a figure capable of bringing men to their knees and blue eyes so direct and passionate they made most people uncomfortable. But he wasn't most people.

He waited patiently for her to zero in on him. A moment later her focus reached the corner where he stood and for an instant neither of them moved, an eternity passing in that split second. A darkness settled in her eyes, like night eclipsing day. Was she remembering their parting? Or was their current situation responsible for igniting the pain he read there?

Her jaw tightened, and with a defiance he couldn't mistake, she popped off another series of photos—this time aimed in his direction. Finished, she started toward him, her sunstruck yellow dress swirling around her knees with each determined stride. Not even the hysteria exploding around her slowed her approach. Skirting one battleground, she thrust straight through another, an elbow to the gut sending a beefy combatant reeling, while a well-placed stab from a deadly pair of high heels put a swift end to any thought of retaliation from his partner.

Gideon left his stance, clearing a path between them with ruthless determination. It wasn't concern for her safety that drove him to meet her halfway, he tried to tell himself. Hell, no. He didn't give a damn what happened to her. His mouth twisted. *Liar.* He made a living bursting other people's delusionary bubbles and here he was creating one of his own. He cared what happened, all right. He cared because he planned to destroy Piper's brother. Unfortunately that meant if Piper got in the way, he'd be forced to either move her out of his path, or take her down, as well.

"Hello, pipsqueak."

She bristled at the nickname. "You son of a—"

He didn't give her an opportunity to finish her greeting. Hell, it didn't take much imagination to figure how it would have ended. Sweeping her camera aside, he thrust his hand into her hair and tipped her into his arms. Then he sealed her mouth with his. She fell into him, her body colliding with delicious force.

She tasted even better than he remembered, hot and sweet and buttery soft, every bit of her edged with a potent vibrancy he'd never found in another woman. Her lips were wide and firm, melding with his as though they'd been specifically shaped with him in mind. Or perhaps his had been shaped just for her. She fit in his arms with a perfection he'd almost forgotten, joining instinctively at thigh, hip and chest.

Her figure had altered somewhat over the years, her legs and belly and arms leaner than the twenty-year-old he'd last held, her breasts and buttocks more lush than he recalled. But that was the only notable difference. All the qualities that mattered, that had attracted him to her in the first place, remained the same. It was there in the tender strength of her touch and the uncompromising determination of her gaze. She even tasted of resilient feminine energy.

He inhaled deeply, drawing her spicy scent into his lungs, absorbing her essence into his pores. Heaven help him, he could drown in her, lose all pretense at common sense and rationality. He traced his hand down her spine, locking them closer together. She didn't fight as he'd expected. Nor did she melt into the embrace as he'd hoped. Instead she ran the heel of her pumps along his calf. It served as an effective warning. He'd already seen the damage she could inflict with that particular feminine weapon.

"Okay, okay. You win this time," he murmured against her mouth.

"Correction. I win every time."

"Every time?" Snatching a final kiss, he fought the primitive urge that demanded he toss her over his shoulder and carry her off to a place where they could bring their renewed acquaintance to a more earthy conclusion. Instead he released her and fought to conceal his craving behind a civilized mask. It wasn't easy. Donning the mask of civilization never had been. Not for him. "Fair warning, sweetheart. That's about to change."

She took a hasty step backward and visibly fought for control. It would seem he wasn't the only one affected. His kiss had more of an impact than she cared to admit. "Dammit, Gideon. What did you do that for?"

"What? Kiss you?" He shrugged. Wasn't it obvious? "I wanted to."

"And whatever the great G.W. Hart wants, he gets. Is that it?"

"Words to live by."

"Words more likely to crash and burn by." She glanced around the room, her gaze falling on the smoldering remains of the dessert table, and she snapped off another picture, her actions both instinctive and practiced. Lifting an eyebrow, she returned her attention to him. "Problem with the caterer?"

He released a sigh. "A small case of pyromania. Negligible, really. Nothing to worry about."

Her mouth twitched and she finally broke down and laughed. The sound stirred something deep in his soul, something beyond his reach—something he'd thought himself incapable of feeling again. "Honestly, Gideon. Why am I not surprised to find you hosting a party where full-fledged warfare has broken out?"

"It's a knack." He gently shifted her to one side as a decanter of extremely expensive scotch soared by, splintering against the far wall. "Would you like some pointers?"

"I'll pass, thanks."

Time to get down to business. "Now, where were we?"

"I was about to call you a son of a—"

"And I took care of that with a kiss." He was pleased to see that his grim warning didn't escape her notice. "I assume you're here on Spencer's behalf?"

"We need to talk." The shouting escalated and she raised her voice to be heard over the din. "Somewhere private, if you don't mind."

He jerked his head toward the door leading from the conference room. "My office."

This time as they traversed the room, Gideon placed

himself between Piper and harm's way. The fighting had slowed, the combatants tiring. Even the couple of swings aimed in his direction were halfhearted at best. That didn't stop Piper from attempting to jump into the fray, no doubt in the hope of ending the conflict. Though she'd never been one to back away from trouble, she'd always tried to find peaceful solutions to even the most disastrous situations. It had been key to her nature when he'd known her and he doubted anything had changed in recent years.

He stopped her from trying to deal with the current battle the simplest and most effective way available to a man of his nature. He clamped an arm around her waist and locked her to his side. It also prevented her from utilizing her camera. "You have to be the only woman I've ever met foolish enough to wade into a fistfight and risk your own well-being out of concern for the brawlers."

"Someone will get hurt if you don't stop them, Gideon."

He shrugged. "That's their choice. If they want to fight through their problems, let them. But I suggest you stay out of it. Fighting other people's battles is guaranteed to get you hurt. I'd have thought you'd learned your lesson the last time you made that mistake."

Pain exploded in her gaze, catching him totally off guard. "Not nice, Gideon. Before you were only ruthless. But I see you've become cruel."

What the *hell* was she talking about? "Explain that—"

Spinning, she evaded his grasp. "Ladies and gentlemen!" she called out. "Listen to me, please. You'll be delighted to know that Mr. Hart has changed his mind. There's no further need for argument.''

For a split second there was absolute silence. Then everyone cheered. One poor man sank to the floor and blubbered like a baby. Piper took a single look at him and turned a gaze so filled with outrage on Gideon that if he'd been any other man he'd have flinched. Did she realize the power of those eyes? She must. Women always took advantage of whatever natural assets they possessed.

The camera went into action again. Not that it slowed the accusations she hurled his way. "You made him cry. You truly are a son of a bitch, Gideon. That's how I'm going to label these shots. 'SOB in action.'"

"No," he corrected. "*You* made him cry. And he'll be crying even harder when he finds out you lied to him."

"You're going to fix this," she informed him in a fierce undertone. "You're going to fix this before anyone else is hurt."

"Like I'm going to fix things with Spencer?"

"Yes."

He shouldn't touch her. Giving in to the impulse offered no advantage whatsoever. Even so, he couldn't resist tucking a silken lock of her hair behind one ear. "You always were a dreamer. It was a quality I liked about you, once upon a time."

Her chin shot up at that. "I was never a dreamer. In fact, I was the most realistic of any of us. But I do expect the best from people."

"You photograph the best within people," he corrected.

"And I still do, maybe because I always hope that

basic goodness will eventually win out over people's more negative qualities.''

"How do you handle the disappointment?''

The whir of the camera paused. "Spoken like a true cynic.'' She slanted him a speculative glance. "It'll be interesting to develop my film. I wonder if I'll find any goodness left in you.''

"Doubtful. But you already knew that, didn't you?'' The man on the floor had stopped sobbing. Climbing to his feet, he made a beeline toward them. "Time to go,'' Gideon announced.

Dropping his arm around Piper's shoulders, he opened the door and left disaster behind. From the chaos of the boardroom, they stepped into a dimly lit corridor filled with an intense silence. It provided a disconcerting counterpoint to the noise and confusion they'd escaped.

"Good grief, Gideon.''

Piper stopped in her tracks in order to absorb her surroundings. The hallway gave the impression of stretching into infinity, an illusion he'd paid an impressive amount of money to achieve. It was as though some unseen entity drew all the light and energy from the surrounding area, leaving behind an unsettling stillness. He couldn't remember hearing anyone speak above a whisper while traversing this expanse. Naturally Piper proved the exception.

"You haven't lost your touch, I see.'' Her voice invaded the far recesses of the corridor, chasing away the shadows. "Always the master at creating an impression.''

He inclined his head. "I do my best.''

"I don't know why you bother, Gideon. You're impressive enough all on your own.''

The observation caught him by surprise. "A compliment?"

"Fact," she responded crisply. "You have presence. You always have, even as a boy."

He didn't know how to respond to her comment, so he lapsed into a remote silence. This meeting wasn't going the way he'd planned, perhaps because he hadn't planned it. At the end of the hallway stood a pair of large double oak doors, stained to a forbidding darkness. He knew how daunting they looked. He'd designed it that way. Piper must have suddenly realized he was still holding her. Sidestepping his arm, she put a discreet distance between them. Her actions irritated him, though he couldn't say why. Over the years he'd become accustomed to people keeping their distance. But coming from her, he found it inexplicably annoying.

Thrusting open the massive doors, he once again clamped an arm around her waist and ushered her across the threshold. And once again she twisted loose and turned to face him. He slammed the doors closed, the sound renting the stillness like a shotgun blast. But aside from an intense wariness that flickered through her gaze, she didn't react with alarm. Rather her expression turned even more combative.

He had to give her credit. Piper Montgomery rarely flinched when confronted with adversity. He liked that. He liked that she wouldn't go down easily. Their battle would be a more equal one, not that it would change the ending. It had taken five years for him to catch her brother, Spencer, at a vulnerable moment in his life and now that he had, Gideon intended to take full advantage.

Piper didn't immediately attack, as she had earlier.

Instead she stood in front of him, quietly assimilating the nuances of both the room and the man. To his surprise, she didn't reach for her camera. But then, she'd never used it as a crutch, never attempted to hide behind its all-seeing lens. Piper had always been too vital for that, too involved in life. Rather, she'd wielded it like a sword of truth, cutting through pretense in order to bare the reality of any given situation. But perhaps this was one situation she preferred not to bare. The results might prove disastrous for both her and Spencer.

Piper offered a cocky smile. "Well? Who goes first?" She gestured for him to begin. "You, I think."

He didn't need to ask the most obvious question—why she'd come. They both knew the answer to that. There were other more interesting issues to deal with. "Didn't you learn your lesson the last time you put yourself between me and your brother?" he offered as a gentle opening volley.

His comment hit hard and Piper felt the color bleaching from her face as it had in the boardroom when he'd warned against fighting other people's battles. She struggled for control, using every ounce of self-possession not to flinch. Unable to continue facing him and also maintain an air of calm, she crossed to a squat antique cabinet Gideon used to conceal electronic equipment. She suspected the uncharacteristic retreat would rouse his hunting instincts, but that couldn't be helped. She needed some breathing space.

"Nice," she murmured.

Sure enough, he came after her. "I said something wrong. What?"

"Is it a Chippendale?"

"That's twice now you've overreacted when I referred to the fight I had with Spencer. I want to know why.''

"It's not a pleasant memory.''

"It's not a pleasant memory for either of us. But that doesn't explain why you look like you're going to faint whenever I mention it. That's not like you. Now what the hell's going on?''

How could he ask such a question? Had he truly become so heartless that he'd completely lost the capacity to feel? Or did he think time healed all wounds? She fought an uncharacteristic wave of bitterness. He should know that wounds of that magnitude never healed. Not really. Sure, the pain eased, but the ache remained, buried deep where the chance of it being hit by careless words or actions was remote.

She gave her full attention to a dark scar marring the door of the cabinet. She'd hoped her own scars were less obvious, but then, she hadn't taken Gideon's powers of observation into consideration. He'd found that deep, dark place with distressing ease. "I didn't realize you'd acquired an interest in antiques,'' she said with dogged determination.

To her relief, he allowed the change in subject. No doubt he'd return to the previous topic, but the temporary reprieve allowed her time to recover her composure. "I'm not interested,'' he claimed. "I acquired this piece when I picked up Ramsey Industrial.''

She sensed he hadn't offered the comment as an offhand remark. There was a point to his supplying her with the information. Typical. He wasn't a man prone to idle conversation. "I didn't know you owned them.''

"I don't. They don't exist as a company anymore.

They're now part of half a dozen different corporations.''

For some reason his description made her think of a jigsaw puzzle, the pieces broken apart and carelessly tossed into the wrong boxes. Those pieces would never again form a complete whole. Nor would they fit the new puzzle they'd been added to. She ran a finger along the elegant curves of the polished mahogany. The thought saddened her and her mouth tilted into a wry smile. It was a silly reaction, she acknowledged. She didn't have a personal connection to either the company or the people involved.

"So this cabinet is all that's left of Ramsey," she observed.

He shrugged. "I suppose you could say that."

She risked a quick glance in Gideon's direction. She'd spent the last twenty minutes doing her level best to remain unaffected by him, to hold the memories of their time together at a safe distance. Closeted with him in an office that formed the base of his operations made it all the more difficult, particularly after the kiss they'd shared. She couldn't hope to escape his influence, not when they were alone together. Sheer masculine power radiated from him, seemingly amplified by the room, as though his essence had invaded every nook and cranny. The thought was an intimidating one, but no more so than the man, himself.

The years hadn't treated him well, she decided. He'd always had an edgy appearance, his features boldly hewn into formidable peaks and hollows. But now they'd settled into a harsh remoteness warning that he'd given free rein to the darker aspects that shaded his personality. Where once laugh lines had eased the intensity of his dark eyes and stubborn jaw, now she couldn't see any sign of the gentler qualities she'd known so well.

He'd cloaked himself in the civilized appearance of a businessman, but Piper knew better. A tailor-made silk suit and tamed black hair may have replaced his jeans and T-shirt and unruly dark waves, yet there lived a primitive soul beneath the surface polish. It glittered in the fierceness of his gaze and the tautness of a body forged into corded steel by years of hard manual labor. Simple outward trappings couldn't hide the truth. This was a man made ruthless by circumstance, a man who lived without compromise or compassion, perhaps because he'd received so little of either in his youth.

There was another truth she couldn't hide from, no matter how hard she tried. She'd had a hand in creating the austere man Gideon had become. She'd failed him at the most crucial moment in his life. She hadn't been strong enough to fight on his behalf and as a result three people had lost everything they'd held most dear. Not that the knowledge changed anything. The past couldn't be altered. But she could change Gideon's plans for the future. Before she'd been too weak. Now she had both the will and gritty determination necessary to do battle.

Besides, she didn't just owe Spence for what had happened all those years ago. She owed Gideon, as well. It was up to her to set right a terrible wrong. And she would, regardless of the personal price she'd ultimately pay. The only question was how to go about it.

A distinctive stirrup vessel held a place of honor on top of the cabinet and she picked it up in an attempt to give herself time to think, not the least surprised to see it was a genuine artifact. It was a gorgeous ceramic piece of a kneeling warrior painted in red and white slip. If memory served, it had been made to hold and serve liquids. "When did you acquire an interest in pre-Columbian artwork? Or aren't you interested in collecting this, either?"

"I'm not interested. That particular piece belonged to Archibald Fenzer."

Her brow wrinkled in thought. "I've heard that name. Didn't he have something to do with steel? I seem to recall reading he went belly-up a few years back."

Gideon stroked the curve of the warrior's battle club, careful to avoid contact with her hand. Was it deliberate? Did he avoid her touch because he didn't trust himself? She instantly dismissed the thought. If that were the case, he'd never have kissed her.

"Fenzer refused to sell his firm," he explained. "Bankruptcy was his only alternative."

"That's not much of an alternative."

Gideon shrugged. "He preferred it to selling out to me."

Oh, dear. "And did you buy the bits and pieces of his business at the bankruptcy auction?"

"No. It wasn't worth bothering with by then."

She was missing something here. "I don't understand. You bought his artwork, right? Why would you do that if—"

"It was his favorite piece." He carefully took the stirrup vessel from her hand and returned it to the top of the cabinet. "And it serves as a good reminder."

"For you?"

"No."

The answer clicked and she struggled not to reveal

her alarm. "You keep it as a reminder for people in a similar position to Mr. Fenzer." He didn't confirm her guess, but she knew she'd gotten it right. "Does it work? Are people more unnerved when you tell them the history behind the piece?"

"We'll find out, won't we?"

She eyed the artifact with distaste. If it didn't have such historic value, she'd see to it that the thing met with an unfortunate dusting accident. Turning, she surveyed his office once again, seeing it in a whole new light. She reached for her camera, curious as to whether her photos would ultimately confirm her suspicions. "Is the entire place decorated from the ravages of other lives, Gideon?" she asked as she set up her shots.

His mouth tightened at her phrasing. "The pieces come from the various companies I've owned."

"Owned...or destroyed?"

"I don't destroy the businesses I buy." A dangerous edge cut through his voice, one she couldn't mistake. "The owners have already done that. I simply pick up the remains at a reasonable price."

She swung around to face him. "And do what with them, Gideon? What happens to the leftovers you collect?"

"I sell them."

There was no reason to get upset. He only confirmed what she'd suspected. "I see. So instead of constructing things as you once did, you deconstruct."

He allowed amusement to override his irritation. "Is that even a word?"

"I'd say you've made it one."

His shoulders shifted beneath his suit jacket, warning of his growing impatience. "We've gotten off the subject."

"No, Gideon. I think we're very much on the subject. You must know I've come about Spence and the contract."

"I figured out that much." A cold pride lent steel to his gaze. "There isn't any other reason you'd come to see me, is there?"

He wouldn't believe the truth, so she didn't bother offering it. "What are your plans?" she asked instead.

His mouth curved into a smile that was a mere ruin of the one she'd once known so intimately. "I plan to deconstruct your brother, of course."

"That contract wasn't with you, Gideon." She forced herself not to plead. She'd never change his mind that way. Years ago she'd have been able to reason with him. But he no longer struck her as reasonable. Too much time had passed and too many hard feelings remained unsettled between them. She knew a man bent on vengeance when she saw one. Hadn't she watched her brother these past five years? "Spence made that agreement with an old family friend."

Gideon nodded. "Jack Wiley. Unfortunately for you, Jack didn't make arrangements to terminate the contract upon his death. Since he didn't, the contract became part of the assets of his estate and came into my possession when I bought Wiley's business from his heirs."

"That wasn't Jack's intention," she attempted to explain. "He was trying to help Spence."

"As I said… He should have made a contingency plan if he didn't want to leave your brother vulnerable."

"So now you're going to call the contract due?"

To her surprise, Gideon shook his head. "Not at all. I simply won't renew it when it expires next month."

Anger flared. "There's a difference?"

"There's a big difference. If I called the contract due now, your brother wouldn't have any options. Giving him an extra month, he can choose how he prefers to go down."

"Generous of you."

Her sarcasm had him closing the distance between them. "Trust me. I'm being more than generous." His voice lashed the still, ominous air with barely suppressed fury. "Your brother did his level best to destroy me. Did you really think I'd let that go, that I wouldn't find a way to pay him back for his kindness?"

"It wasn't deliberate."

"No? I think he saw it as the perfect excuse to separate us. And he succeeded, didn't he?"

More than Spence's accusations had separated them, as Gideon knew darn well. "And because of what happened over five years ago you intend to destroy him?" she demanded.

"Will losing what he's spent the past five years building destroy Spencer?"

"Yes."

Gideon didn't relent. As far as she could tell there wasn't a hint of compassion or forgiveness. Had those qualities been completely driven from him? "Then maybe he'll feel a small portion of what I did. We'll also see if he has what it takes to pick himself up and move on, or if he'll give up."

"And live his life in bitterness?"

A hint of genuine amusement touched Gideon's expression. "Is that what you think I've done?"

"I think you've allowed bitterness to change the man you once were."

"Not bitterness, sweetheart. Try the hard facts of life." And every last one of those hard facts scored his face. "You and your brother put me on this path. Why act surprised when you discover I've followed it?"

Piper shook her head. "Don't blame us for what you've become. We make our own choices in life, Gideon." She turned to examine his office once again. It was tragic to think he'd built his foundation atop the ashes of devastation. How many different firms did all this represent? How many ghosts haunted the various bits and pieces? "Don't you regret any of what you've done?"

He took a stance directly behind her. "I only have one regret in life."

"Which is?"

His hands closed on her shoulders, turning her around to face him. "You haven't earned the right to know."

That roused her curiosity. "Earned?"

All expression vanished from his face and it struck Piper that she'd never sensed such loneliness in a man before. It revealed a vulnerability he'd never have acknowledged. Nor would he appreciate having her pick up on it. She ached to hold him, to ease his pain as she had when they'd been together. But that was beyond her abilities. He'd never allow her to get that close. Not again. Once upon a time he'd have accepted her embrace. But now he'd see it as a weakness, a weakness in need of serious defense measures.

"Years ago I confided my childish secrets to you," he said.

"I haven't forgotten." She regarded him steadily. "But you seem to have."

"They were foolish dreams. Pointless dreams."

"And the goals you've replaced them with are better?"

"Yes."

"Why?"

"Because no one can take away what I have."

This time she did laugh, the sound edged with sorrow. "Oh, Gideon. No one can take what you possess because you haven't built anything worthy of that. And they can't touch you personally because you won't let them close enough to hurt you again."

"Nor will I." His implacability only served to confirm her suspicions. No doubt it would make her job all the more difficult. "Let's get this over with, Piper. You've done your duty. You've come to plead with me on your brother's behalf. And I've rejected your pleas. Go home and tell Spencer that it's time to pay for what he did."

She shook her head with a stubbornness that matched his. "No, Gideon. I'm not here to beg for mercy. Far from it."

"Don't hand me that. You're here about the contract."

"You're right. I am."

He lifted a sooty eyebrow. "Have you come to fulfill the terms?"

"Yes."

Surprise, along with an intense irritation turned his eyes to ebony. "The terms are to either repay the loan or turn over Spencer's property. You don't have the kind of money it would take to pay back the loan. I've checked.''

"No, we don't.''

"Then you plan to negotiate my takeover of the mill?''

"You're forgetting the third alternative.''

It didn't take long for him to come up with their other choice. "You have collateral of equal value to offer?''

She didn't hesitate. "Yes, I do.''

"I'm warning you, Piper. I expect my money's worth.''

"Oh, you'll get it.''

"What are you going to give me?''

She smiled. "Myself. I'm the collateral on the loan.''

CHAPTER TWO

FURY ripped through Gideon. "Is this some sort of joke?"

Piper shook her head, impervious to his anger. "Not at all."

"Let me get this straight. You're offering yourself as collateral for Spencer's loan?"

"What's the matter, Gideon? Don't you think I'm worth it?"

If she knew how close to the edge he was, she wouldn't taunt him. She'd be running flat-out for the nearest exit. "You don't want to know what I'm thinking right now," he warned.

"You were the one who taught me to tackle problems creatively."

She tilted her head to one side, her hair flowing across her shoulder. More than anything he longed to thrust his hands into that silken curtain as he'd done so often when they'd been lovers. His fingers itched to know that distinctive texture again. The opportunity he'd had in the boardroom had only whetted his appetite without coming anywhere close to sating it, and the craving had grown so intense it had become a physical ache. Of course, his weakness only added to his frustration, forcing him to acknowledge how much power she could still wield over him.

"Tackle problems creatively?" he repeated. "What the hell are you talking about, Piper?"

"Don't you remember?" An eager warmth gleamed

in her eyes. Why did she have to be so damn enticing? It drove him crazy. He'd like to be able to dismiss her, to toss her out of his office without a second thought. Instead, every testosterone-driven instinct urged him to lock the doors and keep her. *Keep her.* The words carried a primitive directive that held infinite appeal. "You once told me that when you didn't have the money to purchase what you wanted, you had to find a creative alternative."

"Forget it," he retorted. "I'm not buying."

Her chin took on a defiant set. "I'm not asking you to buy. I'm worth more than that contract. I haven't been idle these past five years. I can be a huge asset to you and your firm."

"Doing what? Taking pictures?"

He hadn't asked the question sarcastically. He respected her abilities. She'd started building a name as a baby photographer when they'd been together, her black-and-white photos capturing unforgettable images that had won her instant local acclaim, even at the tender age of twenty.

She shrugged. "If photos are what you want, I'm happy to accommodate you. Actually I thought my administrative abilities might be of more value. I have a degree in business management, in addition to my photographic skills. Or failing that, I'm excellent with people. I always have been. Perhaps personnel has an opening."

"Not a chance."

An uncustomary grimness settled over her features, the expression sitting oddly on the delicate curves. She'd always been someone who offered a quick laugh, who smoothed over troubles rather than stirring them to a boil. But he'd forgotten how stubborn she could be, particularly in the face of adversity. When she decided to confront a problem, she did it without hesitation or compromise, and with a passion that couldn't be deflected.

"I'm not offering you a choice," she informed him. "I'm telling you that under the terms of the contract it's *our* decision, mine and Spence's. He can either give up the mill, repay the money Jack loaned him or offer collateral of equal value to the amount fronted him. We're selecting the final option."

"And I'm refusing it."

She inclined her head. "That's also your option, in which case the contract is null and void. I suggest you reread the pertinent passages, Gideon. You'll find you don't have any alternatives."

"There are always alternatives."

"Is that what you told the owners of all the companies you've taken over? Did you encourage them to find alternative solutions to the one you were offering?"

He didn't attempt to deny the truth. "Of course I didn't."

To his surprise she didn't respond with either satisfaction or triumph at his admission. Rather, a hint of compassion colored her words. "Think about it, Gideon. If you refuse to renew the contract, we have no choice but to fulfill the terms."

"That's the whole idea."

"Fine. But Spence and I are still left with three options available to us, including choosing collateral of equal value." Her expression turned downright mischievous. "Which means you're stuck with me."

Gideon paced in an effort to walk off his frustration. She hadn't changed one damn bit. She was digging in like the most ornery mule, the same as she'd always done. Sure, she was being pleasant about it, but that didn't change the end result. More times than not her stubbornness caused her greater harm than anyone else. This occasion would prove no exception. Didn't she see that? "I find it hard to believe that Spencer agreed to this. He always preferred fighting his own battles. Or is he hoping you can change my mind?"

Piper shook her head. "We both know that isn't going to happen. Spence understands all about revenge, just as he understands what you and I once had is dead and buried."

"If he understands about revenge, why send you?" He swung around to face her. "Why put you in harm's way? That isn't like him."

Something in her expression gave him pause. It wasn't often that Piper refused to meet his eyes. She had an innate honesty and directness that hadn't changed any more than her obstinacy. Then it clicked. "Dammit, Piper! He doesn't know what you're up to, does he?"

An impudent smile crept across the generous curves of her mouth and she shrugged. "Spence can be almost as stubborn as you. Since he's out of town right now, I decided this was one of those occasions that might be better presented as a done deal rather than an option subject to further discussion."

"Oh, there's going to be further discussion. Count on it."

Her smile faded and a fierce determination took hold. "We're not turning this into another battle like the one you staged in your boardroom."

"I assure you that wasn't staged."

"You put it into motion and did nothing to stop it

from escalating. I'd say that was as close to staging something as you can get."

He lifted an eyebrow. "Are you blaming me because the various owners and representatives of those three jewelry firms couldn't control themselves?"

"Is that what they are? Jewelers?" She nodded. "Yes, absolutely. I blame you for putting people in an untenable situation, one guaranteed to bring out the worst in them. It was deliberate. You know it. I know it. And once those men and women have a chance to sober up, calm down and reflect, they'll know it, too."

"Enough, Piper. There's a limit to how much I'll take."

"Oh, I haven't begun to have my say," she retorted fiercely. "You were once a man I respected more than any in the whole of Mill Run. But you've changed. You're not that man anymore."

Gideon's control vanished, ripped from him with stunning ease by a few careless words from a woman he'd once loved and valued more than anything in his life, even his precious word of honor. "That man doesn't exist anymore! He was torn apart piece by piece until there was nothing left."

"That's an excuse. You can rise above adversity. Isn't that what you always told me?" She made the mistake of approaching. Worse, she put her hands on him. Soft hands. Gentle hands. Loving hands. "You always said that outside influences don't make the man. You said that with drive and determination and by keeping one's word, a person could overcome any hardship."

"A child told you that. A foolish child who hadn't learned the hard, cold facts of life."

"And what facts are those?"

He stared at the fingers clutching his arm. They were so pale, so delicate and feminine against the darkness of his suit. Did she have any sense of her own vulnerability? Did she have any clue how easily he could crush the vibrancy of her spirit? She couldn't or she wouldn't be here. No one was that self-sacrificing. She'd be finding the deepest, darkest hole to hide in until he'd expended his wrath over Spencer's bullheaded skull.

Very gently he removed her hand from his arm. It was either that or give in to the urges that had been clawing at him since she'd first burst through the boardroom door. "The fact is that money and power are the only currency people understand or accept. No one gives a damn about truth, let alone drive and determination. My word of honor meant nothing all those years ago. When put to the test, the people of Mill Run were only too happy to believe the accusations leveled by the town's leading citizens against the son of a drunk."

"How would you know?" she shot back. "You and Spence fought that day and then you took off, leaving havoc behind. How is anyone supposed to believe you when you didn't stick around long enough to stand by your word of honor? Spence told me—"

"*Don't!*" The word exploded from him and it took a full minute to rein in his fury. He lowered his voice, the softness more deadly than anything he might have said in anger. "If you value your life, do *not* quote your brother to me."

"Gideon—"

He flashed her a warning look that checked whatever she'd intended to say. "Enough of this nonsense, Piper. All that was over long ago. Forget the past and deal with the present. We have business to take care of and I suggest we get on with it.''

"Since I'm just collateral, I guess I'm not in a position to argue." She cast him a disgruntled scowl. "Much."

He cut loose with a word that brought hot color to her cheeks. Tugging at his tie, he yanked at the stranglehold it had on his neck while fighting to recover his temper. How the hell did she manage to get him riled up so easily? His reputation for icy calm was renowned throughout the business community and yet all she had to do was open her mouth to break his control. The irony wasn't lost on him.

"I give you full credit for inventiveness," he finally said. "But that doesn't change a thing. Your brother signed a contract with Jack Wiley and I'm collecting what's owed. Whether that's now or in one month doesn't matter in the least. Spencer's going down and you'd be smart to get out of the way."

He thought she might waver, that his anger might have been enough to scare her off. But he'd underestimated her. Taking a deep breath, she held her ground, resolution burning in her eyes. "You're collecting what's owed you right now. And I'm it. As I said, reread the pertinent clauses. You can't refuse my offer, Gideon, not unless you intend to void the contract. I'm the collateral on the loan, which means I'm all yours."

"Interesting phrasing."

Still, she didn't back down. "Collateral isn't worth anything unless it offers full value for your money."

He should refuse her offer, but the more he considered, the more tempted he was to accept. That one kiss had told him a lot. He wanted Piper as desperately today as he'd wanted her five years ago. It had been too long since he'd held her in his arms. Kissed her as he had in the boardroom. Taken her to his bed and made her his. Perhaps his revenge against Spencer would prove sweeter than he'd anticipated. He could accept Piper's offer. He'd be a fool not to. Then, when the workload became too much and she walked out, he'd call the loan due. And in the process, he'd have taken back all that Spencer had stolen from him.

"You're sure you're willing to do this?" he pressed. "I'm not going to make it easy on you."

Amusement resurfaced in her gaze. "It never occurred to me that you would."

"You understand that if your value doesn't match what I'd have realized from the repayment of the loan that nothing you do or say will save your brother?"

"You've made that painfully clear."

"Let me make something else painfully clear." Two swift steps returned him to her side and he drew her into his arms. "The minute I accept your offer, you're going to become my everything. All I want, all I ask, all I demand, you'll do."

"I understand when it comes to business, I'm yours." Her body relaxed into his, as though some unconscious part of her trusted him implicitly. Gideon's mouth tightened. She was foolish to reveal so much, especially to a man like him. "But you'll have to respect the boundaries between a business obligation and more personal demands."

He gave in to overwhelming desire and slid his hands into her hair. He could feel his inner tension loosen, as though her touch had the ability to soothe the demons that drove him. At the same time, touching her provoked a new source of tension, a craving that was fast becoming more and more difficult to resist. "What if my demands involve both?"

"I'm collateral on a business loan, not a personal one." Piper met his eyes with an unwavering gaze, her certainty stirring memories of long-ago events when her faith in him had been absolute. "I know you'll respect that, Gideon, that you won't use our business situation to force something more."

But he wanted that something more. He wanted all she had to give. Not that he'd take it with force. He hadn't fallen that far from grace. "In all the years I've known you, I've never treated you with anything other than respect."

She carefully untangled herself from his arms. "Then don't start now."

The loss of physical contact hit harder than he cared to admit. "This isn't going to work, Piper."

"Why? Because you can't stand the idea of working with me?" She tilted her head to one side. "Or is it that you're concerned you might like it too much?"

He went perfectly still, shoving out a warning from between clenched teeth. "Get out now, while you still have the chance."

She winced. "Pushed the wrong button, did I?"

"You might avoid that one in the future."

"Fair enough. I'll go." She took a step away from him. Then another. "But I'll be back first thing in the morning."

"I suggest you reconsider that decision."

"I can't."

"Because of Spence."

"No, Gideon." She crossed to the door of the office. If circumstances had been different he'd have laughed at the way she had to tug to get them open.

But all thought of humor died when she turned and added, "I'll be back because you need me."

Piper leaned against the closed doors to Gideon's office and fought to draw breath. She'd done it. She'd actually faced him after all these years and lived to tell the tale. True, she'd picked up another few bruises. But they were minor compared to the ones he'd left five years ago.

Heaven help her, how Gideon had changed. She could barely find any remnants of the man she'd once known. He'd all but vanished and that undeniable fact devastated her more than she cared to admit. He'd always been hard, bearing his scars with a stoic resolve that nearly broke her heart. But that hardness had been tempered by a compassion and generosity she'd witnessed from her earliest years. Defender of the underdog, nemesis of bullies, protector, warrior, lover. He'd been all those things and more. But she'd never have guessed him capable of such virtues based on the man she'd met today. His anger lingered too close to the surface, oddly volcanic, his wounds still fresh, even after five full years.

Straightening, she discovered that her legs would actually hold her now and she headed down the endless hallway toward the exit. The artificial hush seemed more daunting this time around, perhaps because she felt a bit more emotionally battered than earlier. She paused outside the doorway leading to the boardroom, wondering if she should return the way she'd come or search for a different exit. Faint voices penetrated the thick wood, taking the choice from her hands. Unable to resist meddling, she entered.

The vestiges of chaos remained, the boardroom a

total disaster. It would take quite a while to get the place back into usable shape. Gideon's little surprise was going to cost a pretty penny in redecoration expenses. Other than the caterer, no one had left yet, the representatives of the various jewelry companies milling around in small, nervous clumps looking decidedly anxious.

"Good afternoon," she said, closing the door behind her. Every last one turned toward her as though she offered imminent salvation. It gave her an idea. "Could you all take a seat, please? I have a few questions I'd like to ask."

Gideon stood in the middle of his office, silently cursing beneath his breath. How did she manage to do it? How did she manage to break through barriers he'd spent years fortifying? With one simple smile she'd nearly brought him to his knees. It was ridiculous. He was the one with the power. Didn't she realize that?

He grimaced, running a hand across his nape. No. She didn't and never had.

Piper Montgomery had a knack for remaining as oblivious to the shoulds and oughts of the world as she remained oblivious to her own vulnerability. She'd always been that way, even as a child. He remembered the first time he'd seen that quality in her. She'd been all of seven or eight and had been standing in front of the candy counter at Murphy's Newsstand, considering her options with the air of a serious chocolate connoisseur. Gideon had also been known to give candy similar attention. The difference between them was that she could afford to buy whatever appealed and he couldn't.

He remembered lounging against a stand overflowing with comic books and watching her, a cocky hellion about to rack up his first teenage year. Of course, he recognized her. Miss Montgomery Mansion, he and his friends called her. She was always dressed with pristine perfection, pulling off what would have been a social disaster in anyone else, with a panache he could recognize, if not name.

There was something about her, he was forced to admit, something that elicited a grudging admiration. Fearless blue eyes confronted the world in a way he secretly envied, even her stance one of absolute defiance. Of course, she could get away with being both fearless and defiant. She was in a different class from Gideon Garbage, her hilltop home as far removed from his rusted-out trailer as it was possible to get. Everything about her reinforced that distinction.

She carried herself like a princess, the dance classes she took doing weird things to the way she walked. Maybe it was because she never walked. She flitted or danced or skipped or twirled. Even when she was in a line at school where everyone had been ordered to stand still, she remained in constant motion, her pale blond head bobbing like the colorful float attached to his fishing line.

She leaned closer to the candy counter and her pale blond hair flowed forward to curtain her face. It was longer and straighter than any other girl's in school. He'd often joked with his friends that her parents wouldn't let her out of the house until they'd made sure that every single strand had been measured and razor-cut to the exact same length. She was cute enough, for a kid, he supposed. Plenty cuter than the brats his mother routinely turned out. And she couldn't help how her parents dressed her, her scrawny arms and legs poking out from beneath a laughable amount of lace and gut-churning pastels. Fact was, her cheerful attitude usually made him smile, a feat that impressed him more than anything else about her.

Staring for so long at the candy made Gideon's stomach grumble and he knew it was time to push off. As much as he'd like to drool over Murphy's selection, he'd have to satisfy his unending hunger with the single bar tucked in his pocket. Besides, he had better things to do than stand around staring at some rich kid—like going by the old mill and snagging a string of trout for dinner.

He pushed off from the comic book stand and headed for the exit. If he didn't have better luck than yesterday, his family would be stuck with franks and beans for dinner again. And anything was better than that, especially since the number of available dogs rarely matched the number of demanding mouths.

"Hey, you! Hart." Gideon had just reached the door when a heavy hand dropped on his shoulder and spun him around. "Where do you think you're going?" the owner of the store demanded.

"I'm leaving, of course. What does it look like?" Gideon attempted to shrug off Murphy's restraining hand. "What's your problem, man?"

"My problem is you." A stubby finger stabbed him in the chest. "You're a damn thief. You're trying to sneak out of my store without paying for your candy."

"What the hell are you talking about?"

"Watch your mouth, boy." Florid color swept into his heavy face. "You're just like your old man. Blood will tell, you know. I should have thrown you out when you first came in here."

"Get off me." Gideon wriggled beneath the crushing hold. Not that it helped. Murphy was one of the biggest, beefiest men in town. "I didn't steal anything."

"That candy bar you've got sticking out of your pocket. You didn't pay for it."

The accusation infuriated Gideon. "Bull. I paid your kid for it. Go ask him."

He glanced at Murphy's son and saw from the smirk on the kid's face that he'd get no help from that quarter. His shouted obscenity didn't help his situation, earning him a swift smack upside his head.

"Call the sheriff, son," Murphy ordered. He grabbed Gideon by the ear, preventing him from running, the old man's grip tight enough to provoke tears. Not that Gideon would ever let them fall. Hell, no. He'd sooner slit his own throat. "It's past time this punk gets his first view from behind a pair of bars. Not that it'll be his last. No sirree, it sure as hell won't be his last. Like father, like son."

"Let him go!"

Gideon would never forget the look of astonishment on Murphy's face when Piper came charging over. She didn't walk. She didn't flit. She didn't dance or skip or twirl. She flew. And she didn't stop until she was right on top of them, a tiny whirlwind of fury that came no higher than the store owner's overflowing girth. Even more astonishing, she smacked Murphy's huge paw of a hand, the one with a death grip on Gideon's ear. It couldn't have stung more than a mosquito bite, yet he jerked his hand back as though his fingers had been set on fire and took a hasty step away from Piper.

"What are you doin', girl?" Murphy's question was more complaint than demand.

She took up a stance directly in front of Gideon, spreading her scrawny arms wide, as though her bony little willow twigs had a chance of fending off Murphy's gnarled oak trees. "Gideon Hart did so pay for that candy bar. I saw him. He gave Timmy a quarter, three dimes and a nickel." She turned her blazing blue eyes on the hapless son. "And if you say he didn't, then you're a liar."

It was the funniest thing Gideon had ever seen and he further confounded Murphy by busting into laughter. At least it helped dispel the tears of pain he'd been so desperately blinking back. "You tell 'em, pipsqueak," he encouraged gruffly.

"My daddy always said a man's word of honor is the most important thing he has. Gideon said he paid and he did. That's what word of honor means, always telling the truth no matter what. All the kids say that Gideon never fibs." A hint of awe colored her words. "Not ever."

It was then that Spencer walked into the store. A couple of years older than Gideon, he sized up the situation with a single look. "Problem?" he asked mildly.

To Gideon's astonishment, Piper didn't rush to her brother's side as he'd half expected. She didn't burst into tears or beg for help or react in any of the ways most girls would have. Instead she held her stance, her gaze never shifting from Murphy's son. "Tell the truth," she ordered. "Tell your daddy Gideon paid."

Timmy wilted beneath her blazing regard. "He paid," the boy muttered.

Murphy exploded, no doubt from sheer embarrassment. "Out. All of you get out of here."

None of them wasted any time. The three were

through the door in two seconds flat. Even Spencer moved with impressive speed. Gideon stood with them on the sidewalk, not quite sure what to do or say next. Shoving his hand into his pocket, he yanked out the candy bar he'd bought and thrust it into Piper's face. "Here."

She shook her head, politely refusing his offer. That might have been the end of it, but her perfectly straight hair caught in an errant breeze and whipped around his arm, shackling him. He'd never felt anything so soft in his entire life and he utilized a gentleness he didn't realize he possessed to pick the strands free and smooth them into order.

The instant he'd freed her, he offered the candy bar again, his discomfort making his words harsher than he'd intended. "Take it, I said."

"No, thank you," she repeated in her best Miss Montgomery Mansion tone of voice.

Gideon could feel his face reddening. Spencer still hadn't said anything, which only made matters worse. Did he think Piper was wrong? Did he believe she'd rescued a liar and a thief? Probably. People tended to suspect the worst of him. "You earned it." He shook the candy bar in front of Piper's nose, deliberately infusing his voice with a hint of impatience, as though what had happened hadn't meant a thing to him. "Come on, pipsqueak. Take it. You didn't get to buy a candy for yourself."

She hesitated for another second, then took the bar and neatly snapped it in half. "We'll share it. That's fair, right?"

"Fair." He must have stared at her outstretched hand for a full thirty seconds. Did she have to be so nice, act so friggin' sympathetic? Like he was a charity case, or something. He didn't know how to respond other than with all the careless disdain an adolescent boy could muster. "Yeah, whatever."

He'd hurt her, he could tell from the way her eyes went all flat and dark. And it made him feel smaller than anything Murphy could have said or done. Spencer dropped his arm around his sister's shoulders in a protective gesture. "Come on, Piper. Let's go." He didn't give her a chance to argue, but turned her toward home. "Next time fight your own battles," he threw over his shoulder as a parting shot.

Gideon stood motionless on the sidewalk for a whole five seconds before going after them. It took every ounce of nerve he possessed to brush Spencer aside and confront Piper. "I forgot to say thanks."

"That's okay."

"No, it's not," he insisted doggedly. "You stood up for me when no one else would have. Timmy wouldn't have told the truth if you hadn't made him. And I won't forget that. If any of the kids at school say anything bad about you, they've got me to answer to."

"She already has a brother," Spencer interrupted. "She doesn't need anyone else defending her."

Gideon refused to back down. "Tough. She's got me now. Nobody's gonna hurt her. Not nobody." He met her eyes, stunned to see something that looked remarkably like hero worship gleaming there. "You have my word of honor."

From that day on, the phrase became his personal motto.

Whenever anyone doubted him, he'd stick to his guns and repeat Piper's words over and over until he'd convinced each and every last person of his sincerity.

And he made sure he backed up what he said, internalizing the true intent behind the expression, externalizing it, eating, drinking and sleeping the concept inherent in her statement until it formed the very core of who and what he was.

That boy survived for more than ten years, a boy from a run-down trailer park on the wrong side of town whose word of honor was his most valuable possession—his only possession. It forged the man he became, a man who fought for his dignity with callused hands and a sturdy back and an uncompromising work ethic. And it lasted right up until a fateful day beside the smoldering ruins of a hundred-year-old mill when he realized that the words he'd honored for so long were just that. Words. They meant nothing. They had achieved nothing. They were worth nothing. And they never would be.

Gideon stared at the huge double doors that separated him from Piper. What the hell had she meant? *I'll be back because you need me.* He didn't need anyone. He hadn't for a long time. Need came from vulnerability and he'd worked long and hard to strip himself of all vulnerability. But apparently, there was one he'd neglected to rid himself of, one he'd have plenty of opportunity to eliminate over the coming month.

A vulnerability named Piper.

CHAPTER THREE

"GOOD morning, Gideon." Piper smiled at the man she'd once loved more than life itself. It was a smile that seemed to emanate from the deepest part of her being and she could no more control it than she could explain why she'd still feel such an intense connection to him after all these years. "Ready to get to work?"

He didn't even look up from the papers scattered across his desk. "I believe that's my line."

Her smile widened. "Then I've already answered it, haven't I? I'm ready, willing and able to—how did you put it?—be your everything."

That caught his attention. His head jerked up and something dark and hungry flickered within his gaze. "Dangerous words, Piper."

"They were your words, Gideon. You said them to me just yesterday. Don't you remember?"

The hungry gleam became more pronounced. "I remember they put you into a flat-out panic."

"Don't be ridiculous," she scoffed. "It takes more than mere words to panic me."

"How about actions?" He tossed aside his pen and shoved back his chair. "Would those panic you?"

"They didn't yesterday, now did they?" She'd pushed him far enough. Despite her gentle taunts she really didn't want him turning a business agreement into something more personal. At least, not yet. "What's first on the agenda? Should I report to personnel? I brought along a résumé, in case. Or have you already decided where I'm to work?''

"Oh, I've decided.''

The grimness of his voice didn't escape her notice. She suspected she knew what had caused it, too. She released her breath in a silent sigh. "I've given you too much time to think, haven't I?''

"Come again?''

She perched on the corner of his desk, a desk as oppressive and foreboding as the rest of his office. The man clearly had something against sweetness and light. One more problem she'd need to address. "I said...I've given you too much time to think. Let's see if this sounds familiar.'' She tilted her head to one side. "You've decided you've made a mistake.''

"A big mistake.''

"Right. A big mistake. You should have gone after Spence directly instead of discussing the contract with me. You certainly shouldn't have let me talk you into this collateral nonsense. But most unprofessional of all, you allowed me to get too close. You kissed me. Me, your worst enemy.'' She paused, lifting her eyebrows. "Sound familiar?''

He stood and planted his hands on his desktop, leaning forward until he'd crowded into her personal space. As an intimidation method, it was very effective. But not quite effective enough—not if his goal was to force her retreat. He probably didn't realize that she liked being crowded by him. Now that she thought about it, she liked it a little too much. She could inhale his crisp, clean scent until she turned dizzy with it, feel the warmth of his body lap over her, hear the steady give and take of his breath. It all sounded and felt and smelled deliciously familiar, like a well-loved treat she hadn't experienced for so long she'd almost forgotten how much she missed it. Now those memories came rushing back, along with a craving so intense she wouldn't be able to resist it for long.

"You have it all figured out, don't you?" he asked.

She forced herself to focus on the problem at hand and ignore everything else. It was quite a feat considering that the "everything else" consisted of Gideon, a man impossible to ignore. "I have some of it figured out." There were still a few missing puzzle pieces that Spencer would need to fill in as soon as he returned from his business meeting in California. "I suspect a detail or two might have escaped my notice."

To her relief, he pulled back. Thrusting his hands into his pockets, he crossed to the windows overlooking the city of Denver. She released her breath in a silent sigh. That was close. A few more seconds and she'd have done something disastrous…like bridge the remaining distance between them and sample a bit of that long-forgotten and well-loved treat.

"This isn't going to work, Piper."

She'd expected him to say that. "It's going to be difficult," she agreed.

"I could sue your brother for the money instead of putting up with all this nonsense."

"You could. But think how much more fun you'll have taking all that pent-up revenge out on me, instead." She gave an exaggerated shiver. "Doesn't the idea of making my life miserable brighten up your day?"

She'd have been happier if he'd categorically denied it, instead of turning to eye her with such predatory interest. "Do you think this is a game?"

His tone worried her. It had become calm and detached, a sure sign that he was feeling the precise opposite. "I haven't decided what it is," she admitted.

"I promise, I'm not playing with you. I also promise if you decide to put yourself in the line of fire, you're going to get hurt."

The words escaped before she could stop them. "I'm used to it, coming from you."

Did he flinch? If so, he recovered swiftly. "I think you have that backward."

Wait a minute. "What's that supposed to mean?" she demanded.

"It means that you and your brother did far greater damage to me than any I might have inflicted on you." He stopped her before she could ask questions, cutting her off with a single sweep of his hand. With his back to the window, she couldn't make out his expression, but his tone was more than enough to guarantee her silence. "Enough, Piper. I suggest you listen to my terms. You can take them or leave them. Personally I don't give a damn. But if you're serious about being Spencer's collateral, you should know what you're agreeing to."

She made herself more comfortable on his desktop, her audacity earning a narrow-eyed glare. "I'm ready. Hit me." She compounded her peril with a cheeky grin. "Figuratively speaking, of course."

"You'll be paid an entry level salary. All of it, after taxes, will go toward repayment of the loan."

"All of it?" That didn't sound right. "You're not going to leave me enough for food or rent?"

"If you need money for living expenses get it from your brother. Or start charging more for your baby pictures."

Uh-oh. She moistened her lips. "I—I don't take baby pictures anymore."

That caught his attention. "You've given it up?" His brow creased in a frown. "Why would you do that? You were good. Really good."

"I've switched to brides and grooms." She managed to make the statement with a nonchalant carelessness, as though it hadn't been one of the most painful decisions she'd ever made. "They're easier to work with."

"I liked the ones you did of babies."

Piper folded her arms across her chest, hoping it didn't make her appear too defensive. "It's not your decision, is it?" She deliberately changed the subject. "So, you're going to keep all of my salary."

He hesitated, as though he'd have liked to continue their previous discussion. Then with a shrug, he confirmed, "Every penny." He fell silent, waiting for her to say something, to protest or complain or argue. There could only be one reason.

She acknowledged his cleverness with a knowing look. "Good try, Gideon, but it's not going to work. You can't get me to change my mind that easily."

"I think it'll work better than you suspect," he warned. "Oh, not at first. You're tenacious. You'll stick it out for a while. But Spence won't let you run yourself into the ground for long before stepping in and giving me what I want. He has too much pride to let his little sister take the fall for his actions."

"You have it all figured, don't you?"

"I want Spencer. One way or another, I'm going to have him."

"We'll see."

Piper stretched across his desk, tidying the papers

within reach in order to give herself time to think. She certainly had her work cut out for her. Not only would she have to find a way to break through the barriers Gideon had built up and free the man she'd once known, but she'd also have to deal with her brother's reaction when he found out how she'd elected to handle the loss of the contract. She shot an uneasy glance toward the windows. Unfortunately Gideon was right.

Spence would do everything within his power to keep her safe from harm, and he'd definitely consider her current predicament—as well as the man responsible for it—harmful to her well-being. With luck, she'd be able to ease her brother's fears long enough to resolve their financial situation before he did something unconscionably noble, like surrendering the mill he'd spent the past five years rebuilding. Addressing all the different problems would be quite a challenge, even for someone as optimistic as she tended to be. But she'd manage.

She had to.

That decided, she returned her attention to Gideon. "Okay, Mr. Hart. I accept your terms." She made certain she didn't betray by word or expression any hesitation or doubt. "Shall we get on with it? What's first on the agenda?"

"You can start by getting off my desk." The order had a bite to it, one she'd be wise to heed. Clearly he'd expected her to refuse his terms. Having crossed him, she could expect him to extract a certain level of retaliation. "Employees stand—or when invited—sit in a chair."

She obediently left his desk and wandered across his office to the antique-topped cabinet. "What's next?"

"Your first assignment is to get together with the owners of the jewelry companies who were at the board meeting yesterday and admit you lied. Then you're to tell them the truth."

She glanced over her shoulder. "And what truth is that?"

"That Hart & Associates will be buying them out and selling off their assets, as I explained at yesterday's meeting. Nothing has changed. You're to make that point very clear. You're not to offer any explanations or reassurances. All questions should be directed to my office." He remained standing by the windows, watching her with nerve-racking intensity. Was he hoping she'd balk at this first job? If so, he'd underestimated her. She'd already guessed what he'd ask. "Since you've given them false hope, it's up to you to correct the situation."

She returned her attention to the artifact, scowling at it. Darn the thing for being so lovely. She'd have been much happier if it were a misshapen lump of clay instead of rich with the beauty of its heritage. She itched to send the stirrup vessel hooking toward the nearest trash can. "Just out of curiosity... What items are you going to keep as trophies for deconstructing these new firms?"

"I don't take trophies."

"Sure you do. Oh, I realize you think they're just bits and pieces salvaged from the companies you've owned." She found herself tracing the scar marring the cabinet door, relating to it on some unconscious level. "But when I developed the pictures I took, they showed something very odd."

His brows drew together. "This conversation is a complete waste of time. I suggest we get to work."

She ignored his dictate, as well as his frown. Something told her it was an expression that came all too easily to Gideon these days. She'd have to see what she could do about changing that, too. Crossing to her case, she yanked out a handful of black-and-white photographs. She placed them close together on his desk, so they overlapped one another, and gestured for him to join her.

"What is it, Piper?" he demanded impatiently.

"The photos from yesterday." She gave him a minute to study the collage of shots. "It took me a while to realize what was wrong. But then I noticed that none of your furnishings matched. See?" She tapped several of the more obvious ones with her fingernail. "It isn't as apparent when you're standing here looking at the actual pieces. But when they're bunched together like this in a series of pictures, it jumps right out at you."

"Your point?"

Did he really not know? She found that difficult to believe. Very little slipped by Gideon's keen gaze. "There isn't anything here that you selected on your own, is there? I mean that you decided you needed and went out and shopped for. Are any of these items personal choices?"

She didn't think he'd answer. After a moment his mouth compressed into a line and he shook his head in a single abrupt movement. "No."

It took her a second to perceive how wrong she'd been. He *didn't* know. "Oh, Gideon," she whispered, compassion washing over her. "You never even realized these things were trophies, did you?"

"I told you. They're not—" He swore beneath his breath. Knocking a chair from his path, he prowled the length of the room, his tension electrifying the air between them. His black eyes glittered with all he longed to express, but fought to control. "Dammit to hell! How do you do it, Piper? You have the most annoying knack of any woman I've ever known for getting under my skin."

She refused to back down, choosing honesty over discretion despite the risk. "I just notice things you don't want to see."

A hint of self-mockery replaced his anger. "So now you're going to be my conscience, as well as my employee?"

She couldn't resist teasing in the hopes of lightening his mood. He definitely had the look of a man on the edge. "Only if it means double the pay."

"Good try."

She lifted an eyebrow. "But, no?"

"Not a chance in hell."

She shrugged. "In that case, you'll have to be responsible for your own conscience." Abandoning the photos, she returned to the cabinet. It drew her with annoying persistence. Was it the stupid scar? Or were ghostly echoes from a life come and gone calling to her? "I've found that taking pictures helps since they have an uncanny knack for revealing the truth. You might consider giving it a try. You can use my camera, if you'd like."

"I'll pass, thanks." He stopped a few feet away, close enough to spark an uncomfortable awareness and yet, far enough away that she wasn't tempted to embarrass herself with an undignified retreat. "I'm sure your attention to those sorts of details will prove an annoying asset for Hart & Associates."

"I can only hope." She removed the stirrup vessel

from the top of the cabinet and opened one of the cupboard doors. Since she couldn't bring herself to destroy the thing, it gave her more pleasure than she could express to shove it out of sight. "Now I have a question for you. Why did you arrange for the owners of all three companies to get together at the same time?"

"Simple. To tell them I planned to gut their businesses."

"I got that part." Piper turned to discover that he'd halved the distance between them. Oh, dear. She forced herself to take a deep, steadying breath. Tension still gripped him, but there was a difference. The anger had dissipated, leaving behind a new, more disturbing turbulence, a visceral awareness that had nothing to do with business and everything to do with an irresistible, burgeoning want. "What I mean is, why all three at once? You could have done it individually."

"I could have. But this way I ended it with one fast meeting."

Piper gave the matter her full concentration—tough to do with Gideon intent on blistering her with so much masculine energy. It positively radiated from him, burning in his black eyes and tensing the sinuous muscles and tendons that not even a tailored suit coat could fully conceal. "Yet something you said or did caused open warfare. What was it?"

He shifted impatiently. "What difference does it make?"

"Humor me," she encouraged, edging away from the cabinet. It wasn't a retreat. Heavens, no. There was no need for that. "Since I'm the one stuck dealing with the various parties, I'd like all the facts."

"You'll still have to tell everyone the truth," he warned, following her. Or was he stalking? "I'll even be generous and let you give them the good news one at a time instead of all together, if you prefer."

"And are you also going to send a bodyguard with me?" To heck with a bodyguard for her meetings. She could use one to protect her from Gideon—or more accurately, to protect her from her own wayward nature.

To her surprise, he took her question seriously. "It might be wise, given their reaction yesterday."

"Come on, Gideon. You still haven't answered my question. What caused the fighting to break out?"

"Okay," he capitulated. "I'll tell you. It should serve as a good object lesson, if nothing else."

"Object lesson?" She wrinkled her nose. "I'm not going to like this, am I?"

"I doubt it." He cornered her near his desk. "I was able to acquire all three companies so easily for one simple reason."

She surrendered to the inevitable, accepting his proximity with a faint sigh that more likely had its origins in sheer pleasure than anything remotely attributable to professional regard. "And what was this one simple reason?"

"They were feuding among themselves and not paying attention to the bottom line. Their battle for domination gained more importance than their businesses. It became more vital than their families, their employees, even their own jobs."

She stared in dismay. It must have been a harsh lesson for the company heads involved. No doubt they'd deserved the reminder. But knowing Gideon, he'd have dished it out without hesitation, compassion or gentleness. "So you brought them all together to make that point."

"After which fingers were pointed, fists were thrown—"

"Dessert tables were set on fire."

A brief smile slashed across his face, bearing only the faintest resemblance to the endearing grin she'd known so intimately. The man she remembered was fading with frightening speed. If she hoped to find him again, she'd have to act fast.

Gideon inclined his head. "Worst of all, I lost most of my cache of scotch, half of which ended up on the walls and carpet."

"A tragedy," she murmured.

"If you'd tasted that scotch, you'd know how much of a tragedy."

"I gather you want me to explain the facts of life to the owners of these three companies a second time?"

"Yes. You can get the necessary names and numbers from my secretary, Lindsey. It shouldn't be difficult to arrange another meeting since they'll be feeling magnanimous, believing all is well with their tiny worlds. After that you're to tell them you're very sorry, but you made a mistake."

"Got it." She lifted an eyebrow. "As a point of interest, I assume I should duck around about then?"

He grimaced. "Either that or hide all the breakables. Particularly the scotch."

"No problem." She gathered up her purse and camera bag. "Leave everything to me."

She must have sounded a bit too accommodating, because he stilled, a ruthless quality entering his voice. "Don't screw this up, Piper. You *will* regret it."

No, *he'd* regret it if she didn't follow her instincts. But maybe she wouldn't explain that to him yet. Somehow she doubted he'd appreciate it. She flashed him a quick, reassuring smile as she headed for his office doors. Interesting. Suddenly she could breathe again. "Trust me, Gideon. I know what I'm doing."

"Why am I having so much trouble believing that?"

Definitely time to leave. "I can't imagine," she retorted. With an airy wave, she beat a hasty retreat before he realized his suspicions were correct—her agenda differed drastically from his own.

"All done?" Gideon asked.

"Everything's been taken care of," Piper assured, shoving the doors closed behind her. "Good grief, these things are heavy. I know you want to impress people, Gideon, but really. Think of your poor secretary, if nothing else."

"She says it takes the place of weight training."

Something in the way he made his comment kept her from laughing. She turned around, attempting to find him in the gloom of the office. His voice, a very exhausted sounding rumble, emerged from a collection of chairs and a sofa near the windows overlooking the city. A soft amber glow emanating from the Denver skyline provided the only illumination in the room. She fumbled her way to the sitting area and found Gideon reclining on the sofa, nursing a scotch.

"I see the rug didn't drink all your precious cache," she observed.

"Not now, pipsqueak." Ice rattled in his glass as he took a sip. "I don't have the energy to fight. If you'll save it for tomorrow, I'll be happy to accommodate."

She curled up in the chair closest to him. Something was wrong. Unfortunately she couldn't begin to guess what it might be. There had been a time when they'd been able to discern each others most intimate thoughts. But those days were long gone and this was a man she no longer knew nor understood. "Problem?" she questioned gently.

"Too many to count. And before you ask, I don't intend to discuss any of them with you."

"Because you're afraid I'll learn too much about you if you open up?"

His quiet laugh nearly broke her heart, the sound rife with pain. "Because it's none of your business. It hasn't been for five years, remember?"

It took her three tries to get the words out. "There isn't a day that's gone by that I haven't remembered," she admitted unevenly.

"Tell me about your meetings."

She didn't fight the change in topic. It was ironic that they both were experiencing similar emotions—a keen sense of loss and the torment that accompanied that loss—and yet didn't dare share their feelings. The danger of doing so was too great. A smoldering desire lingered despite all that had torn them apart, threatening to reignite with one careless word.

"I think the meetings went well." Popping the lens cover off her Leica Rangefinder, she adjusted the settings with practiced ease. "I'm going to take a picture of you now."

"I'd rather you didn't."

"I'm sorry, Gideon," she offered. "But I have to. It's sort of an obsession."

"I know all about obsessions." The comment was little more than a whisper. "I have a few of my own."

A strobelike flash lit the room and she caught a brief view of him. He was stretched out on the couch, one knee bent, an arm tucked behind his head, his bare feet sinking into the leather cushions. Dark hair fell across his brow in rumpled waves, uncovering the rebel beneath the businessman's guise. He wasn't wearing his suit anymore, not even a shirt. Instead he was dressed in well-worn jeans that molded to his hard masculine lines. There was a primitive grace in the way he relaxed that warned of a man not entirely at ease. Tension rippled beneath the surface, reminding her of an animal gathering itself in response to the first whiff of approaching danger, ready to attack at the least provocation.

This was the Gideon she knew and remembered, equal parts casual charmer and wary predator, switching from one to the other with breathtaking speed. Both had been learned responses to his early environment. He'd taught himself to use charm in an effort to become one with the people of Mill Run. But his visceral reaction to threat was a casualty of a childhood fraught with a brutality she could only imagine. With her, he'd lost that wild, defensive edge. He'd let down his guard and opened up.

He'd been the boy who'd taught her how to fish in the river by the old mill and helped her tear the ridiculous mounds of lace off her dresses so she didn't look so prissy. He was the teenager who'd taught her to throw and catch a baseball as well as any boy, and slide into first base without breaking her ankle. He'd also been the only one able to console her when she'd lost her mother to cancer. He'd held her in his arms with a compassion unusual in one so young and allowed her to soak an endless supply of shirts until over the months, her grief had gradually abated. And he'd been the man who'd loosened two of Freddie Collington's teeth when the football jock had decided taking her to the senior prom entitled him to shove his tongue in her mouth against her will while tearing at the most beautiful dress she'd ever owned.

Afterward, when her fear had turned to fury, Gideon had tossed her over his shoulder and carted her off so she wouldn't loosen a few more of Freddie's teeth. Then he'd helped repair her dress and taught her everything she'd ever needed to know about kissing. Real kissing. The kind that had ripped her world apart before setting it right again. He'd been her defender, her friend, her companion, as well as her fiercest supporter. Ultimately he'd become her lover, and she'd thought…her soul mate.

"Gideon," she whispered, aching at the slew of memories. It had been forever since she'd allowed herself to remember.

"Don't, Piper. We can't go there. It's too late for us."

She knew he was right. But there were so many questions that had gone unanswered for so long. Considering all she'd suffered at his hands, didn't she deserve an explanation? She'd come to terms with his callousness, dealt with it in her own fashion and eventually recovered. But handling the emotional fallout from those earlier events didn't stop her from wanting to know the reasons behind his actions. Especially when the "whys" had plagued her for all these years.

"What happened?" she demanded. "Can't you tell me that much?"

"You know what happened." He drained his glass and reached out toward the table nearest to him. The tumbler clattered against the wooden surface. "Spencer happened. He stole the only two things I could claim as mine."

"He didn't steal anything—"

"Stop defending him!" Gideon erupted from the couch. For an instant she thought he'd yank her out of the chair and into his arms. At the last minute he veered toward the windows. Leaning his forearm against the double-glass pane, he gazed out at the city. "You always think the best of people, pipsqueak. But they don't always behave the way you expect. Sometimes they act totally out of character."

Was that all the explanation she'd get? Her jaw firmed. No. She wouldn't accept it. "Are you acting out of character now?"

"Yes."

The word was practically torn from him and Piper left the safety of her chair and approached. It was a risky move, but one she had to take. Every feminine instinct she possessed urged her to explore the broad expanse of his back, while every ounce of reason warned her against such a dangerous action. "How are you acting out of character, Gideon?"

"I'm hesitating. I have the opportunity to take down your brother and *dammit!*" His fist battered the heavy glass. "I'm hesitating like I did all those years ago."

She frowned in confusion. "I don't understand. How did you hesitate then?"

"I let Spencer get away with his accusations." His shoulders bowed, tension rippling across his back and shoulders, cording the powerful muscles. Her fingers itched to smooth away the knots of stress. Or was she simply longing to feel the warmth of his flesh beneath her hands? "I should have taken him down instead of letting him get away with what he did to me."

She stared in disbelief. How could he even suggest such a thing? A fury every bit as turbulent as his own gripped her. "You're wrong! That fight had a bad enough end without your making it any worse."

"No! I should have made certain Spencer ate every last accusation." Gideon spun around, his hands dropped to her shoulders. Despite the fierceness of his words and expression, his touch revealed a gentleness he'd have denied possessing. "Your brother stole my reputation. Hell, Piper, he shredded it. You were there. You know there was nothing I could do to defend myself against his accusations."

"He thought you'd burned the mill. He was mistaken. I did everything I could to make him see that, but—"

He cut her off without hesitation. "My word of honor was all I had. I came from a family of drunks and liars while having the misfortune of growing up in a small town with a long memory. You know I was a marked man from the day I was born. It took my entire life to prove that my word meant something. I didn't have money. I didn't have family connections. I didn't have any outside support. All I had to rely on was myself and the integrity I'd built over the years."

Piper's anger drained away, empathy allowing her to excuse his obsessiveness, even when every word reopened a wound she'd thought safe from harm. Her mouth twisted as she faced the unpalatable truth. She was a fool to still care, but that didn't change the facts. The depth of passion she felt toward Gideon remained, whether she wanted to feel that way or not. Otherwise, she'd never have returned, never have put herself in the line of fire.

Fortunately she'd forgiven him for the harm he'd done her, learned to deal with the injuries she'd suffered and moved on with her life. Apparently Gideon had been unable to do the same, which meant she had to find a way to prevent him from adding to the pain he'd already caused. She refused to allow him to dedicate his life to revenge. He deserved better. And so did Spencer.

"I know how difficult it was for you to overcome your background," she attempted to soothe. "And I admired the way you handled it. You were the most honorable man I'd ever known."

"Until your brother accused me of burning down his inheritance. From that moment on, my word didn't mean squat. The respect I'd spent years earning vanished. In the space of five short minutes I went from being a man of honor to one of those shiftless Harts who'd lie as soon as look at you."

"No, Gideon. There were some who believed in your innocence."

"You're wrong, Piper. They'd been waiting for me to prove I was no different than the rest of my family. It just took me longer to show my true colors."

He was killing her bit by bit. "Don't do this. You're eating yourself up inside over a mistake. You're allowing it to ruin your life."

His hands slid from her shoulders upward, sweeping along the sensitive expanse of her neck before sinking into her hair. "Maybe I could have handled it if Spencer hadn't also taken away something of even more value."

She stared in bewilderment. "More important than

your reputation? There wasn't anything more important.''

''There was you.''

That one simple statement provoked tears. ''No. Oh, no.''

''You sided with him, Piper.'' A bleak darkness emptied the spirit from his eyes. ''You claimed to love me. But you didn't. You couldn't. I sent you a note asking you to leave town with me, to start over. Have you any idea how long I waited for you? What I risked to take you with me?''

I sent you a note... I waited for you... It hurt to draw breath. He didn't know. Dear heaven above, he didn't know. That hadn't even occurred to her. All these years she'd thought he simply didn't care and instead, he'd never been told. ''Oh, Gideon,'' she whispered. ''You don't understand.''

''Understand what?''

She shook her head. ''I need time to think this through.''

His hands tightened in her hair and he tipped her face to his. She couldn't evade his ruthless gaze any more than she could escape the fierce determination she read there. ''Understand *what*, Piper?''

CHAPTER FOUR

PIPER refused to answer, despite the gathering frustration darkening Gideon's eyes. She needed information first. "What note? What note are you talking about?"

His frustration turned to anger. "The one I gave Jasmine for you. She swears she delivered it, so don't try to convince me she didn't. It won't work."

Piper could vaguely recall his youngest sister, a pint-size black-haired savage who'd run wild through the neighborhood, regarding all who approached with acute distrust and a distressing hint of fear. It was possible that Jasmine gave her a note. Her memory of that time was vague, at best. She moistened her lips, seeing a possible way out of their dilemma. "If...if I wasn't in any position to answer your note, would it make a difference?"

"To my plans for Spencer?"

"Yes."

He shook his head, urging her closer. Their bodies fit so well together, it made the emotional distance between them that much worse. "It wouldn't make the least difference. Your brother destroyed everything I'd built in Mill Run. Years of backbreaking work, gone with one unsubstantiated accusation. This isn't between you and me anymore, sweetheart. It's gone way beyond that." His hands still cupped her head. Once upon a time, it would have been a lover's embrace. But not any longer. There wasn't anything the least loverlike about his hold. "Now tell me what I don't understand about the day of the fight. Tell me something that I can give a damn about.''

It hurt. It hurt so much to have the answers he craved but be unable to give them to him. She couldn't tell him the truth, not in his current mood. She didn't dare. It would destroy something precious between them, a final link that still existed despite his denials. Perhaps after they'd had time to work together, after she'd had an opportunity to slip beyond the pain and bitterness, she could make him realize how that day had seen the ruin of them all.

In the meantime, she had to act before he forced an answer from her. Slipping her fingers into his hair in an exact imitation of his hold on her, she tugged his head down and with a gentling murmur, covered his mouth with hers. She could tell she'd taken him by surprise. Tension swept through his body, and for an instant she thought he'd reject her kiss. Then with a rough groan, he relaxed into it.

The unexpected joining was exquisite, every bit as good as it had been in the boardroom. Better. There he'd taken her by surprise and she'd acquiesced. But this time she was the aggressor. A resolve to enjoy her own impetuosity seized hold. The effect was mindblowing. With one simple kiss, she tumbled into emotions she'd almost forgotten existed.

She molded her mouth over his, the damp heat causing a rumble to vibrate deep in his chest. Her lips parted and she invaded his mouth, staking a claim with delicious insistence. She'd never been shy about expressing her feelings. With Gideon, it had been pointless. He had a knack for uncovering her most closely held secrets.

She could only hope that wasn't still the case since

she desperately needed time—time to decide how to answer his demand, time to unravel the problems of their past in slow, careful increments, time to find and reawaken the man she'd once known. Unfortunately Gideon had never been the most patient of men, even under the best of circumstances. And these were far from the best.

"You can't avoid my questions this way," he warned in a voice husky with desire.

"Maybe not." She offered a teasing smile. "But at least it's distracting you long enough to give me a few minutes to think."

"In that case, take all the time you want." Determination gleamed, mingling with the desire. "I'll still get my answers, no matter what it takes."

It made for an effective warning, though one she couldn't bring herself to heed right now. She'd offered the kiss as an excuse to avoid his question. But in reality, it had exposed a very real craving. Unable to help herself, she bridged the distance between them and sealed his mouth with hers once again.

The years they'd been apart had given her the opportunity for comparison. There had been other men in her life, men she'd fooled herself into thinking she could love. But something had kept her from making the ultimate commitment, preventing her from indulging in any sort of serious or long-term relationship. Now she understood why.

Their kisses had never made her lose all self-control. Nor had they caused such a depth of desire that she'd have allowed those others the latitude she granted Gideon. Deep down, in the darkest recesses where brutal honesty prevailed, she knew that if this particular man chose to strip away her clothes and settle her onto the carpet, she'd open herself and welcome him without hesitation or question. She wanted him that badly. Wanted him, despite all that stood between them.

As though he sensed how she felt, he thumbed apart the buttons of her blouse. It gaped and their breathing grew labored, the very air thickening from the urgency of their desire. For an instant time froze, while past and present merged. The Gideon who'd been such a vital part of her heart and soul stared through the eyes of the Gideon who had allowed darkness to consume him—a man who desperately needed her, whether he recognized that need or not. It was a moment of choice and they both knew it. She could either snatch her blouse closed and walk away. Or she could follow her heart and step into his arms. Perhaps if the room had been filled with pitiless light instead of wrapped in protective shadows, she wouldn't have had the nerve to go any further.

But insanity prevailed and she took that final step.

Her blouse dropped to the floor. Next the zip of her skirt gave way, the rose-colored silk puddling at her feet. He backed her toward the sofa, easing her downward. He still wore his jeans, not that they'd last long. Considering his state of arousal, they couldn't be terribly comfortable.

Piper fought for sanity. It wasn't an easy proposition. His flesh was hot beneath her fingertips, the muscles across his back and shoulders rippling with every stroking caress. He groaned, snatching a series of swift, potent kisses. And in between, his hands were everywhere, working the clasp of her bra, following the indent of her waist to the scrap of lacy silk clinging with stubborn tenacity to her hips. She stiffened in his

arms, aware that not even the darkness of the room
would keep her secret safe much longer.

"I didn't mean to distract you quite this well," she
managed to say. The words ended in a soft gasp as
his mouth closed over an erect nipple. "We're going
to regret this tomorrow. You realize that, don't you?"

"Tough. I want you. Just this one last time."

Did he really mean that? "For old time's sake?"
she asked painfully.

"This one night is all I'll need, I swear. After that,
we can keep it as impersonal as you'd like."

A single night wasn't all she'd need. And she
couldn't believe it would be enough for him, either,
despite what he claimed. "After this you'll be satisfied?" She allowed herself a few precious seconds to
reacquaint herself with the width of his shoulders and
powerful contours of his chest. She knew this man,
remembered each taut plane and hard curve. Heaven
help her, how had she survived this long without him?
And how could she ever let him go again? "We can
forget this ever happened?"

"Not forget. Just—"

"Just not let it interfere with the rest of our business?"

He stopped the question with an impassioned kiss.
"This has nothing to do with business."

"What does it have to do with?"

He exhaled sharply, the warmth of his breath bath-
ing her bare shoulders. "Now you want to talk?"

"Before talking struck me as the more dangerous
option." She fought to string words together, horrified
to discover that reason was rapidly slipping away.
"I've changed my mind about that."

"Maybe I can help you reconsider."

He levered upward, allowing a wave of cool air to wash away the scorching heat they'd generated. It afforded her a fleeting moment of sanity, one that vanished the instant he cupped her thighs. He parted them, his thumbs drawing lazy circles across the sensitive skin. Resistance didn't even occur to her, not even when he settled into the juncture. Only his gaping jeans and a thin layer of lace separated them. The rest was sheer heat.

"Do you remember?" he whispered. "Do you remember how it was?"

She shuddered. "How could I forget?" They'd shared warm summer nights, silvered in moonlight and sweetened by endless hours of lovemaking. The river would gurgle at their feet and the mill would creak on the hill while the night serenaded them with the unique music of Colorado's nightlife. Nothing could keep them apart back then. Life offered endless possibilities because they were together and in love. "Do you miss it?" she dared to ask.

"Some days." The door he'd barred against her cracked open, allowing her a brief glimpse of that long-ago man and the anguish he couldn't quite hide. "Some days it's a hunger that won't be sated, a favorite song I can't drown out. A longing. A regret. An ache that nothing can ease."

She held him close, wishing she could give him the solace he so desperately needed. "Then why, Gideon? If what we had meant so much, why can't we work out our differences?"

She could feel the tension return, feel him gathering himself, sense his rejecting her attempts to push past his barriers. "We're not going there, pipsqueak. I'm making love to you. Justify it any way that makes it acceptable. Whether it's for old time's sake, or because we never had the opportunity to say goodbye all those years ago, or because it's been too long since you were with a man. Personally I don't give a damn what excuse you choose. But this is sex, pure and simple. Don't try to pretty it up or give it any special significance. Got it?"

"Gideon, please."

"You want me, Piper. You know you do." His arms tightened around her. The brush of skin against naked skin whispered an irresistible mating call. "It's been too long for us. We need this. Badly."

She couldn't deny it. "I know, I know."

"Then let it happen. You know it's what you want. It's what we've both wanted since you first walked in the door."

"And afterward?"

"Dammit, Piper. Stop putting Spencer between us. Nothing's going to change my mind about him. Not even this."

It hurt to keep talking, hurt to think, hurt to know that all Gideon needed from her was a quick, sordid coupling. She closed her eyes. She was an idiot to think it was more, that it might involve the heart. This had to do with a different part of his anatomy, altogether. "Gideon, we can't do this. Not now. Not until we've had the chance to discuss the situation."

"I'm only in the mood for one thing, and it sure as hell isn't a discussion."

She could have wept with the desperation of her want. "Okay, then answer one quick question."

His mouth trailed from jawline to shoulder blade, before dipping lower. "Fast. Ask me fast."

She went with the first thought to pop into her head,

one she prayed would distract him long enough for her to find where she'd misplaced her common sense. "Whose sofa is this?"

"What?"

"The sofa… It's a trophy, isn't it? Who did you take it from?"

The word he used brought bright color to her cheeks. "Not that again."

"We're making love on top of ruins, aren't we? Tell me whose. Did he want to be taken down? Does he mind that you have his sofa? Was it special to him the way the stirrup vessel was special to Archibald Fenzer?"

"Stop it, Piper."

"Does the pain of others matter so little to you anymore?"

He lifted upward again. This time the cold air that swept between them remained. "You've made your point. You've also managed to kill the moment. But then, I'm assuming that was your plan."

"I'm sorry, Gideon," she said with utter sincerity. "It was the only thing I could think of to stop you."

He escaped the couch. Crossing his office, he picked up her discarded blouse and skirt and tossed them to her. She didn't waste time looking for her bra. Dressing with impressive speed, she took a deep, steadying breath before turning to face Gideon once again.

"We have a lot of issues to deal with," she announced. To her relief her voice didn't betray the tumult of emotions rioting through her. "Not the least of which is what just happened on that couch."

He flicked a switch and stark light engulfed the room, burning a path over every surface and stabbing into every corner. It left Piper painfully exposed, which was undoubtedly his intention. She glanced around, thrusting a hand through her hair. What the *hell* had she done with her bra—or her shoes, for that matter? Maybe if she were fully dressed, she wouldn't feel so vulnerable.

Gideon approached, his expression as remote as she'd ever seen it. "For your information, nothing happened on the couch. Nothing of significance, that is." The ruthless businessman had returned with a vengeance. Whatever doors he'd opened—doors that had briefly allowed her access to his inner sanctum— had been slammed shut, locked, barred and sealed against her. "And the only issue we have to deal with is the manner in which you plan to fulfil the terms of Spencer's contract."

"You're wrong, Gideon." How did she explain all her concerns, especially when he would neither acknowledge nor recognize their validity? "You've changed."

"Let me guess…" His mouth twisted. "It's not for the better."

"Not when all your actions are focused on either revenge or—" She gestured to indicate their surroundings. "Or on deconstructing everything you come into contact with. Including me."

"That's none of your business."

She met his gaze unflinchingly. "I'm making it my business. The Gideon I once knew can't be gone. If it's the last thing I do, I'm going to find him again. Or reawaken him."

A rough laugh broke from him. "You're joking."

"Not even a little."

"You think this is some sort of Sleeping Beauty

story? Only this time it's Prince Charming who's fallen under an evil spell?''

"Something like that.''

He leaned a hip against his desk and folded his arms across his chest. Without a shirt he looked dangerously masculine, the impression intensified by his gaping jeans. There had always been an animal wariness about Gideon, a raw, dangerous quality, as though he anticipated trouble around each and every corner. She had the distinct impression his current occupation intensified that aspect of his personality, honed the edges over the years they'd been apart rather than blunting them. She caught her lower lip between her teeth. What in the world had made her think she could tame such a determined predator? Optimism was one thing, but this...

Tilting his head to one side Gideon studied her with cold dispassion. "What the hell makes you think I want to change?''

All right, so maybe she'd been foolish to think her kiss would reawaken the man she'd once known. And maybe her optimism was downright foolhardy. But she wouldn't give up on him. *She couldn't.* "Your need for revenge has consumed you,'' she argued. "If you keep going the way you are, there's no turning back. It'll change you permanently.''

"So?''

Didn't he understand? "You're not that sort of man. I know you're not. Deconstructing companies, taking trophies, seeking revenge...it's made you hard, Gideon. It's made you ruthless.''

He actually laughed. "And that's a bad thing?''

"Stop it! You know it's not right.''

"That sort of arrogance is going to rebound on

you.'' He left his desk and approached. Grasping her arm, he tugged her close once again. "I've always been this sort of man. You're the only one in all of Mill Run who never realized that. You stuck me on top of a white horse, garbed me in shiny armor and called me a knight. But that didn't make it true.''

Breathing became a struggle. Every sense awoke to him, responded to him. More than anything she wanted to tumble back onto the couch and lose herself in his embrace. "Honor was everything to you,'' she managed to protest.

"And truth, and justice and the American Way. Quaint, but naïve.'' His amusement hurt more than she thought possible. "Honor wasn't everything to me. It was everything to *you*. It was a means to an end.''

"What end?'' The words were painful to utter.

"Getting you.''

For a split second she actually believed him. Believed in his heartlessness. Believed in the darkness shadowing his soul. Believed that he'd taken a path that didn't offer the possibility of a safe retreat. The crippling weight of doubt felt like an impossible burden.

"Gideon,'' she whispered.

"Give me Spencer and you never have to see me again.''

She shut her eyes and fought back a laugh. He'd said precisely the wrong thing. Even if the situation with Spencer hadn't arisen, they'd still be facing this particular confrontation. He just didn't know it. Fate had an ironic sense of humor. She leaned into him, oddly comforted by his closeness. He smelled safe. He felt safe. Even as he hit out with words, he held her with a gentleness she couldn't mistake. He was born to protect, no matter what he said or how hard he fought against his nature.

"So you've turned into a ruthless bastard and there's nothing I can do to change you. Is that it?"

"That's about the size of it. But you don't have to stay here and watch. Nor do you have to participate. Give me what I want and you can leave."

"I am what you want, Gideon."

Muscles rippled along his jaw and he shook his head in futile protest. "You were, once upon a time. But you tried to wake me with your kiss, remember? It didn't work."

"I guess some spells are harder to break than others," she murmured wistfully.

He laughed at that, the sound rusty from disuse. "This isn't a spell you can break, pipsqueak." He swept a lock of hair behind her ear. It was a familiar gesture, one that came with an unconscious tenderness that she doubted he even noticed. "Get out of the way. We had some good times, times I'd rather not spoil by hurting you."

"Too late."

"So you've said. But the hurt you felt all those years ago won't compare to what I could do to you now," he warned.

She fought against the bleakness of memories from years long past. It was a cold, black place she had no desire to revisit. How could anything be as horrible as that? She pulled back to look at him. "You have no idea how wrong you are."

A deadly resolve dropped over his face, settling into the harsh planes with the ease of long familiarity. "Don't challenge me. You'll lose every time. I'm going to get what I want one way or another."

"We'll see."

He released her. "You can't win, Piper. You don't have the money to support yourself while you work for me, and you won't have the spare time to earn what you'll need to stay alive. Starting tomorrow you'll begin deconstructing your very first company. Or you can end it all by backing off and letting me work out the details with your brother."

"Not a chance."

"How's Spencer going to react when he discovers you've been fighting his battles?"

"Not well," Piper admitted. She caught a glimpse of her high-heeled shoes near the couch and crossed to slip into them. For some odd reason the added inches boosted her morale. "But he'll understand once I explain."

"Somehow I don't see Spencer taking your interference very well."

"He won't take it any better than you have—not that he'll have any more choice than you do." She summoned a cheerful smile. "I guess you'll both have to learn to live with it."

"Or you'll have to learn to live with how we negotiate around you. Because the minute I get hold of Spencer that's what I plan to do."

Which didn't give her much time. Fortunately her brother was out of the way in California hoping to attract investors interested in both the mill, as well as the revival of the town. But he wouldn't stay there for long. Two, three weeks at most. If she hadn't found a way out of their predicament by then, Gideon might succeed in his plan for revenge. Spotting her bra draped over the arm of the couch, she snatched it up and stuffed it into her camera bag. One way or another she had to find the man she once knew and set him free—no matter what it took.

"Thanks for the warning, Gideon." Gathering her possessions she headed for the door. Once there, she turned. "Now let me give you a warning. I'm not going to give up on you. You're stuck with me, whether you like it or not. And there are going to be some changes around here. So prepare yourself."

As an exit line, it was pretty good. Piper released her breath in an exasperated sigh. At least it would have been, if Gideon hadn't had to help her open the double doors so she could sweep grandly through them. Oh, well. If nothing else, she left him with a smile on his face. That was worth something, right?

"So where are we going?" Piper demanded.

Gideon maneuvered his car through the traffic clogging the Denver streets and spared her a quick glance. It never ceased to amaze him how upbeat she remained, regardless of the circumstances. After their discussion the night before, he half expected a certain storminess in her attitude. Instead she was sunny bright in perky yellow, her eyes as blue and cloudless as a summer sky. He gritted his teeth. And all he could think about was getting that perky yellow peeled off her and doing whatever it took to cloud those eyes with passion.

Dammit all! His grip tightened on the steering wheel. He wouldn't allow her to keep distracting him this way. *Filing.* That was it. He'd send her to accounting as a filing clerk. Maybe then he'd stop picturing her spread across his couch with nothing but a bit of lace clinging to her hips. After that he'd get rid of the damn couch, too. Because it was clear he wouldn't get much work done with that as a reminder. And then, just to be on the safe side, he'd—

"Gideon? Did you hear me? Where are we going?"

He swore beneath his breath. And then he'd have his head examined to find out precisely what was wrong with him. He'd never had trouble focusing before. At least... Not until Piper showed up. "I want to take a look at a business that's vulnerable right now and see if there's anything worth salvaging."

She brightened at that. "Salvaging. Good."

"Salvaging...as in worth breaking up and reselling for a profit."

Her pleasure faded to a frown of annoyance. "You're going to deconstruct them?"

He shrugged. "Deconstruct, dismantle, dismember. Take your pick."

"How very negative of you, Gideon. I'd think you'd find that very tiring after a while. Don't you ever get the urge to build something?"

He shot her an amused glance. "On occasion. But if I wait long enough it usually passes."

"Oh, very funny." Waves of displeasure rolled off her and as much as he'd like to continue to find humor in her disapproval, his smile faded. Somehow she'd managed to prick his conscience. Strange. He could have sworn he didn't have one anymore. "What sort of company are you investigating?" she asked.

"They're a small ski resort near the town of Happy. They've been in business for a couple of generations, but in the last few years there's been serious competition from other, larger outfits surrounding them. They've been going downhill for a while."

"Happy... That's where the jewelers have their headquarters, isn't it?"

"Yes."

"Are you going to look them over, as well?"

"I did that months ago. Why?"

"Just wondering."

Something in her tone made him suspicious. "Listen to me, Piper. Right now I'm attempting to purchase the Tyler's resort. If you do anything to interfere with the negotiations you'll regret it. Are we clear on that?"

"Very clear."

He'd come down too hard. Not that she let on. Her tone remained calm and professional. But the sudden appearance of her camera and the determined whir of the advancing film as she took a series of pictures warned that she wasn't feeling particularly equitable.

"What are you going to call these?" he asked wryly. "Heartless Hart Hits the Highway?"

"Cute. But I was thinking of calling them Devil Driving."

"Has a nice ring."

"I thought so."

He waited a minute before offering, "It's business, Piper."

"No, Gideon," she corrected. "It's people's lives. I can understand your need to take revenge against Spencer and me. But what did Ramsey do to you? Or Fenzer?"

Not this again. "Are you still obsessing over my office furniture?"

"Yes."

He was definitely getting rid of that couch—before someone told her how it had come into his possession. "Don't. Those men went out of business without any help from me."

"But you could have given them a hand," she argued. "Helped them. Maybe it would have made the difference between their succeeding and their going bankrupt."

He shook his head, adamant. "And by offering that helping hand I could have gone down with them."

"Sometimes doing the right thing comes with risks."

There was something in her voice that warned she spoke from personal experience. Was she referring to acting as Spencer's collateral? He couldn't imagine what else it could be. It sure as hell couldn't have anything to do with the day the mill burned. No one had done right on that occasion.

"I understand what you're trying to do, pipsqueak," he offered gently. "But it's not going to work. I am what I am. Take it or leave it. But I'd rather you did leave than to wear yourself out battling against the inevitable."

"But that would be giving up on you." She gave his knee a reassuring pat and he almost drove off the road. "And I'm not ready to do that."

He was a total idiot. He should have thrown her out when she first showed up. Failing that, he should have stuck her in some obscure division of his company where he wouldn't see her on a daily basis. *Filing.* Definitely filing. He downshifted and darted around a tractor-trailer rig. Yeah, right. That would work. No doubt he'd end up spending half his day reacquainting himself with whatever forgettable corner she occupied. Better to have her close so he could keep an eye on her. That way he could make sure she didn't cause any trouble.

As a rationalization it worked for all of two seconds. "There are some files on the back seat. Get them."

"Yes, sir."

Clearly the request contained a bite he hadn't intended and he deliberately altered his tone. "Do me a favor and read through them."

There. That was better. He'd gone from sounding like a rabid tiger to merely sounding like one who'd caught his paw in a trap. A vast improvement, if he did say so himself. He slanted her a quick glance to see if she appreciated the difference and got a face full of camera for his effort. How he'd managed to get through the rest of the drive without losing his cool again, Gideon couldn't say. Not that Piper appreciated his restraint.

After reading through the file, she snapped it closed and swiveled in her seat to glare at him. "A family?" she demanded in outrage. "You're going to deconstruct over four generations worth of blood, sweat and tears?"

He ground his teeth together. She literally vibrated with righteous indignation which left him with only one option—to react defensively. It was a perfectly natural response. It sure as hell didn't mean he was in the wrong. "I'm thinking about it, yes."

"How can you even consider such a thing? The Tylers are one of the founding families of Happy. They came across the country in covered wagons. They literally carved out a life for themselves from the very earth beneath their feet."

"They were miners. And they did pretty damned well for themselves for a while. Is it my fault they didn't put all that money to good use?"

"The charities they started up wasn't putting their money to good use?" She didn't give him time to do more than wince before continuing. "Even after the mine played out, they were creative enough to come up with a new plan. A ski resort was pretty darned innovative when they first thought of the idea.''

He set his jaw at a stubborn angle. ''And now their new plan isn't working. They're out of options. They just don't realize it, yet.''

''I'm sure you'll take pains to explain it to them.''

Aw, hell. She was going to drive him insane. No doubt that was her plan. So far, it was succeeding beautifully. ''I won't be explaining anything to them until I see whether or not I want to buy their resort. It may not be worth as much as they owe the bank.''

''And if it is?''

''Then I'll make an offer over dinner tonight.''

''Tonight?''

He took in her calculating expression and shook his head. ''Don't even think about it. You're not invited.''

''Afraid of what I might do?''

He shrugged off the taunt. ''Your interference wouldn't change a thing. It would just make the situation more difficult than it needs to be.''

She didn't offer any further comment until they arrived at the resort. What he hadn't expected were the tears that burned in her eyes as she stood outside the rambling mountainside chalet. For some reason they affected him more than anything she'd said so far.

''It's beautiful,'' she murmured after an endless moment. ''No wonder four generations of Tylers have chosen to make their home here. If I'd been born into this, I wouldn't want to leave, either.''

Unable to help himself, he wrapped his arm around her shoulders and tugged her close. ''It reminds you of your family's mill, doesn't it?''

Her chin quivered for an instant before she firmed it. ''Our mill became obsolete the way the Tylers's resort has. Spence's idea to restore the mill as a tourist attraction was a good one, an idea that would have had a huge impact on the entire town. It's too bad these people can't do something similar.''

"I don't see it happening. They don't have enough property to compete with the larger ski resorts in the area. But with serious renovations I bet this place could be turned into a winter home for some Hollywood types.''

She nodded reluctantly. "Or someone who's gotten rich off tech stocks over the past few years and is looking to throw away a handful of his millions.''

"Good idea.''

She released her breath in a long, quavering sigh and it took every ounce of self-possession to keep from comforting her with a kiss. He hadn't lost all his marbles. Not yet, anyway. A single kiss and that pretty little dress of hers would go from perky yellow to grass-stained green. Deliberately he released her and returned to the car.

"So what now?'' she asked.

He opened the passenger door for her. "Now we head back to Denver where I do some more research, crunch some numbers and come to a decision.''

Her hands clenched at her sides. "And then?''

"And then I make the Tylers an offer they'd be wise not to refuse.''

"Unless a better idea presents itself,'' she whispered.

Gideon grimaced. Now why did that sound like a warning? And why did he have a feeling she'd find a way to act on that warning? He shook his head. This was what he got for being such a damned pushover and letting Piper stay. Next time she tried to force him in a direction he didn't want to go, he'd put his foot down. He'd simply tell her no.

Oh, yeah. That would work.

CHAPTER FIVE

"BILL, I don't see that you have any other choice," Gideon explained patiently. "Either you sell out or you face bankruptcy. At least by selling you can realize a small financial gain."

"The bank—"

Gideon shook his head. "Sorry to break the news, but the bank isn't going to help you. They want their money, and they want it now. That leaves me as the only way out of your predicament."

Bill's mouth tightened. "You're buying our note from the bank, aren't you?"

"Yes."

"We've heard about you, Hart," Tyler's son cut in. "And none of it's good."

Jarrett had all the passion of youth and none of the ability to control it. No doubt age and a few hard knocks would correct that oversight. Otherwise, the kid was in for a rough time of it. Gideon could have described some of the tougher lessons he'd swallowed during his years in Mill Run, but it wouldn't do any good. Some lessons had to be experienced firsthand.

"You've seen the bottom line," Gideon continued to address the senior Tyler. "You can't make it through another season. Your choices are limited."

Jarrett thrust his dinner plate toward the center of the table. "What you mean is, if we don't sell, you'll force us into bankruptcy. Well, let me tell you where you can shove—"

The peal of the doorbell drowned out the rest of Jarrett's comment. Not that there was much question about what he intended to say. It was an expression Gideon had heard before and would no doubt hear again in the years to come. He fought back an understanding smile, knowing it wouldn't be appreciated. "Excuse me, won't you?" he said pleasantly.

Considering his apartment was on the top floor of his office building, he didn't often have visitors drop by unannounced. For one thing, the security guards wouldn't let them through without calling first. Which meant there were only two possibilities. Either one of his sisters stood on his doorstep, or—

"Hello, Gideon. Give me a hand, will you?" Piper breezed past. "Could you grab some of my bags? The security guards were sweet enough to help me lug all this stuff up here, but they needed to go back to guarding and securing, or whatever it is you have them doing. I told them you and I could take it from here."

"Take what from here?" He poked his head into the hallway. A half-dozen suitcases, twice as many boxes and an odd assortment of plastic bags and paper sacks littered the area outside his living quarters. "What the *hell's* going on, Piper?"

"Isn't it obvious? I'm moving in." She paused in the doorway leading to the dining room. "Oh! I forgot you were planning to have company this evening."

Gideon gritted his teeth. Piper Montgomery had to be the worst liar he'd ever met. "You knew damn well—"

She ignored him and approached his guests with an outstretched hand. "You must be Bill Tyler." Her greeting came with a natural warmth and openness that

Gideon had always envied. "What a pleasure to meet you. I'm Piper Montgomery, by the way."

Bill studied her with acute suspicion before finally accepting her hand. "You're Hart's woman?"

She laughed in genuine amusement. "Goodness, no."

Next she offered her hand to Jarrett. He hesitated even longer than his father, regarding her with an animosity that was almost a physical presence. For an instant Gideon thought he'd be forced to defend Piper, a confrontation he'd prefer to avoid. Fortunately the kid thought better of saying anything unforgivably rude and took her hand in a quick, reluctant shake.

Turning to Bill, she offered her most brilliant smile. "I'm not Hart's woman. It's far worse than that, I'm afraid. I'm his collateral." She glanced over her shoulder at Gideon and lifted an eyebrow, pure mischief glittering in her gaze. "Have I phrased that right?"

He closed his eyes and swore.

"Oops. I guess not."

Tyler's suspicion turned to confusion. "Excuse me? Collateral?"

She perched on the chair closest to him, making herself at home. "That's right. Collateral on my brother's loan."

Tyler shook his head. "I'm sorry. I still don't understand."

"It's really quite simple. You see, Spence—that's my brother—borrowed money—not from Gideon, but that's another story—and he either has to pay it back or offer something of equal value. I'm the equal value." She eyed the dinner table with unmistakable greed. "I'm starving. Mind if I help myself to a few of those carrots?"

"Piper," Gideon managed to grit out a warning. Not that she listened. But then, why should tonight be different than any other occasion?

"You can't spare me a few measly carrots?" she demanded. Her outrage sounded almost convincing. At least it must have to the Tylers. Obviously sensing a sympathetic audience, she confided, "I haven't eaten dinner. Couldn't afford it, if you want the truth. Being collateral can be tough on the bank account."

Bill's gaze switched from Piper to Gideon and back again. "This is preposterous. How can you be collateral on a loan for your brother?"

Gideon gave up. Folding his arms across his chest, he leaned against the doorjamb and waited with fatalistic interest for Piper to finish destroying his business deal. "Yes, pipsqueak. Tell them what an unconscionable bastard I am. They'll believe it, I guarantee."

She shrugged. "Okay." Snatching a carrot from the bowl, she snapped off a bite. "To be perfectly honest, it was all my idea. I offered to be collateral."

Jarrett jerked upright. "*Offered?* To...to...give yourself to him, you mean?" He stared at her in horror. "Why would you agree to that?"

"Give myself?" She managed a delicate blush and Gideon shook his head in admiration. How the hell did women do that? It must be programmed in their genes. "Oh, no. You don't understand. I'm not *that* sort of collateral."

Jarrett's face reddened, as well. "Then what?"

She explored the contents of a nearby dish and came away with a handful of olives. "You see, my brother needs another year to get his mill up and running. That's what the money was for. To renovate his flour mill and some of the other turn-of-the-century shops and buildings on our property. He's going to turn them into a tourist attraction and save our town from financial disaster by bringing in outside dollars. Then he'll be able to pay off his debt to Gideon.''

Tyler appeared intrigued. ''Interesting idea.''

''I thought so, too. But when Gideon bought out the note—''

''Why does that sound familiar?'' Jarrett muttered.

''You, too?'' she asked sympathetically.

Tyler grimaced. ''It's beginning to look that way.''

''Anyway, Gideon wants his money now, instead of waiting another year. So I came up with a scheme that would allow Spence to keep the mill, while satisfying Gideon's demand.''

''Just for the record, I'm far from satisfied,'' he thought to mention.

She leaned in closer to the Tylers. ''That's because he's impossible to satisfy.'' She offered the observation in an undertone that carried clear across the room, and probably into the next one, as well.

''Not impossible.'' He fixed her with a stare that warned of future retribution. ''I have a few suggestions that would afford me full satisfaction.''

She clasped her hands to her breasts in such a dramatic gesture it should have had everyone in the room cracking up. But as far as Gideon could tell, no one's mouth so much as twitched. ''See what I mean?'' she said. ''How am I supposed to react when he makes a comment like that?''

''My dear, I don't know what to say.'' Bill frowned in concern. ''Surely, there's some other option available to you?''

Piper heaved a heartrending sigh. ''It's only for a year. It won't be too bad,'' she claimed bravely. ''Or it wouldn't if all my money weren't going toward paying back the loan. That's why I'm here. I don't have enough to live on. Either I move in with Gideon or I find a comfortable place to sleep on some deserted street corner."

Bill jerked as though touched by a live wire. *"My God!"*

She went back to snitching food from Gideon's plate, the very picture of the poor, starving waif. He'd have applauded if he thought he could get away with it without having his head handed to him. "I figured since he was taking all my money, he'd have to take me, too."

"I don't get it," Jarrett interrupted. "How can he take all your money unless you agree?"

She batted her big baby blues at him. "Didn't I mention?" she asked with all the innocence of a coiled rattlesnake. "I have to work for him until my brother's debt is paid off. He's my boss. He tells personnel to keep all my money…and they do."

Bill shot to his feet. "This is despicable, Hart. I'd heard rumors about you. But even I didn't suspect you were capable of this sort of depravity."

Gideon inclined his head. "That's me. Depraved to the core."

"It's a shame, you know." Piper filched another piece of chicken from his plate. "He used to be the sweetest man in the world."

"I think 'sweet' is a bit much, pipsqueak."

"Sweet," she maintained stubbornly. Pouring a glass of wine, she offered it to Bill. "It's such a sad story. Why don't you sit down and I'll tell you all about it?"

Gideon stiffened. "Oh, no you won't."

Tyler took the glass of two hundred dollars a bottle wine and swallowed half of it in a single gulp. Then he plunked himself down beside her. "Yes, Hart. I believe she will. Have a seat, Jarrett. I want you to listen to this, too. See how a man starts himself on the wrong path in life."

"Great," Gideon muttered. "I've become an object lesson."

Tyler actually had the nerve to quiet him with a wave of his hand before settling his full attention on Piper. "Now tell me what happened. I'd like to know."

She poured herself a glass of wine, as well, and took an appreciative sip. "Great stuff you have here, Gideon."

"I'm delighted you approve. I'll be sure to pass on your compliments to the Rothschild estate."

Aside from a swiftly suppressed grin, she ignored his remark, keeping her focus centered on Tyler. "This occurred years ago, you understand, when Gideon wasn't much older than your son." Pulling Gideon's plate closer, she helped herself to more of his chicken. "He was accused of a terrible crime. Arson, to be precise."

"Arson!"

"He was innocent, of course," she hastened to reassure between bites. "But it completely destroyed his reputation."

"Destroyed him, huh?"

"After years and years of hard work."

"Oh, for crying out loud." Couldn't they see she was overdramatizing the entire event? "Piper—"

His interruption earned him a glare. "This is my story, Gideon. I'd like to tell it my way."

"Let the girl, speak," Tyler agreed. "No point in squabbling over minor details. If she says you were destroyed, who are you to argue?"

Gideon lifted an eyebrow. "I don't know," he offered dryly. "The one who actually lived through it?"

"Those personally involved aren't always the best judge of these situations," Piper argued.

Tyler nodded in approval. "Quite right."

Satisfied they were in accord, she topped off his glass. "Up until that point, Gideon had spent his youth taking care of his mother and sisters. All six of them. Can you imagine? Providing for them, working his fingers to the bone, doing everything he could think of to prove his worth." She paused in her recitation long enough to examine the broccoli decorating Gideon's plate. With a shrug, she dug into that, too, though with far less enthusiasm than she'd shown for his chicken. "And he didn't just take care of his family. Oh, no. If there was a wrong out there, Gideon was bound and determined to right it."

"This *is* Hart we're talking about?"

Her jaw shot out at the hint of sarcasm coloring Tyler's voice. "He was a veritable knight in shining armor, no matter what he claims to the contrary. I mean the whole package. Got it?" She ticked off on her fingers. "White knight. Shiny armor. Snorting horse. Pointy lance—no pun intended. And all the other stuff knights need in order to do their knighting."

"You forgot the lady fair," Gideon murmured.

To his dismay her mouth quivered. She snatched a quick, steadying breath and inclined her head in agreement. "And a lady fair. And then one day the people in the town where he grew up took it all away from him.''

"Took?'' Gideon straightened from his lounging position, fighting off a sudden flash of anger. "Hell, sweetheart. They ran me out of town. If you're going to tell the story, get the facts straight.''

She swiveled to stare in disbelief, wine sloshing over the brim of her glass. "What?''

Her shock wasn't an act. Interesting. "Didn't anyone tell you?'' he asked softly.

"Oh, Gideon.'' Tears glittered in her eyes. "Is *that* why you left? They made you go?''

"To be honest, I didn't feel much like arguing with the shotgun they shoved in my gut.''

"Shotgun?'' She carefully returned her wineglass to the table. "Are you saying they threatened you with *guns?*''

He shrugged. "Okay, fine. It was only a single gun. But the one they chose was impressive enough to persuade me to go along with their plan.'' He regarded her with a healthy dose of skepticism. "You really didn't know? The way gossip spreads in Mill Run?''

She thrust the plate away and curled deeper into the chair. This time her waiflike appearance looked uncomfortably real. "No one would talk to me about you. Anytime I'd ask, they'd change the subject.''

Bill Tyler's expression filled with parental concern. "So you two knew each other back then? Childhood sweethearts?'' he guessed.

Piper swiped at the tears clinging to her lashes and nodded. "I wish you'd met him in those days, Bill. You'd have been so impressed. He always lived by the motto that a man's word of honor meant everything. But that all changed after he was falsely accused. *He* changed. Now he doesn't trust anyone. And instead of helping people build their lives, he sees everything and everyone as a commodity to be bought or sold. Now isn't that sad?''

"Very.''

Piper smiled through her tears. "I knew you'd think so.''

Gideon thrust a hand through his hair. "I don't believe this,'' he muttered.

"It's the truth,'' she maintained with foolhardy loyalty.

She was wrong and he had to make her see that. He couldn't allow her to continue viewing him through the eyes of an adoring twenty-year-old. He wasn't that man, anymore, and hadn't been for a very long time. "What happened in Mill Run is ancient history. It doesn't have anything to do with our current situation.''

She offered a blinding look of unwavering faith. "Of course, it does.''

Gideon's hands folded into fists. Why? Why did he have to hurt her again? Why couldn't she see him for what he was and play it smart? Any other woman would have caught one glimpse and kept as far away from him as possible. But not Piper. For some reason she desperately needed to believe in him. If it was the last thing he did, that would end here and now. He was going to explain the hard, cold facts, whether she wanted them or not.

"Would you like to know how Hart & Associates got its start?'' he asked.

"You mean, how you decided to deconstruct companies for a living?'' She made herself more comfortable. "I'd love to hear the story.''

Blunt. Brutal. And fast. He'd tell it and get them all
the hell out of his apartment. No doubt they'd be only
too eager to leave. Then he'd polish off the rest of the
wine, and maybe open another bottle for good measure. All this warmth and compassion had put him in
the mood to get stinking drunk. "After I was tossed
out of town, I went to work for a small consortium of
crooks."

Piper swept her hand through the air in a gesture of
dismissal. "You'll never convince me you knew they
were crooks when you took the job."

He shifted impatiently. "Fine. I didn't know,
but—"

"See?" she murmured to Bill.

"Dammit, Piper! Even if I had known, I still would
have gone to work for them. At that point, I really
didn't give a damn. They offered me money and I was
happy to do whatever they asked in order to earn it."

"Because you had to support your mother and sisters, right?"

He gritted his teeth, refusing to confirm her guess.
"This consortium set me up. They were bilking their
customers and planned to use me as the fall guy.
Considering my reputation in Mill Run, it wouldn't
have been difficult to convince law enforcement that
I was the culprit."

"What did you do when you found out about their
plan?" Jarrett demanded, clearly fascinated.

Aw, hell. How had he managed to win over the kid?
That wasn't part of his plan. "I turned the tables on
them. I played them at their own game. I managed to
get damning information on one of the partners." He
shrugged. "There was a reward. And I took every last
penny."

Piper grinned at the Tylers. "Didn't I tell you he was a sweetie?"

"Nice work, Hart," Bill said with an approving nod.

Why weren't they listening to him? What happened to his being a devious, depraved bastard? "I'm not finished. I took the reward money and went after the others involved."

Jarrett pumped the air with his fist. "Excellent!"

Son of a bitch. They still didn't get it. Did he have to spell it out in single syllable words? "I used every devious method at my disposal to make them vulnerable and then take them down," he bit out. "It didn't matter how dirty, it didn't matter whether my methods were on the shady side of the law, it didn't even matter if innocents got in the way. They were going to pay and I was the one who planned to collect."

Jarrett whistled in admiration. "Way to go. Wish I could have been there to see that."

The muscles in Gideon's jaw clenched so tight it was a wonder he could force any words out. "I. Took. Revenge. Don't you understand? That's a bad thing!"

"Yes, it was," Piper agreed. "And you shouldn't encourage him, Jarrett. All that anger and aggression put Gideon on the wrong path. Hasn't it, Bill?"

Comprehension dawned in the older man's eyes. "Of course. I should have seen it for myself." He glanced at Gideon and shook his head in dismay. "No wonder you regard everyone as the enemy. You've been fighting the bad guys for so long, you've forgotten how to deal with the good ones."

"The *hell* I have—"

Tyler actually had the nerve to make solicitous *tutting* noises. "Now don't you worry, son. We'll work with you on this. I'm sure Piper and I can help turn you around.''

Piper nodded vehemently. ''Absolutely.''

''Havin' too much fun walking on the wild side, huh, Mr. Hart?'' Jarrett chuckled. ''I would, too, especially if it meant making those crooks pay for all the rotten things they'd done.''

Gideon exploded. ''Have the three of you lost your collective minds? I'm doing precisely what I want, how I want, and when I want. Dammit, I like what I do.''

''But at least you've realized that it's not what you *should* be doing,'' Piper soothed. ''Not to innocent folks like the Tylers.''

Bill nodded sagely. ''Suggests there's hope for you, my boy,'' he agreed. ''It's a step in the right direction.''

An odd noise escaped Gideon's throat, a low, grating sound somewhere between a growl and a groan. He fought desperately for control. It had taken him a while, but he'd finally begun to understand the problem. Why hadn't he seen it sooner? Piper had infected the Tylers with her own peculiar brand of insanity. It must be contagious. All she had to do was walk in a room and people lost every ounce of reason and intellectual ability. A strange calm settled over him.

''I think my first mistake was opening the door,'' he observed to no one in particular. ''My second was not throwing her out the second she pushed her way in.''

''You do right by this girl,'' Bill admonished. ''It's clear she's been crazy about you for years now. Why, I'll bet she stood by you when no one else would.''

''I tried.'' Regret dimmed Piper's eyes. ''But I didn't succeed.''

Bill patted her hand. "Couldn't have been easy to stand up for him when he'd taken off. Left you all on your own, defending him without a lick of outside help."

"I didn't leave," Gideon protested. "Haven't you been listening? I was *run off*."

"If I were as rich as you, Mr. Hart, I'd have gone back and made them listen," Jarrett said with youthful candor.

"I'm sure he'll come to that same conclusion, eventually. Come along, Jarrett. Time for us to go." Bill pushed back his chair and stood. Crossing the room, he clapped Gideon on the shoulder. "I think you and I can do business after all, once we've gotten you back on the right track. What do you say?"

"I can't even begin to think what to say to that," Gideon admitted with utter sincerity.

"A simple 'you're welcome' will do. You have real promise, my boy. Hang on to Piper this time around and you'll go far." Tyler lowered his voice. "At first I thought you were serious about this collateral nonsense. But now I see it's your way of keeping her close until you can straighten out your differences. Smart move, if you ask me. And how's this...? If you two want to honeymoon at my resort I'll put you up in our best suite, no charge."

"If that day ever comes, you won't have to put us up." If he could only punch something, Gideon reflected. It would really, truly help. "I'll own the resort."

Bill chuckled. *"Ri-i-ight."* He glanced at his son and jerked his head toward the door. "Let's go, Jarrett. We'll give Piper a chance to work out the details with Gideon."

"Don't worry about a thing. I'll take it from here," she promised.

"And I look forward to a call when you've come up with a plan."

"You've heard my plan," Gideon thought to mention.

Bill shook his head in amused exasperation. "I've heard Plan A. I think I'll wait to hear Plan B before reaching any decisions."

Enough was enough. "There isn't a Plan B."

"Maybe not yet." Bill grinned. "But I suspect there will be by the time that gal of yours gets through with you."

There wasn't much point in saying anything further. The instant the Tylers had left, Gideon turned to confront Piper. "Let me guess," she said with one of her pathetic sighs. "First thing tomorrow you want me to call Bill and explain the facts of life to him, too."

"You've got that right." He stabbed a finger at the door, his tone one of utter disbelief. "They were feeling sorry for me."

She stirred in protest. "Not sorry, exactly. But they were definitely sympathetic with all you've gone through."

"Sympathetic? Sympathetic! Dammit, woman!" he roared. "They're supposed to be scared of me, not sympathetic."

Her brows drew together. "Gee…I don't know, Gideon. I don't think trying to scare them is going to work very well."

His jaw came together with a snap and he shoved the words through gritted teeth. "Not after you got through with them, no." He prodded one of her suitcases out of his path. "And what's with all this stuff?"

"I told you. I'm moving in."

"The hell you are."

"You're right. The hell I am. It's all your fault, anyway," she accused. "I wouldn't have to impose if you hadn't been so clever."

"Clever?" He fought to remain coherent. If he didn't know better, he'd swear there was actual steam gathering between his ears. "Sweetheart, if I were so all-fired clever you wouldn't be here, the Tylers would have signed on the dotted line by now and I wouldn't be ready to do serious mayhem to anyone within arm's length."

She took a hasty step backward. "What I mean is… How am I supposed to live without any money? If you want to keep it all, then you're going to have to deal with the consequences."

He glared at the suitcase at his feet. "And I assume those consequences are scattered all over my doorstep?"

"Most of them." She twisted her hands together, the knuckles bleaching a telltale white. "What you see here is pretty much all the possessions I have in the world."

He thrust a hand through his hair. Hell's bells and little fishies. What did she have to go and say that for? "I'm surprised you didn't use that line on Tyler," he muttered.

"I would have if I'd thought of it." She tilted her head to one side and attempted to produce a smile. "What do you think? Too over the top?"

Apparently not, considering the odd tightness that had fisted in his chest the minute he'd heard it. "You're probably the only woman I know who could get away with it," he admitted grudgingly.

Her smile grew, lighting up her face in the sort of

teasing look no one else dared use with him. Not any-more. Until that moment, he hadn't realized how much he missed the camaraderie they'd once shared. It filled some deep, dark hole, feeding a need he wasn't even aware he still possessed.

"And you're probably the only man I know who'd let me get away with it," she responded, a hint of relief underscoring her words.

"You think I'm a pushover?"

She held up her hands in a defensive gesture. "Not at all. I just think your reputation for being rough and tough is exaggerated."

"Exaggerated?" She had to be joking. "If you're basing that impression on the fact that I've indulged you these past several days, I suggest you reconsider your conclusions."

"I don't need to reconsider. I know you, Gideon. You always confront the world with your fists up, ex-pecting the worst. But that's a defense mechanism." She gazed at him with an expression that warned she truly believed what she was saying. "Underneath you're kind and considerate and warm and generous."

She'd managed to steal every scrap of humor from the situation. He didn't want her thinking the best of him or believing in the fairy tale she'd built around him. Calling him a knight wouldn't make it true, any more than describing him in such glowing terms would magically imbue him with those characteristics. He wanted her to see him as he was—the real Gideon—not the mythical man she'd created from quixotic wishes and longlost dreams.

His hands folded into fists. "It would seem I've given you the wrong impression," he said with pains-taking formality. "Clearly I've been too easygoing."

Her mouth dropped open. "You call your actions to date easygoing?"

"Without question." He took a step closer. "Trust me, you don't want to see me any other way. But you will if you keep pushing."

"Sometimes pushing is the only way to get through to you." She glared in exasperation. "Though now that I 'reconsider' the matter, dropping a brick on your head may be an even better plan."

"You know…I'm finally beginning to understand," he said contemplatively. "First you meddled in the contract with Spencer. Then came the business with the jewelers. And now there's this latest disaster with the Tylers. I think I see where I've gone wrong."

"Great. I knew you'd eventually realize your mistakes." She closed the final step separating them. Planting her hands on her hips, she shoved her nose to within inches of his. "Now all you have to do is correct them. Tell everyone you've changed your mind. Tell them you've decided to start constructing instead of tearing things apart and everything will be fine."

He continued as though she hadn't spoken. "I've let you have your way each occasion we've locked horns and you've come to the logical, if erroneous, conclusion that I'll agree to all of your demands. I'll have to figure out what I can do to correct that." He jerked his head in the direction of her suitcases. "Starting with this latest stunt."

"It's not a stunt," she instantly denied.

"You can't seriously expect to move in here?"

"Hel-lo? Weren't you standing here when I explained this earlier? Or was that a different Gideon Hart? Maybe one who actually has a heart." She counted off on her fingers. "No money, no apartment, no food. I guess that means that, yes. I seriously expect to move in here."

"Spencer—"

"Lives in Mill Run. Moving in with him would make the commute a bit lengthy. Wouldn't you agree?"

"Dammit, Piper." His frustration mounted, but other than flinging her out on the streets, he didn't see how he could reasonably get rid of her. "This isn't my problem."

"Maybe not, but it's a problem of your creation."

The woman was being deliberately obtuse. "That was the whole point. You were supposed to be left with no alternative other than to move aside while Spencer and I sorted out our differences."

Her eyebrows shot up at that. "Sorted them out? Cute. You mean, I was supposed to move aside while you took my brother apart piece by piece."

"If it makes you happy to hear me admit it, okay, fine. That's what I meant."

She smiled sweetly. "Too bad. You started this and I'm dumping the situation back on your doorstep where it belongs. Literally. It's about time you learn that actions have consequences."

Now she'd gone and made him really mad. "Is that so? Honey, keep yankin' my chain and you're gonna get a snoot full of consequences."

Aside from a little extra color washing across her cheekbones, she didn't respond to his threat. "Will you help me drag this stuff in here or do I have to do it by myself?" she demanded instead.

"Why the hell should I help? I don't have to put up with this, you know." Yeah, right. Keep telling yourself that, buddy boy. "All I need is one good excuse for throwing you out—just one—and you're gone."

She waved that aside. "I'm sure I'll give you dozens."

He thrust his index finger in the air and shook it in her face. *"Just. One."*

Her eyes flashed dangerously. "One? Great. How about this… I'm going to bed." She bent over and heaved her suitcase into her arms. "I'll leave you to lug the rest of my stuff in all by your lonesome."

"The hell I will!"

"You can kick them around instead of me, if it makes you feel better. But watch the boxes. They're full of my photographs. Harm one picture." She grappled with her suitcase so she could thrust her own finger in the air—not her index finger—and shook it in his face. *"Just. One.* And there will be more than hell to pay."

With that, Piper stalked deeper into his apartment. Unfortunately she'd forgotten one minor detail. Stopping dead in her tracks, she glanced over her shoulder with a chagrined expression. "Normally I'd go to my room and punctuate all that by closing the door just shy of a slam."

Gideon released his breath in a long sigh. "Down the hallway. Second door on the right."

"Thanks." She cleared her throat. "I'm still mad at you, you know."

"I didn't doubt it for a second."

"Okay. I just wanted to make that clear. Good night, Gideon. Thank you for putting me up."

"Night, pipsqueak. And you're welcome."

CHAPTER SIX

PIPER crept from her bedroom and down the hall toward the entranceway of the apartment. Sleep had proved elusive, her insomnia either the result of her recent argument or—more likely—knowing Gideon slept mere feet away. Whatever the cause, she'd needed to get to her photographs. For some reason they managed to relax her, perhaps because they kept her grounded. In her experience, photos didn't lie—at least, not the ones she took. Even when they portrayed an unpalatable truth, at least it was a truth she could trust.

To her surprise, Gideon had brought all her bits and pieces inside the apartment. Well, what had she expected? For him to leave everything scattered across his doorstep? He'd never act in such a callous manner, no matter how much he thought he'd changed over the past several years. She frowned. It bothered her that he considered himself so hard and merciless. Perhaps that explained why he made so many uncharitable business decisions. He needed to prove the accuracy of his own self-image. And perhaps that's what had drawn her to the photographs.

She needed to prove him wrong.

The boxes had been neatly stacked in Gideon's study, next to his desk. It was a far different desk than the one he occupied downstairs in his office and, at a guess, he used it for personal business. Instead of a huge shiny black expanse that crouched on his carpet like a deadly spider, this one was a soothing golden brown fashioned from sturdy, old-fashioned oak. Interesting. It was as though the two desks mirrored the disparate sides of his personality. The surface was barren of papers and she took advantage of that fact to deposit one of her boxes on top before switching on the desk lamp. And that's when she saw him.

"Gideon!" He was stretched out on the couch in a position almost identical to the one she'd found him in after her meeting with the jewelers. And like that other occasion, he wore a pair of faded jeans and little else. "I didn't realize you were in here. Couldn't you sleep, either?"

"No."

"Because of your meeting with the Tylers?" she asked, hoping against hope he'd confirm her guess.

"No, not them."

She snapped her fingers, taking another wild stab. "I know. It's because you've decided to see if your armor still fits before you mount your white horse again and go charging into battle. But since it's been so long, you've forgotten how." She offered an encouraging smile. "Am I right?"

"Not even close."

Too bad. Still… A damsel-in-distress could hope. She shot him a quick glance. With luck, he'd reject her next guess, as well. "Is it because I'm here?"

"Bingo." He stirred, the leather cushions creaking beneath his weight like a well-used saddle. "What *are* you doing here, if you don't mind my asking?"

"Thought I'd go through some of my photos."

"Looking for anything specific?"

Yes. "No."

He clearly didn't believe her, but he let her get away

with the small lie. "If all you're after is killing some time, explain something to me, Piper."

"If I can." She'd have been happier continuing their discussion if she weren't doing it in a thin cotton nightshirt. But then, he'd seen her in far less. And though he stared at her with a certain earthy interest, he didn't appear ready to pounce and have his wicked way with her. A shame, really. A man hadn't had his wicked way with her in the true sense of the word since... Well, since Gideon. She put that thought firmly out of her head before it got her into trouble. "What do you want explained?" she asked.

"Your photographs are magnificent. Why shove them out of sight in a bunch of boxes?"

"Oh, that." She shrugged. "These are duplicate prints I like to go through on a regular basis, so I keep them close by. The actual negatives and proofs are at my studio."

She'd surprised him. "Your studio?"

"That's where I take my wedding portraits. And before you try to question the expense," she added defensively, "the lease is prepaid through the end of the year. Once it's up, you'll have to find a place for all my photographic equipment, too."

"*I will?*"

"Of course."

"Let me guess. Since I'm keeping your money, I'm responsible for the consequences."

She offered a brilliant smile. "Finally. You understand."

A wry expression glinted in his dark eyes. "Sorry it took so long. Maybe it had something to do with the convoluted path I had to follow to get there." He didn't give her time to do more than wince before firing off his next question. "Explain something else for me."

"Do I have to?" There were far too many dangerous discussions for him to choose from, none of which she felt confident enough to tackle tonight. "You're a smart man, Gideon. Can't you figure out whatever it is by yourself?"

"Humor me." To her dismay, he left the couch and approached. If she had her camera she'd have called this snapshot, On the Prowl. She retreated behind the safety of his desk, the hem of her nightshirt fluttering around her thighs. "My secretary gave me some interesting information right before the Tylers arrived."

Oh, dear. Piper made a stab at appearing unconcerned. "Did she?"

"You sound nervous."

She deliberately edged her voice with a touch of irony. "Consider it an occupational hazard. Working for you tends to make me wary."

"A reasonable response."

Piper cleared her throat. "So what interesting information did Lindsey give you?"

"She said you'd applied for a job here a couple of weeks ago and that personnel was on the verge of hiring you. Is it true?"

Of all the various discoveries he could have made, this was the least dangerous. Thank heaven for that. "Yes. I sent in an application for employment," she readily confirmed. "Even if you hadn't gotten your hands on Jack Wiley's contract, we still would have met. We still might have worked together. And we still would have been forced to deal with past issues."

She didn't often see Gideon thrown off balance. But

this had certainly done the trick. "Why? Why dredge it all up again? What's the point?"

"I didn't have any choice." Pain slipped into her voice despite her best efforts to prevent it. "Someone sent me an article about you. In the story they referred to you as 'Heartless Hart.' I had to find out if it was true."

"And if it was?"

"Then I planned to try to fix whatever went wrong."

He folded his arms across his chest, reminding her of an ancient warrior, hard and stalwart and resolute in his course of action. His stance warned that this wasn't a man to be influenced by the vagaries of women. "A rather ambitious project. How were you going to do that?"

She shrugged. "By finding your heart again."

His expression didn't soften as she'd hoped. "You think you know where to find it?"

"I suspect I'll discover that soon enough." She pried open one of the boxes. Her most recent photos were in plastic sleeves on top and she flipped through them until she found the picture she wanted. Next she pulled out a selection of professional shots. "Did I ever mention why I was such a popular wedding photographer?"

He didn't hesitate. "Because you're good."

She flashed him a teasing grin. "Well… That, too. But there's another reason." She fanned a series of plastic-encased photos across the desk. "I'm popular because I see beneath the surface. That's particularly true of the bridegrooms."

Gideon picked up the pictures, one by one. "These

are incredible.'' He flicked the bottommost one in her direction. ''What's with this guy?''

''His is a failed marriage in the making.''

He froze. ''Failed?''

Piper grimaced. ''Kevin doesn't want to be married. He just doesn't know it, yet. Unfortunately, neither does his wife, though that may have changed by now.''

''And this one?'' Gideon fired another across the desk toward her. ''What's he looking at?''

''His bride. He's just seen her for the first time.''

''That marriage is going to last,'' Gideon murmured.

''Yes, it will.''

He released his breath in a gusty sigh. ''Okay, Piper. What's your point?''

''My point is… My photos don't lie.''

''And?''

''And I seem to have a knack for showing men at their most vulnerable.''

Gideon's eyes darkened to obsidian. ''Then it's fortunate that I don't have any vulnerabilities.''

''Really?'' She spun a photo back across the desk at him. It was the evening he'd been lying on the sofa in his darkened office, nursing a drink. She'd snapped the picture over his objections and now she saw why he'd resisted. ''This picture says you do.''

He didn't even look at it. ''You're mistaken.''

''Am I? Or are you simply hoping I'm wrong?''

His gaze remained fixed on hers. ''Wishing I'm something—something I'm not, I should add—won't make it happen. Regardless of what that picture shows, I have no vulnerabilities. I won't allow myself any.

You'd do well to remember that.'' He inclined his head toward the snapshot. ''Take it. I don't want it.''

Picking up the photo, she retreated from the desk. She'd study the picture in private and see if it didn't confirm her suspicions about Gideon. Not that she had any doubt. She knew this man better than she knew herself. But perhaps the photo would offer some insight on how best to reach him. At the door, she paused, a final question occurring to her. She didn't turn, afraid her expression would give her away.

''Were you really run out of Mill Run, or did you say that for Bill Tyler's benefit?'' she asked.

''They ran me out.''

Still she refused to look at him. ''And...and the shotgun?''

''Present and accounted for, with—if you'll excuse the dramatics—an itchy finger on the trigger. You remember Murphy, don't you? I think he was praying I'd give him an excuse to pull that trigger.''

She swiveled to face him at that, thoroughly alarmed. ''You didn't give him an excuse?''

''I'm not that big a fool. I controlled my temper. Just.''

Reassured, she turned to the subject that concerned her the most. ''What about the note you sent me?'' she dared to question. ''What did it say?''

''Piper—''

''Is it so much to ask, Gideon?''

His jaw clenched. ''I told you to join me out by the old Miller place. You always loved that homestead, even though it was little better than a ruin. It seemed the perfect meeting spot for my purposes.''

''Why did you want to meet there?''

His hands folded into fists. "Next time read your notes and you wouldn't have to ask."

"Gideon, please."

The words came grudgingly. "I begged you to leave town with me."

"Is that all?" she whispered.

He shook his head, his gaze as dark and bleak as she'd ever seen them. "I asked you to marry me."

For a second she couldn't catch her breath, couldn't think, couldn't react. Tears she'd sworn she'd never shed filled her eyes. She heard an agonized sound, almost imperceptible, and to her horror realized it came from her. She had to leave—*now*—before she lost complete control.

"Piper?" His voice held a sharp demand she couldn't mistake.

She struggled to push a single word—anything at all—past the constriction in her throat. Something light and reassuring, something that would wipe away the dawning awareness in Gideon's gaze. But it was impossible. She backed up, holding out a hand in half plea, half rejection. The photo slipped from her fingers and fluttered to the floor. She stared at it for an endless moment, seeing the man she loved through a blur of tears.

She was right, came the helpless thought. Down deep where it counted, the Gideon Hart she'd known still lived. The photo confirmed that much. She clung to the knowledge, even as she felt the last bit of her control slipping away. She'd never been the sort of woman to turn and run. In fact, she'd always prided herself on facing up to even the most difficult circumstances. But for the first time in memory, she chose flight, needing to hide from Gideon's astute gaze, needing even more to confront the bitterness of a past she could never alter. Escaping the room, she ran, leaving the photograph behind.

The door slammed closed behind Piper, and Gideon hesitated a minute before picking up the photograph. It was the nighttime shot she'd taken after her meeting with the owners of the jewelry companies and he stared at it, exhaling roughly.

Damn.

It would seem he possessed one vulnerability, after all. She'd caught him stretched out on the couch, one knee bent, an arm tucked behind his head, nursing a drink. Despite his posture, he didn't present the picture of a man at ease, but one of a man in need. It was written in every line of his face—a desperate hunger to possess.

There wasn't any question what he hungered for— or whom. He was staring straight at his greatest need.

Piper.

Piper shivered. She didn't have much longer. The time for absolute honesty was fast approaching. She'd known this day would come, known it when she'd first read the article about Gideon and realized she'd have to approach him.

How would he react when he found out the rest of the truth?

She curled into a tight ball. A few more days. Please. Just a few more days to have him in her life again. To say goodbye in her own way. To come to terms with the past. She closed her eyes against the tears she'd been unable to control.

Just a few more days.

* * *

Where the hell was she? It was nine o'clock at night, well past the time she should have gotten back from her appointment with Tyler. How long did it take to deliver bad news, anyway? Gideon stalked from his apartment down to his office. Snatching up the phone, he stabbed in the numbers connecting him with the security desk by the front door.

"Yes, Mr. Hart?"

"Has she returned, yet?"

"If you're referring to Ms. Montgomery, no, sir, she hasn't entered the building."

"Let me know when she arrives."

"Certainly, sir."

Dropping the receiver onto the cradle, he yanked at the tie anchored at his throat. He couldn't think in these clothes. They constricted his thoughts as thoroughly as his body. They always had. He'd never been a suit-and-tie sort of man. At times like this, that fact came home with a vengeance. He wasn't a native of the business world. And though he'd made a place in it, he'd never felt at home. As a result, he'd learned to compensate. Whenever he had serious decisions to make, he stripped down so he could breathe, so his mind could breathe, as well. Ripping off his shirt, he kicked his shoes to one side. The minute he was barefoot, he padded to the window and stared, unseeing, at the brightly lit city.

Why had she done it? Why had she interfered? She had to know he'd find out, that he'd be forced to act. What was this compulsive need of hers to put herself in the middle of places she didn't belong? And why did he keep protecting her every time she did?

The phone on his desk emitted a soft burr. He ignored it, knowing it had to be security warning him of Piper's arrival. He took a deep breath, hoping to bring himself under control before she reached his office. It wouldn't be easy. Not when his anger competed with a desire so strong it took every ounce of self-possession to keep his hands off her.

A few minutes later, the doors rattled and he heard Piper's muffled voice lifted in complaint. "...open when I tell you to open. Give me trouble again and I'll introduce you to the pointy end of my good friend, Mr. Ax." She tumbled into the office, her Leica swinging from the strap she'd slung over her shoulder. She blinked in surprise when she saw him standing at the window. "Oh, hello, Gideon. Sorry I'm late."

"I've been waiting for you."

"That's very sweet of—"

"It's not sweet. It's business." He slowly approached, knowing it was a mistake to get too close to her, but unable to resist. "Did you think I wouldn't find out, that someone wouldn't tell me what you'd done?"

She actually had the nerve to stick her chin out at him. "Hoped, might be a better word."

"Explain why you did it." The words held a cold bite.

"Certainly." She gave the matter some thought for a moment, before releasing a chagrined sigh. "Maybe you better tell me which bit of business I'd hoped you wouldn't find out about."

"There's more than one?"

She winced at the hint of roar in his voice. "It's possible. I'm new at this job. Heaven only knows how many mistakes I could have made."

"I'm not talking about a mistake." He found himself stepping closer, close enough to pick up the faintest hint of her perfume. "I'm talking about your conversation with the jewelers."

She regarded him warily. "Oh. That."

"Yes. That."

"I don't know why you're upset. I delivered your message. I told them you were still bent on deconstructing."

"You also told them to fight me!"

She dismissed that with a shrug. "It was a reasonable suggestion. You were the one who told me they'd gotten into trouble by refusing to cooperate. All I said was that if they banded together, they might be able to find a way out of their predicament."

"Don't you get it?" he bit out. "I don't want them to find a way out of their predicament."

"Of course I get it." A hint of annoyance sparked in her eyes. "They were the ones who didn't understand how determined you are, not me. It wasn't like I could give them any tangible assistance. All I could do was offer a little advice."

"But you would have helped if you could."

"Absolutely. I like helping people."

A final step brought him up against her and he cupped her shoulders, unable to resist putting his hands on her. "Then help me."

With a nearly inaudible sigh she fit herself to his angles. "Help you make things right, you mean?"

He expelled his breath in a harsh laugh, but didn't release her. Couldn't release her. Not when her mouth hovered so near his own. Not when her heartbeat marched with his. Not when her softness and light filled all the dark, hard places in his soul. "You never give up, do you?"

"Never. Come on, Gideon. You want to help them. Admit it."

"I want those businesses."

Her eyes burned with a desperate passion, a passion that had nothing to do with lust and everything to do with the depth of her conviction. "At any cost?"

"Yes."

The passion now filled her voice, ringing with unswerving determination. "No matter who it hurts?"

"Stay out of the way and you won't get hurt."

She was a flame in his arms, fierce and painfully brilliant. He exulted in what she'd become in the years they'd been apart, even as it saddened him that he hadn't witnessed that final growth. "I won't let you harm them, Gideon," she warned. "And I won't let you harm the man you were meant to be by taking them down."

"You can't stop me."

They'd wasted enough time on talk. There were other, more important matters that needed his attention. He lowered his head at the same instant as she lifted her mouth to meet his. Before he could take what he wanted so desperately, the double doors slammed against the walls and a man charged across the office.

"You son of a bitch! Take your filthy hands off her!"

Gideon reacted instinctively. Pivoting on one heel he swept Piper deeper into the protective darkness of the room and clear of the immediate threat. In the same motion, he slammed the heel of his palm square into the center of the invader's chest. It took him precisely that long to realize he'd taken down Spencer. The knowledge should have brought an immense amount of satisfaction. Instead he had the gut-level certainty that he'd chosen precisely the wrong actions—at least as far as Piper was concerned.

Sure enough, she balled up her fist and socked him in the arm, at a guess doing more injury to herself than to him. "You idiot! What's with the Jackie Chan imitation? For once in your life could you handle things with your head instead of your fists?"

"Doubtful," he admitted. How did he explain that he'd have done whatever necessary—no matter how combative or violent—to protect her? Hell, he couldn't even explain it to himself.

She turned her attention to the man sprawled on the ground. "Darn it, Spencer! What are you doing here?"

To Gideon's immense satisfaction, it took Spencer three tries to get the words out. "Saving you."

"Now why does that sound familiar, not to mention totally unnecessary?"

Slowly Spencer gained his feet, fury mingling with his pain. "Look at him!" He glared at Gideon. "He's half naked. The lights are out. And he was touching you. What was I supposed to think?"

She folded her arms across her chest. "Yes, I can see why you'd need to attack him over that."

"I didn't attack him, I—"

"You charged me like some sort of demented bull," Gideon interrupted.

"I meant to do a hell of a lot more than charge you. I meant to knock you on your ass." With a groan, Spencer bent at the waist, resting his hands on his knees as he struggled to draw a deep breath. "Give me a minute and I'll see if I can't get it right this time."

Amusement vied with a reluctant admiration. "You haven't won any of our other fights," Gideon observed. "What makes you think you're going to win this one?"

"I've had more practice."

"So I've noticed."

The hint of sarcasm provoked an instant reaction. If Piper hadn't stepped between them, Spencer would have charged again. A shame, really. Gideon would have relished another excuse to imitate Jackie Chan.

Spencer must have read his intent because instead of attacking, he draped a protective arm around his sister. "Let's go, Piper."

"She's not going anywhere. I haven't dismissed her, yet."

The provocative words had the precise effect Gideon had hoped. Disbelief glittered in Spencer's blue eyes and he bristled with renewed masculine aggression. "What the hell does that mean, 'dismissed'?"

"Just what it sounds like. As her employer, she has to wait until I give her permission to leave." He allowed that to sink in before continuing. "I haven't given it to her, yet."

Spencer shook his head. "She doesn't work for you."

Gideon bared his teeth in a feral grin. He shouldn't be enjoying this so much, but he was. "Flash bulletin, Montgomery. She started this week."

"Then consider this her first *and* last week."

Piper slipped free of Spencer's grasp. "Has anyone noticed that I'm still here?"

"We'll discuss that soon enough," her brother snapped. "Why you're here… Why you shouldn't be… And why you won't be coming here ever again."

"Cute. But I don't take orders from you."

"Only from me," Gideon goaded.

She turned on him, her expression revealing a protective streak as wide as his own. Once upon a time she'd have defended him with every bit as much passion. He shouldn't miss those days, but he did. "You're not helping," she complained.

"I'm not trying to help. You're not the one I want, if you'll remember."

Piper clutched her camera more tightly, but to his relief didn't pop off any shots. He didn't think he'd appreciate what the developed photos might reveal about his inner psyche—at least, her interpretation of what they revealed. She had a knack for sharing her impressions with a brutal frankness he could live without.

Her expression turned mutinous. "Oh, no, you don't. You're not going after my brother. Our agreement stands despite this latest wrinkle. Spencer was bound to find out about our arrangement at some point." She shot her brother a disgruntled look. "I hadn't expected it to be this soon. How *did* you find out, by the way?"

"I told him," Gideon volunteered. "Or perhaps I should say I told him just enough to get him on the next plane out of California."

She closed her eyes. "Of course. I should have known. How can you fully savor your revenge otherwise?"

"I couldn't."

"Someone tell me what's going on," Spencer demanded. *"Now."*

Piper sighed. "What has Gideon explained so far?"

"Obviously, not enough. Last night I get this crazy phone call from tough guy, here—" he gestured toward Gideon "—who warns me you're holed up in his apartment and if I were any sort of responsible brother, I'd get back to Denver and rescue you.''

To Gideon's annoyance, Piper fixed him with a stare that had him shifting in place like a recalcitrant schoolboy. Hell. He knew that look. She thought there was some special significance to his actions, something—he almost choked—noble about his phoning Spencer. Well, there wasn't, other than as a convenient way to get his hands on her brother. Whatever ridiculous assumptions she was about to come up with to explain what a good guy he was were dead wrong, something he'd take pains to point out at the earliest opportunity.

"Last night must have really rattled you for you to go to so much trouble to get Spencer back here,'' she murmured. "Was it because of what happened at dinner with the Tylers or our late-night conversation?''

"I believe it was the fact that your bedroom door doesn't have any locks,'' he replied blandly.

"Ah. So it wasn't fear, but temptation.'' Amused exasperation gleamed in her eyes. "Very heroic of you to try to rescue me from a fate worse than death, especially considering it would have been at your hands.''

"I haven't fallen so far from grace that I'd use you to even the score with your brother.''

She planted her hands on her hips. "Did it ever occur to you that I might not want to be rescued?'' she dared to suggest. "Or that, despite any temptation you might feel, we both know you'd never try to get even that way?''

He went nose to nose with her, allowing his annoyance to filter through to his voice. "Yes, it did occur to me that you might not want to be rescued. It's one of your most aggravating failings. You keep forgetting that I'm the villain of the piece, not the hero.''

She snapped her fingers. "Oh, right. Silly me. I can't imagine how I could have made such an obvious mistake. How could I have confused you with anything other than a villain?" She returned his glare with one of her own. "Maybe it has something to do with the tights and cape you're wearing, not to mention the way you keep running interference anytime you think I might get hurt."

He thrust a hand through his hair. Piper Montgomery was going to drive him utterly and completely insane—assuming she hadn't already. "I've never yet met a woman in jeopardy who's so determined to tie herself to the railroad tracks and encourage the train to run over her instead of allowing herself to be swept to safety," he complained. He stabbed a finger in Spencer's direction. "Even when I arrange for your rescue, you still don't appreciate it. Damned if you don't throw yourself back down on those tracks and flag the train again. And as for my using you to even the score with your brother, don't fool yourself. I'd have been in your room in a heartbeat last night."

"What stopped you?"

Because I couldn't hurt you like that, he almost said. *Because once I'd made love to you, I wouldn't have been able to let you go again.* He clamped his jaws together, facing the unpalatable truth. No matter what had happened between them in the past, he couldn't deliberately harm her now. Worse, if he'd made love to her, not only wouldn't he have been able to let her go, he'd never have been able to take her brother apart. He glared at Spencer. Dammit all, if he didn't get Piper out of the line of fire, he still might not be able to.

"Hell-o? Would someone *please* tell me what the devil is going on?" Spencer interrupted. "Why are you working for this SOB, Piper? And why the *hell* are you staying in his apartment? Have you lost every ounce of common sense?''

''Probably,'' she said in perfect seriousness.

Gideon folded his arms across his chest. Time to take over this little discussion. He wanted Piper away from ground zero as quickly as possible, while sticking Spencer square in the middle of it. Then maybe he could get down to some serious revenge-taking. ''It's quite simple. I bought out your note.''

''Note?'' Spencer frowned in confusion. ''What note?''

Piper nudged him with her elbow. ''You know. *The* note.''

''That's right,'' Gideon said. ''*The* note. Your contract with Jack Wiley, remember? I recently bought it from his estate and I'm calling it due.''

He had to give Spencer credit. Once he caught on, he caught on fast. Shock swiftly gave way to a blistering anger. ''You son of a—''

''That's getting a bit redundant,'' Gideon baited. ''Can't you come up with anything more inventive?''

Instantly Piper jumped into the fray. ''Calm down, Spence. I'm handling it.''

Would the woman never learn to keep clear of his affairs? Gideon wondered, thoroughly livid. Doubtful, given her track record to date. ''Stay out of this,'' he warned.

''No, I won't stay out of it.'' She kept her attention focused on her brother. ''Gideon can't take the mill if we give him something of equal value. It's in the contract.''

Impotent fury gathered in Spencer's eyes. ''We don't have any other assets. What the hell can we give him that's worth anything close to the value of the mill?''

''I am.''

CHAPTER SEVEN

THE simple words hung between them for an impossibly long minute, impacting on Gideon like a blow. Maybe Piper's comment hit *him* far harder than Spencer because he'd never realized the truth until that moment. She *was* worth more than the mill. His distraction cost him. With a roar of fury, Spencer launched himself at Gideon, catching him by surprise.

The two of them slammed together, clipping Piper's shoulder before crashing to the floor. She fell against his desk, the sound of shattering glass far louder than her soft gasp of pain. But it was that minute sound that brought Gideon to his senses. All thoughts of rearranging Spencer's face fled the instance he realized she might be hurt. He struggled to free himself.

"Pipsqueak?"

Spencer shoved Gideon aside and gained his feet first. "Piper? Honey, are you all right?"

Her camera had fallen to the floor and she slowly knelt beside it, her back to them. "I'd like you to go, Spencer," she said far too quietly.

"No way," he protested. "I'm not going anywhere without you."

"Yes. Yes, you are."

He held out a hand in appeal. "Piper, please. Don't do this. You can't still want to defend him. Not after all this time. And not after what occurred five years ago."

"He doesn't know. He doesn't know about the fight and its aftermath."

"That's bull!"

"I'm telling you, he was never told." She spared a quick glance over her shoulder. The starkness in her eyes nearly sent Gideon into a frenzy. If he hadn't been positive Spencer would attack again, he'd have been all over Piper in order to find out what was causing such agony. "He doesn't know what happened any more than I knew about his being run out of town."

Gideon caught Spencer by the arm, forcing him away from Piper. "You really didn't tell her I was kicked out of Mill Run?"

"Of course not. I'd have been a fool to." He shook off the hold with a quick, impatient shrug. "She doesn't lie. Or has it been so many years you've forgotten?"

No, Gideon hadn't forgotten. He'd simply resisted believing. It had been far easier to think she'd ultimately sided with her brother and allowed the sheriff to force him to leave than to consider the alternative— that she'd never loved him in the first place. That what had meant the world to him had been nothing more than a brief, meaningless fling for her. "Why? Why keep the truth from her?"

"You were gone," Spencer explained grudgingly. "There was no point in her hearing all the details. And after what you'd done to her, I didn't think she could handle—"

"You were wrong to keep it from me, Spence," Piper cut in. There was a desperate roughness to her voice, an unmistakable undertone of pain. "I thought Gideon had left me. I thought he didn't care."

Spencer started toward her and Gideon shifted to

block his way. "Don't even think about it,
Montgomery. The only way you touch her is by going
through me."

"Don't tempt me!" He returned his attention to his
sister. "Piper, listen to me. I'm sorry I didn't tell you
the truth about Hart, okay? But that doesn't change
anything. He wants revenge and he'll take it anyway
he can, even if it's through you."

"You're wrong. He'd never deliberately hurt me."

Spencer swore in frustration. "Don't be a fool.
That's precisely what he'll do. No matter what you
think, he *doesn't* care."

"Maybe not now. But he deserves the truth about
the past and I'm going to make sure he gets it. Then
if he still wants revenge, I'll let the two of you sort it
out."

Her determination must have finally penetrated because Spencer's shoulders sagged in defeat. "How
long?"

"Just a few days. That's all I'm asking. I need time
to explain everything in my own way."

Gideon refused to stay quiet another minute. There
were nuances to this encounter that he was missing.
He felt like a player without a rule book or a clue as
to what game they were playing, and he didn't like it
one little bit. "Explain what, Piper? What are you two
keeping from me?"

She didn't answer, instead curling into a tighter ball.

Something was wrong and he suspected it had little
to do with a broken camera lens. Gideon jerked his
head toward the door. "Get out, Montgomery."

"Please go, Spence," she begged. "I'll call you
later and give you the details about the money we
owe."

"Piper—"

"Please."

Gideon had never heard her so close to the edge before. Without a word, he crossed his office and opened the doors. His look warned that he'd use physical force, if necessary, to eject Spencer. Piper's brother hesitated a moment longer before turning and following.

"Hurt her and it'll be the last thing you ever do" came his parting shot.

It took every scrap of Gideon's self-control not to lay hands on Spencer again. "If you don't want her hurt, fight your own damn battles. I want that mill. Give it to me and she's all yours."

Spencer inclined his head in acknowledgment. To Gideon's surprise, he added in an undertone, "I didn't tell her the truth about why you left town because she would have gone chasing after you."

"It wasn't your decision."

"I made it my decision. You were bad news then, and you're even worse news now." Spencer invaded Gideon's space, his statement low and intense. "Just so it's clear between us, I don't believe for a minute that you didn't know the full extent of the damage you left in your wake."

"For the last time… I didn't burn your mill," Gideon stated through clenched teeth.

"I'm not talking about the damage you did to the mill. You think I give a damn about that in comparison to my sister?" A smoldering fury settled over Spencer. "The only reason I'm leaving now is because Piper insists and I'd do anything for my sister. But she's all that's stopping me from putting you down so hard you wouldn't be able to get up in a month of Sundays. I'm also telling you flat out. You're not getting the mill and you're definitely not getting my sister. I won't have you ruin either one. Not again.''

With that Spencer disappeared through the doors. Gideon closed them with more force than necessary and glanced at Piper. She remained hunched on the floor beside his desk, her back to him, cradling her camera in her lap. Aw, hell. This couldn't be good. He was at her side in two seconds flat. Crouching behind her, he folded his arms around her in a comforting embrace and hugged her to his chest.

''I'm sorry, sweetheart. I didn't mean for your camera to get broken. How bad is it?''

She shuddered in his grasp, her breath coming in short, shallow pants. ''I need a towel, please. A damp towel, if you don't mind.''

The starkness of her request left him feeling as though he'd been sucker-punched. ''What's wrong?''

''Gideon…please.''

The words were barely audible, but they had him instantly reacting. He carefully released her and charged into the bathroom adjoining his office. Ripping a towel from the bar, he thrust it under the faucet. A half-dozen swift strides returned him to her side. He saw it then. She held her left hand clasped tightly to her right arm. His office was too dark to distinguish color very well, but even in the subdued lighting he could tell her fingers were bright with blood.

A single, brutal word escaped before he gritted his teeth and stooped beside her, pressing the damp towel to her arm to stem the flow of blood. ''What the hell happened?'' he demanded.

''It was my fault. I tried to catch the camera before

it dropped and I slipped against your desk. My arm caught the corner. I didn't want Spencer to see I'd been injured. He...he wouldn't have taken it too well.''

"My *desk* cut you?"

She managed a broken laugh. "Apparently some of your trophies are even more dangerous than the man who collects them.''

He flinched at the comment. "Dammit! I can't see what I'm doing. Come on. Let's get you into the bathroom.''

He didn't wait for her to stand, but simply scooped her up and carted her into the connecting room. Setting her on her feet, he turned on the water and eased her arm beneath the faucet. Then he gently pulled away the towel.

"How bad is it?" she asked, refusing to look. There wasn't any expression in her voice, but she'd turned deathly white.

"You didn't cut an artery, if that's what you're asking.'' How he managed to sound so steady and in control, he'd never know. "But we need to get you to the hospital so they can stitch this up.''

"*No!* No hospital.''

"Be sensible, Piper.''

"No hospital,'' she repeated. Her refusal contained a quality he'd never heard before, warning that she was far more upset than he'd first thought. "Clean it with soap and stick a bandage on it. Tomorrow I'll see the doctor in his office. But I'm not going to the hospital.''

"I've got news for you. You're not going to wait until tomorrow to see a doctor, and that's final.''

She began to shake. "Drop the tough guy act. You can't bark orders and expect me to obey."

"As your employer, that's precisely what I can do. But if it makes you feel any better, I have an in at the local emergency room. Lucy—do you remember my younger sister?"

He'd succeeded in momentarily distracting her. "Of course I remember her. When I was little I thought you two were twins."

"Well, she's an ER doctor now. I'll give her a call and have her meet us at the hospital. She owes me a favor or two."

"I still don't want to— Ouch! That stings."

He dabbed cautiously at the wound. "Sorry. I didn't mean to hurt you."

"Oh, shoot." Her breathing grew shallow and rapid. "Gideon?"

"What is it, pipsqueak?"

"I really do apologize."

If the circumstances had been different, he'd have found her formality amusing. "Hell, woman. What do you have to apologize for?"

"I'm either going to get sick or faint. Maybe both."

He should have realized how bad off she was a lot sooner. Wrapping a clean towel around her arm, he pulled her close and lowered her to the tile floor, cradling her against his chest. She fit as perfectly as she always had, as though she'd been born for his embrace. "Rest for a minute. Then I'll call Lucy. She doesn't live too far away."

"I don't want—"

"We're going to the hospital and that's final." Piper didn't answer, but simply turned her face into his shoulder, a sigh shuddering through her. He'd never

known she had a fear of hospitals. Perhaps it had
something to do with her mother's death. He vaguely
recalled it had involved cancer. No doubt that sort of
illness would have required lengthy hospital stays that
would have had an adverse effect on a young girl.
"I'm going to carry you to the couch now. Then I'll
give my sister a call."

Within thirty minutes they were at the hospital, the
three of them closeted in a small cubicle. "Of course
you did the right thing bringing her here," Lucy
groused. "I can't believe you even bothered discussing it. That's not like you."

"We're in shock," Gideon offered blandly.

"Right." Lucy dismissed him with an irritated
shrug and gave Piper a professional smile. "It's not
deep, fortunately. Only a couple of stitches necessary.
I'll also update your tetanus shot. I assume Gideon can
keep an eye on you tonight?"

"Yes."

Lucy groaned. "I was afraid you'd say that. But if
my brother wants to make a fool of himself over you
again, that's his business. I can't stop him."

"That's enough, Lucy." Gideon cut in. "I'm dealing with the situation."

She gave his bare torso and low-slung jeans a
pointed look. "Yeah, I see how you're dealing with
it. She made your life a misery once, why in the world
would you let her do it again?"

"Would you like to put the stitches in crooked?"
Piper offered.

Lucy stared in confusion. "What?"

"Would it make you feel better if I let you put the
stitches in crooked? Or you can forget the stitches altogether and let it scar."

"I'd never do that," Lucy protested. "I try to help people, not hurt them."

"And I'd never hurt your brother. Not deliberately. I never have and I never will." Piper's gaze didn't waver. "I didn't know your brother was run out of town. If I had, perhaps these past five years would have ended differently."

Gideon went very still, her comment prompting a memory. *He doesn't know. He doesn't know about the fight and its aftermath.* Once before he'd had the impression he was playing a game without having all the rules. The feeling grew stronger, clawing at him with an urgency he couldn't ignore. Piper's injury had prevented him from demanding an explanation. But one way or another, he'd force the truth from her. And he'd do it tonight.

"Fix her up," he ordered. "I want to get out of here."

Lucy's mouth tightened. "No problem." It didn't take long to close and bandage the wound. The minute she'd finished, she gave Gideon a list of instructions. Standing to leave, she glanced at Piper and released her breath in a long sigh. "Fair warning. I'm going to hold you to that promise not to hurt my brother. Mess it up and you'll have some very angry sisters to deal with."

Piper smiled. "My brother said more or less the same thing to Gideon. Maybe we should all get together and compare notes. I'll bet we have more in common than you might think."

Lucy returned her smile with less reluctance than she'd shown to date. "I'll give you this much... Leaving Mill Run was the best thing that ever happened to us. We owe you for that, if nothing else."

On the car trip home, Piper remained strangely quiet. Even on the elevator ride to his apartment, she refused to be drawn into any discussions. It wasn't until they were in the living room, recovering from their ordeal with a small splash of brandy that she turned to Gideon. "What did Lucy mean by that? About leaving Mill Run being the best thing that ever happened to you?"

He hesitated, cradling the snifter between his hands. This wasn't a story he'd planned to repeat to anyone. But there'd been enough secrets between them. She deserved the truth. "After I was thrown in jail, there was no one to protect my mother and sisters from my father."

She stared in horror. "Oh, Gideon—"

"Don't feel too bad. It finally gave my mother the incentive she needed to gather up the girls and leave. Until then, they had nowhere to go. When I was run out of town, they followed. Somehow we muddled through, though that first year almost destroyed us."

He saw the tears come, like dark clouds marring a perfect blue sky. He found the sight unexpectedly wrenching. "It was a long time ago, Piper," he said gently.

She swiped at the tears that fell. "You say that like it's over." Her response had a fierce, impatient edge. "If it were, you wouldn't still hold a grudge. What happened back then changed something fundamental inside of you. And look at the path you've chosen as a result."

He fought against an irrational surge of anger. "That path has provided my family with a livelihood they wouldn't have otherwise enjoyed. It put all my sisters through college, paid for Lucy's medical training and gave my mother the first home she's ever known. Before that she'd lived her life in squalor, barely subsisting inside of a run-down trailer that wasn't fit for pigs. It also gave me the drive to make more of myself than I could have if I'd stayed in Mill Run.'' He swallowed the last of his brandy and set the snifter aside, the glass clattering discordantly against the wooden table. ''And it showed me what happens when you allow yourself to be vulnerable. Vulnerabilities make you weak.''

''Was I one of your vulnerabilities, Gideon?'' she demanded. ''Was our love? Did that make you weak?''

He stood and crossed to the windows, staring out at the city nightscape for a long moment. ''You were my only vulnerability,'' he confessed. ''And my greatest weakness.''

''And you won't make that mistake again, will you?''

''Not a chance.'' He glanced over his shoulder, fixing her with an implacable gaze. ''I want to know what you've been keeping from me, Piper. Now. What information do you and Spencer have about the day of the fight that I lack? What are you hiding?''

He could see her debating how best to answer. Then she joined him at the window, standing dangerously close. Desire swirled between them, driven by forces beyond his control or resistance. It was as though a connection existed on some alternate plane, as though some primal awareness formed between them whenever they were together. He could feel the ancient weaving begin, the swift formation of silken bonds that shimmered with a primitive imperative to join. To mate. To form a necessary whole from emotions which had remained separate and incomplete for far too long.

"All right. I'll explain everything, but I'm not sure you'll appreciate the explanation," she warned.

"Let me worry about that." The lingering traces of a hospital odor clung to her and his frustration grew. Or perhaps the unique bonding he sensed between them added to his distress. She shouldn't smell like a medicine cabinet. He knew her distinctive perfume and it wasn't this. If he had his way, she'd never carry this scent again. "Answer me, Piper."

With a reluctant sigh, she slipped her hands around his neck. "No, Gideon, don't move," she warned the instant he reached for her wrists. "You'll reopen my cut."

He stood rigid within her embrace. "What are you doing?"

"Answering your question...in my own way." She smiled up at him with an invasive warmth that overran every barrier he possessed. "Or has it been so long that you're no longer familiar with this mode of communication?"

She pressed herself against him. She was so soft. So feminine. So imbued with a warmth of body and spirit. He fought to hold perfectly still instead of molding her close as he'd have liked. He clenched his hands at his sides instead of filling them with her lush curves and exploring all that he'd once known so intimately. Her actions brought home an unpalatable fact. No matter what he claimed to the contrary, she remained his only vulnerability and greatest weakness.

"I seem to remember your using this method last time you tried to avoid my questions. It worked that time.'' The words grated. ''It's not going to work again.''

''I know. But let it work for a minute longer. Please, Gideon. Give me this one, brief indulgence and then I'll answer your question.''

He found it impossible to refuse her request, not when he craved to have her mouth beneath his, her lips spread in welcome. Intense desire swept over him and every masculine instinct urged him to seize what he wanted, as though she were a business acquisition to be taken by force. Instead he cautiously cupped her face and stole a kiss. Gently, tenderly. Rather than demanding a reaction, he found himself coaxing it. And when he'd won the softest of sighs and the most generous of responses, he found himself doing something he'd have sworn he'd lost the ability to do.

He gave back with all that he had.

She held him for a moment longer, as giving as he'd tried to be, succeeding far better because she was more generous by nature. A different quality entered the kiss and it took him a moment to realize what had changed. And then it hit him. He couldn't explain how he knew, but he had a gut-level certainty that she was saying goodbye—and that was why she'd kissed him before offering the answers he craved. Because once she explained it would somehow change their relationship. Suddenly he didn't want the answers, couldn't even remember the questions.

''No,'' he muttered against her mouth. ''Don't stop now.''

''We have to. I made a promise and I'm going to keep it.''

''Piper—''

She took a deep, steadying breath. "Thank you for helping me tonight."

"It doesn't have to end," he insisted.

"Yes. Yes, it does."

He couldn't explain the desperation he felt. Desperation suggested an unfulfilled need. And he knew better than to need anything or anyone. Hadn't he told Piper that he wouldn't leave himself that open again? "At least spend the night with me. Let me make love to you. We can talk in the morning."

"No. We have to finish our discussion tonight. I might lose my nerve by morning." She escaped his arms with a reluctance even he couldn't mistake and crossed to the doorway leading to the bedrooms. There she paused. "I never answered your question earlier. And you deserve to know."

"Know what?"

Her throat moved as she swallowed. "You asked what Spence and I were keeping from you. What we knew about the fight that you didn't."

"And?"

"During the fight I fell off the embankment and was injured." She shrugged as though it were no big deal. "That's why I didn't realize you'd been arrested. Or that you'd been run out of town. I was in the hospital."

A minute later he heard the soft click of her bedroom door closing.

Gideon couldn't sleep. He kept hearing Piper's words. *During the fight I fell off the embankment and was injured. That's why I didn't realize you'd been arrested. Or that you'd been run out of town. I was in the hospital.* There was more. Far more than she'd told him. He could tell from her expression and from the bleakness in her eyes. And he suspected he knew what it was.

Escaping his rumpled bed, he climbed into his jeans and headed downstairs to his office. Rescuing Piper's camera from the floor, he examined the damage. The lens had shattered and would have to be replaced. He'd leave a message for his secretary to get it taken care of first thing in the morning, even if she had to have the new part flown in overnight from Germany.

After cleaning up the shards of glass, he made his way back upstairs. Silence reigned, the lack of sound oppressive. For some reason, he wanted to throw things, to pound the pavement in a mind-numbing run, to utilize every muscle in his body in the sort of hard, physical labor he'd known during his days in Old Mill Run. Anything that would drown out the voices in his head. Anything that would leave him too exhausted to think. Instead he paced from room to room until he found himself standing outside of Piper's bedroom, drawn by forces he refused to acknowledge. The pull proved irresistible.

Grasping the knob, he shoved the door inward, light from the hallway vanquishing the darkness. It spilled across the carpet, rushing toward the bed where it extinguished the last of its radiance on the form curled beneath the covers. He could tell from her breathing that she slept, her injured arm propped on a pillow.

A painful tightness closed his throat. Why did she have to be so foolhardy? She shouldn't have put herself in the middle of two men bent on doing serious physical damage to each other. She'd been hurt because she had a ridiculous need to protect Spencer—as though her brother required protection. Gideon shut his eyes, acknowledging the bitter truth. Rationalizations wouldn't work any longer. He'd wanted a confrontation, thirsted for the opportunity to tell Spencer his plans for revenge face-to-face. And he'd gotten that opportunity. But at whose expense?

Dammit all! What the hell had he done?

When had his need for vengeance become so all-consuming that it allowed him to harm the woman he'd once loved more than anything in this world? He approached the bed and gazed down at her, a slight smile easing the rigid muscles knotting his jaw. He'd adored this woman from boyhood and despite the changes he'd undergone—changes that clearly distressed her—she'd remained constant. In fact, there was little he could see that was different.

She was still as strong-willed as she was generous, and just as determined to battle for the underdog as she'd always been. Even her hair had stayed the same, the thick blond strands as ruler-edge straight as ever. He gathered up a handful. And it still had the softest texture he'd ever felt. His smile faded as he allowed her hair to sift through his fingers.

Tomorrow. Tomorrow he'd get the rest of the truth from her. He'd find out how she fell from the embankment and ended up in the hospital. Until then, he'd stay well away from her before he did something they'd both regret.

Silently he crossed to the door.

"Gideon?"

Piper sat up and stared in confusion. Gideon stood in the doorway of the bedroom, his back to her. At the sound of her voice, he stiffened, his sudden tension communicated itself in the rigid set of his shoulders and the stiffness of his spine.

"Go back to sleep," he told her without turning around.

"What are you doing here?"

"Checking to make sure you're all right."

"I'm fine." But he wasn't. Something was very wrong. "What is it, Gideon? What's happened?"

Still he didn't face her. "Nothing you need to worry about. Go back to sleep," he repeated.

She drew her knees to her chest. "You can't fool me. I know you too well. Something's upset you. Is it your fight with Spencer?"

He turned then, the light stabbing across his profile for a brief moment. It betrayed the torment in his dark eyes and the grim set of his jaw. Furrows cut a path from the corners of his mouth to the harshly arched cheekbones. "Not the fight. It's the results of the fight."

"My arm?" she asked gently.

"You shouldn't have put yourself in the middle. I warned you about that."

"Yes, you did," she promptly agreed. "My mistake. You once said I had to be the only woman foolish enough to wade into a fistfight and risk my own well-being out of concern for the brawlers. I guess this proves it."

"Don't make light of it!"

Good heavens. He really was upset. "How am I supposed to react?" she asked reasonably. "How was I supposed to react when you and Spencer started fighting?"

"By staying out of it."

"Ah. But you don't understand."

He glared for an instant before releasing his breath

in a slow sigh. "Okay, Piper. I'll bite. What don't I understand?"

"I couldn't stay out of it. How could I? You're the two men I love most in all this world."

The words were stated with breathtaking candor and Gideon flinched as though he'd been struck. "You can't. Not any longer."

She simply laughed. "Of course I can."

"Spencer, sure. But not—" His throat moved convulsively and he shook his head.

"I fell in love with you when I was eight years old. It was when you promised to protect me, promised that no one would ever hurt me again. You gave me your word of honor, remember?"

"You're not eight anymore." His words grated. "And I broke my word long ago."

"Not deliberately. You protected me as long as you could. I didn't expect more than that."

He banged his fist against the doorjamb. "Dammit, Piper! Stop trying to make me into something I'm not. I don't know the man you keep describing, but it isn't me."

"I know who you are. It's you who's forgotten."

He swept that aside with a wave of his hand. "Fine," he said wearily. "Believe what you like, if it makes you feel better. All I ask is that you get out of my way. Spencer and I can take things from here."

"Not a chance. Neither of you are rational about this issue. I'm not going to let you take Spence down, any more than I'm going to let him harm you. There has to be an alternative and I intend to find it."

"Piper—"

"Next subject, Gideon."

He looked like he intended to say more, but then he

shrugged. "As long as you're awake, I need to ask you something."

Uh-oh. The glitter in his eyes warned that she wouldn't like this topic any better than the last. "Tonight? It can't wait until morning?"

"No, it can't wait. Not if I want to get any sleep."

It didn't take much guesswork to figure out what was troubling him. She gave in to the inevitable. "Okay. Ask your question."

"You said you fell off the ridge by the mill." He took a deep breath as though steeling himself for her response. "How?"

She gave him a final out. "You really don't want to know."

"It was my fault, wasn't it? I don't know how or why, but—" A muscle bunched in his jaw and she could see him struggle to push the question past clenched teeth. "But somehow I'm responsible, aren't I?"

"It was my fault."

"*How?*"

"I tried to stop the fight, same as tonight. Sound familiar?" Her mouth tilted into a wry smile. "I'm beginning to suspect this is an aspect of my personality that needs some work."

His brow creased and she could tell he was struggling to recall the details. Finally he shook his head. "No, you weren't anywhere near the fight at the mill."

"Not at first, because I couldn't get to you. There were too many people in the way and they wouldn't let me through. But then you broke through the circle, remember? Everyone scattered."

"How could I forget? That's when someone knocked me off my feet. I cracked two ribs."

"Oh, Gideon." She hadn't known that part. Unfortunately a lot of the specifics had escaped her notice. "How in the world did you manage to keep going?"

"I didn't have any choice." He shifted position and the light played across the drawn planes of his face, warning of emotions kept rigidly in check. "Tell me the rest, Piper. How did you get hurt?"

"When you stood up, I knew from your expression that either you or Spencer was going down and which-ever one of you it ended up being would get badly hurt." She lowered her voice. "You two were so close to the drop-off. I was terrified you might be killed."

"Finish it, Piper!"

The words came in a desperate rush. "I made a terrible mistake. I grabbed your arm. You didn't know it was me. I'm sure you thought I was the person who'd tripped you."

"I vaguely remember someone grabbing me right before I knocked Spencer out. I shook him—you—off."

"I lost my footing. That's when I fell."

CHAPTER EIGHT

GIDEON swore with such guttural fury that Piper flinched. Then he was across the room, sweeping her into his arms. "There were rocks down there. Sharp rocks."

She made an unsuccessful stab at humor. "So I discovered."

"I'm sorry. I'm so sorry."

"You didn't know it was me. And it was over a long time ago."

"How bad was it?"

Just thinking about those dark days caused helpless tears to threaten. She didn't dare let Gideon see them. She blinked hard, fighting to keep all hint of pain from her voice. "Don't think about it," she whispered. "I don't."

"How bad?"

She didn't know how to answer him, what words would reassure him when they hadn't succeeded in reassuring her. Silence seemed her only option. He must have read some of what she was feeling in her eyes. He eased her back against the pillows, gently subduing her instinctive attempt to escape. Slowly, with an implacable determination she didn't have a hope of fighting, he released the buttons of her nightshirt, one after another. She caught at his hands, trying to stop him, but he wouldn't be deterred. He was too strong, too purposeful. Sweeping the thin cotton from her shoulders, he examined her. She didn't attempt to hide herself from his gaze, but remained motionless, naked and exposed.

His breathing changed the instant he found what he sought, the give and take acquiring a harsh, shallow quality. Gideon cupped her shoulder, tracing the thin, silvery line that tattooed her in a sicklelike curve. "Did you break your arm?"

"My...my collarbone."

"Is there more?"

She clenched her teeth and waited. Tossing the shirt aside, he shifted their positions so they lay directly in the path of the light filtering in from the hallway. It gilded her in gold, pitiless in what it exposed. She stared at the ceiling, the tears she tried so hard to suppress sliding from the corners of her eyes and dampening the hair at her temples. The thundering of his heartbeat filled her ears, his raspy groan an expression of such agony she didn't think she could bear it. Then he touched her again, his fingertip finding the jagged scar at its starting point high on her hip. Without a word he followed it, inch by excruciating inch until he reached its ending point, low on her belly.

Her breath escaped in a shuddering gasp at the intimate touch. No one had seen that scar, other than her doctors. But Gideon was intent on exploring every bit of it. When she didn't think she could stand another second, he lowered his head. His hair brushed across her stomach, his breath gusting on her skin. And then his mouth closed over the scar. A quiver started deep inside, directly beneath his lips, spreading a warmth that had once been a vital part of her life.

"Gideon!" His name burst from her, a plea for something she didn't dare put into words.

"I did this to you."

"It was an accident."

"I put these marks on your body." He lifted his head and stared at her. If she could have looked away she would have. The frenzied bitterness in his eyes was beyond anything she'd ever seen before, his pain even greater than her own. "If I could transfer them to my own flesh, I would."

She believed him. "I know you'd never deliberately hurt me."

"Not then."

"And not now." The words came without doubt or hesitation.

He traced the scar a final time. "Right now hurting you is the furthest thing from my mind." Devastation scored his face. "I'm so sorry, pipsqueak."

Piper reacted instinctively. Closing her arms around him, she gathered him close, simply holding him. There weren't any words that would comfort him. At least none that had successfully comforted her. She'd dreaded this moment, when he'd find out how their worlds had been destroyed that day by the mill. It had been one of the reasons she'd stayed away from him for five lonely years. But no longer. He needed her every bit as much as she needed him. The time had come to heal old wounds.

"We all made mistakes, Gideon. But they're passed. What we have to decide is how we go on from here."

"Let me show you how...."

A fierce resolution settled into his expression and he communicated his intent slowly, without words. His mouth closed over hers with delicious insistence. The touch felt hesitant, almost experimental, yet filled with a tenderness she'd thought lost to him. A freshness invaded the kiss, a tentative sampling, as though he were tasting something untried and novel. She'd never experienced such an erotic sensation—a virginal newness combined with a sensual familiarity. It reminded her vividly of their first time together when forever had stretched before them in unlimited possibilities.

He must have thought the same. "Do you remember?" he whispered. "Do you remember the first night we made love?"

She hadn't forgotten a single moment. How could she? Her world had changed that night. He'd turned girlish fantasies into a reality she'd kept sheltered in her heart to this day. Whether he realized it or not they were forever joined, and part of her would remain in his possession until the end of their days. "You didn't want it to happen," she reminded.

"You were too young. I shouldn't have touched you." Then, as though in unconscious denial of his own words, his hands sought her softness and he filled his arms with her. "But once I did, I couldn't stop."

"I didn't want you to stop. I still don't."

He groaned. "Dammit, sweetheart. What the hell am I going to do about you?"

She lifted upward until her mouth hovered just shy of his ear and she whispered a suggestion that left him shuddering. "How about trying that?"

It took him a moment to shove free an answer. "It's a distinct possibility."

She traced the hard curves of his face. "We'll start again. Touch me the same way you kissed me. No past. No pain. No sorrow. Just a night that's new and fresh and untouched. Is that too much to ask?"

"You want an illusion?" His voice hardened. "You

prefer the fairy tale with all the pretense that goes
along with it?''

Yes! she almost said. But she realized it wasn't the
truth, could never be the truth. How could they appreciate the present without acknowledging all they'd
gone through to get there? The past had shaped who
and what they were, the good as well as the bad.

''I want whatever you have to give me,'' she told
him. ''As long as it's honest.''

''Fair enough. If it's honesty you want, it's honesty
you'll have. I'm not the person I was and I refuse to
pretend I am. But I'll give you what little is left of the
man you remember. And—'' He hesitated, his throat
moving convulsively. ''And I'll never lie to you.
You...you have my word of honor.''

''Oh, Gideon—''

He stared down at her, his gaze more determined
than she'd ever seen it. ''I haven't said those words
since the day the mill burned. But I'm saying them to
you, for what it's worth.''

She couldn't control the tears then. ''Not in all these
years? Not even once?''

He shook his head. ''There hasn't been any point.
I guess I figured you of all people deserve to hear them
one last time.''

''Not the last,'' she begged. ''Please don't say it's
the last time.''

His mouth twisted. ''Honor's not important to anyone but you, pipsqueak.''

''It is important!'' she instantly refuted his claim.
''To *you.* Haven't you figured that out, yet?''

''You asked for honesty and I'm giving it to you.''
He thumbed the tears from her temples with a gentle-

ness he'd have undoubtedly denied. "Sure you don't want the illusion?"

Her lips formed a stubborn line. "We've never pretended with each other and I don't intend to start now." She traced the breadth of his shoulders, reacquainting herself with each familiar ridge and hollow. "Now are you going to take me up on my suggestion, or aren't you?"

She'd provoked an instantaneous reaction. He strained backward, the hallway light cutting a path across features taut with desire. Color rode high on the ridges of his cheekbones and his eyes blazed with a ferocious night-dark glitter. He left the bed and stripped away his clothing with an economy of movement. And then he rejoined her, his hunger impacting like a physical force.

She welcomed him with open arms. It had been so long. Too long. Despite the fact that she'd dated in the past several years, the desire she'd experienced on those occasions had stolen through her veins in bland, distant waves. The temptation to take the moment further had been easy to resist. What she felt now had little to do with such mild, sedate emotions. And the temptation to take the moment as far as possible proved overpowering.

Want stormed through her, ripping her universe into incoherent bits. Only Gideon remained within the center of the chaos, anchoring her in the moment. Once the raging had subsided, they'd talk and she'd tell him the rest. All of it, regardless of what happened as a result. But tonight was for them, the closing of a volume from the past and—she hoped—the start of a new one leading toward the future.

Her fingers dipped into his hair and she tugged him

down to meet her. His mouth was firm and sure, parting to welcome her home. With a soft moan of pleasure, she claimed him as her own. She bit at his lower lip, then soothed it with the tip of her tongue. He reacted to the silent duel with exquisite aggression, initiating a thrust and parry that stoked a white-hot fire, the blaze igniting in the pit of her belly and spreading relentlessly outward.

"Don't stop, Gideon." Stirring beneath him, she fitted herself to him with an instinct undimmed by the years. "Don't ever stop again."

He took her mouth over and over, his kiss becoming one of desperation. "I didn't know," he muttered. "I swear to you, I didn't know it would be the last time."

He sounded so troubled that she hastened to soothe him with an easy smile, a smile that became part of their kiss. "That what would be the last time?"

To her concern, he didn't respond to her reassurance. A darkness settled over him, one she'd have done anything to erase. "The night before the fight, when we made love by the mill. I didn't know it would be the last time we'd be together, the last time I kissed you. I didn't know we wouldn't have a tomorrow. That when I touched you, when I held you, when I heard you whisper my name, when I felt you climax in my arms, that those would be my final moments with you. I didn't know I wouldn't have you close again for five years, or I'd have stamped every second of that night in my memory."

"Oh, Gideon," she murmured, clutching him tighter. "Don't you know I felt the same way?"

He lowered his head, as though bowed beneath an impossible burden. "Afterward... Afterward I tried to remember. I tried to hold on to every moment I could. But it slipped away, faded into echoes.''

"It happens, Gideon. Memories do fade.'' She captured his face once again, forcing him to look at her. "Make love to me and we'll create new ones, ones we'll never forget.''

Her gaze never left his as she slid her hands downward, following the contours of his chest. Tracing the muscular ripples to the flatness of his belly, she reached the source of his desire. He surged against her hand, groaning an encouragement that escaped as half plea and half demand. She didn't need further prompting. She cupped him, stroked his length with slow, indulgent sweeps, reacquainting herself with every scorching inch. He felt incredible, far better than five-year-old memories.

"You're killing me.'' His words escaped through gritted teeth.

She laughed softly. "I'm doing my best. Are you enjoying it?''

"More than you can imagine.'' He pressed her into the pillows, settling into the warm delta between her legs. "Allow me to return the favor.''

He forked his widespread fingers through the tight curls between her thighs until he reached the tip of her scar. Then he backtracked, dipping into her moist heat. Swirling. Stoking. Plying the silken folds until she trembled beneath his hand.

"No more,'' she begged. "I can't bear any more.''

"Sure you can.''

And he proved it by catching the peak of one breast between his teeth, tugging with delicious insistence. At the same time he buried a finger into the very core of her. Every muscle in her body arched in response and a cry caught in her throat. A fluttering began, deep within, and she closed tight around the sweet invasion. She gazed helplessly up at him, silently pleading for the completion that hovered so close. To her profound relief, he didn't hesitate.

"You're mine," he stated, positioning himself between her thighs. "You always have been and you always will be."

"Gideon."

His name finally escaped, the single word an expression of both confirmation and unwavering commitment. He pressed inward, joining them with gratifying speed. She could sense the urgency gathering in him, the overpowering drive to take her, while a conflicting directive forced him to go slow and savor each and every second.

His control was phenomenal. He sheathed himself in her warmth, driving home in a single, powerful stroke. She lifted to meet him, matching the silent cadence with a primal rhythm that sang from the depths of her soul. It must have sung within his, as well, for each of his thrusts matched every one of her parries. They came together again and again, their joining more than a mere mating. Each touch formed a bond, each murmured word a promise, each look a pledge.

Piper clung to him, wishing the moment could last forever. But it slipped away far too soon, the song completed before it had barely begun. Contractions rippled, fisting around him. With a roar, he buried himself to the hilt, spending himself within her. It was all she needed to send her over the edge. Her climax hit hard, the release a painful rapture.

"What have you done to me?" The question burst from her.

He collapsed into her embrace. "I've given you what we've both been after from the moment you came storming back into my life. Whatever you do, don't tell me it was a mistake."

She closed her eyes, unable to move or think, let alone regret. "It wasn't a mistake, I promise. In fact, I'm wondering why we waited this long...and when we can try again."

A noncommittal noise rumbled deep in his chest. "We'll see if you're still feeling so charitable toward tonight's events come morning. I've found the cold light of day often brings a change of heart once the head takes over."

Why would she have a change of heart tomorrow when she hadn't changed it in five impossibly long years? Exhaustion closed around her and she resisted long enough to reassure him. "Come morning my head will be every bit as happy as the rest of me." She even managed a teasing glance. "You have my word of honor."

He cradled her close, snagging the covers and pulling them around her. For a long time he simply watched her. She curled into him, a smile of intense satisfaction curving her mouth. He smoothed her hair away from her face, knowing the time had come for more honesty. He closed his eyes, wishing he'd had the nerve to tell her sooner. "Sweetheart?"

No answer.

"Pipsqueak?"

Her breath came in a soft sigh that spoke of deep sleep and sweet dreams. It didn't matter. Saying it while she slept wouldn't alter the truth any. And hadn't he just promised to always be honest with her? He leaned into her, imprinting the feel of her on his flesh, drinking in the scent of her until he was dizzy with it, tasting the potent nectar of her essence. He branded her in his heart and mind until it burned straight down to his very soul. Something shifted inside of him, offering up a lightness and easing he didn't deserve, but welcomed nonetheless. After being sentenced to what felt like an eternity in pitch darkness, he stepped into reaffirming sunshine.

"I don't know why you still care," he whispered. "I don't know what I've done to deserve such loyalty, considering I'll never be the sort of man you deserve. But I love you, Piper. I always have. And I always will."

A bewildering sense of wrongness woke Gideon. To his amazement, morning had arrived hours earlier. He couldn't remember the last time he'd slept so late. He glanced at Piper, tucked snug within his arms. She hadn't stirred the entire night. It was as though she'd come home and had no intention of moving ever again. He'd had time to sleep on what she'd told him about the fight, and he'd gradually become aware of an elusive "something" that he'd missed during their discussion, a strange insistence growing inside that urged an immediate response.

Gently he eased Piper from his shoulder and onto the pillow. Her breath escaped in a contented murmur and he swept his thumb over the flushed curve of her cheek. Now that he had her back in his life, he'd make certain she stayed there. Once she understood that he wasn't a project requiring a serious overhaul, everything would work out.

Escaping the bed, Gideon padded silently to his study and flipped on the light. His restlessness increased, along with an awareness that he was missing something important. She'd explained about her fall, but a nagging sensation continued to trouble him, a gut instinct he'd learned to trust through painful experience. There was some key bit of information she'd told him on another occasion that held a vital significance—a puzzle piece he needed in order to complete the picture. But he was damned if he could figure out that one final detail.

Piper's boxes were stacked neatly on the floor by his desk and he picked up the first one, opening it. A certainty solidified inside him. Somehow he knew he'd find what he was looking for here, hidden within her photographs.

An hour later, he'd finished sorting through the majority of them. They were all stunning, every last one, revealing an intimate connection with the subjects. He'd long considered it a hallmark of her personal style. But he still hadn't pinpointed what was missing, and it was driving him crazy.

Once again, he scanned the prints he'd spread across his credenza, the ones from her early days. They expressed a raw talent under development and consisted of hundreds of photos of Old Mill Run. Not a single resident had escaped Piper's attention. There were dozens of her family. There were also a handful of the town council. They were all hanging around their favorite gathering spot, the bait and tackle shop, indulging in their favorite activity—a heated discussion over the merits of fishing lures versus live bait. Another showed Mrs. Watz standing in front of her chalkboard expounding on the intricacies of geometric theory and he smiled, remembering how much he'd hated her class—and how much he'd learned from the old bat.

And finally there was his mother, tired and drawn, hanging up the laundry while his youngest sister played in a wicker basket at her feet.

What he wanted wasn't there and he scowled. Dammit all! Come hell or high water, he'd get to the bottom of this. She'd told him something significant and he was positive it related to her photographs. Crossing to the coffee table by the couch, he sorted through the pile of her most recent shots. He stirred in discomfort as he studied them. She'd snapped off an entire roll that first day when she'd interrupted his board meeting.

"The not-so-happy people of Happy," he murmured.

There was so much emotion. Anger. Fear. Sorrow. Emotions he'd caused. And then there were the shots taken after Piper had announced that he'd had a change of heart. Joy. Relief. Excitement. Next, he flipped through pictures Piper had taken of his office, and of their contentious drive to Happy when he'd tried to justify buying the Tylers's resort. Last of all, he came across the one of himself stretched out on the couch, the one that showed him at his most vulnerable. Still, he didn't see anything to explain his disquiet.

Returning to his desk, Gideon examined the photos from the years he and Piper had been apart. Most were professional portraits of brides and grooms. To his surprise, there weren't many personal pictures, far fewer than she'd taken during her early years. He paused to peer closely at a couple of photos from right before the fight had broken out, as well as several stark shots of the gutted flour mill. There were also a handful that must have been taken in the months afterward.

Several showed Spencer exhausted and aged beyond

his years. And there was even one of Piper. Gideon's brows drew together as he studied it. She sat curled in a protective ball, her face half turned away from the camera, her hair hanging in limp disorder. Had Spencer taken the photo? If so, why? It wasn't a flattering shot. In fact, she looked downright ill.

The phone burred softly beside him and he rested his hip on the edge of the desk. Still staring down at the photo of Piper, he snagged the receiver. "Hart."

"Gideon, thank goodness. Tyler here. I hope I haven't caught you at an inconvenient time?"

"Not at all." His frown deepened as he studied the photograph. "What can I do for you, Bill?"

"Bad news, I'm afraid. The bank's decided to foreclose on our resort. We were given the news first thing this morning."

That captured Gideon's attention. "I'm sorry. I know you were hoping they'd hold off a little longer."

"I…I wondered if you were still interested in doing business."

"I'm still interested in buying you out, yes."

There was a long silence and then Bill spoke again, his voice gruffer than before. "That's all you're prepared to offer?"

Quick and brutal, that had always been Gideon's style. But for some reason he found it more difficult this time around. "I'm afraid so. I don't see any other option."

"All right, fine. I assume you're still willing to pay a fair price?"

"Yes."

"Okay, we accept your offer. And…and thanks."

For some reason, Gideon felt strangely guilty. It didn't make a bit of sense. What the hell did he have to feel guilty about? The man needed help and he was getting it. It might not be in the form Tyler preferred, but that was business, plain and simple. Just like life, it could be harsh and cold and not always pleasant.

"Give me a couple hours to make arrangements at this end and then I'll be in touch," Gideon said.

The minute the conversation ended, Piper opened the door to the study. Coming up behind, she wrapped her arms around his waist and released her breath in a slow, gusty sigh. "Mmm. You feel good."

He turned and folded himself around her, greeting her with a lingering kiss. "Good morning to you, too." Realizing she was dressed, he lifted an eyebrow. "Going somewhere?"

"I'm late enough for work. I'd rather not be any later by lazing in bed the rest of the morning." She smiled at him, her eyes an incandescent blue and filled with the sort of loving expression that eased deep into his soul. "What are you doing?"

Gideon held up the photograph so she could see for herself. "Looking at a picture of you."

He felt her sudden tension. Tiny lines edged her mouth and a bleakness dimmed her gaze. "I didn't realize I'd kept that one."

Interesting. "It's not very good. Who took it? Spence?"

"Yes. About six months after you left town."

She'd confirmed his guess. But what he'd really like to know was... "Why did he take it?"

"As a wake-up call." She shrugged, the irritable movement of her shoulders lacking her usual grace. "He wanted me to see what I'd become."

"Which was?"

"Withdrawn. Emotionally disengaged." She gestured impatiently. "It's all there in the picture."

"Photos don't lie," he repeated.

"As much as I tried to deny it at the time, no. They don't." She stepped farther into the room and glanced around in surprise. "You have my pictures out. Why?"

"I'm looking for something."

She shot him a swift, disconcerted glance, one almost of panic. "In my photos?"

Every internal alarm he possessed went off and his sense of wrongness intensified. "Yes," he confirmed slowly. "I can't get over the feeling that there's something missing. I don't suppose you know what that might be?"

"Not a clue." She plucked the photo from between his fingers and tossed it aside. "Who was on the phone when I first walked in?"

Hell. When she turned the tables, she did it with a vengeance. This was *not* how he'd planned to start his day with her. "Bill Tyler."

She looked up eagerly. "And?"

"And he wanted to let me know that the bank has given him official notice. They plan to start immediate foreclosure proceedings."

Her excitement switched to distress. "Oh, no. Gideon, this is terrible. What are you going to do?"

Quick and brutal, he reminded himself. "Buy his resort." With luck he didn't sound too defensive, though poking out his jaw at a belligerent angle may not have helped his case any.

"Buy the note from the bank, you mean." The optimism in her eyes cut to the bone. "Give him time to turn things around, right?"

Gideon didn't bother to pull his punches. "No."

He'd never realized how painful it would be to witness the death of hope, especially in the gaze of someone he loved more than life itself. She laced her fingers together in a white-knuckle grip. "Gideon, please."

"You're putting yourself in the middle again, Piper," he warned. "It isn't a place you belong."

"Someone has to be there."

"Not you." He picked up the photo she'd discarded, determination taking hold. "If you want to lend me a hand finding what I'm searching for, I'd appreciate the help. But I'm not going to discuss Tyler with you."

She hesitated and he could see how desperately she'd have liked to argue. She must have read his resolve for her expression changed, mirroring the one in the photograph. To his concern an unsettling combination of despair and defeat settled over her. "Are you sure you wouldn't rather let that subject drop, too? Are you positive you want to pursue it?"

"I'm not sure of anything. But gut instinct tells me I'd better figure it out."

"And you always listen to your instinct."

It wasn't a question. "Even when the results might be unpleasant," he confirmed. Her mouth quivered ever so slightly and the truth struck him. How could he have been so blind? She knew. Whatever it was, she knew what he was looking for. He snagged her chin with his index finger and gently tipped her face up to his. "What am I missing, pipsqueak? What's not here?"

He didn't think she'd answer. Then she stepped free of his touch and wrapped her arms around her waist, her breath coming in a long, shuddering sigh. "You were close, Gideon. You followed the progression of the photos. But you've forgotten something. Something from the early days."

"What?"

She gestured toward the corner of the room. "You're missing some pictures. They're in that box on the floor."

He glanced at it. It was a small, dusty carton set apart from the others and carefully sealed shut with endless yards of packing tape. He hadn't even realized it held any photographs. It had the look of something that had been closed up tight and shoved into the far corner of a closet where it could remain forgotten. "I thought I had them all. These are the ones I'm missing, aren't they?"

"Let it go, Gideon," she whispered.

"What's in the box?"

"You don't want to go there."

Without a word, he carried it to the desk and sliced it open with a pair of scissors. Slowly he drew out a handful of stills. "Your baby photos," he murmured. The missing piece locked into place. "How could I have forgotten them?"

Piper didn't say a word.

"I remember you saying you didn't take baby pictures anymore. For some reason that comment stayed with me. But why are they boxed up like this? It's almost like you're hiding them." He frowned, perplexed. "*Why?* Why hide baby—"

She simply stared at him.

It hit him then. He looked at the pictures again and shook his head. If he'd been a praying sort of man, he'd have been down on his knees. "No." His voice broke on the word, the sound eerily similar to the cry of a wounded animal. "Please, no."

CHAPTER NINE

THE photographs tumbled unnoticed from Gideon's hands and he braced himself against his desk, locking his knees in place to keep them from buckling. "You were pregnant when you fell?" He fought for breath, fought to push out words that never should have been uttered—wouldn't have been uttered, if not for him. "You lost the baby? Our baby?"

Tears flooded Piper's eyes, her distress every bit as great as his own. "I'm sorry. I'm so sorry."

His jaw worked for a moment. It took three tries to get the statement out. "I killed our child."

"No!" She was in his arms in an instant, wrapping him up in the sort of loving embrace he didn't deserve. "Spence said the same thing, blamed himself, too. But it was an accident. The mill shouldn't have burned. My brother shouldn't have blamed you. You and he shouldn't have fought. And I shouldn't have interfered. Don't you get it? None of it should have occurred."

He could hear his voice come from far away. "But it did."

"Yes, it did. And no matter how badly we try to change the past, we can't."

"What happened? Just tell me that much."

She opened her mouth, then closed it again. He could feel her start to tremble and he bowed his head until his jaw nestled into the softness of her hair. He wanted to sink into her, lose himself in her. That's all he'd ever wanted. Instead he'd hurt her. The knowledge struck with brutal force. *He'd hurt her.* The one person he'd have protected with his life, he'd left broken on the rocks, their child never to draw breath. And it was all his fault. He shuddered, unable to escape the horrific image.

"Please, Piper. I need to know."

Her arms tightened around his waist and she burrowed into his arms. "After I fell, they took me to the hospital. But all I could think about after the accident was getting to you," she whispered. "No one would tell me where you were or how you were. I should have insisted. I realize that now."

"And I should have found you, regardless of the consequences." A sudden thought occurred to him. "Jasmine swears she gave my note to you. If you were in the hospital—"

"I wasn't. Not the entire time. After they immobilized my shoulder and sewed the cut on my abdomen, I left the hospital against orders." She rested her head on his shoulder, a single tear splashing onto his chest. "Oh, Gideon. It was such a foolish thing to do. I went home to change before tracking you down. That must have been when Jasmine found me. I don't remember getting the note. Or what it said. I must have blacked out right after she left."

Gideon's fingers tangled in her hair and he massaged her nape, absorbing every bit of her pain that he could. "And then?"

"Spencer found me shortly afterward. When I woke up, I was back in the hospital and the baby—" Her breath hitched and it took her a minute to continue. "The baby was gone. I didn't even realize I was pregnant. Apparently there was a delay with the lab results or they'd have known sooner about my condition. If I'd stayed at the hospital, maybe they could have prevented what happened. Maybe our baby wouldn't have—"

She broke down completely, crying in heartrending silence, as though the pain came from someplace so deep even sound couldn't escape. Tears burned his own eyes and his chest grew tight and full. More than anything he wanted to howl in torment, to give voice to all that Piper had locked away inside. He shook with the need to make it better, to ease both their agony. But there were no words. Even simple speech was beyond him. He didn't say anything for a long time, but simply held her close, trying to give her what strength he had left.

When he felt capable of speaking again, he asked, "You blamed yourself, didn't you? That's why Spence took the picture?"

She fumbled in her pocket for a tissue and swiped at her wet cheeks. "You have no idea how many times I've gone over the 'if onlys.' All it does is drive you insane. It happened. There's nothing that can be done. It took me six months to figure out that simple fact. And even then, Spence had to force the issue."

No wonder he'd been so protective of his sister. And so angry at the man responsible for her anguish. "If I'd known you'd been injured, I'd never have left you, despite the shotgun and no matter what the sheriff threatened."

She looked at him, startled. "You forgot to mention the part about the sheriff. What did he threaten?"

Gideon shrugged. "He gave me an alternative. I could face charges of arson, attempted murder, resisting arrest and anything else they could think of to throw at me. Or I could leave town.''

"So you left."

He shook his head. "Don't you believe it. They gave me an hour to pack my stuff and go. Instead I hid out in the woods for two days waiting to hear from you. I didn't give up until Murphy tracked me down and forced the issue.''

"If it makes you feel any better, he's gone now." She stroked the bunched muscles of his arm, her touch one of solace. He wanted to protest, explain that he should be comforting her. But somehow he couldn't summon the words. "Not long after the fire, Murphy sold out and left town with his son and daughter.''

"Forget Murphy. Mill Run is better off without his kind." He tipped her face up to his. Even such an innocuous caress gave him intense pleasure. "Now I have a question for you.''

"Anything."

"What would you have done if you hadn't been injured? If you'd gotten my note?''

She didn't hesitate. "I would have asked you to stay and fight. Mill Run was dying. It still is. It needs someone with your drive and determination—the same sort of drive and determination that Spence has—to help fix that. And you needed the family and community that you couldn't find at home. So do your mother and sisters. That hasn't changed, either.''

"You're wrong. I don't need anything or anyone." *Except for Piper.* That small truth had become inescapable and he didn't back away from it as he would have days ago. He released his breath in a long sigh. "That's bull, pipsqueak. I need you. I always have and I'm willing to bet I always will.''

The pain eased from her face and she offered up a smile that reminded him of the first hint of dawn breaking through an endless night. Or was it five years of endless nights? ''We've always felt the same way, haven't we?''

''About most things.'' He hesitated, facing facts she still wasn't willing to. ''But not about everything.''

She made a face. ''I know. It would have been difficult to change popular opinion, mainly because Spence was so certain you'd destroyed the mill.'' An urgency threaded her words. ''But we could have done it, given time. You still could, Gideon. Together, we can make a difference. Not just in Mill Run. We can help people like Bill Tyler and the jewelers, too.''

He closed his eyes, hating what he was about to do, but knowing that if there were any chance for them, he didn't have any choice. Piper would continue to interfere until he physically moved her out of harm's way. ''That's not going to happen.''

''Please, Gideon—''

''It's not going to happen because I'm letting you go.''

Every scrap of color drained from her face. ''What are you saying?''

''I know you want to help Tyler. And the jewelry companies. And your brother. But you can't.''

''*You* can,'' she argued.

He shook his head. ''I'm going to tear up your brother's note. As of this minute, he doesn't owe me a dime. You don't have any reason to continue staying here. I'll see to it that personnel cuts you a generous check for your services to date.''

''No!'' Her grip tightened around him. ''Don't do this, Gideon.''

"Tomorrow I'll have your things delivered to whatever address you request."

"Did last night mean nothing to you?"

His control almost broke. "It meant the world to me," he rasped. "I love you, Piper. I flat-out adore you. And I want you in my life."

"But?"

"I can't be the person you want."

"You're already the person I want. You're not hard or cruel," she insisted urgently. "I know you're not."

"I am when it comes to business."

"You can't be or you wouldn't forgive Spencer's note."

She was grasping at straws and they both knew it. "I'm doing this for you," he said. "I'm doing it so we have a chance."

"But you won't help the Tylers or any of the others?"

He shook his head. "Which means you need to think long and hard about the future. You have to accept me as I am, flaws and all. You can't put yourself in the middle every time you disagree with one of my decisions."

She smiled sadly. "Don't you get it? That's who I am." Her smile wobbled. "The girl in the middle."

"And I can't let that continue. I can't have you throwing yourself in the tracks of every oncoming train you see. One of them is bound to run you down. After what you told me about the baby—" His jaw worked. "I can't have you hurt again. I want to marry you. I want to rebuild a life together. Have…have children that can know our love instead of being destroyed because of it."

Her arms fell to her sides. "In that case, I think we both need to think long and hard about the future."

"You don't want marriage?"

She shook her head. "It's not that. *You* may not want to marry *me*." She stepped free of his hold and backed away. "The baby photos, remember?"

He glanced toward the box, his brow creasing in confusion. "What about them?"

"I didn't stop taking pictures because I lost your baby." She paused by the door. "I stopped because I can't have any more children."

"What the hell are you doing, Hart?"

Gideon swiveled to glare at Spencer, his breath coming in exhausted gasps. "I might ask you the same question, considering this is my office and you're here without an invitation."

"Blame your secretary. She phoned Piper. I intercepted the call and came instead." Spence took in the condition of the office with a lifted eyebrow. "You've been busy. Redecorating, are you?"

"That's none of your damn business," Gideon bit out, his tone just shy of a snarl. "Now that you're here, you can turn around and get the hell out."

"Sorry. Can't do that. Maybe if you hadn't torn up the note, I'd be willing to go. Or if you hadn't turned Piper into a weepy mess again."

"Piper?" That snagged his full attention. "I've been trying to find her all day. Where is she?"

To his silent fury, Spencer ignored the question. He turned in a full circle, clicking his tongue in admonition. "You really are in bad shape. This place is a disaster." Strolling farther into the room, he halted by a pile of kindling that decorated the middle of the carpet. "I assume that's your desk. Or what's left of it. I also assume this is why Lindsey called in such a panic."

"My furniture. My ax." Gideon hefted the tool in question, his muscles screaming in protest at the prolonged abuse they'd suffered. He gritted his teeth against the pain and managed to push out a final sentence. "And my choice to use one on the other."

"Can't argue with that logic. Just out of curiosity... What did it do to you? Refuse to deconstruct on demand?"

"Deconstruct?" Gideon's breath escaped in a rush that was part groan and part rough laugh. "You've been talking to Piper."

"She's my sister. Of course I talk to her."

Gideon tossed the ax into the middle of the rubble. It clattered discordantly, gleaming dully amid the ebony remnants. "What are you doing here?" he asked tiredly, massaging his chopping arm.

"Thought I'd have another go at you now that Piper's not around." He stooped beside the remains of the desk. "You really need to do something about your temper, Hart. Why would you want to destroy something this nice?"

"It injured your sister."

Spencer lifted an eyebrow. "Come again?"

"During our...discussion last night," he muttered. "She fell against it and cut herself."

"And because of that you chopped up your desk? A rather drastic response, don't you think?"

Gideon's jaw inched out. "No."

"What about this other stuff?" Spencer gestured toward the rest of the demolished furnishings. "Did all these other pieces attack her? Or was destroying them a preemptive strike in case they went after her, too?''

''Indirectly, yes.'' Once he'd laid waste to his desk, it had seemed a natural progression to go after the remaining items. Now he wasn't so certain. ''At the risk of sounding repetitive, what are you doing here, Montgomery?''

Spencer slowly stood. ''I thought we could talk. I mean really talk. Without Piper in the middle.''

''Good idea.'' Gideon inclined his head toward the steps that led to his apartment. ''Come on upstairs. As long as you're here, there's something you should see.''

Spencer followed him to the study. ''First let me say that I appreciate your forgiving the note. I realize it's to move Piper out of harm's way and not because you were overcome by an uncontrollable urge to help me. Even so, I intend to pay back every dime.''

''I don't give a damn about the money,'' Gideon retorted.

''*I* do. If I mention it's a point of honor, maybe you'll understand.''

Gideon paused at the door to the study. ''Be smart for once in your life, Montgomery. Don't go there.''

''Touchy about that issue, are we?''

''You might say that.'' He crossed to his desk and sifted through Piper's photos. Uncovering the ones he wanted, he tossed them in Spencer's direction. They were a series of shots she'd taken right before the fight had broken out. ''I know you don't believe me, so I won't waste my breath repeating this more than once. I didn't burn down your mill.''

''So you've said,'' Spencer replied in an expressionless voice.

Gideon fixed him with an unwavering stare. "I've said it because it's true."

After a long moment, Spencer inclined his head. "Okay. If you didn't do it, then who?"

It was time to put all his cards on the table. Either Spencer believed him or he didn't. At least by presenting his case, he'd have given it his best shot. He couldn't even say why it was so important to convince Piper's brother of his innocence. It simply was. "I have an idea who might have started the fire. But to be honest, we'll probably never know. Not for certain. I wish life were tidy enough to wrap up in a neat little package. But it isn't. It's messy and confusing and full of loose threads."

"You're saying this will always be a loose thread?" Cynicism colored Spencer's tones. "I should simply take your word about the fire, is that it?"

"Personally I don't give a damn whether or not you take my word," Gideon shot back. He gestured toward the photos. "But you might want to look at these. Maybe you'll have the same reaction to them I did."

Spencer joined him by the desk and studied the pictures. Residents from Old Mill Run had crowded close to the burning mill, staring at the leaping flames in shock and panic. "These are Piper's," he murmured. "You can't miss her style. I'm not sure she ever showed them to me before."

"They're…unnerving. She might not have wanted to upset you."

"No doubt." Spencer frowned. "Okay, I give. What am I supposed to see?"

"At the start of the fight you claimed someone had witnessed me setting the fire. I thought you were deliberately lying because no one *could* have. Now I'm curious. Who told you it was me?''

''Trish.''

''Trish Murphy. Your girlfriend.'' Gideon tapped a corner of one of the photos. ''She's here.''

''Of course she's there,'' Spencer replied impatiently. ''She was a witness.''

''Look who's standing behind her.''

''Her father. Old man Murphy. So?''

''Check out his expression.''

Spencer peered closer and swore softly. ''I don't believe it!''

''You see it, too, don't you?''

''He's the only one who doesn't seem horrified.''

''Horrified? Hell, Spence, he seems damned pleased with himself. I can't help wondering why.''

''I can't say for sure. I know he didn't like the Montgomerys any more than he liked your family. You were trash and we were too uppity for our own good. I assumed that changed when I started dating Trish. He didn't seem to mind the idea of his daughter benefiting from a possible marriage.'' Spencer shook his head. ''Who knows why he's looking so pleased. Maybe he enjoyed seeing me taken down a peg or two.''

''Especially if I was taken down along with you.'' He gave Spencer a few more minutes to examine the picture before asking his next question. ''Is there any reason you can think of why he'd try to drive a wedge between us?''

''More of a wedge, you mean?'' Spencer picked up another photograph. ''I see where you're going with this and it doesn't make sense. Do you really think he was twisted enough to burn down my mill to cause trouble between us? Sorry, I can't buy that.''

Gideon shrugged. "I wouldn't put anything past the man, not considering how much he hated me and my family. But I have to admit, I can't figure what his motivation would be, either. I was hoping you might have some idea. Is there anything? Anything at all?"

Spencer started to reply, then hesitated. "Trish was always trying to convince me to sell out and leave Mill Run," he admitted slowly. "Her father even took a stab at changing my mind. Said we could pool our money and start over somewhere else. I flat-out refused. My father had been committed to rebuilding Old Mill Run into a booming tourist town and I wanted to ensure his dream became a reality. Not long after I told her there wouldn't be any insurance money, she broke off the relationship. The three of them packed up and left town within the week."

"Is it possible they thought the mill was insured? Could they have burned it in the hope of forcing your hand? Burn the mill and maybe they'd have a better shot at convincing you to leave Mill Run, money in hand. After all, what would be left to rebuild if the key tourist draw no longer existed?"

"This is what you meant about our never knowing for sure, isn't it?"

"I have to admit, it's sheer supposition on my part and I could be totally off the mark. But the minute I saw these pictures..." Gideon's laugh had a bite to it. "What does Piper always say?"

"Photos don't lie."

Gideon nodded grimly. "My gut says that what we're seeing here isn't a lie."

"So's mine." Spencer swallowed. "All this time I thought— I was so certain that you were the one."

"Why? What the hell did I ever do to you?"

"It wasn't what you did."

"It was who I was."

Spencer looked him square in the eye. "I'm not talking about your father or how you grew up. I'm talking about your nature. Piper never saw you the way everyone else did. She only saw the good."

"And you?"

"I saw a dismantler of worlds, never a builder of them. That hasn't changed. At least, not that I can tell." He edged a hip onto the desk. "Piper's told you everything, hasn't she? About the fall and the baby?"

It took Gideon a minute to reply with anything approaching equanimity. "Along with the fact that she can't have any more children. Yes, she's told me."

"And what was your response?" Spencer didn't wait for Gideon to answer. "You took an ax and chopped your desk into kindling."

Gideon's mouth tightened. "Your point?"

"You haven't changed, Hart. And that's a shame. Instead of finding a constructive way of dealing with your pain, you chose the most destructive route available." Straightening, Spencer tossed the photographs onto the desk. "That's why I've worked so hard to keep you two apart. I don't want my sister deconstructed by you. The last time nearly killed her. I won't risk that ever happening again."

Hours later, Gideon returned downstairs and grimly surveyed the ruins of his office. What had Spencer said? That it was in Gideon's nature to dismantle the world around him? Looking at what he'd done to the furnishings, he was forced to admit the truth. It came easily to him. Instinctively. But Spencer had been wrong about one vital fact. Piper hadn't seen only the good in him. She'd seen all of him, the flaws as well as the potential. And still she'd loved him, believed in him.

He realized something else. When she'd put him on that white horse and garbed him in knight's armor, she'd been silently telling him that he could choose to be the hero instead of the villain. It boiled down to choices. He could continue to take, to build an empire on the ruins of the companies he'd dismantled. To deconstruct. Or he could build a future with Piper.

Slowly he stooped beside the remains of the Chippendale cabinet and picked up the stirrup vessel. Miraculously it had escaped damage. Choices, he reminded himself. Was this what he wanted from life? He glanced out the windows and toward the stalwart mountains in the distance.

Or did his future lie along a different path?

He found her by the stream that ran alongside a newly renovated flour mill.

Piper lay in the grass near the water, sound asleep, and Gideon stooped beside her, frowning in concern. Lilac semicircles shadowed her eyes and a tension gripped her, one clearly not eased by whatever dreams she was experiencing. Tenderly he swept a lock of pale hair from her brow, his knuckles brushing the delicate hollow at her temple. She appeared exhausted. Another sin to lay at his feet.

"Pipsqueak?" he murmured. "Wake up, sweetheart."

Her lashes quivered. Stretching, she looked around, blinking in surprise. "Gideon?" Awareness struck and a dozen different emotions darkened her face. None of them were ones he wanted to see. "What are you doing here?"

"I've come for you, of course." He settled at her side, depositing the present he'd brought in the grass between them. "Did you think you'd escape me this easily?"

She stirred in protest. "I wasn't running away."

"Weren't you?"

"Well, maybe I was. But all things considered, I think it can be excused this once." She pushed herself upright, facing him with typical directness. "If this is about what I told you—"

"That's part of it."

"You're not responsible, okay? It's not your fault. I don't expect anything from you. You can go your way and I'll go mine. Are we clear?"

Ever so gently, he threaded his fingers through her hair. She felt so good. So right. He'd loved her first as a boy, then as a teenager, and finally as a man. But somehow he found himself falling for her all over again. Did she have any idea? If not, he'd make sure he explained it in no uncertain terms. "Oh, we're absolutely clear."

At his touch, she released her breath in a long sigh and leaned into him. He accepted her weight with a small smile, reveling in the feel of her. "Why are you here?" she demanded into his shirtfront. "What's left to be said?"

"There's a lot left to be said. But first I have something to give you." He deposited the gift he'd brought in her lap. "Did I mention? It's a wedding present."

She didn't make a move to touch it. "Funny. I don't recall your asking me to marry you."

He winced. "I'm asking, pipsqueak. Hell, I'm begging." He nudged the box. "Open it. Please."

Reluctantly she picked it up. With slow deliberation, she removed the ribbon, followed by the wrapping paper. After what seemed like an eternity, she opened the flaps and pushed aside the protective packing. "The stirrup vessel?" She appeared less than ecstatic. "Most men go for something more traditional. Like an engagement ring."

"Most men aren't marrying you."

Her jaw tightened. "Let me get this straight. You're giving this to me? You're giving me one of your trophies as a present? And I'm supposed to be pleased? Happy? Or were you hoping to impress me?"

"No. We'll be returning that particular trophy to Archibald Fenzer on our wedding day. Then you're supposed to be pleased, happy—and not to mention—impressed as hell."

She stared at him, stunned. Clearly she hadn't seen that one coming. "Why?" she demanded unevenly. "Why would you do that?"

"Because it's my promise to you," he stated. "A promise that goes even deeper than the promise of an engagement ring."

She stared at him searchingly. For the first time, a spark of hope gleamed in her eyes. "What sort of promise?"

"A promise that I've finally figured out how to climb back on that white horse again. A promise that together we can build a future instead of deconstructing one. A promise that I'll love you to the end of my days." He slipped his other hand into her hair, cupping her head. "We lost our future the day the mill burned. I don't want to lose you, too."

"No, Gideon. We lost one potential future." She lifted her face to his, her breath warm and sweet against his skin. "You'll see. We'll build a new one."

"You can count on it." He couldn't resist any longer. He took her mouth in a slow, passionate kiss and she responded with unstinting generosity. It was a long time before he remembered his other present. "By the way, I have a second wedding gift."

"A ring?"

Aw, hell. He shifted uncomfortably. "No. Not exactly. But that's next on my list. Honest."

She grinned. "It's not another trophy, is it?"

"Nope." He hesitated, struggling to be absolutely honest. "At least... That wasn't what I had in mind when I bought it. I was thinking of making you happy."

Her understanding was instantaneous. "Then it can't be a trophy," she reassured calmly.

"It's the old Miller homestead. I was thinking that after we got married we could move in there and fix it up. I know how crazy you always were about the place." He glanced at her uncertainly. "It'll take a lot of work. But I figured that together we could pull it off."

Tears of joy filled her eyes. "And the resort?" she demanded the instant she recovered enough to speak. "What are you going to do about that?"

"I put Tyler together with the jewelers. Bill's not making it running a ski resort and the others aren't making it in competition with each other. I figured with a little financial backing they could pool their interests. What if we offered a retreat where people could come and mine for their own silver? Meet with local artisans who can design and make handcrafted jewelry from that silver?"

"It's a wonderful idea, Gideon."

"Bill liked it. So did the others. During the summer

they could have conferences for jewelers and designers. Hell, anyone in the business. And in the winter, the Tylers can still run a skiing operation. Happy could become the jewelry capital of the western U.S." He shrugged self-consciously. "It could happen, don't you think?"

"Yes." She laughed through her tears. "It could happen. Miracles happen every day."

An easing began deep inside, years worth of tension slowly unknotting. "Sure they do."

"What changed your mind, Gideon? You were so determined to continue deconstructing."

He took a long time to answer. "It was the baby." His throat moved convulsively and he wrapped his arms around her, resting his forehead against hers. "I kept thinking… What if he'd lived? He'd be more than four now. He'd be at an age where he'd start asking questions. And when I looked at my life and what I'd done with it, I wasn't sure I'd want to answer those questions."

"Why, Gideon?"

His voice grew rough with remembered pain. "You once told me that no one could take away what I possess because I hadn't built anything worthy of taking. That isn't the legacy I'd planned to pass on to my children."

At the reminder, a shadow moved across her face. "I wanted so badly to have your children, Gideon," she murmured unsteadily. "You know that, don't you?"

"Of course I know." His arms tightened around her. "What did the doctors say? Is there any hope?"

She shook her head. "They used words like little to no chance and one in a million and miracle."

"Miracles can happen, Piper."

"You don't understand." She smiled up at him and in that moment he knew nothing mattered as long as he had this woman at his side. "I've already gotten my miracle. You're the only miracle I'll ever need. I love you, Gideon. That's all that's important."

He gathered her close. The sweet odor of the grass beneath them provided a perfume he'd nearly forgotten. At their feet, the creek gurgled a familiar serenade, while the creaking of the mill above them and the gentle chirping of the crickets made him realize something vital. He'd missed this. Missed it more than he'd have ever suspected. At some point, when he hadn't been paying attention or been too self-absorbed to care, the essence of Old Mill Run had crept deep into his bones. It had lodged there, quiet and enduring, remaining even during the years he'd been absent. No matter how hard he'd tried to deny it, the town and his experiences within its boundaries had forged the man he'd become. And he realized something even more vital.

He'd returned home and he didn't intend to leave ever again.

"I love you, too, pipsqueak," he whispered. "And I swear, I'll do everything in my power to make you happy. You have my word of honor."

Piper closed her eyes, her happiness complete. His last few words had slipped out with breathtaking ease, as unconscious as they were heartfelt. Whether he knew it or not, they were the ultimate proof that she had, indeed, received her miracle. It had been a long, rough road. But now that they had made it back home, she truly didn't need anything else.

EPILOGUE

During the years that followed....

TWILIGHT had settled over Colorado, blanketing the foothills in peaceful shades of rose and lavender. Golden light flickered to life throughout the thriving community of Old Mill Run, spearing outward toward the more remote homes found on the outskirts of town. It spread across Spencer's Mill, now in operation and a huge tourist draw, and across Hart Construction, which had at one time been a run-down trailer park.

The name was something of a misnomer because it wasn't an operation that constructed buildings, but was owned by a man who had an uncanny knack for turning the most disastrous companies into successful operations. Businessmen from all over the country came here for advice, and occasionally a helping hand, both of which were provided with unstinting generosity.

A few miles out of town, one house in particular glowed with life, tucked close into the embrace of the Rocky Mountains. It was the old Miller place, a huge homestead that had been left to suffer into ruin. But loving hands had changed all that, renovating it over the ten years since its purchase.

The exterior reflected the most obvious changes. Gardens profuse with flowers wreathed the house and fresh paint gleamed on the clapboard siding and surrounding buildings. Prosaically a porch swing stirred gently in the breeze, creaking a welcome to approaching visitors. And the stained-glass front door showed a boy and girl sitting side by side fishing in a stream that ran alongside of an old mill.

The interior had seen as dramatic a change as the exterior. A photographic studio occupied what was once a dusty attic. Black-and-white photos abounded, including many that had won national awards. And though it was off-limits except to a select few, the dictate was an unusual exception in an otherwise warm and accommodating home.

A huge, modern kitchen had become a natural gathering place for friends and relatives, and what was laughingly referred to as the formal dining room was anything but. Nor did the spacious living room offer any such decorum. The only suggestion of formality came from the framed photos that lined the walls. But even that small pretense was negated by the poses.

The first was of a naked baby standing in an old metal washtub. A black-eyed glare warned of a pugnacious nature, as did the cheeks flushed with temper. Most telling of all, a bright red washcloth winged a path toward the photographer. The second picture was of a young girl—no more than four—dressed in her mother's wedding clothes. She stood on wobbly heels, a string of pearls encircling her neck and hanging to her knees. Her pale blond hair fell ruler-edge straight from beneath a cockeyed veil that nearly obscured her face. But it couldn't obscure the sweetness of her smile or the enormous light blue eyes that peeked out from beneath the mounds of ivory lace and tulle.

Next came a photo of a young boy, his wayward dark hair ruffled by a breeze as he hammered home the finishing nail into an impressive tree fort. The camera had caught that final moment of accomplishment—

the boyish chin set at a determined angle that hinted at the compelling man he'd someday become, his blue-gray eyes awash with jubilation, his grin one of ultimate triumph.

And last of all was a photo of a girl, clearly the oldest of the four. She was dressed in jeans held together by holes and sheer determination. Her shirt was missing more buttons than remained, and it had been haphazardly shoved into her jeans. Her light hair hung in uneven braids to her waist and her black gaze warned of a ferocious energy. Around her neck hung her very first camera and she crouched beneath a tree, preparing to take a photo of a fledgling screech owl's inaugural flight.

The first impression most visitors received when they saw the photos was the skill with which they'd been taken. Their next comment came the second they noticed that the pictures were no longer completely black-and-white—a departure for this particular photographer. The faintest hint of color had invaded the shots, adding depth and light and joy to each. Some preferred the old style. Others relished the new. But to a person, they agreed on one vital fact.

These were photographs of miracles. And the four "miracles," as they were affectionately called, were raised by parents who adored them, in a town that became known to tourists far and wide as a modern-day Brigadoon. It was a timeless place, built into prosperity by the Hart and Montgomery families, a place where love abounded and happiness was guaranteed. For through their love for each other Piper and Gideon discovered one simple truth.

Miracles do happen.

*Isabella Trueblood made history reuniting
people torn apart by war and an epidemic.
Now, generations later, Lily and Dylan Garrett
carry on her work with their agency,
Finders Keepers. Circumstances may have
changed, but the goal remains the same.*

*The legend continues with the first book
in our exciting new continuity series,*

TRUEBLOOD, TEXAS

*A year's worth of stories where long-lost relatives
are reunited and new lovers find each other.*

Watch for

THE COWBOY WANTS A BABY

by Jo Leigh

Coming next month.

Here's a preview!

*Ailing Eve Bishop desperately wants to find her
estranged grandson and heir before she dies.
Lily Garrett is on the case. Now all Lily has to
do is find a way to hog-tie a lone wolf and get
him back to Grandma's house. Gossip says that
dangerously handsome Cole Bishop is going to
pay someone to have his child, which gives this
Little Red Riding Hood an idea....*

CHAPTER ONE

LILY CLOSED her bedroom door, then slumped against it, her heart beating frenziedly against her chest. "I am in *so* much trouble here. And I've only known him three hours."

She pushed off the door and flung herself across the bed. That little tango in the kitchen had nearly done her in. The jerk had some nerve testing her like that. For all he knew, she was going to be the mother of his child. It wasn't nice and it wasn't fair, and oh, my God, how she'd flunked.

This attraction to him was something outside her experience. Her body had never reacted as it just had with Cole.

She turned over and looked down at her boobs. "Bad body," she scolded. But there were no immediate apologies. Maybe she should call Dylan and talk it over with him. No. This was not something she wished to discuss with her brother. Ashley? Uh-uh. Somehow, somewhere, it would come back and bite her on the butt.

The other options were her two closest girlfriends, Denise and Sandy, but Denise was in Europe on a business trip and Sandy was too much in love with Paul, her babe du jour, to give sensible advice.

What a pickle. The intelligent thing would be to march out there, tell Cole that she was a private detective, that she'd been sent by Eve, yada, yada, yada.

Then he'd tell her exactly what she could do with Finders Keepers, and she'd be staying at the Jessup Motel.

Plan B? Keep her wits about her, find out all she could about Cole and, when the time was right, explain the situation, if it seemed prudent. If he really was a nutball, she didn't want to turn him on Eve.

And then there was Plan C. Which was forget about the case, forget about her vow to stay chaste until she was completely over Jason, and attack Cole in the middle of the night. Make love until the paramedics were called, then spring her true mission on him when he was too weak to argue.

Plan C had some merit. She just wished she'd paid attention when Sandy had talked about rebound guys. There was something every woman should know about meeting men right after a big breakup, but for the life of her, Lily couldn't remember what it was. Sleep with them? Don't sleep with them? It was one of the two.

My goodness, but this was not how she'd thought her day was going to go. However, there was a little part of her that was unapologetically excited. Curious as hell about what was going to happen next. She honestly didn't know. Would he make another move? Would he ignore her?

She had the feeling if he really meant to kick her out she would have been kicked by now. No, despite the Granite Man demeanor, the guy was probably as confused as she was.

Wanting to hire a wife. For heaven's sake. What a dumb thing to do. Maybe she was supposed to be here to knock some sense into the big guy. Show him that he couldn't be in control of everything. And that money and the love of a mother didn't mix.

Sighing, she sat up, looked at the clock. Another forty minutes and it would be dinner. She was definitely hungry. But there was time to shower, to cool herself down and gather her composure. Assuming, that is, that she could stop thinking about those shoulders.

In August 2001

New York Times bestselling author

DEBBIE MACOMBER

joins

DIANA PALMER

&

Patricia Knoll

in

TAKE5

Volume 1

These five tender love stories
are quick reads, great escapes
and deliver five times the love.

Plus

With $5.00 worth of coupons inside,
this is one *sweet* deal!

HARLEQUIN®
Makes any time special ®

Visit us at www.eHarlequin.com

HNCPV1R

Harlequin Romance®

Capturing the world
you dream of

Save $2.00 off the purchase of any 3
Harlequin Romance®
series titles.

$2.00 OFF!
any three Harlequin Romance series titles.

RETAILER: Harlequin Enterprises Ltd. will pay the face value of this coupon plus 10.25¢ if submitted by customer for this product only. Any other use constitutes fraud. Coupon is nonassignable. Void if taxed, prohibited or restricted by law. Consumer must pay any government taxes. Nielson Clearing House customers submit coupons and proof of sales to: Harlequin Enterprises Ltd., 661 Millidge Avenue, P.O. Box 639, Saint John, N.B. E2L 4A5. Non NCH retailer—for reimbursement submit coupons and proof of sales directly to: Harlequin Enterprises Ltd., Retail Marketing Department, 225 Duncan Mill Rd., Don Mills, Ontario M3B 3K9, Canada. Valid in Canada only.

Coupon valid until December 31, 2001.
Valid at retail outlets in Canada only.
Limit one coupon per purchase.

52603293

HARLEQUIN®
Makes any time special®

Harlequin Romance ®

Capturing the world
you dream of

Save $2.00 off the purchase of any 3
Harlequin Romance ®
series titles.

Visit us at www.eHarlequin.com
T5V1CHRUS
© 2001 Harlequin Enterprises Ltd.

HARLEQUIN
Makes any time special ®